Praise for Toni Shiloh

"I love a romance populated with characters you can truly root for. And this one has that and more. Coupled with Toni Shiloh's winning voice, it's a story not to be missed."

Oprah Daily on *In Search of a Prince*

"This romance with a touch of mystery will stay with you long after The End."

Rachel Hauck, *New York Times* bestselling author, on *In Search of a Prince*

"Toni Shiloh brilliantly weaves a romantic tale."

Vanessa Riley, bestselling author of *Island Queen*, on *In Search of a Prince*

"Shiloh has penned yet another adorable and charming royal romance!"

Melissa Ferguson, bestselling author of *Meet Me in the Margins*, on *To Win a Prince*

"Shiloh offers a sweet romance with a strong dose of spiritual truth."

Pepper Basham, award-winning author of *Authentically, Izzy*, on *The Love Script*

"Toni Shiloh delivers another soulful, uplifting romance. . . . A swoon-worthy romance readers will adore."

Belle Calhoune, bestselling author of *An Alaskan Christmas Promise*, on *The Love Script*

"Another winner that readers will enjoy from start to finish."

Vanessa Miller, author of *Something Good*, on *To Win a Prince*

"Shiloh delivers a fun, contemporary romance delightfully full of favorite romantic tropes that also conveys serious messages of faith and destiny. It is refreshing to see dynamic Black characters in the genre, and readers will be eager for this modern-day fairy tale."

Library Journal starred review of *In Search of a Prince*

a RUN at LOVE

LOVE IN THE SPOTLIGHT

a RUN at LOVE

Toni Shiloh

BETHANYHOUSE

a division of Baker Publishing Group
Minneapolis, Minnesota

© 2024 by Toni Shiloh

Published by Bethany House Publishers
Minneapolis, Minnesota
BethanyHouse.com

Bethany House Publishers is a division of
Baker Publishing Group, Grand Rapids, Michigan

Printed in the United States of America

Library of Congress Cataloging-in-Publication Data
Name: Shiloh, Toni, author.
Title: A run at love / Toni Shiloh.
Description: Minneapolis, Minnesota : Bethany House Publishers, a division
of Baker Publishing Group, 2024. | Series: Love in the spotlight ; 2
Identifiers: LCCN 2023053554 | ISBN 9780764241512 (paperback) | ISBN
    9780764243172 (casebound) | ISBN 9781493446582 (ebook)
Subjects: LCGFT: Christian fiction. | Romance fiction. | Novels.
Classification: LCC PS3619.H548 R86 2024 | DDC 813/.6—dc23/eng/20231120
LC record available at https://lccn.loc.gov/2023053554

Emojis are from the open-source library OpenMoji (https://openmoji.org/) under the Creative Commons license CC BY-SA 4.0 (https://creativecommons.org/licenses/by-sa/4.0/legalcode).

This is a work of fiction. Names, characters, incidents, and dialogues are products of the author's imagination and are not to be construed as real. Any resemblance to actual events or persons, living or dead, is entirely coincidental.

Cover illustration and design by Jena Holliday, Spoonful of Faith.

Author is represented by Rachel McMillan.

Baker Publishing Group publications use paper produced from sustainable forestry practices and postconsumer waste whenever possible.

24 25 26 27 28 29 30   7 6 5 4 3 2 1

To the Author and Finisher of my faith.

PROLOGUE

JUNE, LAST YEAR

breathed in deeply, inhaling the intoxicating combination of horses and hay. Today was going to be a good day. I just knew it.

My folks had sent me and my best friend, Tucker Hale—who also happened to work for them as one of their assistant trainers—to come to today's livestock sale in their stead and purchase another racehorse. They were hoping I'd take over their farm and racing operation one day.

Only, I had my own plans, which was why I'd registered myself as a potential buyer under my new farm name. And since I wanted to avoid a potential conflict, I'd asked Tuck to register for Bolt Brook Thoroughbred Farm and act in my folks' place. I'm sure he thought the request strange, but until I found the perfect horse, I'd keep the *why* to myself.

Before walking into the stables, I'd pored over the information in the catalog, studying every horse's stats. Some were quite impressive, like Emperor Whethers, whose stall I stood in front of now.

"Can you bring him out?" I asked the stable hand.

"Sure." He opened the door and grabbed the lead hanging from a hook on the wall. Then after clipping it to the two-year-old's halter, he walked the colt into the aisle. Instead of calmly following, he tossed his head back and forth as if trying to break free of his hold.

"He's very spirited," the stable hand said.

Mm-hmm. Not a horse my folks would appreciate but one they'd listed as a potential nonetheless. I went down the list they'd sent with me, marking my opinions in the catalog after inspecting each horse out of the stall. I also kept out an eye for any I might like.

I had the budget for one good horse. One I believed could take me all the way to the Kentucky Derby and launch my own aspirations, giving me the independence I so desperately wanted—*needed.* Before flying out here, I'd entered the contract stage of purchasing a farm. I was merely waiting to see if everything would be processed smoothly before calling myself an owner.

So far today, I'd starred two Thoroughbreds that would make perfect additions to my folks' farm. Tuck had already been through the stables as well, a tactic we'd establish long ago. We each examined the horses on our own so we wouldn't influence the other's opinion, then discussed the pros and cons of each one before the bidding process started.

Except this time I had no plans of asking Tuck's opinion on the purchase of my own racehorse. I'd know the perfect one when I spotted him.

I reached the last stall.

"This here is Dream. You wanna see him?" the barn hand asked.

"Yes, please."

I sucked in an inhale as Dream stood before me. He was absolutely magnificent.

"May I touch him?" My fingers itched to run along his strong, sleek lines.

"Sure can. He won't mind."

I put my palm face up below Dream's muzzle. His nostrils widened, and a puff of air caressed my hand as the colt took my measure. Slowly, I ran a hand down his shoulders and along his flank, reveling in the softness of his coat but also assessing his muscular structure. He didn't shy away from my touch and held a calm disposition.

No, not calm. Regal.

I continued my assessment by running my fingers along his knees down his cannons to his fetlocks, my hands allowing me to feel what I couldn't see. His repository had shown he was injury free. All the X-rays and other medical tests had shown him to be a healthy horse, but I wanted to feel for myself.

"Why are they pushing you this early?" I whispered softly. Why had his current owner decided to give up on Dream being a Derby contender? His ears flickered backward, listening to my voice. I caressed his neck, keeping my volume low as I spoke. His racing speed hadn't been as fast as the others that ran the eighth of a mile, but he was no slouch either. I could see the promise in him.

Perhaps his regal personality kept him from getting in the trenches with the others? I wanted to ask the handler, but I would have to decide this on my own. Everything I saw of Dream showed me he could go the distance.

"You could be mine," I whispered.

I stepped away, noting other potential buyers filling the stables. I didn't want anyone to think I was attached and try to drive up the price later on. Because deep down I knew I'd bid on Dream.

The next day I found myself in the auction room, waiting impatiently for the start.

"First up is Hip 340." The auctioneer read the highlights of the dam's family as well as the colt's breeze time.

Then when I saw Dream on stage in the auction ring . . . well, something in my heart clicked. He was it. Dream was *my* horse. He would help me make my own dream come true. One that involved no one telling me how to live or how to dress. I didn't want to run a three hundred acre stable like my folks'. Something much smaller and less formal was more my speed.

I leaned forward, heart pounding within my chest. Once again, I couldn't get over how stunning the two-year-old was. If he did well in the Derby, he could go on to sire many winners after him. I'd prayed all last night for wisdom regarding him and one of the other horses I'd marked as a potential purchase.

I swallowed and looked at my best friend. "I want to buy that horse," I whispered.

"Your parents didn't mark him down, did they?" Tuck's brow furrowed as he stared at his copy of the catalog.

Goodness, he was a fine-looking man. "No." I shook my head—pushing away attraction to him that shouldn't be present. "Not for them. For me."

"Wait, what?" Tuck placed a hand on my arm as if to keep me from raising my finger.

I wanted to sigh as the warmth of his palm heated my arm with little electric pulses. But now wasn't the time to think of all the ways I loved Tucker Hale. After all, I'd made a commitment to myself to never admit to him the depth of my feelings. I couldn't—*wouldn't*. Tuck was my person, and I wanted him to stay my person. If I told him how I felt, and he rejected me . . .

Well, I'd never know if his rejection of me was as a woman or a Black woman. Either outcome was one I didn't want to navigate. Not when we were so good together as BFFs—my moniker, not Tuck's. He claimed the term *BFFs* was too feminine.

"I've been thinking," I said.

"Uh-huh . . ." His warm blue eyes studied me.

"I want to be more than just the daughter of Ian and Jackie McKinney. I want to make my own way in the racing world." I held my breath, waiting for his reaction.

"And buying this horse is a way to do that?"

The auctioneer opened bids. I bit my lip, waiting to see if someone would raise their hand or nod to accept the price.

"Yes. I've been dreaming of running my own Thoroughbred farm, but something a lot smaller than my parents' big ol' estate." *Big ol'* was a complete understatement. Their operation was a huge undertaking.

"So why this guy?" Tuck motioned to Dream.

"Look at him." I flinched as first one person, then another, bid. "Obviously, I'm not the only one who agrees."

"I won't stop you, but I will caution you."

That was Tuck. The one to hesitate and plan out everything before taking a plunge. While I could appreciate that fine character trait, I wouldn't let it prevent me from going with my gut feeling. I caught the auctioneer's eye and raised my finger. Adrenaline surged through me as he acknowledged my bid.

Tuck gaped at me. "You already registered, didn't you?"

"Yes." I grimaced inwardly. "That's why I asked you to register my folks."

"I would've never guessed." He shook his head, looking stunned.

"Please bid for them."

"Pipsqueak, come on. Let someone else buy this colt. We can talk about your plan before you go diving in headfirst."

I raised my finger again. "Tuck," I whispered out the side of my mouth, "I'm not jumping into anything I haven't tested the temperature for. This has been a long, thought-out plan. I have a vision board and everything."

"Oh no, not a vision board."

I suppressed a laugh at his dry tone. "Besides, I've been sitting on the sidelines of my own life for far too long."

"Why didn't you tell me you were thinking about this? I thought we told each other everything."

I turned toward him just in time to see hurt flash through his eyes. A pang throbbed in my chest. "I'm sorry. I just . . . I didn't want to say anything until I had the wheels in motion."

"And the wheels are moving?"

I nodded and raised my finger once more.

The auctioneer continued chanting at the speed of lightning flashing, but it looked like no one else was going to raise the bid.

"Is this really happening?" Tuck asked.

"I hope so." No need to tell Tuck I was in the process of buying a farm as well. Purchasing a racehorse was probably too much of a shock for him right then as it was.

The auctioneer slowed his speech, then named my bid as the final call. This was it. This was my move toward freedom. Dream—*my* dream.

This colt would be my first official major purchase as an adult. Up until now, my parents had bought almost every single thing I owned, including my truck. Getting my own place, purchasing my own racehorse . . . all done to move me toward independence and help me stand on my own two feet regardless of what the folks of Eastbrook, Kentucky, thought best.

Being adopted was a gift I'd never take for granted. But I was tired of letting it keep me from living life on my own say-so. All my life I'd listened to my folks' suggestions for navigating the tricky waters that were often part of a transracial life. Plus, the people in Eastbrook pressed upon me the need to behave in a way that would express gratitude to my folks. After hearing from so many neighbors how grateful I should feel throughout my childhood, that obligation was second nature to me now.

I needed a change. Somehow I had to get past the double looks I received because of my race. Even at this auction I'd earned second glances. As if the thought whispering in other people's minds was *Why is a Black person at a horse auction?*

As if I couldn't love horse racing just as much as anyone else. I was tired of people questioning my motives. I just wanted to do something that brought me joy.

And that was owning my own farm, making my own way in this industry. Not as Ian and Jackie McKinney's daughter, but as Piper McKinney, owner of Maisha Farms. I'd run a place that let me be . . . me. But there was one person I wanted alongside me.

I turned to my friend. "Tuck?"

"Hmm?"

"Will you come work for me? Be the head trainer at my farm?"

"You're going to own a farm now too?" He took off his Stetson and ran a hand through his dirty-blond locks. "My head is spinning."

This time, I placed my hand on his and leaned forward. "Tucker Hale, who else would I want beside me as I take the racing world by storm?"

● ● ●

JULY

Tucker Hale always had a plan.

Granted, agreeing to train Piper's new colt meant he'd had to alter his old plan and start a new one. But he had to admit, this might be his best plan yet.

He stared at what he'd written in his planner.

Win Piper McKinney's Heart

1. *Increase annual income by 30% and have a six-month emergency fund*
2. *Get Dream to the Derby*
3. *Win the Derby*
4. *Tell Piper how I feel*
5. *Marry her*

Tuck stared at the words, trying to decide if he was missing some steps.

Now that he was no longer working for the McKinneys, he had to figure out other ways to provide for Piper. Yes, she had a trust fund and likely didn't *need* his money, but at the end of the day he wanted to provide some type of income. He could add more horseback riding lessons, maybe even see if he could train other horses besides Piper's.

He nodded slowly, then thankful he'd left a few lines blank after each number, he added a few bullets under step number one. Of course, he wrote in pencil, because you never knew when a plan needed to be altered. He wasn't so bullheaded that he'd write in pen. But seeing the list come together loosened the tightness around his chest and gave him hope.

Tuck had loved Piper ever since middle school, when he finally saw her for the beautiful girl she was. That love had only grown over the years. But he'd never been able to tell her. Unfortunately, he'd always felt inferior to her.

He wasn't rich like her folks. Hadn't owned his own home until the beginning of the year. And up until she hired him, he'd been only an assistant trainer. Not one of the headliners who got to have their names listed next to the racehorse and a bona fide win added to their résumé.

Tuck prayed that was all about to change. He'd poured out his heart to God when Piper asked him to train Dream, praying for wisdom to know if leaving Bolt Brook was the right thing. When he got the yes, he panicked a little, immediately wondering how he'd make his mortgage payment and other bills that must be paid.

So he kept praying that God would provide until the itchy feeling under his skin abated and calm restored. He still wasn't fully surrendered and at peace, but at least he could breathe.

I trust You, Lord, and I know You'll get me through. I pray this new plan will bring me ultimate happiness.

Because being with Piper—as the love of his life and *not* merely his best friend—was all he really wanted. More than a Derby win, more than any plan he'd ever created. It all meant nothing if he couldn't win Piper McKinney's heart.

One

*L*aissez les bons temps rouler!

Somehow Tuck and I had driven right into the beginning of Mardi Gras season. We'd been in the car for more than ten hours since leaving Eastbrook and making our way to the Risen Star Stakes held at Fair Grounds Race Course in New Orleans. We planned on attending the race to check out Dream's competition.

I couldn't quite express what it felt like seeing purple, green, and yellow beads hanging from the branches of the trees. Surely that was just something from the movies, right? Had parade participants thrown them up there on purpose, or was it a bead toss gone wrong?

"Can you believe this?" I asked.

"The sights or something else?"

"That we made it on the Derby trail."

Dream had done well in the early prep races, and now he'd be participating in the championship series, consisting of sixteen races that would lead to twenty horses on the field of Churchill Downs to run the Kentucky Derby.

"You mean when you asked me to train Dream, you didn't

actually think you'd make it on the Derby trail?" Tuck smiled at me from the driver's seat.

My breath hitched at those perfectly curved lips and baby-blue eyes. Why did my best friend always have to make me feel like I was in need of a fainting couch?

I swallowed. *Focus on his words.* "I'd hoped. But now that we're here . . ." I shook my head. "Seriously, Tuck, how did we get here?"

Risen Star was the first race on the Derby trail, but we'd chosen to instead participate in the Battaglia Stakes at Turfway Park in two weeks. Each race awarded a certain number of points for the first through fifth winners. The twenty horses with the most points were eligible for the Derby.

"Hard work."

His hard work. Sure, I'd picked the horse, but I hadn't been the one spending hours and days and weeks training the colt. Tuck had. Though I did give my opinion here and there.

"I can't begin to thank you enough." My fingers itched to squeeze Tuck's hand like I'd done numerous times. But I needed to get my heart rate back to normal and push those affectionate feelings aside before I could touch him platonically.

"No thanks necessary, Pipsqueak."

Well, there went those loving feelings.

Since Tuck and I had started working together, our friendship had taken a strange path. We'd gone from sharing everything with each other to Tuck putting up an invisible brick wall between us. He treated me more formally, like he'd once treated my dad, his old boss. Yet every now and again, the wall lowered, and he'd choose to call me by my childhood nickname. I couldn't remember how often he called me Pipsqueak prior to training my Thoroughbred, but now I heard the unflattering nickname way too often.

More than once I'd considered confessing my feelings to Tuck, but the longer I remained mute, the longer it seemed taboo to me. Tuck would most likely reject me with all the love and kindness that existed in him, but that goodness wouldn't lessen the blow. No matter how he cushioned his words, telling me I would simply remain his best friend would shatter my heart.

Unfortunately, I wasn't sure his returning my affections would be the best thing either. We'd never been anything but Tucker and Piper, the two kids seen running across my folks' estate, playing hide-and-seek or, once we got older, racing our horses. We were always together, and people naturally assumed that meant we were like brother and sister.

Only there wasn't a single ounce of sisterly affection for Tucker Hale in me. I stuck my hand out the window and let the warmth from the sun soothe me. It had been a lot colder in Kentucky when we'd left my farm.

I'd bought the property last July, throwing my folks for a loop. I could still remember the shocked look on my mother's face when I enlightened her regarding my plans.

"Piper, honey, we didn't even get to look at the place. What if they upped the price because you're a McKinney? How could you make this step without our guidance?"

Dad had winked at me. *"Now, Jackie, we raised Piper to be smart. I'm sure she handled it beautifully."*

I sighed as the memory faded.

"You're thinking awfully loud over there. Thinking 'bout your folks?"

"Yeah," I murmured.

Tuck sighed. "They show their love the only way they know how."

Which begged the question, How did I need to be loved? Was it ungrateful for me to want them to let me stumble a bit? As soon as they'd learned of my plans, they'd tried to step in and help. They'd offered to find a jockey to race Dream and even tried to pay for my farm. I'd had to beg them to let me be independent and trust I could handle the responsibility.

"I might be smothered by the end of the season."

Tuck laughed. "Jackie McKinney is a fashion icon in the Derby world. Surely her picking out outfits isn't all that bad."

I just stared at him while he tried to dial down his laughter.

"Okay, the last outfit made you look like a Stepford wife."

"It's not me." I shuddered thinking of the pale pink tweed skirt suit Mama suggested I wear at our last race.

"Keep gently reminding her of that, and she'll eventually get it."

I rolled my eyes. Maybe I needed to have a conversation with Dad. He was great at playing mediator when I thought Mama's guidance a little overbearing. I tried so hard not to show her how upset her suggestions made me.

"Don't slouch. People will wonder why you can't walk with confidence."

"Don't wear those colors. They're not good with your complexion."

"Always use the manners we raised you with. We don't want others to complain."

She was so focused on what other people thought. And I got it. I was, too, but I saved myself a little breathing room. Of course, I couldn't be mad at her, because she adopted me. Wasn't it ungrateful to be mad at a parent who'd done more for you than your biological parents had?

My bio parents had dropped me off at an orphanage in Ọlọrọ Ilé—an island country in the Gulf of Guinea—and left me without a backward glance. Believe me, I know. I had that one childhood memory of their departure to torture me. Their retreating backs and my wails were all I could recall of them. On the other hand, my adoptive parents had continuously poured their love and monetary blessings on me. I'd never wanted for anything . . . except a little more autonomy.

As the parent of an only child, a little breathing room wasn't something Mama knew how to give. She loved fiercely and with a side of a little-overbearing presence. She'd been unable to have biological children, and Dad said after the two long years of waiting for my adoption to finalize and for me to actually arrive in the States, it was too much turmoil to go through again. So I became an only child to wealthy parents who were royalty in the Kentucky Derby scene. Their horses had sired past Derby winners, and they enjoyed selling the foals to the highest bidder in hopes that history would repeat itself.

"I don't know when, but I have no doubt your mom will learn how to parent an adult and give you some space." Tuck's voice broke my silence.

"I hope you're right." Because I didn't look forward to another ten years of feeling like a child past the age of eighteen.

Tuck slowed the truck to idle in front of our hotel.

I looked up at the white building with a black awning over the front entrance. "These buildings are gorgeous."

"And right downtown where you wanted to be."

"That's because I was thinking of my stomach." I grinned. "I've been dreaming about gumbo and beignets ever since I've known we were coming."

Tuck laughed. "Are we going to try to catch a Mardi Gras parade or two as well?"

I shrugged. I was there to scope out the competition, and I hadn't really made any plan other than that. Knowing Tuck, he'd taken care of that for the both of us.

"What's your plan?" I asked him.

"I'll share with you. Don't worry."

"Okay."

After we found the guest parking lot, skipping valet service, I followed Tuck up the hotel steps. He handed our baggage to a bellboy, and then we went inside to check in. My eyes took in the swanky details of the place, and I recalled the first time I traveled with my parents. They always stayed in five-star hotels for the best accommodations. I had to admit, the hotel snobbery bug caught me. Only now it was my money paying for my room as well as Tuck's.

"We going to eat right away?" I asked.

"Definitely. I don't want you getting hangry."

I loved that crooked grin on his face. What would he do if I let my wobbly knees tip myself right against him where lips could meet? I turned away, feeling heat in every pore on my face.

The memory of our first meeting came to the surface.

"You the new kid?"

I'd tilted my head back, the sun silhouetting a kid's frame. Someone sat down next to me, and a young boy's face came into focus, showing blond hair and blue eyes. The complete opposite to my black eyes and short black hair. His skin was pale where mine was dark.

"Yes," I said, English feeling foreign on my tongue.

He stuck out his hand. *"I'm Tuck. My dad's the horse trainer."*

"Piper." We shook hands, and something clicked right into place.

I hadn't realized it then, but Tucker Hale had stolen my heart before I even knew what love was. From that day forward, I followed him around Bolt Brook on a daily basis. Tuck taught me how to skip rocks at the water hole. He was right next to me when I rode my first horse. He was there to wipe my tears when I fell off and to cheer me on when I got back up.

I hooked a thumb over my shoulder. "I'm gonna go shower and change, then."

"Sure thing."

Good grief. Attending races together now proved to be a lot more difficult than when we worked for my parents. I thought removing my family from the equation would make work easier, but it had only added a weird tension.

After checking out my room, I grabbed a fresh set of clothes and toiletries from my suitcase. I wanted to look my best for

Tuck just in case he ever decided to open his eyes and see that we could be more.

At least, I think that was what I wanted. My mind was so conflicted. The risk of losing him as a friend or being rejected because of my ethnicity was too much. Mentally, I knew Tuck had never given me reason to believe my race was an issue. But when you spent the majority of your life being the only Black person in nondiverse spaces, you couldn't help but believe people were just keeping their racial judgments quiet.

I didn't want to believe that's what Tuck did, and for the most part, I could assure myself he wasn't like that. But then a little voice would whisper in my ear, and doubt would ensue.

Most of the time, I could be myself around Tuck without race entering my mind. Fortunately, he seemed to accept all of me. After all, this was the same guy who watched rom-coms with me because I liked them, not because he would choose that genre.

So how could I risk the one friendship I could never bear to lose?

I couldn't.

Wouldn't.

Right?

I shook my head and turned on the shower. Surely those troubles would be waiting for me another time, another day. I wouldn't give them any more headspace . . . for now.

Two

Tuck stared at the texts from his friends. These guys were his prayer support and often a source of entertainment. Chris was a wildlife conservationist who had his own YouTube channel, spreading information on how to help wildlife and conservation efforts. Lamont was a Hollywood actor who'd been named *People*'s "Sexiest Man Alive" at one point. How they were friends with him was beyond Tuck's understanding.

His thumbs flew over his phone screen.

Tuck
All's well.

Chris
That literally tells me nothing.

Lamont
Maybe we interrupted him when he was gazing at his ladylove. You know, the one he claims is just a friend?

Tuck shook his head. Lamont had gained a girlfriend the Hollywood way—by pretending to be in love for the tabloids.

Fortunately for them, their relationship turned into the real deal. They were disgustingly sweet and now engaged. Of course Lamont saw romance everywhere.

Tuck
We're just friends.

Chris
Right. Aren't you two on vacation together?

Tuck
Business trip.

Lamont
Oh yeah? Which race is Dream participating in?

Tuck
You know why we're here.

Chris
Maybe, but do you?

Tuck
I maintain our status: just friends.

Chris
Guess I'm stuck being the fifth wheel.

Lamont
You could always find yourself a good woman like me and Tuck.

Tuck
Hey! Piper and I are just friends, so that doesn't make you a fifth wheel or me listed as "in a relationship."

Chris
Sure 😊

Lamont
This ^

Tuck was tempted to come clean. The guys had taken to regularly asking him when he'd admit his feelings for Piper. He often debated letting them in on his game plan to win her heart, but he chickened out each and every time. Admitting it out loud made it seem more real with a higher risk, so he kept his thoughts to himself.

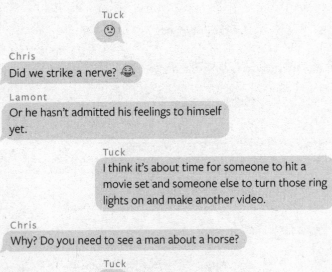

Rather, he needed to see a woman about dinner.

A smile drifted over Tuck's face as he pictured Piper. The woman was absolute perfection in his opinion. From beautiful looks—her flawless ebony skin and the cutest chin—to her absurdly smart mind. The way she kept horse-racing facts in her brain and rattled them off with ease was nothing short of amazing.

She could recall Derby winners, their trainers, and their jockeys at any prompting. When she was younger, her parents would show off her stat wisdom to their colleagues. Probably helped them sell horses better as well. Who wouldn't buy from the McKinneys when their own daughter was so steeped in equine knowledge?

After a hot, steaming shower, Tuck dressed in a button-down, jeans, and boots—the only footwear that ever made it onto his feet. He grabbed his going-out Stetson and wallet, then headed down the hall toward Piper's room.

He'd been having a tough time maintaining friendship propriety ever since they signed a contract stating she'd be signing his paychecks. Tuck had never worked for her personally before. She was no longer simply Piper McKinney, daughter of *the* McKinneys. Now the very same Piper McKinney was his boss. Something about the new title had shifted things for him. To keep his head straight, he'd pulled back little by little as he tried to process the change in their relationship. It didn't even matter that she wasn't his only client.

Tuck taught horse riding lessons and was training another horse for the Kentucky Oaks. Though Piper was hoping for some professional exclusivity in the future. She wanted to be a smaller operation than her parents' but still operate in a similar matter, which meant having an on-site trainer. Granted, she didn't have a track on her land yet, so all training was conducted at his Hale Tier Farms on its dirt oval. That was one of the reasons Dream stayed at his farm, although occasionally Tuck transported him to Piper's place when there was a gap in the training schedule.

The first day he'd visited her new farm had been a shocker. Turned out they were next door neighbors with nothing but a fence preventing them from being on each other's property in a matter of seconds.

Tuck rapped his knuckles against Piper's hotel door. The sound of a dead bolt turning pricked his ears, and he took a step away as the door swung open.

He almost staggered backward.

Piper wore a pale pink dress that fell to her knees and had those puffy sleeves. Did she know how gorgeous-yet-playful she looked? He wanted to tell her she looked pretty, but he'd never done that before.

He cleared his throat. "You ready?"

"Yep." She gave him a once-over. "Got your clean Stetson, huh?"

"You know it." He could do this. Talk about things that didn't matter if only to maintain a friendly façade. "The other one is in the truck. Never take it out so I don't end up mixing the two."

Piper rolled her eyes but kept the grin on her face. "Let's go find some food."

"Do you want to walk, or should I get the truck out of the parking lot?"

"Walk. I can't imagine driving around when we're downtown. Plenty to see by foot."

"So we're going the tourist route?"

"Yes." She hooked her arm through his.

The urge to turn and nuzzle his nose in the curve of her neck and smell the sweet scent that always clung to her overwhelmed him. He felt heady. All he wanted to do was tuck her into the curve of his body and hold her tightly.

Instead, he let her guide them through the lobby and out onto the streets. Tuck would follow Piper. Anywhere. Anytime.

The sun had started its descent, so they walked the downtown streets of New Orleans under the evening glow. Not to mention how the old-fashioned streetlights heightened the ambiance. Tuck often wondered what it would be like to date Piper. They were together so much, did a lot of things couples did, but always under the umbrella of friendship. Yet as they passed other couples walking with hands clasped, Tuck could almost imagine this was real and not a zone he couldn't drag himself out of.

They headed for Decatur Street, which the concierge had assured them everyone wanted to see, as it was part of the French Market. Tuck didn't mind the walk, as it gave him time to discreetly take peeks of Piper. Plus, some of the shops were fun. Piper dragged him into one that sold various heat levels of hot sauce. Another sold pralines—which she purchased.

"Oh! What about this place?" She pointed at a restaurant that had a line coming out the door. "There's a menu on the bricks if you want to make sure there's something you'll like."

"When in Rome." He shrugged a shoulder. He really didn't care what they ate just as long as they were together and he could see her pretty smile.

You've got it bad.

He thought back to the Usher song, and Tuck almost laughed at how true the lyrics were. Only, that was about being in love. Could Tuck call what he felt for Piper romantic love? Yes, because he did want to marry her. But it probably fell under the unrequited category, and that made his stomach tense.

"Should we get on the wait list?" Piper asked.

He ran a hand over his beard, then nodded. "If it's long, we can continue walking around and make our way back here."

"True."

Tuck walked ahead, making sure those in line had already been helped. He gave his name and cell number, then made his way back onto the street. "Ready?"

They continued their stroll until they hit an outdoor market area. Piper walked up and down the aisles, oohing and aahing over the wares.

"You gonna buy something?" he asked.

"You don't think I have enough?" She held up the three shopping bags of items already purchased.

Tuck laughed. "Tourist shopping is about the only kind you like." He knew for a fact she hated shopping for clothes and antiques. Her mom went overboard in both areas. Piper, on the other hand, used some online company that picked out clothes for her. If the company was responsible for that pink dress, then praise them.

"I did see this pretty necklace I think Mama would like." She reached for the white statement piece. It was very Jackie McKinney.

31

"Go for it."

But he could practically hear Piper's thoughts. If she gave her mom jewelry, then her mom would think it was fine to continue buying jewelry and clothing to dress Piper in. The one thing that really got under her skin.

"Or not," Tuck added.

A myriad of thoughts crossed Piper's face. Finally, she picked up the necklace and went up to the merchant. Tuck let out a breath and sent up a prayer asking God to help Piper navigate her relationship with her folks. Being an only child had been difficult for her, not just because she was the only kid but because she'd been the only minority in her home, their school, and almost the entire town. Still, she flourished under the love of her parents. She just didn't know how to communicate what she wanted for her future.

Tuck remembered the day she told her parents about purchasing Dream and the farm. Her father had shown up at his home unannounced.

"*You saw her horse?*" Mr. McKinney had folded his arms, looking like a guard as he stood in the middle of Tuck's living room.

"*Yes, sir.*"

"*And?*"

Despite the older gentleman's formidable presence, Tuck had been hesitant to spill the beans when he couldn't decipher the man's intentions.

"*Are you asking as her dad or . . .*"

"*Or what?*" Mr. McKinney had taken a step forward.

Tuck straightened to his full height. "*Or her competition?*"

"*Tucker Hale, what in tarnation are you accusing me of?*"

Tuck raised a hand as if trying to soothe a spooked filly. "*I just want to make sure you're asking as a concerned father and that's it.*"

Her folks had only ever wanted to make sure Piper would

never be taken advantage of. By the same token, they wanted to give her anything and everything she could ever ask for. Just because she was twenty-eight didn't mean they treated her as a grown woman.

As far as Tuck was concerned, the day she turned eighteen—well, maybe twenty-one to be fair—Piper had been free to make her own decisions and live with the consequences, good or bad.

He watched as she added another bag to her arm. No matter what happened in the future, whether Piper rejected him when he finally laid his feelings bare, or they lost the Derby—whatever trial, Tuck would always be there for Piper McKinney. She was his friend for life. She deserved to have someone who would help her dreams come true and see her for who she was.

"Should we start back toward the restaurant?" Piper asked. "They may ring us soon."

Tuck nodded. "Yeah, we can do that." His back pocket vibrated. He pulled out his cell and held it up. "Looks like you're right. Table will be ready in ten minutes."

"Good. I'm starved."

Tuck smiled. Piper was always hungry and could pack away the food. It was one of the things he loved about her. But that was a thought he'd have to keep to himself just a little while longer.

Three

Aaron Wellington III looked nothing like I'd imagined an award-winning journalist would. He'd casually draped his lanky form over the dining chair in the restaurant where I'd chosen to meet him. Now that it was time for Dream to race in the March stakes at Turfway Park, my stomach was doing little dips. Maybe meeting a journalist on one of Dream's biggest race days wasn't a smart thing to do.

I took the seat across from Aaron, trying not to be obvious in my perusal. It wasn't often I got to sit across from another Black person. The urge to catalog his features to see if they were similar to mine niggled at the back of my brain, but that was a tendency I could push away. I stopped playing the where's-my-family game once I understood that I didn't live on the same continent as my blood relations.

"Thank you for meeting me," he said, pulling me from my thoughts.

"Of course." I smiled. "You have an impressive résumé." I wasn't sure why someone like him wanted to write a magazine article about someone like me.

His black eyes met mine, and I noted the brown skin with the red undertone. Somehow his suit seemed at odds with the shaggy 'fro he sported. He reminded me of someone, but I couldn't put my finger on who.

"And you have an intriguing history," he said.

"How did you hear about me, again?" I took a sip of the ice water.

"Friends in various places know what captures my attention. This particular friend saw Dream in a few prep races. He made the connection between you and your adoptive parents."

His grin somehow reassured me that this meeting was all very normal, but modern media reminded me anyone could be dangerous. I needed to proceed with caution.

"How could my *intriguing history* possibly be newsworthy?"

Dream hadn't won the Derby. Wasn't writing an article about me and whatever potential success he had premature? Aaron was known for writing lengthy feature articles on Black Americans who'd broken the racial barrier. Surely I fell in the watch-and-see category, not award-winning.

"You'd be surprised what the public wants to know." He stroked his mustache. "For instance, you're a transracial adoptee. That alone would pull in a certain audience. How do you feel about racial tensions in the US? Was it an issue growing up? How did it impact your identity? Et cetera."

Ugh. So he basically wanted an answer to all the questions that continued to plague me? "What about the racing aspect?"

"If Dream continues an upward trajectory and lands in the Derby or Breeders' Cup, you're breaking a barrier that's previously been seen only in the jockey world. It's a whole lot different telling the tale from the owner's box."

"How does this work? If I were actually interested?" I resisted the urge to ring the cloth napkin in my lap.

"I'd ask questions. Come to certain races like today's. Incorporate a little of the personal with your business life, and the article will practically write itself. I could even talk to your friends and family who'd be willing to lend a quote."

My heartbeat pulsed in my neck. What would my folks say about this? Would they feel exploited or a little unnerved to have me tell the adoption story? Would I—we—feel exposed?

I rubbed my forehead. "I need to think about this."

"How about a little sample of how it all works?"

"Um, sure?"

"How nervous are you for today's race?"

"I can't quantify it," I responded.

"Try."

I searched my brain for the right words. "Part of me wants to throw up, and the other wants to jump up and down cheering." I lifted a shoulder. "It's hard to express if you don't have a dog in the fight."

"Why horse racing? Why not any other sport?"

Because the equine life was in my blood. But seriously, since I was adopted, did that phrase even apply?

"Horses are part of my earliest memories." Much better than the ones of me in the orphanage . . . alone. "I feared them for a time because they seemed so big and imposing. Now I love them with every breath in my body."

"I see."

Yet something in Aaron's tone told me he didn't *get* it. "Do you?" I studied him.

A chagrined expression covered his face. "Not really."

How could I explain the thrill of watching the three-year-olds burst out of the gates and down the track? Seeing the pure agility and horsemanship of the jockeys as they coaxed the Thoroughbreds closer to the finishing post. Not to mention the inexplicable pride that surged through me knowing I was here as an owner.

I wasn't a jockey—though I'd been mistaken for one in New Orleans—and I certainly wasn't a stable hand. My name was listed as owner of Dream. I wasn't going to let my ethnicity or gender keep me from enjoying the sport. I refused to be the token Black girl and instead aimed to be one of the African American trailblazers paving a way in the sport for people who looked like me.

"Penny for your thoughts?" Aaron asked softly.

"They're worth more than a penny."

His grin crooked. "Good. Then maybe working with me will show you how I can bring out your love of horses, showcase the lack of diversity—"

I opened my mouth to interject, and Aaron held up a hand.

"But the growing interest in ethnic circles would be discussed as well."

"And my faith."

Aaron blinked. "You believe in God," he stated, skepticism in his tone.

"I do." I straightened to my full height, chin lifting just a little. I wasn't ashamed of my faith, and I wouldn't let anyone make me feel less than because of it. "Is that a problem?"

"I wouldn't say problem." He rubbed his stubbled jaw. "More like an added layer to delve into."

"A layer that makes you uncomfortable?"

He shrugged, tilting his head with the movement as well. "Nothing that would impact my professionalism."

"Fair enough. I'll let you know once I make a decision."

"I appreciate that. I'll be in Kentucky for a while, so the timing is really ideal for me."

Could I say the same, though?

"Piper?"

The sound of Tuck's voice had me turning in my seat. "Tuck!" My heart lightened at his approach. Just seeing him soothed the jittery nerves flowing through me—as if I'd drunk one too many cups of coffee.

"Hey, Pipsqueak. I didn't realize you had a meeting." He glanced at Aaron, and a look flashed in his eyes. One I couldn't quite place because I'd never seen that expression on him.

Remembering my manners, I stood and introduced him to Aaron. "He's interested in doing a feature article about me in *Glass Breaker*."

"Wow. Nice to meet you." Tuck shook his hand.

"Likewise." Aaron slid his hands into his pockets. "How do you know Ms. McKinney?"

Was he already in investigative mode? Would he be mentally labeling people in my life like a genealogist with a family tree?

"She's my best friend. We grew up together."

Something sparked in Aaron. I could see his little writer hamster rubbing his hands together in glee. "So you'd be the man to talk to if she accepts my proposal?"

Tuck glanced at me, asking me with his eyes if it was okay to divulge a bit.

I dipped my head.

"Guess so. I'm probably the one who knows her the best."

"Not her parents?"

"Her parents know childhood Piper."

Actually, that was probably an apt statement. It's not like I didn't want my folks to know me as I was now, but I didn't spend as much time at home now. I was usually at my own place or Tuck's.

"I see." Aaron met my gaze. "I'll let you two catch up. Please reach out when you have an answer." He picked up the check. "I'll handle this."

"Thank you."

I gestured for Tuck to join me, then sat. "Did you come to eat?" Tuck had mentioned grabbing a bite midday, but I told him I had something to do. Not that I was necessarily being secretive, but I wasn't sure how the meeting with Aaron Wellington III would go.

"No. Saw you through the window and thought you looked a little uncomfortable. I wanted to make sure everything was okay."

Did he have any idea what he did to my heart?

What would it be like to gaze into each other's eyes while holding hands and whispering sweet nothings? Though the image was almost sickeningly cliché, it didn't make my heart pound any less. Plus it didn't hurt that he looked impressive in the tan sports jacket, matching cowboy hat, and dark-wash jeans.

Time to shove Tuck back into the role he'd played for the majority of my life.

"You're such a great friend," I said.

Something that looked very much like a wince flickered across his face. "I try." He sat back. "So a feature article, huh?"

"Yep." My lips smacked at the *p*. "Sounds ridiculous, right?"

"Not at all. You have an interesting beginning and, depending on how far Dream goes, a potentially explosive future."

A shiver racked me. Wasn't that what I wanted? Yet the thought of being thrust into the spotlight before I knew how to handle my everyday had me reaching for my glass of water. I downed the contents and dabbed at my mouth with my napkin.

Tuck's eyes glimmered. "Thirsty? Or are you nervous at the thought?"

"Terrified." I liked the little anonymity I had. So far Tuck had been the one journalists wanted quotes from. They loved talking to trainers. "Teetering frontward and backward. Though that may be a passing-out feeling."

Tuck laughed. "Even when you're nervous, you make me laugh."

"Glad someone is." I certainly wasn't. "I have no idea if I'm supposed to say yes to the article."

"You'll make the right decision for you." Tuck reached out his palm.

I placed my hand over his, and he squeezed it. "How do you always calm me down?"

"I've had practice." He winked, then slid his hand back.

Tuck winked often in my dreams, but I also followed up the action with a kiss. Too bad this was reality.

"Pipsqueak, you listening?"

"Sorry, what did you say?"

"The race will start in about an hour." He made a motion toward the exit. "You ready to go?"

"Yes." As if it had gained permission, my brain immediately switched to worrying about my Thoroughbred.

Four

As the announcer began his spiel, Tuck slid his palms against his jean-clad thighs. He didn't know if his nerves drumming away was due to the impending race or the way the journalist had studied Piper. The looks were reminiscent of how Tuck knew he watched Piper, letting the longing seep out just enough to keep it from completely spilling over and making him profess his hidden feelings.

Seeing them seated at a table for two had left Tuck uneasy—even if Piper had looked unsettled. Just the little visual forced Tuck to ask himself for the first time ever, *What does Piper want in a boyfriend?*

That was something they actually never discussed. She didn't talk about any dates or point out who she thought was good-looking. He didn't know if she wanted a man her same race or if that didn't matter to her at all.

Did she want someone accomplished like the journalist? Or would Tuck, as a first-time lead trainer, be good enough for her? It was one thing to be friends, but a lot of women seemed to want men who were wealthy and ambitious.

Don't be ridiculous. Piper isn't materialistic.

The announcer continued speaking, and Tuck pulled his thoughts off himself and onto the track.

Lord God, please help Dream place. Let this be his best performance yet. Tuck wanted the accolade of having a winning horse under his belt. He'd get more clients, which meant more income, and hopefully another step in winning the girl's heart.

Piper's jiggling knee entered his peripheral vision.

"It'll be okay." He placed a hand over her kneecap.

"Fifth place and two points okay or better than that?"

Thank goodness she'd asked a legitimate question to break his focus off the warmth of the touch. "You know we won't know until he crosses the finish line. Gabe has done well working with Dream in the mornings, and I've put him through a regimen that's gotten him this far." *Thank the Lord.*

A few races early on in the road to the Derby had sent Tuck falling to his knees in regret, thinking he hadn't done enough and doomed all Piper's chances of winning that blanket of roses.

"I know," she mumbled.

He squeezed her knee, then let go. He flexed his hand, feeling the residual warmth from her.

"And they're off!" the announcer called.

Tuck leaned forward as the horses left the gate. He looked for the maroon top Maisha Farms' jockey, Gabe Moreno, would be wearing.

"Dream is pulling up from the outside into fourth with a half mile to go. AlwaysaWinner, on the inside, is still in the lead."

"Remember how we trained," Tuck muttered under his breath.

Tuck had given Gabe strict instructions on when to spur Dream to race faster. If he gave the signal a moment too soon, the colt could run out of steam before reaching the finish line. Tuck's jaw clenched as his heartbeat seemed to sync to the rhythm of the race.

"Come on, come on," Piper urged beside him.

"Dream is pushing from the outside into third. Alwaysa-Winner maintains the lead as they head into the home stretch and . . ."

Tuck watched, breath stuck in his chest as Dream neared the finish line.

"Dream sweeps past AlwaysaWinner to win the John Battaglia Memorial Stakes!"

"Yes!" Tuck jerked his fist downward in victory.

"Oh my word!" Piper shouted as she jumped into the air.

He turned to her and wrapped his arms around her waist, lifting her. "You did it," he murmured.

"*We* did it." She squeezed his neck.

His eyes closed, reveling in the moment. Unfortunately, his mind quickly realized their embrace was running a little long, and he opened them. A dazed look had Piper's ebony eyes glowing. Tuck would love to assume their closeness had put that expression there, but that would be pure arrogance. Dream had just secured twenty points toward the Derby trail. Historically, forty points would be enough to earn him a spot. If he won another race, they'd be heading to Churchill in May.

Thank You, Lord!

Tuck blinked, realizing he'd get ten percent of the $150k purse money, as would their jockey. Tuck had been using the winnings from the earlier races to make renovations around his place. When he first purchased his farm, all his money and time had gone into perfecting the horse facilities. Nowadays, he spent his off time refinishing floors and buying furnishings for the interior of the house.

When he got home, he'd have to look at his renovation plan. He couldn't recall if this win would be enough to finish everything or if he would still need another one. But he was certain if he had more days like today, he'd be able to mark off item one in his Piper plan and be a better provider.

Get real, you'll never match her trust fund.

43

"I need to go down to the winner's circle." Piper looked up into his face. "You coming?"

He nodded. "Yeah."

Tuck placed a palm on the small of her back and used his other arm to keep people at bay as they made their way to the track.

Flashbulbs flared in their faces as a few photojournalists took pictures of them. After today, Piper's phone would probably be ringing off the hook as the media clamored for a soundbite. He still couldn't wrap his head around how many times his phone rang from horse-racing magazines wanting an interview. One of the track's social media managers had even asked Tuck for a video of Dream's morning work to upload to their YouTube channel. That had been a strange day, one that had Tuck reaching out to Chris for advice on angles and natural light.

A man pushed through the crowd. "Ms. McKinney, how does it feel to be the first African American owner to win the Battaglia Stakes?"

Tuck's mouth dried. How would she answer that? Piper had shared a little with him about how unnerving it was when people kept bringing up her ethnicity. Especially once they made the connection between her and her folks. He wished he could shield her, but all he could do was step closer and remind her she wasn't alone.

"I may be the first owner, but I'm certainly not the first African American to win a stakes race." She flashed a smile and continued walking.

"Great answer," Tuck said, keeping his voice low.

"You think so?"

"Yes." He squeezed her hand, then let go, hating the loss of her warmth.

"So many reporters," she whispered.

"You're handling it all beautifully." Tuck slowed to a stop and pointed ahead of them. "Go get in that circle."

"Aren't you coming?"

He grinned and gave her the same answer as always. "Nah, this is your moment."

"Tucker Hale, you're Dream's trainer. You belong in that circle as much as I do."

"You know I don't like the cameras." Chris and Lamont ribbed him every time Tuck hit the news. Then again, it was only fair considering how much he'd joked when Lamont hit the newsstands last year.

"And I do?"

His lips quirked. "Right. Okay." He let out a breath. "Let's go."

They walked into the circle side by side, fake smiles across their faces as they waved to those hoping for a newsworthy shot. Finally, they dropped their arms, and Piper turned and hugged her winning Thoroughbred around the neck. Tuck hoped someone snapped the shot, because that was gold in his book. He took out his cell to capture the moment before she moved.

Wouldn't that look amazing blown up and hanging above his leather sectional?

In your dreams.

All too true.

A few more reporters asked for a quote from Piper—and Tuck, too, once she identified him as Dream's trainer. Eventually, the noise from the crowd faded as they got closer to the stables and behind the grandstand.

"I'm tired," Piper said in a grouse.

"Then let's load up and go home." The drive to Eastbrook was only about an hour and a half.

"Did you see my folks, Tuck?"

"I didn't." He hadn't been looking. Anticipation of the race had crowded out all other thoughts. "Did they say they were coming?"

She nodded. "Dad had a couple of horses racing." She shook her head. "I didn't even see where they placed."

Tuck pulled out his phone. "Give me a sec and I'll tell you." He scrolled through the listing. "Third and fifth."

Silence greeted his ears, and he glanced over to see her shoulders drop. "What is it?"

"Do you think they'll hate that Dream came in first?"

"Of course not. They'll be too happy for you." At least that's what he'd guess. Ian McKinney loved his daughter, and Piper was definitely a daddy's girl.

"Will they?" She laid her head on his shoulder.

Times like these reminded him of how perfectly she fit into the crook of his arm. *Remember, keep it platonic until you check off the first three items in the plan. Only then can she know how you feel.*

Tuck squeezed her shoulder, then reluctantly moved in a way that had her shifting her head off him and creating space between them. "They will. They love you."

"Why does reaching for my dream feel so lonely sometimes?" she mused.

Tuck stopped in his tracks and took her by the shoulders. "Listen to me. As long as I draw breath in my body, you will *never* be alone."

Tears welled in her eyes, wrenching his heart.

"Promise?" she whispered.

Tuck stuck out his pinky. "All day, every day."

"You're the best." She hooked her little finger with his.

"Don't I know it." He cracked a smile, hoping to see her melancholy fade.

She tutted. "Be sure to let some of that ego out, or you'll be riding back in the trailer with Dream."

"Then who would listen to your random horse-racing stats?" He nudged her forward, resuming their walk.

"What year did Apollo win the Kentucky Derby?"

Tuck racked his brain for the answer. His love of racing stats didn't measure up to his love of horses. Or maybe he just didn't have that much room in his brain. "I give. When?"

"1882."

"How do you remember that?"

"Because they thought Runnymede would win, but Apollo made a rush toward the end and won by a half-length."

"Your brain is impressive."

Piper laughed. "Nope. I just want to impress people."

"Sure." He didn't believe that for a second. She'd always been able to remember random facts with seeming ease. He admired that.

Piper paused, her brow furrowing.

"What is it?"

"Don't you ever feel like you have to prove yourself?"

All the time. He swallowed. "Yes."

"Remembering random stats, as you put it, is the same. I always wanted to make sure my folks didn't regret adopting me. I wanted them to be proud of me."

Tuck blinked, shock coursing through him. "Is that why you remember those things?"

She nodded. "When I was young, I pored over racing books from Dad's library and made notecards. Anything to show that I belonged to the McKinneys, that I wasn't just an adopted child but their *real* daughter."

"Oh, Piper." He tugged her close, tightening his arms enough for her to know she was safe with him. "Love is what makes you theirs. Nothing else matters."

He saw a single tear as she buried her face in his shirt. Dampness spread, and he knew she'd released the rest of them. He wasn't sure how long they stood there, but even when Piper's shoulders stopped shaking, he held on to her a little while longer.

Five

Sometimes a girl just needs to be one with her horse.

I ran a brush along Dream's side as he munched on his lunch in his stall at my farm. I couldn't believe how well he'd done at the Battaglia Stakes last week. I'd been praising the Lord ever since they announced Dream the winner. Though I knew he couldn't possibly win all his future races, my hopes were high and my mind was firmly on cloud nine.

"Tuck's done great things with you, hasn't he, boy?"

Dream's ears flickered, but his muzzle never lifted from the feed. I smiled, continuing to let muscle memory glide the brush over his soft hair.

"I don't know what my life would be like without Tucker Hale." I sighed. "Part of me is afraid to ask for more. It's enough that you won your race and that I've got my farm and the love of two adoring parents."

I *knew* I was blessed, yet discontentment niggled at me. I wanted to marry—in my fantasies, Tuck was always leading man—and have a family of my own. I wanted a separate identity from being the adopted daughter of Ian and Jackie McKinney. Not that the label was bad in any way, but how old did I have to be before I felt like my own person? When could I shed the societal expectations thrust on me from the day the judge announced me a McKinney?

Was I being ungrateful?

Counting my blessings and at the same time bemoaning what I didn't have just because I wanted more made me seem exactly that. Entitled. Spoiled. *Ungrateful.*

I laid my head against Dream. The rhythmic rise and fall of his side soothed me. The barn was my happy place outside of being around Tuck. It was the one place that usually quieted the petulant child within me and helped me focus on what mattered. I needed to focus on the next race and my upcoming appointment with Aaron Wellington. A quick glance at my phone showed I had a few minutes before he was due to arrive.

Yesterday, I'd called my dad and asked him for advice on the magazine feature. He'd readily agreed to talk with Aaron and said he'd help Mama see the benefits of speaking with a journalist, especially since Aaron Wellington III wasn't some tabloid reporter. Dad had assured me it'd all be just fine.

Maybe I should have texted Lamont or Nevaeh. They both knew how to have the press eating out of their hands—even when they'd admitted to fake dating and then truly falling in love.

I hung up the brush and let myself out of the stall. "See you later, boy."

Dream's ears flickered again, and this time he tossed his head before digging back into the oats. I left him with the right amount of food so he wouldn't overeat. No way I wanted to cause any intestinal issues. I needed my winner healthy and ready to get back to his training schedule next week.

I tracked across the yard from the stables to my home. A cold breeze blew through, and I zipped my jacket closed. Oh yeah, I needed to change before Aaron arrived. A T-shirt and jeans didn't necessarily seem like proper attire to wear to an interview. Or had Mama drummed that kind of thought into my mind?

Now wasn't the time to have a crisis and wonder if I held a thought of my own. I threw the shirt into my laundry basket and grabbed a blouse from my closet. A spritz of the perfume Mama bought me—good-smelling scents were one thing we could agree on—and I was ready to be interviewed.

Still, my palms remained damp, my heart beat much too fast. My mind filled with a buzzing that could only be related to worry. I had no idea what kinds of questions Aaron would ask despite his so-called sample he'd given me at our last visit. But I was saying yes to the interview because I wanted to show the world how great horse racing was. It was one of the oldest sports in history, capturing the attention of both royals and the common man. Surely a sport that could bridge the class gap wasn't all that bad.

Yes, there were flaws, but too many people fixated on them. I wasn't saying ignore them, but they certainly shouldn't dominate the discussion. Everything should have a balance. If we ignored every good the horse-racing industry brought, we'd continue to see only the harm.

My phone buzzed, showing a visitor at the iron gate that kept out trespassers. I pressed the open button on my security app to allow Aaron to drive through. Knowing how little time it took to drive from the gate to my house, I rushed into the kitchen. After pouring two glasses of sweet tea, plating my favorite cookies, and then setting it all on the coffee table in the living room, I was prepared for company. Mama would be proud.

The doorbell pealed through my home.

"Here goes nothing," I whispered.

Aaron beamed at me from the other side of the threshold. "Piper McKinney. You might be my favorite meeting to date."

"Uh . . ." I stepped back. What was I supposed to say to that?

"Come in. We can talk in the living room." A quick walk past the foyer wall and I turned left.

My home was clutter free. Everything had its place, and I was thankful Mama had always shown me the importance of cleaning up after myself. I didn't have to worry about Aaron seeing anything unruly. Instead, he'd peer at the white shiplap walls holding various paintings of horses and their jockeys.

Like the one of Aristides and Oliver Lewis, the first Black jockey to win the Kentucky Derby. More importantly, the first jockey to win the Kentucky Derby since he participated in the inaugural 1875 race. Aristides had even had a Black trainer in Hall of Famer Ansel Williamson.

Aaron's obvious perusal of the paintings turned to the Thoroughbred lampstand on my end table to the glass-top coffee table, whose legs were fashioned from horseshoes, and then to me.

Okay, so maybe he would judge me on décor. What could I say? I was an equestrian lover.

"Have a seat." I gestured to the cream armchair as I took a place on the couch.

"Thank you."

"Tea? Cookies?" I reached for the glass on the wooden tray and passed it to him along with a ceramic coaster that held a depiction of a horse painted in watercolor. Okay, maybe I overdid the horse theme when I moved in, but it was *my* house and solely brought about by *my* wishes.

"Appreciate this," he said. He took a sip, then stared at me over the top of the glass. "May I record this meeting?"

Why did that make me want to run from the room? I simply nodded and watched as he pulled a recorder from his jacket and set it on the coffee table.

Aaron took another sip, then placed his glass on the coaster. "I have to admit, I don't know what to think of you."

"What do you mean?" Did journalists study their subjects

like a scientist studied bacteria growing in a petri dish, fascinated but ensuring they were gloved up?

"You've lived a comfortable life here in Eastbrook. I've seen pictures of your parents' estate. It's obvious you didn't want for anything growing up. Yet . . ." He rubbed his mustache.

I crossed my arms, then motioned for him to continue before tucking my hand back underneath my forearm.

"Yet you were adopted. That alone makes me wonder how life as an adoptee was. I read you were adopted at five, I believe. Did you ever feel like anything was missing? Were you able to maintain contact considering the vast distance between the two places?"

So I was the petri dish. Now I rubbed one wrist, trying to formulate a reply. Then I met Aaron's gaze. "What question do you want an answer to the most?"

He leaned forward, resting his elbows on his thighs as he grasped his hands together, a contemplative look on his face. "Honestly, I want to know what it was like growing up in a fishbowl."

"Do you mean because my parents are well-known?" Then again, outside of Kentucky and horse-racing circles, who cared about them?

"No." He stared right into my eyes. "I mean being the only Black person in a white area. I roamed the streets of Eastbrook, and it's quite obvious they're not used to seeing people of color. If the whole town didn't know you were adopted, one or two people probably would have asked if I was related to you."

I sighed. Why couldn't his question be about my chances of going to the Derby? *Lord, how do I answer something I'm not even sure I've entirely processed?*

"I don't know." I stared at Aaron, my thoughts one jumbled mess. "I don't mean to be vague, and I'm not trying to ignore your question, but honestly, I don't know. When I was a kid, obviously, I figured out the differences between me and everyone else pretty quickly. But it was like I was constantly weighing that against what I'd gained. A family. A best friend. Clothes on my body. Food in my stomach."

I had the barest recollection of being hungry at the orphanage. Only, I wasn't sure if it was a legit memory or my mind trying to create a backstory that made sense.

"Eventually the stares and mean comments stopped. And I accepted that I'm an only in the sea of a majority. But every now and again, someone does something to make me feel like I don't belong. Like I'm here only by happenstance."

"So how do you handle that? Does that sink you into depression? Are you bitter? Because you seem pretty joyful, at least there's"—he waved a hand in the air—"something about you that says you don't let those thoughts rule."

"Trust me, I spiral just like everyone else. But I then remind myself of what God says, so those thoughts *don't* rule."

He shifted in his seat. Was this where I lost the journalist? Would a path toward God make him bolt, or would he forge ahead?

"What does God say?"

Lord, please give me the words to plant a seed or to water what's already been sown.

"I'll recite Scripture from the Bible, like Jeremiah 29:11, where it talks about the plans God has for us. No matter my beginning, my middle, or whatever ends up being my end on this earth, God has His hand in it. He saved me from the orphanage. He's saved me in ways I'll never know. He's also blessed me in too many ways to count but never to forget. I remind myself of those things so I don't continue to spiral but instead reject the unhelpful thoughts. A verse in the book of Philippians talks about focusing on the good. I hold that close to me as well."

Aaron nodded, and with that answer, he steered the conversation to horse racing and how I caught the fever. The mention of my faith probably made him uncomfortable, but I wasn't worried. Instead, I would pray, asking that something about my life would speak to Aaron so that he'd be curious enough about God to seek Him for himself.

Six

Tuck studied horse and rider as Gabe jogged Dream around the track. In a couple of weeks, the team would be traveling back to Turfway Park for the Jeff Ruby Steaks—named after the owner of Jeff Ruby's Steakhouses. The possible points earned would be five times more than at the Battaglia Stakes, enough to cement a place at Churchill Downs.

The jockey slowed the colt, ending their twenty-minute jog. Jogging the Thoroughbreds before a gallop was a new technique gaining popularity in Japan, and Tuck had been itching to try it. So far it seemed to be working well for Dream.

"You ready for me to race him now?" Gabe asked.

The Latino was five-one and one hundred fifteen pounds soaking wet, yet the slight build was perfect for his position. Not to mention, the man had a great way with horses. Tuck could only continue to pray it would be a winning way with Dream. The thought of failing Piper when she'd placed so much trust in him to train the Thoroughbred had had him on his knees before the Lord ever since the season started.

"Yeah, take him to the gate."

Gabe pulled on the reins, directing the colt to the three-horse-wide starting gate. Tuck couldn't help but grin at the thought of the track, gate, and farm all under his ownership. If a few years ago you'd asked him if working on his own was a future goal, he would've adamantly said no. But now he found the experience filled him with pure joy.

He opened a horn app that mimicked the sound used on race days. Once the jockey signaled the okay, Tuck pressed the button, and Dream burst out of the gate.

Tuck analyzed the Thoroughbred's form and speed and the jockey's riding position. It all mattered. Gabe didn't use a whip to urge Dream to go faster, merely his hands to guide the colt.

They would probably go up a few days before the event to get Dream reacclimated with the Tapeta track. Tapeta comprised a mixture of silica sand, wax, and fibers to simulate the root structure of turf. It did pretty well in wet weather. Getting familiar with the surface conditions would help the young horse be better suited for racing conditions, especially considering Tuck's track was just dirt.

Once Gabe and Dream crossed the finish line, Tuck looked at the stopwatch.

"What was the time?" Gabe asked.

"1:02:2."

Gabe patted the colt's neck. "Thatta boy. But we need to shave off some time."

He wasn't wrong. Last year's winner, Two Phil's, had run a career best in the Derby, coming in at fifty-nine seconds.

"We'll try again next week," Tuck said.

The jockey nodded.

"Thanks for all your work."

"Want me to take him to the stables?"

Before Tuck could respond, his phone rang. He gave a thumbs-up, then hit the green accept button. "Hey, Mom, how's it going?"

"I'm just peachy. Do you want to come over for supper? Lasagna's on the menu."

His mouth watered at the thought of her famous dish. She

made the best lasagna in Eastbrook as far as he was concerned. "That sounds great. Thanks for the invite."

"You know you can come over whenever you want," she said. "You bringing Piper? We haven't seen her in a while."

By design. Tuck was still trying to figure out how to be her employee as well as her friend. Not to mention he still felt a little off-kilter since seeing her and Aaron Wellington at that two-seater table. Knowing the thoughts around the image filling his head were irrational did nothing to make them dissipate, so he'd kept to himself as much as possible, hoping they'd fade. "Not sure. Just saw her yesterday, but I can text her."

"I'm sure you're busy. I'll text her."

His stomach clenched. Piper would think he was upset with her. But if he texted her, he'd get a guaranteed yes. He blew out a breath. "I promise it's no trouble. I'll text her." If he said that enough times, maybe his brain would believe it.

It's not time to tell her. Stick to the plan.

"You sure?"

"Mm-hmm."

"Good. Then see you later."

He opened his text messages and clicked on the thread between him and Piper.

> Tuck
> Wanna eat at my folks' tonight? #lasagna

> Piper
> Oh man, I'm supposed to meet Aaron again tonight to talk about my childhood. 😩 Let me text and see if I can change the time.

Tuck wanted to reply a clipped *Don't bother*, but then he'd have to admit he was jealous. Had Piper picked up on that? He hoped not. But if she had, maybe she'd think his behavior merely a fluke. Which meant he had to be careful in his response.

> **Tuck**
> If you can, great. If not, I understand. You want the article to go viral.

> **Piper**
> I don't have to go viral, but knowing there will be a readership helps. Give me a sec.

Tuck headed to the stables. He needed to cool down the colt and get him some feed. Maybe even a sugar cube for his great efforts.

His phone chimed.

> **Piper**
> Okay. Aaron can meet earlier, so I can come. You picking me up?

> **Tuck**
> Don't I always?

> **Piper**
> 😳

> **Piper**
> Oh brother. Are you in a snit, or are you using your charming smirk I can't see?

His neck heated. She thought his smirk charming? Did that mean she saw more than friendship, or was she just being complimentary? *Ugh.* He hated thinking like this, dissecting every comment, look, and little detail of their relationship. He couldn't assume Piper had romantic thoughts like he did. But hoping she did made the thought of confessing his feelings easier.

> **Tuck**
> I'm always charming.

> **Piper**
> Keep telling yourself that. 😄

See! That right there was something a best friend or sister-type would say. He wanted to chuck his phone in frustration, but he just slid it into his back pocket. He'd talk to her when suppertime rolled around and he'd mentally prepared himself to not act like a love-sick fool.

Because being around Piper McKinney always had Tuck cataloging the ways he loved and wished for a perfect relationship. Knowing there was no such thing as perfection kept his mouth shut every time. Though sometimes . . . he wanted to take the risk.

● ● ●

Tuck turned his truck into his folks' subdivision. Though they lived a little more of a suburban life than he and Piper, their neighborhood was still made for horses. Trails that came with communal stables intertwined throughout the community. Most of the horses in the neighborhood were older, retired racehorses.

Piper bounced in her seat. "I can't wait to see your folks. It feels like forever."

"My mom thought the same thing." He spared a glance to take another peek at her pretty face. "She's probably made your favorite dessert since you're coming."

"She would have made one for you—if you had a favorite."

Good point. His mom was kind that way. Only Tuck didn't really care for desserts.

He stopped at the red-brick home in the middle of the property belonging to his parents. Every home in the neighborhood was blessed with one to two acres of surrounding land. His folks had about one and three-fourths acres.

Before he and Piper made it halfway up the front walk, his dad stepped out onto the porch. "Two of my favorite people. How are you, son?"

Tuck met his dad's embrace, then tried not to wince at the vigorous pats on the back. His father might be aging, but there was no sign of waning strength in his hugs.

"I'm good, Dad."

"Glad to hear it." He turned to Piper. "How 'bout a hug from my honorary daughter?"

"Of course." Piper slid her arms around his dad and hugged him tightly. "Sorry I haven't seen you in a bit. Life's been busy."

"Well, I'm always here. Feel free to stop by and bother this ol' hermit. Thanks to retired life, I'm at the whim of the missus. She's either dragging me to run errands or letting me sit out back all day."

"Oh, please, Leslie. You act like I'm your warden." Tuck's mom stood in the doorway and rolled her eyes.

"*Warden, wife,* both start with W's. Ain't a coincidence."

Tuck bit down on his tongue to keep his smile hidden. Choosing sides was never an option.

"*Husband, headache* . . . Yes, I see what you mean," Mom shot back.

Piper met Tuck's gaze, eyes dancing with suppressed laughter.

They followed his dad and mom back inside, and Tuck shut the screen door behind them. Smells of basil, garlic, and something else filled the air. Tuck wanted to race to the dining table and start eating, but his parents would probably amble their way while picking Piper's brain or asking Tuck questions that could instead be shared over dinner.

"How's the training going, son?"

See.

Tuck turned to his dad, who'd fallen back while the women walked ahead of them in the hallway. "Good." He swallowed. "I'm a little nervous."

"You've done great. I'm proud of you." His dad laid a hand on his shoulder.

"Thanks. I appreciate that."

"What are you two talking about?" Mom said, turning around to interrupt them.

"Just giving Tuck accolades for his training efforts. I'm sure Ms. Piper's pleased, aren't you?"

"Definitely." Piper shot him a grin. "Tuck's the best."

The best what? Trainer? Friend? Or . . .

Tuck pushed away his thoughts so he wouldn't analyze them to death and worry about heat traveling from his neck to his face, giving his inner thoughts away.

"Sit, sit," his mom said, now shooing them along.

Dad took the head of the table, and the rest of them filled in the four-chair seating. "Smells good, Caroline."

"Sure does, Mrs. Hale," Piper said.

After they'd said grace, filled their plates, and spent a few minutes just eating the delicious meal, Mom broke the silence. "Piper, I think it's just absolutely amazing what you're doing in the racing world."

"What do you mean?" Piper dipped her garlic bread in the lasagna sauce oozing on her plate.

"Why, going the distance with a horse that others underestimated." His mom clapped her hands and sighed. "You're an inspiration to many, dear. Most people wouldn't want to put in all that work."

"I may have an idea how being underestimated feels. No one wants to feel less than."

Piper's words came out nonchalantly, but everything in Tuck tensed. Had her conversations with Aaron Wellington forced her to relive moments of feeling less than in the orphanage? Why hadn't he thought to ask how everything went with the man?

Because you were protecting yourself, that's why. But what had his silence cost Piper?

He stared at her, taking in her short afro, pretty ebony eyes, and dark brown skin as smooth as velvet. Not a single hair was out of place nor did any sign of farm life linger on her simple shirt and jeans. If it weren't for his cataloging every single detail, he might've missed the hurt lingering in her eyes.

"Well, isn't that the truth?" his mom continued. "Some people have no problem casting aside the undesirable."

Tuck tried to catch his mom's eye, but she seemed oblivious to the undercurrents in the room. At least both he and Piper had finished what was on their plates, and he doubted she wanted seconds any more than he did.

"Uh, Mom, can we be excused? I think we could use a ride around the neighborhood." He met his dad's gaze. "Is it okay if we ride the horses?"

"Sure thing." His dad cast a worried glance at Piper. "Take your time."

"But come back for dessert," his mom said. She eyed Piper, blinking rapidly as if now realizing something was off. "I made your favorite."

"Will do," Tuck said, assuring her they would.

Seven

Want to tell me what's bothering you?" Tuck asked. I glanced at him from Dorcus's back. We'd saddled up his parents' horses and were now ambling down the trails in the subdivision.

"I'm not sure I have the words."

My mind wouldn't stop cataloging moments I'd experienced rejection. From Mama, whenever I tried to become a little more independent. And from Tuck—though was it really his fault if I never told him how I felt about him? Not to mention every single time I walked into a space as a minority and others assumed I had no right to be there. When would the world stop rejecting me?

"Was it something Mom said? Me?"

I shook my head. "You're great. You never get on my bad side." *Much.* Again, I couldn't truly fault him for treating me like a friend if I never expressed a want for anything different.

It's better this way. If Tuck remains your best friend, then he'll never disappoint you in that area.

"Because I'm not a fool," Tuck said.

I chuckled, feeling a little brightness push away the darkness.

"Except that one time in middle school when you asked if I was on my period." My lips pursed, and I stared at him, daring him to remember the full error of his ways.

Tuck's face turned red. "I blame that on my newfound education. It only seemed to make sense because you were so moody."

"Oh, and you forgetting my birthday didn't factor into it?"

"Well, no. I'd forgotten it, remember?" He smirked.

How I loved that expression on him. No one should make smug look that adorable. "Whatever, Tucker Hale." I made sure my scoff came out loud and over the top so he wouldn't suspect the hidden feelings I chose to set aside.

"So who got on your bad side? Aaron?" he asked cautiously.

I studied Tuck, then decided it was better just to tell him everything. "Not necessarily. Hearing your mom talk about being cast aside triggered some memories." Not to mention, being reminded that Dream did live up to the potential I saw in him.

"Which ones?"

I held on to the saddle, staring off into the evening sky. I didn't discuss racial issues with Tuck that often. Never really felt a hundred percent comfortable divulging my deepest fears to those I loved, not even to the man who knew me the best. "Aaron asked how big of a factor race played into my upbringing."

Tuck's blue eyes flickered across my face as if searching for my true emotions. "What did you tell him?"

"At first I tried to avoid answering. But honestly, talking to him about it felt kind of safe." My gaze darted to Tuck's. How could I explain that the safety came from Aaron being in the same minority bracket, not from a close relationship?

Tuck looked taken aback. "You trust him that quickly?"

"Not really. But being in the same ethnic group makes a difference." I hid the wince that wanted to crawl onto my face.

Tuck turned away, his jaw rigid. Had I upset him? Was he hurt that I didn't share that part of me with him so readily? "Tuck?"

"Hmm?"

I guided Dorcus closer to his horse. "I never wanted you to feel uncomfortable."

Tuck faced me. His brow was furrowed and his mouth down-turned, yet I had no idea what the expression on his face meant. It wasn't his angry one or even a sad one.

"Tuck?"

"What does that cost you?"

I blinked. "What do you mean?"

"What does not sharing how you truly feel about a subject because I'm white . . . what does that cost you?"

Tears welled in my eyes. No one had ever asked me that. Not Mama, not Daddy. I bit my lip, searching for the words.

"I want to be there for you." Tuck sighed. "I hope you know that's all I've ever wanted. To be someone you can trust with *everything*. Even if you think it'll make me uncomfortable. I don't want comfort at the cost of yours."

My throat ached from unshed tears. I wanted to fall into Tuck's arms and share every single emotion coursing through me. But I couldn't let the romantic feelings out. How could I say what I needed to say without showing that?

I wiped at an errant tear. "You *are* that person. Just because I shared something with Aaron doesn't mean I value him more than you." I gathered courage and looked Tuck in the eye. "Be-cause of who you are, I'm able to share more of myself with you than anyone else."

"Then know you can talk about racial issues. I won't die of shock. I sincerely hope I won't ask insensitive questions, but I ask you to check me if I do. Is that okay?"

Could I share that part of myself with him? After all, Tuck's rejecting me as a love interest because of my race was one of my biggest fears. But if I shared, maybe I could see how he handled things. I could see if sharing my feelings for him was actually a possibility.

"Okay, Tuck."

He gave me a cautious smile.

"Ask me anything." I threw my hands into the air, symbolizing throwing caution to the wind. Only I could tell how much my insides quaked.

Tuck didn't say anything immediately. Knowing him, he was measuring everything flitting through his mind before deciding what was best to say.

"Do you ever think your parents made a mistake adopting you?" he asked quietly.

Too many times. More tears sprang to my eyes. "I don't want to answer that."

Tuck leaned across Jedidiah and pulled on Dorcus's reins. The horses came to a stop as his gaze met mine.

"God knew who would raise you, Piper McKinney. He knew every struggle you'd go through. But remember this, none of it's wasted. God'll use it all for good. *All* of it."

A tear slipped down my cheek. "I just feel so lost sometimes. Like I don't know who I am, but I do, but then that version isn't good enough for people."

"Who? People like those in the media? They're only chasing after a story. All that matters is what God thinks. Not a single person on this side of heaven, including me and your folks, matter. You answer to God."

But I wanted my parents to matter. I wanted Tuck's opinion to have weight as well. "Y'all are my people, though." I hated hearing my voice crack, knowing a full crying session would be coming if I didn't take in steady breaths.

"And we always will be." Tuck's lips softened into a smile. "I've got your back, Piper. I don't expect you to conform to some ideal version of who I think you should be. Be yourself.

Be who God made you to be and how life circumstances have shaped you. Value every dip in the valley and every rise up the mountaintop."

I wiped my face with the hem of my shirt. "You always have such a way with words." I took the reins and blew out a breath. "Thanks."

"Of course."

We guided the horses back into a walk. "Tuck?"

"Hmm?"

"Do you think my mama will ever see me as an adult? Do you think she'll stop caring about what society thinks and let me just be?" As much as I wondered if my folks made a mistake adopting me, I couldn't forget how much I loved them and they loved me. They were my parents, and nothing would change that.

"I don't know what drives your mom to be that way. She'd wrap you in a bubble if she could. Having you work for them, keeping you in the same house . . . When you moved out, you took the control away from her. She either has to adapt or . . ." He shrugged.

I hated that he was right. I guess it was the need to please my parents that made part of me want to move back home. "I'll always be their daughter. I simply want to be the adult I am and live the story God has for me." Then again, my folks were part of that story. God knew how Mama would be.

"You are." He gave me such a look of pride that my heart filled my chest cavity to the brim. "I believe one day God'll make the paths straight. Just keep praying."

"I will." I'd pray as soon as I got home. Maybe I just wasn't letting Mama know how much her so-called suggestions bothered me.

"You feeling better?"

"Yep."

He gave me a cagey grin. "Then want to race?"

"To the sign?" I leaned forward, already getting into position.

"Yep."

"You're on." I squeezed Dorcus's sides and whooped as she took off, leaving Tuck behind.

Of course, he wouldn't stay there. Tuck loved competition, and we'd been racing since we learned how to ride. The wind blew across my face, and I looked over my shoulder. Tuck rode low over Jedidiah, and he neared Dorcus's hindquarters. Pretty soon he'd be in the lead if I didn't urge the mare to go faster.

"Come on, girl," I whispered.

Her ears flickered backward, and she surged forward. Before I knew it, we'd come to the subdivision sign ahead of Tuck and Jedidiah. I threw my hands into the air, cheering as we came to a canter, then slowed to a stop.

Tuck shook his head. "Had no idea Dorcus had it in her."

"Ha! That's what you get for underestimating her." I rubbed her side, murmuring encouraging words.

"Such a good girl," I whispered. "You showed them."

It was my hope that Dream would do the same thing. Continue to show up, race after race, and beat the odds.

"Want to race back?" Tuck asked.

"No way. I'm going out on top, Tucker Hale. You won't take my win from me."

He threw his head back and laughed. "You're so suspicious."

"Am I?" I arched an eyebrow. Tuck was always trying to race again after I beat him.

I would end this day on a good note. Spending time with him, eating delicious food with his folks . . . It would keep me from dwelling on the things I couldn't change.

"All right, then. We'll head back. I'm sure Mom is ready to serve the dessert."

"I hope she made her bourbon pound cake." Living in Kentucky, you could figure out how to add bourbon to just about anything. But the way Tuck's mom made her pound cake was divine. You got the taste of the bourbon without the effects of alcohol. I considered it a win.

"Fine. Race you there," I called over my shoulder, laughing as Tuck yelled, "No fair!"

Eight

Famous Bolt Brook Thoroughbred Farm under Investigation for Illegal Substances

What in the world? Tuck clicked on the notification on his phone. Thanks to internet algorithms and cookies, ever since purchasing a smartphone, he constantly received alerts related to horse racing. Only Tuck never imagined seeing a photo of the McKinneys under *that* particular headline.

He quickly scanned the article, and with each passing line, Tuck's stomach tensed, and his heart drummed heavily in his ears. He clicked on the comment section of the article.

How dare they endanger those horses.

Tbredfan4life

No surprises here. That's how all those big farms make their money. I wouldn't be surprised if all the horses needed drug testing.

HorsesRtheReason

Maybe they should investigate the daughter as well. She owns her own farm now.

KYBlue2

Everyone who has ever worked for them needs to be investigated.

Not4Sportz

Tuck grimaced.

"Everything okay?" Mordecai asked.

"Uh, not sure." Tuck glanced up at the vet. He'd forgotten the doc was there to check out Tuck's animals. "Do you need me to stick around?" He needed to get to Piper's before she found out about her parents by internet alert or worse.

"No. Everyone looks good. I doubt there will be a problem. If so, I'll call."

"Appreciate that, Mordecai." Tuck tipped his cowboy hat, then rushed out of the stables. Normally, he'd hop on one of the horses and head to Piper's place that way, but since they were getting their checkups, he'd take his truck.

Lord, I don't know if what the article claims is true, but please, help Piper through this. The media will be reaching out for a comment if they haven't already.

He winced. Aaron Wellington would certainly be getting fodder for his magazine feature. Would the journalist make life more difficult for Piper or become an ally?

Tuck put the truck in gear and thought about how emotional Piper had been after her last conversation with the man. He could only pray that he would be the exception and not meet all the stereotypes Tuck had for reporters. Surely working for a magazine made the man more inclined to report the truth.

Piper would be devastated at the allegations against her parents, true or not. *Lord, please let them be false.*

Even though Tuck had worked for the McKinneys—part-time as a teen and full-time once he'd received his degree—he'd never seen anything to suggest Ian McKinney allowed illegal substances for Bolt Brook's horses. Then again, Tuck hadn't been high up on the chain. It was certainly possible to do something illegal without everyone at the farm in the loop. After all, the fewer people who knew, the easier it would be to pass as legit, right?

Don't speculate.

Tuck punched the code into Piper's security system, waited for the iron gate to open, and then drove up the black asphalt and parked. He ran up the sidewalk, but his senses took hold before he pounded on the door. If she hadn't seen the article, he didn't want to rush into her house like he was being chased. Pulling every ounce of reserve, he knocked twice.

His boots tapped a mindless rhythm as he waited for the sound of a lock turning, but nothing came. He rapped his knuckles against the wood louder. "Come on, Pipsqueak," he murmured. After a few moments more, he checked his watch.

Maybe she was riding? Or doing something around her farm?

Was it possible she was with Aaron Wellington?

Please, no, Lord. I have a feeling he'd just make the situation worse.

Tuck went around the side of the house. Scanning the horizon didn't show her on horseback. Every step across the grass brought him closer to Piper's stables but no closer to an answer. Just as he was about to take another step, a sniffle hit his ears. He froze, eyes darting to the left where the small goat barn stood.

There sat Piper, holding her white Pygmy goat, Ice Ice, while tears streamed down her face. The other goat, Baby, brown with white patches, nuzzled against Piper as if trying to comfort her. Tuck's heart dropped to his toes like an anvil from a four-story building.

She knew.

He trudged over to the barn and unlatched the gate. At the sound of his steps, Piper looked up. The moment she saw him, sobs tore free. She let go of the goat and launched herself into his arms. He pulled her to him, surrounding her with his arms as tight as he could while she buried her face into his chest. They stood there until his shirt dampened and Piper's sobs settled to hiccups.

"Want to go inside?" he asked. "I'll make you some tea." She always drank tea when something upset her.

She sniffed. "Tea sounds good."

Tuck wrapped an arm around her shoulders and tugged her toward the house. He didn't know what to say. Should he tell her it would be okay? What if it wouldn't? What if her parents had done what they were accused of? Should he offer a Bible verse to give her comfort?

Which one, though?

His mind remained as blank as a sheet of paper. He led Piper inside and headed for the kitchen, where she sat down at the round table taking up space to the far left. She had a dazed look on her face that tugged at Tuck's heart.

He grabbed her teakettle resting on the stove and filled the navy-blue pot with water. After turning on the gas burner, he perused the tea offerings, then selected an herbal one. He wasn't a tea drinker, but he'd seen Piper drink tea enough to know this was the one she reached for the most. That and the low quantity gave him a clue.

"Want to talk about it?" he asked.

Her eyes darted to his face, then away. She shook her head.

Maybe she needed a snack too. No telling when she'd eaten last. He opened the fridge and assessed the contents. He grabbed some already cooked bacon, a tomato, and fresh lettuce. After toasting two slices of the sesame bread she had, Tuck made his favorite comfort food—a BLT.

He placed the sandwich in front of her as the kettle began its soprano ascent to a screech. He readied her tea and set the mug on the table before her, pleased to see half her sandwich already gone. Tuck took the chair opposite her and watched as she began sipping her tea.

"A reporter called me this morning. Asked me if I wanted to make a comment regarding the accusations against my parents." Piper's voice was low and shook every few words as if she were holding back more tears. "You can imagine my shock."

"I was hoping I'd be the one to break the news."

Piper tilted her head as if to say, *What can you do?* "I definitely would've preferred that."

"Did you make a comment?"

"No. I hung up and turned off my cell, then searched on my laptop for an article."

Tuck winced inwardly. "You didn't read any comments, did you?"

"Maybe . . ."

"Piper." He groaned.

"I know. I know. But what was I supposed to do when I saw it trending on X? Of course I clicked on the hashtag."

Did he even want to know? "There's a hashtag?"

"Oh, you must have clicked on a news outlet like an old person."

Tuck chuckled, thankful she could still crack jokes. "It's the only way to get reliable news."

"Maybe so, but X will have you know #McKinneyGate is not a surprise. Obviously, my parents only produce such champion Thoroughbreds because they use blood-doping agents."

Well, if the world had assigned a hashtag, the news was worse than Tuck had anticipated. He thought it would only stick to the horsing community. "Did it say how many tweets were associated with the hashtag?"

"About ten thousand."

Tuck let out a low whistle. Last time he saw that much noise was during Netflix's live reunion for season four of *Love Is Blind*. A live reunion that didn't happen live and ended with fans upset with one of the cohosts. Tuck knew horse racing had a huge base tuned in to either watch or bet. But was it really that many who tweeted this morning?

"Have you called your folks?"

Piper's eyes flashed. "Like they called me to inform me they were facing a criminal investigation?"

"Maybe they were trying to spare you."

She threw her hands into the air. "My parents are being accused of tampering with champions. If they're found guilty—" She swiped at the tears now running down her face. "Why wouldn't they tell me something this huge, Tuck?"

"You know they've always tried to shield you from too much media attention."

"I'm an adult!"

Tuck sent up a prayer asking for wisdom. He understood where Piper was coming from, but he also understood the desire to shield a loved one from drama.

"I know that. So do your parents. But you'll always be their child, no matter how old you get. Believe me, my mom tells me that often. Your folks are great at shielding you from unwanted public attention. How do you think you got to be so normal while some of the other trust fund babies became brats?"

"I hate that you're right." She sniffed. "It just hurts. Feels like another exclusion."

Could he just tuck her into the crook of his arm and never let go? Probably not. Seemed like shades of her parents . . . 2.0 style.

He stroked his beard. "I imagine it does. Try thinking about what they're feeling. Their whole lives are on display for the world to see and become judge and jury. If anything paints them in an untrustworthy light—regardless if it's true or not—the public will use that to execute them on social media. It's sort of like what Lamont went through."

Lamont was practically a monk. So even though pictures of

him and Nevaeh had been plastered all over the internet suggesting he wasn't representing a Christian walk, Tuck had never doubted his innocence. Once he heard the true story, Tuck had been grateful to live in Kentucky and not under a microscope like Lamont did in Hollywood.

But apparently, the spotlight had now been directed toward Eastbrook, with Piper's folks under the hot lights.

"I'm so self-absorbed," Piper murmured.

"No, you're not. You're human. Anyone would react the way you did."

Her lips pursed. "So you'd run into your fields, grab a goat, and sob your guts out?"

"I don't have any goats." He winked. "But I did go grab the girl and let her sob her guts out somewhere a little more comfortable than sitting in dirt and grass."

Piper tossed her balled-up tissue at him, and he juked to the side, letting it sail past him.

"Do you want me to take you to Bolt Brook?" he asked as he stood.

"Yes, now that you've talked some sense into me."

"You'll get through this, Pipsqueak."

He held out his arms, and when she walked into them, Tuck said a little prayer of thanks that he could be there for her in this way.

In any way, honestly.

* * *

Lamont
I don't even know what to say. Know Nevaeh and I are praying for Piper and her family.

Chris
Same. I'm sure the media storm is hard right now, but God's got her.

Tuck
Appreciate y'all more than you know.

Nine

Silence filled the truck's cab as Tuck passed through the wrought-iron gate of Bolt Brook Thoroughbred Farm. It would be a half mile until we reached the white house—painted that particular shade where shadows and light made the color appear warmer or darker—that had been my childhood home. The house—well, mansion, really—was more than sixteen thousand square feet and had made for a great place to play hide-and-seek with Tuck in our younger days.

However, passing the parked news vans and photojournalists trying to get a shot of the comings and goings had put a damper on my happy memories. Fortunately for my folks, their estate comprised three hundred and twenty-five acres of rolling bluegrass. Unless one of the media companies came equipped with a drone, they wouldn't get the photos they were hoping for and still maintain the no-trespassing laws.

I prayed my parents' legacy would overcome the accusations currently hurled in their direction. Bolt Brook had always been where horse legends were bred, trained, and became winners for their future owners. My breath shuddered when the sprawling house came into view. Tears pricked at my eyes, and I blinked multiple times trying to keep them at bay. Tuck had seen me blubber enough.

He parked in the circular driveway and then peered at me. "Want me to come inside with you?"

Boy, did I. Yet I had no idea what I'd be walking into. For some reason, I wanted to shield Tuck from that—or maybe save myself the embarrassment. "I think I got this."

"You sure?" He reached over and squeezed my hand.

I wanted to grip his hand and hang on to the lifeline he offered. Even let him whisper words of comfort and assure me this was all a bad dream. His holding me as I poured out my heart in tears earlier had been the most achingly tender thing he'd ever done. Not including the care he'd shown by making me tea and a sandwich.

But if I leaned on him one more time, my worries would fall by the wayside, and I'd be confusing the feelings that had risen in his embrace—thanks to the delicious woodsy cologne clinging to him—with something that had only been meant to bring comfort. Yet I couldn't shake his scent from my memory. Breathing in his essence reminded me of roasting marshmallows at a bonfire or snuggling under blankets with a fire crackling in the hearth. Tucker Hale was my weakness.

Back to the issue at hand.

I'd been trying to tell my parents how independent I truly was. If Tuck came inside, surely that would be proof I wasn't. Not to mention the very real fear I'd be sucked right back into the place I'd been trying to leave since I turned eighteen and craved more freedoms.

You can do this. Walk in there, find out what's going on, and then return to your own home.

The thought bolstered me. I wasn't dependent on my parents now. I owned my own property and business. I could go in there, support them, and not feel the need to turn into a people pleaser that would have me moving in, in an effort to console them.

I drew in a deep breath and let go of Tuck's hand, immediately missing its warmth. "I'll be fine." God was with me, but I'd have to repeat that statement over and over to let my anxiety-filled brain remember the truth. "Just please pray for me while I'm in there."

"Already started."

The sincerity in his gaze made me forget my rules as I wrapped my arms around his neck. "You're the best . . . *friend* ever." I let go. "I'll text you if I decide to stay long." No use making him wait out here forever.

"Roger that."

As I walked up the outdoor stairs, I whispered my own prayer. "Lord God, please give me the words. Please let me know what to say to my folks. How to help. Please be in the midst of our conversation. Amen."

I entered the double-paned glass doors and stopped in the foyer, listening for sounds of occupancy. Then I pulled out my cell to text my dad. Maybe he could tell me where he was so I wouldn't end up wandering from room to room.

"Piper?"

My inner child sighed in relief at the sound of Mama's voice, and I turned and stared. Her gorgeous red hair was pulled back with a headband that matched the cream-colored sweats she wore. My mother rarely dressed down, so to see her face free of makeup and with dark circles under her eyes pricked every sympathetic nerve in my system.

"I saw the news." I still stood near the doors, unsure of what to do. Should I hug her and tell her it would all pass over?

"Pretty sure the whole world has seen it." The derision in her voice broke my heart.

Again, I wanted to kick myself for not considering what my folks were going through and focusing only on feeling left out. "I thought I'd come offer support or comfort or . . ." I shrugged.

Mama crossed the hall and wrapped me in her arms. I buried my face in the crook of her neck as she started rocking us back and forth. Her arms held me tightly as her body started to shake.

"I can't believe anyone would accuse us of such a thing," she wailed.

Somehow, we'd switched places. I was now the comforter as I patted her back and whispered nonsensical words in her ear. The same way she'd soothed me when I was a child waking up from nightmares or crying over a scraped knee.

After a while, Mama drew back and stared at me. "You shouldn't have come. What if they photographed you and display your picture all over the media too?"

Of course she was concerned about me. I offered a small smile. "You're my mama. Of course I'm coming over when I read such headlines. You know I care about what affects you and Dad."

She nodded. "Still, I wouldn't want them to add mean comments about you."

Obviously, she wasn't reading the comments on the articles. The judgments had already been thrown. "I'll be fine, Mama."

"Your father's in his office." She sighed. "He's been staring at his trophies ever since the news broke."

I wasn't too sure why my parents called the shrine room—my nickname—Dad's office. Sure, a desk and chair occupied some of the space, but so did tons of trophies, ribbons, and framed photos that were a testament to Bolt Brook's legacy. I doubted he did any actual office work while sitting in there.

"Have y'all had lunch?" I asked.

Mama shook her head. "I can't eat."

"Maybe you should try."

"Maybe." She sniffed. "You want to join us for lunch?"

"I'd like that." Even though I'd had a BLT, I'd eat again to be surrounded by my loved ones. I hooked my arm with hers and guided us to the kitchen.

"The chef has the day off. I didn't want the staff to have to drive through the reporters."

"It's fine." I'd rather cook for myself, though having a chef had been a perk growing up here. Yet if I had the budget, I'd pick a cleaning service over a chef. Cleaning took too much time I'd rather spend outdoors.

I let go of Mama's arm and pulled out my cell to text Tuck. He'd been sitting in the driveway long enough. I'd find my way home later.

"Who are you texting?"

"Tuck. He gave me a ride here."

Mama stopped walking. "Is he still outside?"

"Yeah." I met her gaze. "He was waiting to hear if I would need a ride home."

"Piper Imani McKinney, tell that boy to come inside. No sense idling out in the driveway when we have enough seating to host another friendly face."

"Are you sure?"

"Yes. Tell him to come on in." She made a waving motion with her hand, then moved toward the fridge. "I'm assuming he'll be hungry too?"

"He always is." I'd never seen Tuck turn down a meal.

> **Piper**
> Mama said to come inside.

> **Tuck**
> I don't wanna encroach on family time.

> **Piper**
>

> **Tuck**
> Lol, all right. I'm coming.

> **Piper**
> Good. Head to the kitchen.

"Did you tell him where we are?" Mama asked.

"Yes."

She looked up from the stove. "How've you been?"

"Busy."

"You ready for the next race?"

Yes and no. I didn't really have to do anything to be ready. Tuck was the hard worker in this scenario. But sitting in the owner's box, having reporters come talk to me . . . It all made me anxious despite my love for the sport. "Somewhat."

"I can only imagine. Have you bought more horses? Is that your plan?"

"Yes. I don't want to own as many as y'all, but I do have two purchases in the works." Thanks to Dream's previous wins, I could afford the bill. "Of course, I'm hoping Dream will go the distance so I can use him as a stud in the future."

"I'm sure he'll do well enough."

Well enough. Did Mama expect me to fail? Was that why she was always giving me tips and suggestions? Because she didn't believe in me?

I didn't have the heart to ask the questions mulling inside me. I'd never really told Mama how insecure I felt the majority of the time. And now I just smiled and continued listening to her as she flipped the tuna melt in the skillet.

"I love your melts."

Her eyes crinkled with her grin. Though Mama chose to keep dying her hair the color of her youth—her words, not mine—everything else on her was slowly aging. Sometimes it was weird to watch her get older. Other times it made me wonder what I'd look like as I aged. I couldn't base the information on Mama's own looks, and at times that fact hurt my heart. I was missing the connection of genetics on a daily basis.

Yet I couldn't deny that I had my father's temperament and my mother's love for rom-com movies. You'd think having those would lessen the desire for the DNA portion, but the yearning in my heart never went away.

The sound of footsteps interrupted my dive into melancholy, and I breathed a sigh of relief when Tuck stepped into the kitchen.

"Afternoon, Mrs. McKinney."

"Hey there, Tuck. Thanks for bringing Piper over."

He nodded, then came to sit next to me. His blue eyes searched mine, and when I gave him a small smile, letting him know I was fine, his lips quirked up in response.

"Do you want some lunch?" Mama asked.

"Yes, please. If it's not too much trouble."

"Tuna melt okay?"

"Yes, ma'am."

She glanced at him. "How are your folks?"

"They're good. Enjoying the retirement life."

"I bet. Piper, why don't you be a dear and go see if you can convince your dad to join us for a meal?"

I bit my lip. Was she purposely splitting Tuck and me up? I glanced her way, then his. He motioned for me to go.

"Sure. Be right back."

When I got to the doorway, I turned to look over my shoulder, and unease sprouted in every unspoken worry. Mama was up to something.

Ten

A s soon as Piper left the room, Jackie McKinney faced Tuck and stared him down. He resisted the very strong urge to swallow.

"Tell me the truth. How'd she handle the news?"

Huh. Not what he thought she'd ask. Would answering be violating best friend codes? Finally, Tuck settled for "Not well."

She shook her head. "Life hits Piper harder than it does most of us." Mrs. McKinney assessed him. "Then again, I suppose you know that."

"Yes, ma'am." He always knew Piper hid some of her feelings. Oh, she wasn't afraid to cry in front of someone, displaying some measure of how much something affected her. But hearing the words, her actual thoughts? That was an entirely different story. Often an untold one, so Tuck had to ask God to help fill in the blanks.

"Please watch over her, Tuck."

He wanted to ask if the headlines were true, but he didn't. Instead, he nodded to let her know he was still listening. "I'll always support her."

Her lips wisped up into a smile. "I know. Anything you want to tell me in that arena?"

"No, ma'am." If he was going to confess, it wouldn't be to Mrs. McKinney first.

"You know, we've always had big dreams for her."

"She knows that."

Now her lips pursed. "But does she understand it? Sometimes I feel like I failed her as a mom."

"I think most parents feel that way, Mrs. McKinney." At least, Tuck's mom had expressed that to him a few times.

"That's true." She paused. "I don't want to get in the way of her dreams, but I also don't know how best to support them."

"I know she appreciates it when you attend the races."

"That's such a small thing." She waved it off like an invisible gnat had entered her orbit.

"Not when presence is the one thing she craves." He grimaced inwardly. That felt like breaking the friend code. He probably should have kept that tidbit to himself.

"Piper needs more friends."

"She made one in Nevaeh." At her blank stare, he explained. "Lamont Booker's girlfriend."

"How on earth does she know her?"

"Uh . . . Lamont's my friend."

Tuck appreciated his friendship with Lamont and Chris. At times, he forgot Lamont was a famous actor and Chris had his own fans as a YouTube influencer. Though they both lived outside Kentucky, Tuck knew they were only a text or FaceTime away. In fact, maybe the time had come to finally share his feelings about Piper with them.

Hearing Mrs. McKinney ask him to look after her reminded Tuck he'd been doing that ever since he became Piper's friend. He'd always be in her corner. He just wanted the right to be *more*.

"I didn't know you knew him." She looked at him as if remeasuring his worth.

That was the thing about Mrs. McKinney. She'd never treated

Tuck badly per se, but he had a feeling she judged him never-theless. Considering he came from horse trainer stock and the McKinneys came from Millionaires' Row, the two weren't des-tined to meet. But horse racing had changed, and the million-aires weren't always the owners. Famous trainers had accrued as much thanks to the rise in stakes.

At least Chris and Lamont had never belittled him for being "just a horse trainer." In fact, Lamont saw enough value in his occupation to pick Tuck's brain for a movie role Lamont played. Could Mrs. McKinney look at Tuck and see his true worth?

I know your worth.

Chills pricked the back of his neck, and Tuck almost looked up toward the ceiling. It wasn't an audible voice so much as an inner stirring that sounded very much like God's still, small voice.

Thank You, Lord.

"Maybe you can help Piper make friends with someone local."

"Why do you want her to have more friends?" *Or is it just me you don't want her to hang around?*

Mrs. McKinney sighed. "I want her to have a community around her. They'll be there for her when the time gets rough . . . like today." She'd whispered the last part.

"Isn't it better to have true friends than ones who merely live nearby and might be around only because of your net worth?"

"Maybe." She met Tuck's gaze. "But dressing the part, sur-rounding yourself with influential people . . . it all helps. I want Piper to settle down, have children. I want to plan a wedding so lavish others will be jealous. I want the world for my daughter."

"What about what she wants?" he asked softly.

"I'm sure having a family of her own is a dream of hers."

"Is it?" He hoped the same, but that was neither here nor there. He had a point to prove. "Seems like she moved out because you weren't willing to listen to her dreams or help put them in motion."

She drew back. "Oh, and you did?"

"It's why I'm training a horse for her, and that's why she can practically reach for the fruition of her dreams now."

"It's her trust fund that gave her the leg up to begin with."

Why was it always money with Mrs. McKinney? "Maybe so. But what she needs is your understanding, not your credit card. She wants you cheering in her corner."

"I'll always cheer for my daughter."

"Then make sure she knows that."

"Of course Piper knows that."

Was he talking in circles? He rubbed his chin, searching for the words. Then the sound of footsteps had him looking over his shoulder.

"Dad's hungry," Piper chimed cheerily as she entered the room.

Seeing the happy look on her face told him she'd had a good conversation with her father. She was such a daddy's girl, but in the way that had Tuck hoping he'd be just as good of a father to any children he and Piper had.

Hold on, man. You have to date her, then marry her before you can talk about those 2.5 kids.

"Oh good. Lunch is ready," Mrs. McKinney said. She wiped her hand on a dish towel, eyeing Tuck out of her peripherals.

He wasn't sure if that look meant *I'm not done talking* or *Say nothing about this conversation.* Regardless, Tuck was done with their talk. He'd said his piece, tried to get Mrs. McKinney to consider Piper's wants. It was up to her and God to do the rest of the work.

As Tuck sat at the kitchen table, he watched Piper as inconspicuously as possible. He searched for anything that would give him a hint of her feelings. *Lord God, could You show me something?*

What if Piper cared for him the way he cared for her? Could he skip some of the steps in his plan, make a play for her heart, and still come out smelling like roses? Or was it better to show Mrs. McKinney and anyone else watching that he could make something of himself and provide for her?

"What were y'all talking about in here?" Mr. McKinney asked when he came in. "Looks like it was a serious conversation."

"Tuck was just expressing his concern over the news." Mrs. McKinney waved a hand. "I told him your lawyers have everything under control."

Okay, so the look had meant *Say nothing about this conversation.*

"You have lawyers?" Piper asked.

"Of course we do. The same ones we use for business are helping us out with these ridiculous accusations," Mr. McKinney said.

Tuck studied his former employer. Ian McKinney had aged overnight. Deep grooves lined his mouth and creased his forehead. Not to mention it looked like his hair had become more salt than pepper since the last time he'd seen the man.

For the first time since Tuck read the news article, he wondered how it would affect Piper if Bolt Brook was actually found guilty of using blood-doping agents. Trying to increase the number of red blood cells in a horse was a huge no-no. Yeah, the drugs could possibly increase the horse's oxygen capacity and performance, but they could also increase the risk of stroke and heart attack.

This wasn't just about the legalities of horse racing but the humanity of raising horses. Piper loved the sport, but she loved horses more. If her dad had any hand in this, she would be crushed. Not to mention the impact it would have on her own reputation.

Lord, what's the truth? I pray it's revealed sooner than later so I can help in whatever way I need to.

Tuck kept quiet as Piper chatted with her folks. He took a bite of his tuna melt and prayed right there. Everyone was trying to act normal, but the unknown had his shoulders rising toward his ears and his pulse drumming way too quickly. Because even though it was quiet, almost serene, inside the house, Tuck couldn't forget those cameras stationed outside.

"How's the training going for your colt?" Mr. McKinney looked to Piper for an answer.

"Dream is just that. A dream. Don't you think, Tuck?"

He swallowed. This was not a conversation he wanted to have in front of her parents. Like it or not, Mr. McKinney had a couple of horses going up against them in the next race. That is, if the racing commission allowed him to. Tuck didn't see him as the enemy, but he certainly wouldn't give away any trade secrets.

"Maybe we should talk about something else?" he said.

Piper's eyes roamed his face as if trying to read his thoughts. He arched his eyebrow.

"Right. We should probably talk about something else." She looked hesitantly at her father.

"That's okay, sweetheart. If Tuck thinks my integrity holds no weight, we can certainly change the subject for him." Ian McKinney gave him a hardened stare.

"Now, Mr. McKinney, that's not what I'm suggesting at all." Tuck dropped his fork. "You have two colts in the next race. No one talks about how their horses are doing with their fellow racers. It has nothing to do with today's headlines. *Nothing*." He couldn't stress that enough. He didn't want his future in-laws—*Lord, please let that be true*—upset with him or thinking he didn't believe in them. He just wanted to make sure Dream had a fair run.

Mr. McKinney scoffed. "Sure, it has nothing to do with our name being plastered all over the papers and across the internet for all to speculate on our principles."

"Dad, you know Tuck thinks highly of you. I'm sure being wrongly accused is tough, but don't take it out on your support system."

Mr. McKinney's jaw bulged.

"Dear . . ." Mrs. McKinney said, cajoling him.

The man blew out a breath. "I apologize."

Tuck nodded.

Mrs. McKinney looked at him, then toward her husband. "I think your point about changing the conversation is warranted."

If the tension in the room wasn't so thick that it felt like he'd walked into a sauna, he'd laugh. Instead, Tuck searched for the right response. "Yes, ma'am."

The conversation went smoothly then, but the antsy feeling crawling through his middle didn't leave until Tuck was back in his house . . . alone.

All the way home, he'd thought about Piper. How she allowed him to comfort her, how she *knew* he was in her corner. If the world was gonna start hurling insults and tarnish her reputation, Tuck wanted her to know just why he was always in her corner.

He stared at the text message that sat waiting for him to hit the send button. For some reason, telling the guys the whole truth felt like a big deal. Like once he let it out, Tuck wouldn't be able to contain his feelings. Surely that wasn't right, right?

First saying a quick prayer, Tuck hit the button and waited to see what his friends would say.

Tuck

I'm in love with Piper.

He had a reply in no time.

Chris

'Bout time you admit that!

Lamont
Hallelujah. I think the angels are rejoicing. Had to be the most denied feelings in the history of man.

Tuck
So glad y'all are amused.

Chris
More like happy for you.

Lamont
What he said.

Tuck
I've got a plan.

Chris
You and your plans. Just tell her.

Lamont
Again—what he said.

Tuck
Not sure I'm good enough for her. Shouldn't she want more than a horse trainer?

Lamont
There's a new show for farmers who want to find wives. They seem to be a hot commodity.

Tuck
I train horses.

Lamont
On a farm.

Chris
Lamont: 1 Tucker: 0

Eleven

I stared at the clothes hanging in my closet. On one side were the items I loved and suited my personality and style. On the other side were all the ones my mama had bought. Every now and then, she managed to find something I liked, but those made up a small section on her side. The rest made me feel like a woman in her sixties—or what I imagined they wore. After all, all the country club members Mama associated with wore a similar fashion.

It wasn't often that I was stuck on what to wear. Mama wasn't around to strongly suggest an outfit, so why was I staring at her side of *my* closet?

The security gate chimed, and I jumped.

I opened the app that let me access the video feed to see who was there. My heart dropped to my toes at the badge being held up in front of the camera.

"Yes?" Thank goodness there was no video feed on my end. Still, I clutched my robe closed.

"Piper McKinney?"

"That's me."

"I'm Bob Tracker from the Racing Medication and Testing Consortium. The RMTC. Can I come in to speak with you, please?"

Did I have a choice?

"Sure." I pressed the button to open the gate, then grabbed a pale blue T-shirt from the shelving at the end of my closet and reached for some jeans. After dressing, I made my way to the front door.

Was Mr. Tracker the same guy who was investigating Bolt Brook? Would Tuck be next on his list to interrogate? The questions tumbled in my brain as I struggled to draw in a slow breath and not let anxiety have full court in my mind.

Breathe and bring every thought captive under the obedience of Jesus Christ. Don't conjure up endless possibilities that may never occur. Breathe.

I tacked on a *Help me, Lord* because I wasn't feeling any calmer by the time I opened the door and stood face-to-face with Bob Tracker.

"Ms. McKinney. Sorry for the intrusion."

I motioned him forward. "May I get you something to drink? Glass of water? Sweet tea?" I would've offered coffee, but my percolator broke last week, and I hadn't found the opportunity to buy a new one. Not when I knew I could just ride over to Tuck's and grab a cup if I was really desperate. Fortunately, I wasn't a huge bean drinker.

"No, thank you, ma'am. I promise this conversation will be short."

Would it really? I sat across from him, slipping my hands into my lap so I wouldn't be tempted to fidget. "How can I help?"

"Are you aware of the allegations against Bolt Book Thoroughbred Farm? Especially regarding Ian McKinney, your adoptive father?"

"Not the full extent, but yes, I saw the news like everyone else."

His head tilted. "Interesting. They didn't tell you prior to the media being made aware?"

Had they been informed before that? Was that why they seemed so distant the past few weeks? My mouth dried. "No, they didn't."

Mr. Tracker wrote in a notepad, and this time my stomach dropped to my toes.

"Have you ever witnessed them giving illegal substances to their animals?"

"No, never." At least I could be assured of that. Though the judgmental stare in Mr. Tracker's brown eyes suggested he wasn't impressed by the clarity in my voice.

"Will you submit your horse"—he looked at his notes—"Dream to testing?"

"What? Why?" My pulse kicked into a gallop. Did I need a lawyer present?

"We're aware of the wide reach of the McKinneys. Considering you're their adopted daughter and a former employee, we'd like to be assured you're not continuing in their practices."

I reared back. "You concluded your investigation already?"

"Well, no, but results are due back any day."

Oh no, oh no, oh no. What do I do? Say?

If I told Mr. Tracker no, would he think I was hiding something? Was it better to consult a lawyer first?

Lord?

"Ms. McKinney?"

"Fine." I licked my lips. "You can test him."

"Where is he currently stabled?"

"He's with his trainer, Tucker Hale." *Sorry, Tuck.* "He lives on the farm next door." I pointed instinctively as we both stood.

"Good. You can take me there, and I'll draw some blood for testing."

"All right. When will you get the results?" I slid my sweaty palms against my jean-clad thighs.

"In a week or two."

"Will this prevent him from racing in the Jeff Ruby Steaks?"

"No. You can race, but if the results come back positive, any win may be taken away."

Good thing I knew Dream was clean of illegal substances. "Will my name end up in the news as well?"

Mr. Tracker's bushy eyebrows rose. "Our department wasn't who alerted the press. I'm assuming that was just a reporter doing their job."

Great. So if someone was snooping around my property and saw the RMTC emblem on Mr. Tracker's car, they'd drag me through the mud too?

When we stepped outside, I locked the door behind me and headed for my truck. "You can follow me."

"I'd rather not. I don't want you alerting Mr. Hale to our arrival." He gestured toward his vehicle. "I can give you a ride there."

I held back a huff but got in the passenger seat of his car.

By the time we pulled into the driveway, Tuck was walking up, his face a perfect mask of indifference. His gaze flicked to mine, roaming up and down my body as if to assure himself I was okay. I gave a slight nod of my head and quirked my lips to show I was more annoyed than anything. Tuck's shoulders dropped, and he turned his attention to the RMTC agent.

"You're Tucker Hale?" Mr. Tracker asked.

"Yes, sir."

"With Ms. McKinney's cooperation, I'm here to take a blood sample from her horse, Dream. He needs to be tested for illegal substances."

"I see. Do you plan on testing my own horses as well?"

Mr. Tracker pursed his thin lips. "That's not necessary considering you don't own any racehorses. However, considering you're a former employee of Bolt Brook, it could shed a good light on you and other employees. After all, we *will* find out if laws have been broken and who did so—however many guilty parties there may be."

Yikes. Why was this guy spreading doomsday propaganda so eagerly?

"I also have a few questions for you," Mr. Tracker continued. "It'll all go very quickly, I assure you."

Right, because taking me from my farm to Tuck's was so quick.

Y'all are neighbors.

Could I tell myself to shut up?

"Very well," Tuck said.

He led Mr. Tracker to the stables. As we walked, the RMTC agent asked Tuck the same questions he asked me. After taking samples from all the horses, Mr. Tracker left with a wave.

"Unbelievable," I muttered.

"The wave or the drug tests?"

"All of the above?" I turned to look at Tuck. "He told me not to call ahead."

"No worries." Tuck shrugged. "Not like we have anything to hide."

"It still feels invasive." I wrapped my arms around myself.

Tuck looped an arm around my shoulders. "God's got us. Mr. Tracker and the RMTC will see we don't dabble in that stuff and all will be well. We'll ride off into the sunset, headed for Turfway Park."

"I can't believe how this day started." Could I lean into his shoulder? Drop my head on it and relax into his embrace? Surely those were friendly reactions.

Keep telling yourself that.

"Life's always full of surprises," Tuck said.

"Hey, Mr. Tracker told me the RMTC didn't talk to the press."

"Then who did?" Tuck drew back, looking into my eyes.

A certain journalist had repeatedly asked me invasive questions searching for the "good stuff." The drama that would sell. But other than being adopted by white parents, my story was pretty boring. Could he have found out about the RMTC and created this drama?

My body flashed hotter than the fireworks at Eastbrook's annual Fourth of July festival. "Aaron Wellington the third," I growled through my teeth as I flung Tuck's arm off my shoulders.

"Why would he do that?" Tuck mused.

"I'm going to—"

He grabbed the back of my shirt before I could stomp away. "Deep breath, Piper."

My breath came in spurts as I attempted to keep marching forward.

"Piper Imani McKinney." Tuck wrapped an arm around my waist. "Don't go making a scene."

I froze. Couldn't help it as my insides turned to liquid fire under his touch. Though Tuck was just trying to keep me from going off, the hold was effective at turning on my hormones and alerting me to a man worth swooning for.

I swallowed. "I'm okay now."

"You sure?" he asked, his breath caressing my cheek.

Great, now I'd have to get away to hide the goosebumps pebbling my skin. "Peachy."

He dropped his arms, and I took a couple of slow steps away from him until I could turn and face him without either wanting to look demure or like I was objectifying him. That was wrong, right? Men didn't want to be treated like a piece of meat and the whole gambit, but holy Hannah, my insides were still taking repeated falls onto a fainting couch.

Don't ask me how that's possible. Just recognize it is.

"You don't look peachy." He leaned forward, studying my face. "Your eyes look glassy or something." He placed the back of his hand against my forehead. "You're kind of warm too."

Yes, Tuck. Glassy eyes and heated skin is what happens when a woman is attracted to a man. Ugh. Why did he have to be genuinely concerned?

"Tucker Hale, get back," I snapped. I moved his hand off my forehead, acting offended. Seriously, what was a girl to do when the man who made her pulse race kept encroaching on her bubble?

"Good grief. It's Aaron you're mad at, not me."

"I'm not mad. Besides, what if I'm wrong?"

Tuck snorted. "Always a possibility, but that guy . . . I don't know, but I'd proceed with caution."

"He's an award-winning journalist."

"And I go to church every Sunday." Tuck smirked. "Doesn't mean a thing. Either one of us could be thinking or acting in the flesh."

I laughed. "Tuck, you don't think or act in the flesh. I'm pretty sure you have heaven on speed dial with the way you handle things. Slow and methodological. I bet you check with God on everything."

"Listen." His eyes darkened. "Just because I don't go around running off at the mouth or acting hotheaded doesn't mean I don't have my battles."

He took a step forward, his gaze taking in my every feature. At least, that's what his attention looked like. It was all I could do to keep myself from swaying forward.

He raised his hand, then stepped back, letting it drop to his side.

I stood there for a moment, too stunned to do anything. What was that? Had he been about to . . . Was he looking at me like . . .

My brain restarted, and I gathered some wits. "I'm sorry, Tuck. I shouldn't have assumed life is easy for you."

It's just that from the outside looking in, his life seemed idyllic. Parents who loved him and helped him grow into the wonderful man he was. A farm that was a tad better than mine.

I mean, he already had a racetrack. Not to mention he was friends with a Hollywood A-list actor and a YouTube star.

"Don't worry about it. I know you were mostly teasing." He ran a hand over the back of his neck.

Despite his show of grace, my insides were still unsettled. Whether it was because Tuck had seemed irritated before that strange show of . . . *attraction?* Or something else? I didn't know.

"Are we good?" I asked softly.

"Always," he said solemnly.

Twelve

Where do you want me?" Tuck prayed his cheeks weren't turning red at the question.

A perfectly innocent question, but at the mention of want, Tuck couldn't help but spin a dream or two of him and Piper living in this place as husband and wife.

"Just sit in my office." Piper fluttered around her living room, straightening accent pillows and draping a tan-colored blanket on the back of her couch. She'd let Aaron Wellington in the gate mere seconds before.

"How will I know if you need me? Do you have a code word?" He slid his hands into his jean pockets.

Piper sighed and flopped onto the couch. "I don't know, Tuck. I just know I don't want to confront Aaron alone."

"Then let me sit on the couch like a normal person instead of sequestered away in the office. Eavesdropping seems wrong."

She closed her eyes, then quickly opened them. "Won't that feel like an ambush to him?"

The fact that Piper was worried about the reporter's feelings when she was the one being ambushed was one of the reasons he loved her. She still cared for others even if she was being wronged.

"Fine. I'll be in the office *listening*."

She smiled at him. "Thanks, Tucker."

And now his cheeks were heated from her simple sincerity.

Lord God, whenever You're ready to green-light me, I'll tell her how I feel. Just please give me the words at the time so she'll know how serious I am. I don't want her thinking it's a game.

The doorbell rang, and Piper made a shooing motion. Tuck nodded, then walked out of the living room and around the corner of the hallway into her office. It wasn't a perfect place to be, but thanks to the vaulted ceilings, he'd hear every word of their conversation.

"Thanks for coming over," Piper said.

"Sure. I'm surprised you have time to talk today. I know you leave for Turfway Park next week."

"I just had a question for you."

"Okay. But the article is coming along great. Keep winning, and it'll go viral."

"About that."

There was a long pause and Tuck gripped the doorjamb. *Lord, please give her the words.*

"Did you leak the news about my parents to the media?"

Why did his chest feel so tight? His grip tightened as he waited to hear the journalist's answer.

"It's not quite like it seems."

"Is that a yes?" Shock filled her voice.

"You see, I have a friend who works at the county paper."

"Uh-huh."

"And, well, he might have told me he saw the RMTC vehicle at Bolt Brook. He knows I'm writing an article about you. So I asked him to dig around and find out what was going on."

"And then?"

"Once he did, he took the info to his boss."

"How could you?"

Tuck leaned his forehead against the wall. He'd hoped Aaron wasn't behind the leak.

"I did my job. Having this bit of information will only make your story more appealing."

"Is that all I am? A story? Do you not realize actual *people* are being affected?

"Look, if you can't handle the limelight, don't reach for glory."

Tuck straightened, one foot crossing the threshold. *Wait*, he reminded himself. *She asked you to just listen.* His jaw clenched.

"If you think you can hurt the people I love under the guise of good journalism and believe I'll answer any more of your questions, you have got to be under the influence of some pretty good drugs."

"Are you calling me crazy?"

"More like senseless." There was a pause, then Tuck heard footsteps. "You can leave."

"Piper, come on. People will learn the truth behind the accusations. If you let me tell your story, they'll get that."

"No, they won't. I'm Maisha Farms, not Bolt Brook. Leave."

As soon as he heard the door close, Tuck bolted and entered the living room to see Piper pacing back and forth. He could practically see the steam leaking from her ears.

"That man had the *nerve* to think he can still write my story."

Tuck raised one eyebrow. "You cleared that up pretty quick."

"Does he actually think just because he has a way with words I have to put up with his willingness to do anything to get a good story?"

"I think he does."

"I never want to see him again."

"And you don't have to." He sat down to watch her pace. Was it bad he was happy Aaron was out of her life even though he knew she saw him as just a journalist?

"But how can I share the greatness of horse racing with the masses now? How can I get people who look like me interested in the sport? We need more diversity."

"So you still believe he should tell your story?"

She turned those big ebony eyes his way. "Help me, Tuck. Was I right to turn him away?"

He really hoped so. He'd had enough of that guy. But Tuck prided himself on acting on wisdom, not feelings, so he said a quick prayer while running a hand through his hair.

"He's a good writer, and he claims the article will pull in millions of readers to learn about you and horse racing. That's great, but what's the cost?" Tuck paused, trying to gauge Piper's reaction. At her silence, he continued.

"How will you be portrayed to readers? Will he tell the un-biased truth or the truth he wants readers to believe? Sounds like he wants to include the business with Bolt Brook. Will he sensationalize it to make a name for himself?"

"I prayed before giving him an answer the first time he asked to tell my story. I prayed God would give me the wisdom and, after consideration, I believed letting him write about me was the right decision."

"And now?" Tuck held his breath. *Please, let her be done with him.*

"Now I'm wondering if I misunderstood God. Or is it one of those situations where it was right to say yes then, but now I need to cut my losses?"

"Or maybe Aaron needs to see the power of God." *No, Lord. Why did that just come out my mouth?*

Piper scrunched her nose. "I hate when you say something that feels right but makes me want to be selfish. It's not fair for you to be so wise."

"Any wisdom you think falls from my mouth is all God. Believe me. I'm on the selfish train of thought more often than not." *Like now!*

"Sure." She rolled her eyes, then propped her chin onto her hand. "Unfortunately, you make a lot of sense. Maybe the yes all along was for Aaron's salvation. He seemed increasingly irritated about my faith and my linking it to some of the questions he asked me."

"Then show him God is real. Show him you won't be shaken despite the paparazzi camping outside your parents' estate and the RMTC coming to your farm. You'll stand firm on the Rock and praise Him while the world watches and waits to hear more about Bolt Brook."

"What if I *am* shaken, Tuck?"

He held out one palm. When she placed hers face down, he wrapped his fingers around her hand. "Then you reach out to someone who can lean on God and lift you up in prayer."

"Why are you always there for me?" Piper's gaze searched his as if she could see the answer for herself.

"Because you're my person."

His mouth dried at his vulnerability. She could take the declaration at face value, realizing how much he cared as a friend, or she could see the truth he couldn't always admit to himself for fear of bursting the dam holding him in check. He loved her. Always her and only her.

"I always will be." She squeezed his hand, then let go.

He wanted to take her hand back, tell her how much he needed her in his life. Only knowing this wasn't the right time kept him from spilling the beans.

"Want some lunch?" Piper asked.

"Please."

She made grilled cheese and bacon sandwiches. Then he grabbed the plates while she grabbed a couple of Ale-8s from the fridge and set the dishes on her coffee table.

"You know we have to watch a rom-com now, right?"

Right, because watching a movie about love with the woman he couldn't tell he loved her was something he wanted to do. "I'm sure we can find a rerun of a race." He reached for the remote.

"Nope. Pass over the remote," Piper quipped.

He gave it a light toss, and she caught the control expertly, then blew the top like a sharpshooter in the Wild West. With a click of the button, her streaming service popped up.

"What's online for the torture fest?" he asked.

Piper clicked on Julia Roberts's face.

He groaned.

"What? This movie is the best."

"*My Best Friend's Wedding* is *not* a rom-com."

Piper watched him with an amused expression. "Please. Do tell. Tell me how this doesn't have romance or doesn't make you laugh."

"Oh, I'm not disagreeing with those things. But you're taking them out of context."

"I am, am I?" She folded her arms across her chest.

Tuck leaned forward. "You are. Because Julia Roberts doesn't get the guy." And he had no desire to watch the movie and wonder if such a scene would play out in real life. Tuck could be the guy losing out on the girl if his own failures got in the way.

"But—"

Tuck shook his head. "No buts. It's not a rom-com. She loses the guy, and that's not a happily ever after." If Lamont or Chris heard him using these terms on a regular basis, they'd laugh way too hard. But Tuck had spent years watching '90s rom-coms plus any new ones the movie industry put out. If a film looked like it had romance and comedy, Piper was dragging him to the theater or one of their living rooms to watch it.

"Does that mean you don't want to watch that one?"

"Vehemently not."

"It doesn't sound like those two words go together."

"Sounded a lot better in my head."

Piper laughed. "Then which movie should we watch?"

"Does it have to be from the '90s?" That was usually her criteria.

"Yes, please."

"Let me think." He scrolled through the mental Rolodex of rom-coms they'd watched over the years, searching for any that would be halfway decent.

"*Clueless?*" Piper suggested.

"'As if,'" Tuck scoffed.

Her lips twitched. "Fine. What about *The Wedding Singer?*"

"Made in the '90s but it's really an '80s rom-com. Nope."

"*The Best Man?*"

"Who didn't deserve to be one? Pass."

"*Drive Me Crazy?*"

"One of the many remakes of *Can't Buy Me Love*, which is an '80s film. Nope."

Piper sighed and bit into her sandwich. "You're making this difficult."

"Choose something better and it won't be."

"*Runaway Bride?*"

"Are you on a Julia Roberts kick? I'd rather watch Sandra Bullock."

Piper sat up. "Good. Then choose one of her movies."

"Her best ones were made in the 2000s."

"No way. What about *While You Were Sleeping?*"

"That's a Christmas movie." He pointed outside. "It's not Christmas."

"You can watch that any time of year."

He shook his head slowly. "Can you really?"

"Ugh," she groaned. "You're the worst."

"Just minutes ago you were telling me I'm the best."

She chucked a throw pillow at him.

He caught it in the air and tucked it behind his head.

"*Miss Congeniality?*"

"Made in 2000."

"How do you know that?"

"You were on an early 2000s kick all through high school. That was number one on your list."

She pouted. "You're right."

"I know."

"Fine." She chuckled. "Then what do you want to watch?"

"That's a trick question, but how about *The Proposal*?"

"But it's not 1990s."

"Then *Never Been Kissed*."

"Why do people like that movie? It's a high school teacher falling in love with a student. It's all kinds of wrong."

"A *fake* student."

He didn't necessarily like that film, but he knew how much it annoyed Piper. He shrugged waiting to see if she would cave to his suggestion or pick something else.

"Fine. Let's watch *Never Been Kissed*."

Phew. Because watching Josie "Grossie" survive the living nightmare of high school twice would ensure Tuck had no compulsion to erase the distance between him and his best friend and end up cuddling with her.

Thirteen

END OF MARCH

Walking into Turfway Park was what I imagined walking into a Vegas casino would be like. Slot machine noises went off around me as I squinted to see in the dimly lit building. Last time we came to Turfway, I'd barely peeked inside the main building. This time, I was meeting Aaron.

He'd asked me to hear him out. I couldn't help but remember Tuck's comment about Aaron needing to see Jesus. Did that mean I should continue with the article? I feared I'd spend too much time trying to shield my parents from any hidden agenda Aaron had.

Not to mention that talking about my feelings around transracial adoption wasn't as freeing as it was initially. I had known the topic would come up—I was an African American with Caucasian parents—but talking to another minority about my upbringing ended up making me feel less than. Aaron was a whole lot more in touch with his ethnicity than I was, and toward the end of our sessions, I was left feeling more uncomfortable than safe.

I'd always been an oddity. Thankfully, people in Eastbrook

had long since stopped staring at me when I walked by, but that didn't mean I didn't still get peculiar looks when I ventured out of our small town. If I was with my parents or Tuck, there was a higher chance of stares and whispered comments—some subtle and others more in your face.

I wished I was used to the unwanted *and* unwarranted attention. I wished I could say they no longer bothered me. But I had yet to arrive at that level of self-assuredness. Often my twenty-eight-year-old self still felt like the insecure kid from Ọlọrọ Ilé waiting for my biological family to reach out to me or for my newly adoptive parents to ask how it felt to be the only Black person in our town. As much as I loved my dad, his response had always been not to engage. Unfortunately, that didn't really address the issue.

And Mama . . . Well, I'm not actually sure how she felt. As I was growing up, she'd tried to connect me to my roots. She thought it was important to understand my birth country. As a kid, I even had a few pen pals from Ọlọrọ Ilé. Dad thought it unnecessary since we lived in America, the melting pot. He believed being raised by loving parents was all that mattered. Which I could agree with to an extent, but he didn't have to grow up in a skin many shades darker than those around him.

I'd lived for the moments I got to leave Eastbrook and see people who resembled me. Representation was often the reason I'd reach for a book that had a lady on the cover with the same dark brown skin as mine. Knowing there were authors and cover designers willing to give minority voices representation touched me in ways I didn't share with many. Representation colored my social media account and everything around me. But so did my Kentucky roots and love for bluegrass and country music. I was the very definition of a *melting pot*.

Now if only I could boldly say that to Aaron so he could understand that these were my sum-total parts.

Perhaps I should start practicing being vulnerable with my

BFF so talking with strangers wouldn't cripple me. Wasn't I tired of keeping my thoughts close to my chest? How would Tuck react if he could read my every thought? Wouldn't I like the opportunity to read his?

When we'd watched *Never Been Kissed* a week ago, Tuck seemed more quiet than usual. No, not quiet. *Introspective.* Like he had something on his mind and wouldn't share it unless I pried with all my might. The thing was, I rarely pried. I understood what it was like to want to keep your thoughts safe from those who could be hurt by what you were contemplating.

I blew out a breath when I saw Aaron. He stood by the restaurant entrance, hands in his slack pockets. He turned and froze as our gazes met. Too bad the eye contact didn't have any meet-cute vibes. Instead, I was trying very hard to maintain a neutral expression. I hadn't forgotten that this man was the reason my parents' names were being dragged through the mud. Tuck's suggestion was the only reason I was still talking to Aaron Wellington III.

"You're looking good, Piper."

Why would I need to hear that from him? "Do they have a table ready for us?"

"Yes. I was just waiting for you. Didn't want you to get lost looking for me."

Right. Like I couldn't ask the hostess where he was sitting. The urge to let my eyes rotate in their sockets was strong, but the Holy Spirit kept me from activating the action.

The hostess maneuvered through the tables and sat us at a table for two with even dimmer lighting. I hung my purse over the back of the chair and placed the cloth napkin across my lap. *Manners, Piper*, Mama would surely say if she were present.

"You wanted to talk?" I asked.

Aaron smiled. "Let's chat first."

Why? What was with the oil-salesman vibe he was emoting? But my thoughts remained just that. "Fine." I folded my hands and tilted my head. "Have you talked to your reporter friend about getting his colleagues to vacate Bolt Brook's premises?"

"Now, Piper, it's already all over the national news." Aaron gave me a placating smile. "There's nothing he can do about it. His media outlet won't leave until everyone else does."

I *detested* patronization or mansplaining.

My phone hadn't stopped ringing since the news broke. I could only imagine the toll on my folks. Mama would probably need counseling after this was all said and done. "Can't you make them leave sooner?" Surely reporters called in favors to others.

Then again, in the movies they seemed to actively hate one another.

"That's not how the news works."

"It should. It's not like my folks will give a statement, nor will the media find anything by camping outside their farm."

Aaron leaned forward. "Be realistic. If they did something illegal, they should be held accountable."

The nerve! My folks would never do anything to jeopardize Bolt Brook. No one who worked for them would do something so heinous either. "They are *not* guilty."

"Are you sure?" Aaron's eyebrows rose. "Most folks have blind spots when it comes to those close to them. I'm surprised the RMTC hasn't looked into your trainer."

If I were a cat, every hair on my spine would be standing at attention and my paws ready to strike. "You sincerely think Tuck could ever do something like that?" I stared at him. "Are you the reason the RMTC came to our farms?"

Something shifted in Aaron's gaze. "What? When did that happen?" He placed his arms on the table, his lanky frame bent over.

"An RMTC agent tested our horses last week."

"I didn't start that." Aaron blew out a breath. "I wouldn't. You're my subject."

Subject? Very telling. Funny how I ever thought this man was kind or sincere. "Did you or did you not call someone to look into my parents, putting this whole ball into motion?" Ugh, I hated using clichés, but this one was so apt.

He rubbed the back of his neck. "I suppose you want an apology."

"What am I even doing here, Aaron? You said you wanted me to hear you out. I thought you'd start with an apology. Maybe even tell me why you were still the right person to tell this story." I swallowed. "I genuinely believed you were the right person to talk to. I *prayed* over this before I said yes to you. I had some idea you'd shine a light on a sport I love dearly and show how important inclusion was. Instead, I get the feeling you'd rather stir up trouble than document facts."

His expression hardened. "Excuse me if I don't want to jump on the white savior train. Doesn't it bother you that white people adopt kids who look like us and then stick them in a small town where they don't see anyone who looks like them? You can't tell me that hasn't done something to your psyche. You love a sport no one cares about only because of who adopted you."

My chair screeched back, and I was on my feet before the movement even registered in my mind. "You can't tell me that being raised by loving parents and having all my needs met isn't better than rotting away in an orphanage where want is all that's in abundance." I had my issues. Who wouldn't with my background? But no one would ever make me believe my parents were wrong for wanting to love a child.

"I'm done." I grabbed my purse.

Aaron stood, coming to stand by me. "Come on, Piper. We can talk about this. You and me, we understand each other."

"No, we don't. I thought you'd see me for me. I thought you'd be able to give me something I've been longing for." *Identity. Representation.* I'd been so foolish. But man couldn't be the source of my identity. Only God could fulfill that role.

I straightened my shoulders. "You see only your agenda and nothing else. That doesn't make you a good writer. That makes you a good salesman. Consider this article dead. Don't contact me again."

I purposely tilted my chin so he could see me walk away with my head held high. Only, my bottom lip trembled. I wasn't a fan of confrontation, but Aaron Wellington wasn't the man I thought he was.

Following the signs to the hotel rooms, I made it to the elevators before a tear spilled over my cheek. It was pointless to cry over this, but I couldn't seem to make my tear ducts agree. I pressed the number for my floor while trying to hide the waterworks.

The elevator doors whooshed open, and I let out a sigh of relief. No one was in the conveyance, saving me the embarrassment of explaining my sorrow. I peered into my purse, searching for the key card to my room. Why was this thing like a black hole, swallowing up whatever landed in it?

"Piper? Is your meeting over that fast?"

I made a show out of digging in my bag as I came to stand in front of my door. "Mm-hmm." If I said anything else, Tuck would know something was up.

When a brush of air caressed my nape and his scent enveloped me, I knew it was too late to hide my tears.

"It didn't go well?" he whispered.

"Not now, Tuck." I tapped the key card and pushed open the door to my room.

Tuck stayed me, his warm hand lightly holding my wrist and turning me to face him. "Did he say something to upset you?" The scowl that overtook his handsome face almost did me in. "I'll go find him."

Now I was the one holding on to Tuck. "Please don't." I didn't want him coming to my rescue right then. I just wanted to wallow in pity.

"I have to do something," he said. "You know I can't stand to see you cry." He wiped a tear away with his thumb.

The dam broke, and I threw my arms around him, sobbing into his shirt. Why couldn't life be easier? Why couldn't all the answers I'd ever needed be found in an instant?

Tuck pulled me tighter into his embrace and cradled my head, then let me just be. Tuck never tried to change me. Tuck had never not encouraged me. Tuck had always been there, and right now, loving him as merely a friend tore me up inside.

I cried for losing an imagined connection with Aaron. I shed tear after tear for not being honest with Tuck. I cried for my folks and the awful reality they were going through.

When I lifted my head from Tuck's chest, I found myself in the sitting area of my suite. Tuck had maneuvered us onto the couch with me bundled into his arms on his lap. I hadn't even been cognizant of his moving us from the doorway.

"How long did I cry?"

He shrugged. "Until your heart said what it had to say."

"Thank you, Tucker Hale." I laid my head against his chest.

"Anytime." He paused. "Do you want to talk about it?"

"Not really. Aaron's a jerk." I sat up. "But I told him how I felt in a really classy way."

Tuck's eyes twinkled. "Yeah? How did he take it?"

"I don't know. I didn't look back."

"That's my girl."

"I wish."

Tuck went rigid under me.

I lifted my head to stare into his wide blue eyes. "What? What's wrong? Oh my goodness, am I too heavy?" I jumped up.

But he pulled me down until I flopped back onto his lap. "What. Did. You. Say?"

"I asked if I was too heavy." I stared in confusion. "Why do you think I tried to give your lap a break?"

Tuck snorted. "You weigh less than some jockeys do. That's neither here nor there. What did you say before that?"

I racked my brain, relaying our conversation.

"That's my girl."

I wish.

My breath hitched.

Lord, please tell me I didn't say that out loud.

"What did you hear?" My heart thumped.

"Don't play games with me, Piper McKinney. Repeat it. *Please.*"

I licked my lips. "I wish."

Tuck surged forward, and his lips crashed into mine with such passion I instantly warmed from the inside out.

Fourteen

Piper's lips were pillowy soft and so smooth Tuck might have lost his head a little bit. He'd often imagined what it would be like to kiss his best friend. What he hadn't imagined was the instant heat or how eagerly she would return his kiss.

Her arms circled around his neck and pulled him closer as he deepened the kiss. His heart pounded with every touch as time slowed and his insides sung the "Hallelujah Chorus." Then just like that, imaginary ice water dumped over his head, and he jerked back.

They were in Piper's hotel suite, and his thoughts were edging toward the impure. His Adam's apple bobbed as he tried to slow his breathing and detangle himself from her.

"Why did you stop?" Piper wore a bemused expression.

At least she did in the brief second his eyes managed to meet hers before landing on her plush lips. He cleared his throat. "We're in your hotel room."

She looked around as if just as surprised by their surroundings.

"I should go." He slid her off his lap and stood. Realizing she was still within reach, he took another step back.

"But shouldn't we talk about that?" She pointed a finger toward her lips.

Her sweet, beautiful—

Tuck shook his head. "Maybe tomorrow. Outside." He swallowed. "Where it's safe."

"Tucker Hale, what's going on inside that brain of yours?"

Not much, but enough that he was hoping this was God's neon sign of escape. *Don't miss it, Hale.* If he didn't leave now, he could guarantee they'd both come to regret what happened next.

"Tomorrow. Promise." He whirled around and hightailed it out of her suite and into his room right next door.

Thank You for no connecting door.

Tuck slid down a wall, lowering his head between his knees.

They'd kissed. And it was a heated kiss that shook him to his core and made him want to buy a ring all in one fell swoop.

"I wish."

Once more Piper's response to his "That's my girl" echoed in his mind and filled him with a heady sensation. She wanted to be his. He couldn't have been happier to get that big of a hint.

Tuck's phone buzzed, breaking into his sappy thoughts. He pulled it from his back pocket and clicked on the text from Piper.

Piper
Why did you leave?

Tuck
Didn't trust myself to stay any longer.

Piper
😮

Piper
So this wall between us is necessary?

Tuck
Very

> **Piper**
> That was some kiss.

> **Tuck**
> Understatement of the century. Think my boots shook.

> **Piper**
> I know mine did.

This woman! He wanted to march next door and demand she go out with him right this instant. Only he'd never been the impulsive type. Kissing her had messed with his timetable. He needed to regroup and figure out what in the world he was supposed to do next.

Any suggestion other than going over there and kissing her again.

> **Piper**
> You promise we'll talk about it tomorrow?

> **Tuck**
> Yes

> **Piper**
> Ok

He waited for the three dots to appear, but after a few minutes, nothing. Tuck placed his cell on the floor and dropped his head into his hands. He could perfectly visualize his plan to win Piper.

1. *Increase annual income by 30% and have a six-month emergency fund*—☑
2. *Get Dream to the Derby*—*in progress*
3. *Win the Derby*
4. *Tell Piper how I feel*
5. *Marry her*

Tuck had always assumed kissing the girl went along with declaring his feelings and the in between before getting to number five. But he hadn't gotten Dream to the Kentucky Derby yet. Granted, he wasn't doing too shabby. The Thoroughbred was winning races leading up to the big one.

Now that Tuck had jumped the gun—not that it hadn't been better than his imagination ever conjured—there was no going back. Not the way Piper had leaned into the kiss and met him at every tempo. The way their lips had fused suggested they'd been practicing the sport for years, not seconds.

But Tuck still hadn't figured out how to prove his worth. That was the whole point of winning the Derby. How could he convince Piper he was husband material if all he had to show was the farm and an emergency fund? Compared to Bolt Brook, Hale Tier Farms was running an ant-sized operation with two ants. Bolt Brook was more like the whole ant colony. He couldn't see the McKinneys blessing his and Piper's relationship unless he could call himself a Derby-winning trainer.

Lord God, my mind is spinning. I'm torn between elation and mortification at showing my hand too early. How can I explain to Piper that I need to prove my worth before I'm ready for a relationship with her? I don't know how to go forward, but I certainly don't want to go backward.

He just couldn't.

Holding Piper in his arms felt so right. Kissing her with all the longing he'd been storing up had been as easy as breathing. How could he tell her he wasn't mentally ready? Thinking about her and their relationship was all he did when his mind wasn't focused on things equine in nature. It was horses and Piper. That was it.

He should have stuck to his plan. After all, that's what made him a good trainer. He knew how to get a horse to offer more and show the horse when to go and when to conserve energy. Because Tuck *planned* it. This thing with Piper . . . well, he'd jumped out of the gate early like an overeager two-year-old colt.

His phone rang. If that was Piper . . .

But relief—and disappointment—filled him at the sight of Lamont's name.

"Hey, Lamont. What's up?"

"I don't know. You tell me."

"What does that mean?" Tuck forced a laugh.

"Had a feeling something was wrong, so I thought I'd check on you. You okay? Training all right?"

"Yeah, training is going well. You know how it is." It was funny to say that to an A-list actor, but coaching Lamont on training horses had been Tuck's job for a while. The actor really did get it.

"I'm glad to hear it. Nevaeh and I are coming out for the Derby. I think Chris is going to try to come as well."

"What if we don't make it?"

"You will. I know it."

How? Even with Dream winning stakes in the past, Tuck still had doubts. "Appreciate the faith, man."

"So now that we've made small talk, you going to tell me what's really up?"

"I kissed Piper."

"'Bout time."

Tuck laughed, which quickly turned into groaning. "Bro, it was too soon. I saw her crying, and next thing I know, I'm kissing her before the thought that I was a few steps ahead of my plan entered my mind."

"You know, Tuck, I think it's great that you plan ahead. God definitely gave you a talent for that. But tell me, are you leaving room for God to act?"

Tuck gripped the phone. "What are you saying?"

"If you're always planning every step and coming up with contingency plans, are you really trusting in the Lord? Maybe kissing her now was the right moment and not a misstep in some grand plan orchestrated by you, not God."

Ouch. Tuck rubbed his chest, where conviction pricked. "I trust the Lord."

"Do you?" Lamont paused. "Then if He asked you to throw away every to-do list, every plan, every schedule, and lean on Him for guidance, you wouldn't break out in a cold sweat?"

No, because Tuck already was. Just imagining that scenario had his sweat glands working overtime. "That's a cruel question."

"Maybe because you know I'm right."

"I'll never admit it."

Lamont laughed. "You don't have to. I know I am."

"There's that Hollywood ego." Tuck smirked.

"On the real, let go of your plans, and let God order your steps."

"I hate when you're right."

He didn't want to admit he was terrified at the idea of scrapping his plans and letting the Lord direct His steps. What if God's steps took him away from Piper? Then what would he do? Or what if the steps required more than he could give?

As much as he hated the idea of losing control, Tuck hated the idea of disappointing God more. Ever since he'd proclaimed Jesus as his Savior, he'd tried to live for God. But now he was starting to realize his plans had become his idol.

"I don't know how to let go," he murmured.

"Then ask God to show you. I had to wrestle with the fact that I had no control over my mom's health. Hiring the best doctors, nutritionists, and even yoga instructors was all designed to prevent her from getting sick again. Then I realized I actually had no control over that. She would either get cancer again or she wouldn't. Once I accepted that, it was easier to lean on God for wisdom, strength, and guidance. Trust me, I'm not throwing shade, only trying to give you a leg up based on personal experience."

"Thanks, man."

"Of course. We wouldn't be friends if neither one of us offered the truth even when it hurt."

Good point. Tuck remembered offering advice to Lamont when he entered into a fake relationship with Nevaeh. And again when he entered into a real relationship with her.

"How's Nevaeh doing?"

"She's great. She's excited to see Piper again in person."

"Is y'all's visit a surprise, or should I tell Piper?"

"Let's keep it a surprise. That way we can see the look of shock on her face when we show up and cheer her on in person."

"Sounds like a plan." Tuck paused. "Hey, I gotta go."

"Gonna tear up those plans?"

"Something like that."

"Good on you."

Tuck rose to his feet and walked over to his planner. He was probably the only guy he knew who owned one. At least it didn't come with stickers or any coloring pages. It was just a no-nonsense black planner with black-and-gray styling inside. He opened it to the page that held his plan to win Piper and ripped it out.

He winced at the sound, at the meaning behind the action. *Lord, this is me showing that I trust You. I trust that Your plans are good. That You are good. I trust that You want the best for me, and by ripping up this plan, I'm allowing Your will to be done.*

Whew.

His skin prickled at the offering. It was huge to just trust God's will. It felt like standing on a ledge, then jumping off. But if that's what God wanted from him, Tuck would use blind faith. Faith guaranteed by Christ.

Fifteen

The next morning, I pressed my fingers against my lips for the umpteenth time, like I needed to reassure myself that the kiss—the most amazing, mind-blowing thing ever—had actually happened. With one touch to my lips, my mind swirled at the memory, leaving me feeling weightless and warm all at once.

That did happen, right?

I'd stared at every offering in my luggage, debating on what I should wear to breakfast, but nothing looked pretty enough. Surely I could find something better than jeans to wear when I sat face-to-face with Tuck to talk about the monumental shift in our relationship. The dress I brought for race day wasn't a garment I wanted to wear twice. Which left me with an offering that included a couple of blouses and a black pencil skirt I'd thrown in at the last minute. If I chose the skirt, wouldn't it be glaringly obvious I was trying to impress my best friend?

Ugh. This is Tuck. Does it really matter what you wear considering he's seen you look your worst?

Like last night when salt tracks had covered my face from all the crying. All the while, I'd been encased in jeans and the shirt from my interview. Though said shirt would now earn top-shelf tier after being the one to earn me a kiss. Still, I wanted to look decent in case Tuck needed a reminder that I was all in for a romantic relationship. Knowing him, his mind had already urged him to take two steps back from one. Now that I knew he liked me as more than just a friend, I was ready to latch myself to him.

I clicked the power button on my cell to glance at the time. It wasn't *so* early that I couldn't text Nevaeh for outfit advice. Since we'd met in person last year, we'd become long-distance friends, just like the guys. Still, she could be sleeping, as she was on West Coast time.

> Piper
> I need to make an outfit that will impress Tuck.

> Nevaeh
> Morning to you too.

> Piper
> Sorry. Good morning. Help!

> Nevaeh
> Why are you trying to impress him? He obviously likes you. Just show up to wherever you guys are going.

> Piper
> We kissed last night.

I laughed out loud at the screaming GIF Nevaeh sent.

> Nevaeh
> Was it amazing? How did it happen? When will you do it again?

> Piper
> More than amazing. With our lips. Hopefully after he sees me in an outfit that makes me look desirable and not like I'm going to hang out in the stables.

> Nevaeh
> Let's FaceTime.

124

My cell rang, and I clicked the video option.

"Hey, girl. Show me what you've got."

I flipped the phone's view around, pointing its camera to the bed where my clothes lay strewn about. "This is all I have."

"Hmm. What kind of look are you going for?"

I flipped the view back to my face. "I want to look pretty but not like I tried too hard. Just, you know, better than my everyday look."

"Got it. Let me see the clothes again."

I did as asked.

"Is that cashmere?" Nevaeh squealed.

"Yes. You're talking about the sweater, right?" I held up the sweater, flipping the view once more.

"Oh, Piper, that's perfect. Pair that with the light-wash jeans. What kind of jewelry did you bring?"

I walked over to my travel bag and showed her the choices.

"Go with the blue beads. It'll bring some color to your face and contrast with the top but give a nod to the jeans."

"Really?"

"Yes. Put that on, and Tuck won't know what hit him."

I grinned. "Thanks, Nevaeh."

"Anytime. And make sure you call me tonight and spill the tea."

"Deal."

We hung up, and I quickly put on the combination she'd recommended. By the time I rubbed on a rosy shade of lipstick—to match my eye shadow, obviously—a knock on my suite door sounded. Nerves gathered in my middle like when I'd ridden a horse for the first time. Granted, that had ended with me in the dirt, but Tuck had been the one to help me to my feet.

My lips curved at the memory.

This was going to be okay. I wasn't sure what would happen when we talked, but I'd been praying God would give me the words and that Tuck wouldn't retreat—his go-to maneuver.

Lord, please be in the midst of us. Please let us get everything out in the open.

Because if Tuck had been interested in me as long as I'd been interested in him, I would need to keep my composure instead of lamenting the lost time.

When I twisted the knob and opened the door, my breath hitched at the sight of Tuck wearing his standard jeans and a blue button-down shirt. The shirt I told him made his eyes look sky blue. The way they practically smoldered now had my lips curving even wider.

"Good morning." His deep voice broke the silence.

"Morning." Ack! Why was my mouth suddenly so dry?

"You ready for breakfast?"

I was and I wasn't. I wanted to hear what he had to say, but I also wanted his lips on mine again, which probably meant I needed to close the door behind me.

"Uh, sure." I shut the door, letting out a low exhale. "Where are we going?"

"Found a breakfast place that's all about the biscuit."

I nudged Tuck with my elbow. "Was that pick on purpose?" He knew how much I loved biscuits.

"You know it." He squeezed my elbow, then slid his warm hand down my arm until our fingers interlaced.

My heart picked up speed as tingles spread through my arm. I wanted to sigh and squeal all at once. We were holding hands. *Holding hands!*

I never thought Tuck was huge on affection, but this one move made my heart swoon and fall at my feet—or maybe his.

"You ready for today's agenda?" I asked. Surely I could say the things I normally would to my BFF and not make a big deal about our hands being pressed together.

"Sure am. It's only racing days that makes me want to hug the commode and pray to God my stomach stops hurtling toward my throat."

Training was always better because you still had opportunity before you.

"You never look nervous."

"That's because I'm smart and get it all out of my system before we sit in the stands. It wouldn't look very manly of me to lose my breakfast in front of you."

My head slowly turned until I was staring at Tuck's profile. "Being manly in front of me is often a concern of yours?"

"I can't answer that with you staring at me so intently." His lips twitched.

I faced forward. "How about now?"

"This is going to be awkward, isn't it?" Tuck sighed and came to a stop in front of the elevators.

"We don't have to let it be." I certainly didn't *want* it to be.

"Maybe not."

Tuck cupped the side of my face and leaned closer, then placed his soft lips against mine in a move that was so tender I clutched his shirt.

"Tuck," I whispered, "are you trying to undo me?"

"No," he replied just as quietly. "Just saying a proper hello."

"Well, hello to you too." I wound my arms around his neck and kissed him back.

And kissing was what we did until we heard the chime of the elevator. When we parted, I smirked at the rose stain on his lips, then rubbed at them. "Sorry. Lipstick hazard."

"No worries." A crooked grin etched across his adorable face.

We held hands the entire elevator ride down and all the way to the parking lot, where he let go of my hand only to open the passenger door of his truck for me. Before I stood on the steps to get in, I placed my hand over his heart. "Can I expect more hand holding and door opening?"

"I've always held the door open for you."

"The hand holding is new."

"This is true. Then yes. You can expect more."

Was it too early to cheer? I really expected a more reticent Tucker Hale than the cinnamon-roll man standing before me. "Are we still going to talk about . . . things?" I asked hesitantly.

"At the diner. I'll probably be too distracted trying to steal kisses and holding hands before then to do so."

My heart lightened with his answer. "I'm glad to know I'm not the only one thinking of those things."

"Should we make a bet on who can think about holding hands the longest?"

"No. It won't be a competition you can win, Tucker Hale." I twined my fingers through his. "Because this has long been a dream of mine."

"Can't be longer than mine, darlin'."

My eyes unexpectedly smarted with tears. "Am I going to be *darlin'* instead of *Pipsqueak* now?"

"Get in the truck," he said, laughing. "Or else we'll starve as you dissect everything that happens between us."

I only sat down because he wasn't wrong. Already my mind was trying to come up with reasons he switched to *darlin'* from *Pipsqueak*. Then I wondered why *darlin'* and not *babe*—ew, I didn't like the sound of that, so maybe that's why—or *honey*.

Wait, and you'll get your answers.

Tuck would probably pull off the bandage achingly slow, but I truly was in no hurry. We weren't due to hit the racetrack until noon, and that was a good three hours away.

My stomach rumbled the moment we stepped into the diner and the smells of biscuits, butter, and bacon hit my senses. I rubbed my middle while discreetly peeking at all the tables to get an idea of the menu offerings. Sometimes it wasn't until I saw what a meal actually looked that I could choose what I wanted.

And boy, did this place have my mouth watering. One person was eating biscuits topped with white gravy and an egg over easy. Another person's biscuit looked like a sandwich with a piece of fried chicken between the bread. I also saw waffles and hash browns.

"You're gonna have to roll me on out of here, aren't you?" I nudged Tuck, glad he'd picked up the hand holding as soon as we got out of the truck.

"Not if I don't get rolled first." He pointed to someone's plate. "Do you see the size of that chicken over there? Makes the biscuit look like one of those cookies they serve with tea."

I chuckled. "But that's the one you're getting, isn't it?"

"We'll see."

The hostess sat us at a corner booth for two, then filled Tuck's cup with coffee and mine with hot water for tea. After getting her recommendations, Tuck and I ordered.

I added creamer and two sugars to my black tea, then took a sip. Warmth filled me as I stared across the cup's rim and into the gaze of my best friend. The man whose eyes had barely left my face since we sat.

"You know"—I set my cup down—"I'm surprised at you."

Tuck arched an eyebrow. "Why?"

"I thought you'd pretend like nothing happened and this would be us trying to go back to friend-zone mode."

"I thought about it." He nodded slowly. "Still thinking about it, honestly." He glanced out the window, then turned his eyes back to me. "But that kiss . . . It keeps playing in my mind on repeat. As much as I want to go back in time and wait a little bit, even I can recognize how ridiculous that option is."

I didn't love that he had doubts, but I understood. "So what plan did you settle on?"

"Actually . . ." He smirked. "I'm just winging it."

Tucker Hale winging it? "Who are you, and what did you do with my best friend?"

Sixteen

Tuck had to fight a smile at the look of incredulity on Piper's beautiful face. Man, did she look perfect this morning. Not that she didn't always look great, but something about her practically glowed. He could only hope he was even partway responsible.

He shook his head, focusing on the conversation at hand. "Maybe I should explain a little."

Piper nodded.

"I ended up talking to Lamont after a moment of crisis."

"Wait." She held up a hand. "Did you have a plan that involved telling me how you feel?"

"Yes," he drawled, cheeks heating with embarrassment.

"So the moment of crisis was you realizing you deviated from that plan?"

"Yep." His lips made a popping noise.

Yet censure didn't come his way. Instead, Piper threw her head back and laughed. After a moment, she reached for the diner napkin to dab at her eyes, then motioned for him to continue.

"Like I was saying before someone so rudely mocked me—"

"Not mocked. Laughed." She held up a finger. "There's a difference."

"Yeah, sure." He nodded as if he believed her. "Does that difference involve laughing until tears appear?"

"Of course. I would never laugh while mocking someone. It's impossible to do both."

He rolled his eyes, then threw his balled-up straw wrapper at her.

"Boys. They never grow out of throwing stuff."

"Do you want to hear my revelation or not?"

She batted her eyelashes. "Yes, please."

This woman. She could make him laugh despite himself and make him feel like the most important person in the world all in the span of seconds.

"Lamont challenged me about making plans and not leaving room for God to act." He sighed. "Kind of convicted me."

Piper's face turned serious. "I never thought about that. I mean, I know you believe in God and pray often. I guess I never considered your plans might be a barrier."

"Same. But what Lamont said made a lot of sense. Then I talked to God about it until I couldn't keep my eyes open any longer."

She chuckled.

"This morning I determined to let God direct me. Hence the reason I didn't pretend like nothing happened." Though now that they were talking about it, his stomach was more knotted up than a fishing line.

What if Piper started dating him, then realized he didn't have a whole lot to offer? Sure, he could train her horses, and sure, he could watch rom-coms with her. But he couldn't pay for the suites they were currently staying in. Not if he wanted to get his farm paid off and make sure he also paid taxes and had health insurance and other basics.

"So . . ." Piper placed her chin on her hands. "Let's talk about this kiss and your feelings."

Oh boy. Did she expect him to bare his soul, or could he

maintain a surface level until assured she was as gone for him as he was for her? Tell her he had more-than-friendly feelings, yes. Tell her he was pretty sure it was love, no.

"Tuck?"

He cleared his throat. "Let's talk."

"How long have you had more-than-friendly feelings for me?"

Now his insides felt like live bait was squirming around. "Probably since middle school at the end-of-the-year dance. Tommy Blake was supposed to take you, but he backed out when he discovered his mom didn't like your mom. So I took you, which I wanted to do in the first place. But since I was in my freshman year of high school, I technically didn't have a reason to go to an eighth-grade dance."

Her mouth parted. "You've liked me since then?"

"Yes." He blew out a breath. "You looked so pretty in your pink dress."

"Tuck . . ." Her ebony eyes sparkled. "I had a huge crush on you then."

"Before then . . . or only then?" And dang if he wasn't holding his breath while waiting for her to answer.

She bit her lip. "Before then. . . ."

All this time? "Why didn't you ever say anything?"

"Well . . ." A solemn expression covered her face. "I was afraid the difference in our race would be an issue."

He sat back against the seat. "Piper, we're best friends. If I had an issue, don't you think it would have stopped our friendship from even happening?"

"People might be friends with someone outside their ethnic group, but that doesn't mean they'd actually *date* them."

"Darlin' . . ." He hated that she thought that. That she would ever feel any kind of lack. He was the one deficient. He was the one who couldn't offer her the world.

Tuck reached for her hand and gazed steadily into her beautiful face. "I'm not eloquent in speech, so I'm asking the Holy Spirit to give me the words. I want to be crystal clear and pray you have ears to hear." He paused. "You being born in Ọlọrọ Ilé is a non-factor for me. Not because I don't see how beautiful the color of your skin is and don't care how that's shaped you, but because who you are on the inside is what matters the most to me." His thumb stroked the back of her hand as words poured forth.

"You are faithful to Christ, loyal to family and friends, and you make me laugh as much as you make me want to be the man you deserve to have by your side. Your personality matters more to me than your looks. Like it says in the Bible, beauty is passing. One day, I may be bald with hair coming out only my ears and nose. But I hope you'll still care about me because my personality had long since endeared me to you."

Did that make sense, or was that another microaggression version of *I don't see color*?

Piper stood and came to his side of the booth, perching half on the seat and half in his lap. Then she wrapped him in a hug, whispering softly in his ear. "Thank you for seeing me for me."

"Always." He kissed her cheek, then nuzzled his nose right in the crook of her neck.

He could have happily stayed that way for hours, but she moved back to her seat in a matter of seconds. A moment later, their server brought their food.

Tuck offered to say grace, thankful he could say the blessing as a couple now. Wait, *were* they a couple?

"Lord God, please bless this food and please bless our relationship. Amen."

"Amen," Piper echoed. She tilted her head. "So what are we?"

He grinned. "Best friends." That he could say without a doubt.

"Is that it?" Her gaze narrowed.

"Is that all you want it to be?" Tuck could barely contain his amusement as a glower flared her nostrils.

This time, Piper threw something at *him*. He caught her napkin in midair and handed it back.

"Piper McKinney, I'll be whatever you want me to be." If that wasn't the truth.

"Then *boyfriend* it is . . . for now."

His heart quickened at the "for now" comment. "Okay . . . girlfriend."

She grinned and took a bite of her food. "Oh my word. We have to eat here every morning until we leave."

"That can be arranged."

"Thank heaven." She took another bite, shimmying with delight.

Tuck didn't know what he'd been expecting, but the rest of their breakfast was much the same as their time together had always been. They joked and laughed, talked about Dream and the other contenders for the Jeff Ruby Steaks, and then left after paying for their meal. The only thing different was the amount of hand holding and shared looks.

He actually really enjoyed the change even though panic wanted to creep into his mind here and there. Like when Piper mentioned something her mom had said. Immediately, he wondered what Mrs. McKinney would think. Would she believe Tuck was good enough to date her daughter? Have a serious relationship that would—God willing—lead to marriage? Or would she urge Piper to pick some other man just like she managed to get her to wear something she wasn't comfortable in?

Not to mention how a win with Dream at the Derby would change things. He'd always assumed he'd needed Dream to win that race before Piper would even think of him in a more-than-friends kind of way. Now that he knew that wasn't the case, he wasn't really sure what to do next.

Remember, God will lead.

Piper tugged on his hand, pulling him from his thoughts quite literally. He followed and told his brain to relax.

"Will Gabe be at the track this afternoon?" Piper asked.

"Yeah. He wants to work the colt once over the track."

"How's your other horse doing? The one who has a chance at going to the Kentucky Oaks?"

Tuck smiled. The filly was doing really well. "She's great. I can't wait to see how she places."

"I'm so happy for you." Piper squeezed his hand. "It's about time the world found out how great of a trainer you are. I'm only sorry my parents never offered the lead trainer position to you."

He wasn't. He liked owning his own farm. Liked choosing who he worked for. Basically liked everything there was about working for himself. "I think it was for the best."

"You think?"

He nodded. "I really do. I wouldn't get to direct my own hours if I were still working at Bolt Brook."

"That's true."

"Plus, it's showed me that a change of plans isn't always a bad thing." He winked.

In truth, Tuck had been worried that leaving his position as associate trainer at Bolt Brook when Piper asked him to train Dream would be a foolish move. Still, he gave her offer some serious consideration. After praying and praying, God had told him to move forward with Piper and not her folks' farm. Now he could see how much better being his own boss was.

See, you laid down your plans for God's will.

"I'm so glad you decided to train my Thoroughbred. Honestly, you were my only choice. I'm not sure who I would have asked if you'd said no." Her nose scrunched up as she peered up at him.

"I've got a question." She nodded, so he continued once they were both in the truck and he had started driving. "Did you pick your farm because it was next door to mine, or was that a mere coincidence?"

"Sort of a coincidence." She twisted in the seat to look at him. "I was looking for farms with specific criteria, and Maisha Farms was one of three I found. One was outside of Eastbrook, which was a little strange to me. I mean, I was open to the move, only the land was in rough shape, and the buildings needed a lot of reno work. The other farm was also in Eastbrook, but honestly, it was too close to my folks. So I chose the one next door to yours."

"Me or your folks, huh?" Whoa. Now that he heard it out loud, it almost felt like a premonition.

"Well, my folks will always be my folks. But before that kiss, I always figured my time with you was limited, so having you as a neighbor would be better than nothing."

"What do you mean *limited*?"

She huffed. "Tuck, I thought you'd fall in love with some girl and marry her, and then I'd be forced to pretend I liked her. Not to mention that once she realized how much time you spent with me, she'd quickly squash that. What girl wants her man to be besties with another woman?"

"No woman?" he said cautiously.

"Exactly."

Tuck laughed. "Good to know you were a little jealous."

"You call it jealousy, I call it smarts."

"Well, in this case, it might be the same thing."

He wanted to promise he'd never give her a reason to be jealous, but who knew what went on in a woman's mind when that feeling arose? He once saw a girl get jealous of another girl because they were wearing the same shirt. Looked different on each of them, but that didn't matter to the one turning green.

Instead, Tuck squeezed Piper's fingers and continued his way to Turfway. They'd get Dream out of the stables and acclimate him to the track, so he'd be ready for the race on Saturday. And he and Piper . . . well, one step at a time.

Seventeen

M s. McKinney, how does it feel to have Dream land in first place?"

I smiled at the reporter. Not because I was trying to look friendly, but because I couldn't keep the grin from forming every time I thought about Dream crossing the finish line first. "I'm elated. I'm so happy he's doing well this season." I wanted to glance over at Tuck and see how his interview was going, but I needed to stay focused.

"Where will you go next?"

"He'll be racing at the Mountain Laurel Stakes next." Dream didn't necessarily need the points from that race, but it would keep him tuned up.

"Do you think he'll win?"

"I certainly hope so." I clasped my hands in front of me, presenting a calm front, but inside I wanted to dance, jump up and down, and yell in jubilation. Dream was going to the Kentucky Derby this year. *Ahhhhh!*

"One last question. Do you use illegal substances like your parents do?"

Heat infused every feature of my face, zapping my joy. "No comment."

"Come on, Ms. McKinney," the journalist said, trying to

cajole an answer from me. "You must have something to say regarding the allegations against your adoptive parents."

"My *parents*," I snapped.

"Yes." He sneered. "Do you believe they're innocent? Has the RMTC investigated your own farm and conducted blood tests?"

"No comment," Tuck said, coming up to stand behind me. He glanced down at me. "You done with this interview?"

I nodded, slipping my hand into his.

"Then let's go." He turned his back against the reporter and guided me away.

Relief filled me, and the outrage that had thickened my throat slowly abated. I looked up at Tuck. "Did they ask you something similar?"

"Yeah. But I said *no comment* just like you."

We walked away from the track toward the stables to the left of the grandstand. "Have you seen Dream?"

"Briefly. Gabe will be handing him off to the stable hand. I'm sure he needs to unwind just like the colt does."

"I can help the stable hand. It's my horse, after all."

Tuck smirked at me, so I rose on tiptoes to kiss his cheek.

"What was that for?" he asked.

"I've always wanted to do that when you smirk. It's adorable."

He rolled his eyes. "Smirks aren't supposed to be adorable. They're supposed to be a little arrogant and superior."

"But you look cute. Your blue eyes sparkle when you do it."

Tuck stopped in his tracks. "Darlin', no man wants any part of him to sparkle. Ms. Meyer has hoodwinked a generation of women."

"Maybe, but my bookish heart just swooned because you know who Stephenie Meyer is."

"Oh, is Stephenie her first name?" He smirked again, then winked.

"Ugh." I strode off, trying to keep the laughter at bay. But when Tuck swung me around, it bubbled out of me. You'd laugh, too, when your new boyfriend assumed you were mad and wore an expression like the one you get when you stepped in animal droppings.

"For a moment, I thought you were actually upset." Tuck breathed out a sigh of relief.

I wiped my eyes as my laughter slowly subsided. "Your face said as much."

"What am I going to do with you?"

Love me. But saying that week one of our being official seemed a little bit like getting ahead of myself. I didn't want to scare Tuck with the depth of my feelings. "Buy me some bourbon balls, and we'll be good." There was never a wrong time for chocolate.

"You've always loved those."

"What self-respecting person doesn't?"

Tuck shrugged.

I picked up speed as we walked into the stables. Dream's stall was in the middle on the right. I waited to see his head pop over the gate, but when I stepped in front of the door, the stall was empty.

"He's probably getting cooled down."

I nodded. "Right."

The stable hands would take a hose and spray water all over the horses after a run to aid in lowering their core temperature. Dream was probably enjoying the cool down.

Once he returned to his stall, I gave him a treat, then Tuck and I headed back to the main building. We walked in silence, hand in hand. With any other person, I always felt the need to fill the quiet and make small talk. With Tuck, I could just let my mind be still and be thankful for the companionship.

Lord God, thank You so much that Tuck likes me back. It's such a relief to hold his hand, a hand that warms every part of my being.

It seemed like such a small thing to focus on, but I couldn't help but repeat it over and over. My hand felt cherished and cared for within Tuck's larger grasp. When we turned a corner to go in the front entrance of the casino-hotel, his hand kept me upright as a swarm of reporters surrounded us before I could even blink.

"Ms. McKinney, are you surprised that Bolt Brook is guilty of using blood-doping agents?"

"Ms. McKinney, over here! Do you have a comment to give us?"

"Mr. Hale, did you ever administer blood-doping agents while working for Bolt Brook?"

My breath came in spurts as camera flashes went off in our faces. Questions pummeled me from all sides as my brain tried to understand what was happening. Bolt Brook had been found guilty? Were they lying? Sensationalizing a small fact to turn it into a breaking-news story?

Tuck gripped my elbow and shielded my body as he pushed his way through the throng of reporters. Like a scene from a movie, slow motion had been fully activated, and it took us several minutes to get through.

This was no rom-com, though. Reality had been served with some horror plot twist of continuous camera shutters, accusations hurled by reporters, and a sinking feeling that my relationship with my folks would never be the same.

By the time we escaped the horde—thank you, Turfway, for not letting them into the casino—my ears were ringing from all the commotion. Or maybe that was shock. Was that a side effect?

Tuck guided me into the elevator, then to my suite, where I dropped onto the couch in a daze. Then he paced a track in front of the TV while his fingers flew across his cell screen. A few moments later, he froze. Then his gaze darted from his phone to me, then back to his phone.

"Spit it out." My voice sounded weary.

"Multiple articles state the RMTC found conclusive evidence of Bolt Brook's use of illegal substances and that blood work showed multiple horses with the agents currently in their system."

I choked on an inhale and bent over as if I'd been literally socked in the abdomen. As I gasped for air, my eyes filled with tears.

"Breathe, darlin', breathe."

Tuck's calm tenor enveloped me, and I became aware of warmth surrounding me. Eventually, the haze receded from my eyes, and I saw the warmth came from Tuck. Concern etched into the lines of his forehead and those framing his mouth.

"I'm okay," I whispered.

"Are you sure?"

I nodded.

He cupped my cheek. "I'm so sorry."

"So am I." Tears spilled over. "Do you think it's true? I can't hope they were framed or something like that?"

"I mean, anything is possible, but how possible is it in this scenario?" A pained look crossed Tuck's face. "Maybe it wasn't your dad. Yes, the farm could be guilty, but that doesn't mean your dad administered the drugs or knew about it."

"I really hope you're right, Tuck." What would I do if either one of my parents willingly betrayed everything I believed in and the sport I loved so much?

And what would Mama do if she found out Dad had known? They'd been married for almost forty years.

"What am I going to do?" I asked.

"First, let's pray. Then once we're home, you can call your mother and get more details."

I nodded, thankful for a plan of action. Trust Tuck to already have one at the ready. "I still can't believe it could be true."

"Bolt Brook wouldn't be the only farm to ever use illegal substances on their horses."

"I know that, but I thought better of my folks. They're supposed to be Christians and uphold integrity."

"Until either one of them admits to knowledge, don't assume the worst."

"Come on, someone had to know something."

Tuck rubbed his chin. "I agree. But Christians aren't perfect, Piper. Remember the recent lie Nevaeh and Lamont perpetuated? Just because we believe in Christ doesn't mean we're flawless—merely forgiven."

I sighed. "You're right." I looked at my best friend. "Do you ever need to be forgiven?"

"Of course. I don't always use the best language."

"Like when Baby escaped the pin and made you chase after her?" Giggles rose within me at the image of Tuck chasing one of my goats around the farm to capture her and bring her back to the goat enclosure.

"Exactly. Slipping in the mud and then her darting just out of reach pulled a word out of my mouth that would make my gran blush."

I laid my head on his shoulder. "Sometimes I feel like I need forgiveness for wishing I knew my birth parents."

"Why's that? You don't think it's natural to want to know them?"

"Maybe it is, but it makes me feel guilty, nevertheless. Like the want means I don't appreciate everything my folks did for me by loving on me as if I were born of them."

Wasn't that what made my identity so tricky? I have mannerisms from my parents because they're who raised me. Yet somewhere out in the world someone was walking around with my small button nose and chin that slightly jutted out.

"Wanting to know pieces of your DNA makeup doesn't mean you love the people who were there for every knee scrape and bedtime prayer any less."

"I'll try to remember that." Because I'd been battling guilt ever since I knew what the word meant. "Do you know what my biggest fear is?"

"What?" Tuck asked softly.

"That my folks'll be guilty, and then I'll be without any parents to claim."

"Oh, darlin', you'll get through this. Whatever happens and when you talk to them, I'll be there. Not to mention the Lord is walking every step with you."

Tuck's words comforted me, just as I'm sure he intended. I needed to be reminded that God was with me and that I wouldn't be lost if my folks really had done the unthinkable. I certainly didn't want to sever ties with them, but I also didn't know how I'd react when I faced them. If they'd committed a cardinal sin in the horse-racing world, that wouldn't be a sin that stopped at their doorstep. It would taint every single person who'd ever worked at Bolt Brook.

Eighteen

Lamont
Heard the news. How are you guys holding up?

Chris
Praying for you and Piper and her parents.

Tuck closed his eyes as he tried to decide how to respond.

Tuck
She's not taking it too well.

Chris
How are you taking it?

Tuck
Most of my clients have canceled their horse-back riding lessons. And a couple of owners no longer want me training their horses.

That pretty much summed up the craptastic morning he was having.

Lamont
Man, I'm sorry about that. Will you be ok financially?

That remained to be seen. Tuck hadn't had the opportunity to assess the monetary impact of the whole affair. He'd been too busy dodging reporters and sleeping in from the drive home.

Hence the reason he was now in his office instead of spending time with his girlfriend.

Thanks to his previous association with Bolt Brook, news journalists were now camped outside his gate. Didn't seem to matter that his horses were cleared of any illegal substances. That wasn't a narrative they were interested in telling.

Unfortunately, Piper had more than a few measly journalists at her door. Since it was her folks in the news, the vultures had been camping out on the public yard across from her gated entrance.

Tuck
I'm praying so. But we'll see.

Chris
Man, if you need anything, don't be too proud to ask.

Lamont
What he said. We got your back.

Tuck
Thanks

Tuck slid his cell near the top of his desk and exhaled. Now to deal with the rest of the voicemails piling up on his office phone. He'd already listened to a few that made him wince at the disdain coating his clients'—ex-clients—voices as they assured him they'd never set foot on his property again. The fallout from the McKinney scandal was enough to have him dreaming of climbing back into bed to restart the day.

Too bad ignoring his problems wouldn't get them solved or make them disappear. Knowing his luck, he'd end up in some torturous version of the movie *Groundhog Day*.

Lord God, what do I do? If I don't have lessons and training to supplement my income from Piper, how will I earn enough money?

He shook his head. As much as he appreciated Lamont and

Chris offering to help, Tuck didn't know if he could swallow that much pride and ask for their assistance. Considering Lamont's net worth could be found with one internet search, it seemed foolish not to ask for help. Still . . . Tuck didn't want the man to think he just wanted a handout from a movie star. He wanted to maintain their friendship, and the idea of borrowing money from him seemed like it would muddy the waters.

But what else can I do?

He shoved the thoughts aside and pulled up his budget. Eliminating the horseback riding income from the eight out of ten clients who'd called him would give him an idea of what he was working with. Maybe he should just erase the income from everyone, including the horses he was training, in case everyone decided to seek services elsewhere. Just because they hadn't left a nasty voicemail didn't mean they would maintain ties with him.

After deleting the numbers, Tuck looked at his monthly expenses and compared it against his monthly income, then groaned. Losing these clients would put him in the red unless he could cut some expenses.

He glanced at the items like his streaming service, haircuts, and how much he regularly put into his savings account. He could also adjust his tithing amount if his income was falling. Plus, no one said he needed to save as much as he was. His goal of a six-month emergency fund had been met. After updating the numbers, the bottom of the spreadsheet stayed red. Would he have to dip into his savings to cover the deficiency until the McKinney scandal became old news?

Fortunately, if Dream placed at the Derby, Tuck would get some of the purse money.

Of course! He'd be receiving his percentage of the purse income from the race they'd just won, not to mention any future races where the colt placed.

Tuck let out a breath and whispered a praise to the Lord.

How had he so quickly forgotten that the purse money would be coming in? Since the Thoroughbred had placed first, that was around seventy grand in his pocket, though Tuck would have to account for taxes. Still, a good amount could go to his savings with enough left to go back into the farm. He'd be financially stable as long as he didn't splurge too much.

His ringtone broke the quiet. Tuck jumped, then snatched up his phone, swiping quickly to silence the noise.

"Hello?"

"Tuck, this is Aaron Wellington."

Tuck's lip curled. "Yes?"

"I'm sure you're surprised to hear from me." The man cleared his throat. "I need to pass on some news."

"To me and not Piper?"

"Yeah. Look, Piper was upset that I put things into motion. She blames me for all the bad press her parents are receiving."

Of course she would. But now that something shady had happened at Bolt Brook was confirmed, Tuck could see Aaron's side of things.

Ugh. Don't give me another perspective, Lord. "I'm aware."

"Are you aware of who first alerted the RMTC?"

Tuck straightened. "No, I heard it was an anonymous tip."

"Yeah, that's what I heard as well. But I did some digging."

After a long pause, Tuck spoke. "And? Who was it?"

"Your father."

"What?" Tuck sank back in his chair. "No way."

"Yes."

"Why should I believe you?"

"I just wanted to help Piper. Let her know I'm not just after a story. Only this new information would make everything worse."

Tuck was shaken, but he wasn't going to take the reporter's word for it. He needed to see his dad. "Who else have you told?"

"No one."

Tuck swallowed. "Thanks."

"You're welcome." Then after a pause, "I'll be rooting for Dream in the Derby. I'm sure he'll do great."

Tuck said nothing more as the phone went silent.

Lord God, please say it ain't so. If his dad really reported someone at Bolt Brook . . .

Tuck groaned and laid his head in his hands. How could he possibly tell Piper her folks were under fire because of his dad? He needed to find out if that was true.

> **Tuck**
> You home?

> **Dad**
> Where else would I be? You plan on coming through?

> **Tuck**
> Yeah. I'll be there in a half hour. Mom home too?

> **Dad**
> Nah. She's at a crafting market.

His mom loved collecting homemade items from craft shows. Tuck always thought it was a boring hobby, but right then, he was thankful she wouldn't be home. He had no clue if she knew what his dad did—allegedly. He could only pray Dad would tell the truth, not lie.

Please, Lord, let the truth come to light.

He wasn't sure yet what he'd do with the information. The thought of telling Piper made him sick. Surely this would have her breaking up with him before their romance even started.

If he drove to his parents' place, the reporters would see him, maybe even follow. But if he left on horseback, then he could cut through both his land and Piper's and use the county's horse trails to get to his folks. That should keep him out of the paparazzi's view.

Nutcracker whinnied as Tuck entered the barn.

"Hey, boy. How are you?" Tuck offered him a sugar cube. He laughed as the gelding lapped it up like it was a Tic Tac. "Wanna go for a ride?"

He stroked Nutcracker's mane and offered him another treat before starting the process of saddling him. The Thoroughbred stood still as Tuck cinched up the saddle.

"All ready?"

Nutcracker tossed his mane.

Tuck put on his helmet, then mounted the horse. "Let's go." He squeezed his legs against the horse's sides and led him out of the stable in a walk. Then once they cleared the building, Tuck urged Nutcracker into a canter.

The canter was where his horse excelled and the reason he made a good teacher for Tuck's lessons. He'd have to make sure he took the ol' boy out every day so he wouldn't be sad at the lack of visitors.

As the cool breeze of the day feathered against Tuck's face, he began to see the top of the fence between his and Piper's land. He'd bought the horse from a previous cross-country rider, so the gelding knew how to jump, but it had been a while since they'd done so.

As they neared the fence, Nutcracker adjusted his speed for the height of the fence. Tuck loved how aware his horse was as he prepared himself for the jump. Tuck moved to forward seat with just his knees touching the horse. He loosened the pressure on the reins, then bent his hips so his chest would lower toward his body. Nutcracker rocked back on his hind legs, and they sailed through the air and over the fence, landing in rhythm. Tuck whooped, feeling the sun shining down on them as Nutcracker moved assuredly beneath him, already adjusting his speed to a canter rather than maintaining the gallop from the jump.

"Attaboy."

He patted Nutcracker's mane as he settled in his seat once more. But then the horse squealed, then shied to the side in a move so unexpected that Tuck lost control of the reins. He was about to get thrown.

Time slowed, and Tuck prepared himself, kicking his feet from the stirrups. As he flew through the air, he tucked his chin and knees toward his chest and curled his arms over his head. He landed on top of the grass with a thud that stole his breath, but he tried his best to let his back take the brunt of the impact.

Only, he must have anticipated incorrectly, because he heard a pop. The heat radiating from his shoulder didn't stop him from attempting a roll, but as soon as he hit his right shoulder again, his body stopped momentum on its own accord.

His eyes squeezed tightly shut as the ache in his shoulder intensified.

"Tuck!"

Piper's voice sounded so far away. He wanted to assure her that everything would be okay, but the only noise that made it past his lips was another groan. Why was the pain getting worse? Had he broken something? Nausea tossed his stomach. Everything hurt, and he just wanted to give in to the darkness beckoning him.

Tuck closed his eyes and let out a sigh.

Nineteen

The sound of sirens had my shoulders sagging with relief. Time had crawled to a stop since I'd called 911. While I waited, I'd prayed over Tuck as he lay unconscious. Thankfully, he was breathing with the occasional moan of pain mixed in.

"The ambulance is coming. You're gonna be okay," I whispered.

I stood, waving my arms in the air as two EMT members pulled a gurney behind them.

"What've we got?" Ted asked.

Seeing his face put me at ease. We'd graduated from Eastbrook High together, and he'd always been the guy to help someone in need. Thank goodness a stranger hadn't shown up.

"Tuck fell off his horse. I think he landed on his right shoulder, because he reached for it at one point."

I could still remember the horror of seeing him fly through the air. I didn't even want to imagine what would've happened if I hadn't been out in the field getting some QT with the goats. Baby had taken off on a run, and I'd just proceeded to chase her when it all unfolded.

"I didn't move him." Lord knew I'd wanted to. "He doesn't

appear to be bleeding from anywhere external. He's still breathing. Um . . ." I tried to think. "Pulse seemed steady from what I could tell."

"Do you know what caused him to get thrown?" Hannah asked, scanning the area. She'd graduated from high school a few years ahead of me. Last I heard, she was married to a local farmer and had two kids.

"The goat startled his horse." I pointed to Baby, who stood a few yards away.

"Darn goats," Ted mumbled.

Before today, I would've laughed and made him hold Baby so he could see how charming she truly was. Now I wanted to scold Baby and apologize to Nutcracker before begging Tuck's forgiveness. I had no idea the goats would scare his horse. It's not like Nutcracker hadn't already seen them escape from their enclosure the few times Tuck had ridden him over here and kept him in my stables.

"Give us some space to work on him. You can follow us to the hospital," Hannah said.

I nodded, tears smarting.

I turned toward Baby and cautiously walked forward. I needed to get her into the pen before I could leave. Maybe she understood the gravity of the situation, though, because she just let me scoop her up. Fortunately, my part-time barn hand had already taken Nutcracker to the horse stables. As soon as I had Baby back in the goat house, I unlocked Tuck's cell phone.

The man still used a pin code—claimed if he were ever mugged, they wouldn't be able to use his thumbprint or face to unlock it. He watched too many true-crime shows. But right now, I was thankful I knew the code and he'd never converted to fingerprint or facial security. I needed to let people know what happened so they could pray.

"Hey, son," Mr. Hale said in greeting.

"Um, Mr. Hale, it's Piper." I drew in a shaky breath. "Tuck's been hurt."

"What happened?"

"He was thrown from his horse. Ambulance is getting ready to take him to the county hospital."

"I'll let his mother know. We'll be up there as soon as we can."

"Okay."

"Was he conscious, Piper?"

My mouth dried. "No, sir."

"Lord have mercy," he whispered.

"Drive carefully."

"You too."

I hung up, then opened the text thread between Tuck, Chris, and Lamont.

> **Tuck**
> This is Piper. Tuck was in a riding accident. Horse threw him. He's unconscious and on the way to the hospital.

> **Chris**
> Praying. What can we do?

> **Lamont**
> 🙏 Should we fly out there?

> **Tuck**
> I'd wait until the doctors give us more information. Thank you so much for the prayers.

Then I opened my own phone and sent a similar text to Nevaeh. She wasn't in the guys' group thread, but that was okay since we had our own stream going.

> **Nevaeh**
> No! Praying right now. Do the guys know?

> **Piper**
> Yes.

Nevaeh
Keep me posted.

Piper
Will do.

After grabbing my purse so I'd have my license, I hopped into my truck and rumbled out the gate. Flashes went off, but I ignored the photojournalists. I'm sure they had much to speculate about as the ambulance had left the house before I did. They didn't matter. I just needed Tuck to be okay.

Please, God, I pray he has no brain trauma. No concussion. No spinal injuries or internal bleeding. Let every body part be well and whole. Please. Please. Please.

I bit my lip, trying to keep from crying. Right now, I needed to see, and shedding tears for my boyfriend might put me in an accident and in the room right next to his. Surely he would be okay. He had on his helmet, so it wasn't like his head hadn't been protected. But remembering his groans of pain and how he reached for his shoulder before passing out had me thinking something was wrong. A broken bone? Could you even break your shoulder?

Ugh. That was probably a ridiculous question, wasn't it?

The silence of the truck's interior threatened to overwhelm me, so I pressed the button for my cell's music playlist. Maybe hearing some inspirational music would keep my mind from spiraling and me acting like Chicken Little. Though an acorn hadn't fallen from the sky, I still felt like the world could be ending. Despite living with the realization that riding injuries were a guarantee in this field, I couldn't recall the last time Tuck had been seriously injured. Maybe a sprained tendon or a bite, but this . . .

Stop. Listen to the music. Praise God.

My voice warbled as I matched it with the artist's. Holiday Brown had firmly left the pop field and now sang only contemporary Christian music. I'd admired her switch and the sincerity of the words that weaved around my soul and gave me comfort. I wasn't alone. Tuck wasn't alone. God would see us through.

• • •

My head jerked forward.

I jolted, realizing I'd fallen asleep in Tuck's room. My neck was stiff and my bottom sore from sitting in the hard hospital chair for so long. I stretched my arms toward the ceiling, letting out a breath. Then bringing my arms back down, I looked at my smart watch. It was eight in the evening. *Oh man.* The cafeteria was probably closed.

My nose scrunched.

"You always look so cute when you do that," Tuck rasped.

"Tuck." I raced to the side of his bed and smiled at the sleepy look on his face, then brushed his hair back from his forehead. "How are you feeling? How long have you been awake?"

"Just a few minutes. Enough time to watch you snooze." His mouth crooked into a smile.

"Can I get you some water?"

"Please."

I grabbed the insulated cup the nurse had left when Tuck was first moved to the med-surge floor. By God's grace, he didn't have anything wrong with his spine or noggin. And the helmet had done its job so he was concussion free. Though apparently you could be concussed—the reason for his blackout—but not have a concussion. Who knew?

Unfortunately, he'd broken his right shoulder and would need surgery. Thankfully, a top-notch surgeon was willing to perform the procedure. She just wasn't able to come in until tomorrow. That meant they were keeping Tuck medicated and hydrated so he'd be ready first thing tomorrow morning.

I held the straw to his lips. "Drink slowly."

"Are you gonna activate that naggin' gene women are so well-known for?" Tuck's eyes sparkled at me. Or maybe I should think of another term since he claimed real men didn't sparkle.

"Not if you know what's good for you." My lips twitched.

He laughed, then groaned when the movement jostled him. "Sorry."

"No worries. I'll be fine. You heard the ER doc. Just a broken shoulder."

"That needs surgery."

I could feel my brow furrow just thinking about it. The doctor would have to insert pins and screws. I could only imagine the amount of pain Tuck would be in after that.

Chris and Lamont had been relieved it wasn't anything worse than a broken bone. Nevaeh too. Tuck's parents had come and gone and would return tomorrow.

"The important thing is I'll be able to work with Dream before the Mountain Laurel Stakes."

"Are you *serious*?" I reared back. "Do you not remember being thrown from a horse? Maybe they need to run that CT scan again, because you're acting like you took a hit to your frontal lobe." I slid my hands onto my hips. "Not to mention you'll be in a sling for who knows how long."

"Darlin', there's nothing wrong with my cranium." Tuck squeezed my hand with his on his good arm. "A concussion would've put me out of commission, but a slinged shoulder is merely a little inconvenient."

I glared at him. He was speaking nonsense. "What if my colt thinks you look strange and doesn't want to get close to you or, worse, hurts you?"

"That's why we have grooms and exercise riders." Tuck rolled his eyes. "It's not like I'm riding him myself."

I leaned close to Tuck and said through gritted teeth, "You better not get on a horse anytime soon, you hear me?"

But he didn't respond. Just reached out and closed the distance between us. "I love that you're worried and want to take care of me. But I promise you, I'm okay." He pressed soft lips against mine and held them there until all my objections floated out of my head.

Who could think when all I could feel was the heat between us and the love I had for this man?

We broke apart, and Tuck grinned. "Now I know how to win an argument."

"You don't fight fair, Tucker Hale."

He trailed a finger down my cheek. "And I don't plan on doing so anytime soon."

"Well, I've been forewarned, and I think you should be too."

He stared into my eyes. "What's that supposed to mean?"

I did my best attempt at a wink. Judging from the smolder in Tuck's eyes, I was successful and didn't look like some damsel with an eyelash in her eye.

I straightened just as a knock sounded on the door.

"Come in," Tuck said.

The night-shift nurse walked in. "Oh, goodie, you're awake. How are you feeling?"

"Drugged."

"Mm-hmm. That would be the pain meds. Narcotics can make a person feel loopy."

"And sleepy?"

"That too. Do you remember hearing you're having surgery tomorrow?"

"Yes, ma'am."

"That means nothing to eat or drink after midnight."

"Why? Will I turn into a gremlin?"

I snickered behind my hand.

The nurse shook her head, but her cheeks were bunched in amusement. "Don't worry. I'll see if I can snag you a sandwich or a snack before then. You'll get a full meal tomorrow. If not lunch, then definitely dinner."

"Will I be back in this room tomorrow?"

"Yes. And I'll be back on shift tomorrow night, so don't you worry. I'll take good care of you."

"I appreciate that."

"Sure thing." She turned and looked at me. "I'm sorry to tell you this, hon, but visiting hours are done at eight thirty. You'll have to come back tomorrow at eight a.m."

"Will his surgery be before then?" I wanted to be with him when he met the surgeon.

"They may have him prepped before then."

"Can she please come in early?" Tuck pouted.

I bit back a laugh.

"Well, hon, since she's not your wife, I doubt that'll be possible."

"I understand that, but I'd really appreciate being able to see my girlfriend's face well before I go under the knife. My first broken bone."

"How's that possible, Mr. Hale? I've seen you on the news interviewed about training horses and whatnot."

"Only got bumps and bruises before now."

"Hmm. Sounds like God's blessing. I'll see what I can do about your girlfriend."

"Thanks"—he glanced at her name tag—"Winnie."

"If you leave your contact information with me, Ms. McKinney, I'll make sure I notify you about the surgery time."

"Thank you." I paused. "Um, can I bring his parents with me? Maybe not to be in his room but to wait in the waiting area?"

She nodded. "They're more than welcome."

Winnie finished taking Tuck's vitals, then left the room.

I walked over to his bed. "Guess I'll see you tomorrow."

"Hurry back." He kissed the palm of my hand.

Twenty

Tuck's hospital room's door opened, and in strolled a good-looking Black woman with shoulder-length braids. He tried to adjust the bed so he could sit up, but doing so with his left hand proved to be a little awkward.

"You don't have to move." The woman's face curved upward in a way that somewhat resembled a smile but didn't actually look like one. "I'm Dr. Erykah Kennedy. I'll be your surgeon today."

The stethoscope and scrubs were a dead giveaway. "Nice to meet you, Doc."

"Dr. Kennedy is just fine." She gave that awkward-looking smile again.

Okay, Tuck was going to call it a grimace. He just had to, because it looked like she was forcing her face to move in a way that pained her.

"How long will the surgery take?" he asked.

"Based on the X-rays and amount of damage you did to your arm, I suspect three hours." She looked up from the iPad the hospital used to store patient charts. "Do you have any questions?"

Lots. But before he could ask them, a quick knock sounded, then Piper walked in.

Tuck smiled at her. She was a beautiful sight for so early in the morning. "You made it."

"Yeah. Sorry I was late. They directed us to the waiting area, then I had to convince them I was listed to be here for this conversation."

Dr. Kennedy turned, and her eyes widened as she took in Piper. Tuck didn't know if she was simply shocked he was dating a Black woman or if she disapproved. Either way, he didn't care as long as the doc maintained respect.

"Hi, I'm Piper. Nice to meet you." She held out her hand to the surgeon.

"Hello. I'm Dr. Erykah Kennedy. You're the girlfriend?"

Piper nodded. "Am I too late? Did you already tell him everything?"

"Just how long the procedure is. Mr. Hale was about to ask questions." Dr. Kennedy turned back toward him, an expectant expression on her face.

Tuck searched his mind, and Piper came to stand by him, sliding her hand into his.

"How long is recovery?" he finally asked.

"You'll be in a lot of pain for the first couple of weeks. But I'll administer a nerve block, so you'll have at least the first twenty-four to forty-eight hours pain free. Once the nerve block wears off, though, I recommend using the pain medication I'll prescribe. If you don't start taking it before the block wears off, you may be in more pain than you anticipate or can handle."

Great. Tuck hated pain. He sighed. "When can I get back to work?"

"What do you do, Mr. Hale?"

"I'm a racehorse trainer."

Her eyes narrowed. "Do you plan to get on the back of a horse? Because if so, I highly advise against it."

"No, I don't need to ride. I have a couple of exercise riders who can do that. But I do need to be on the track giving instructions." Surely that wouldn't be too bad.

"Then when you feel the pain isn't debilitating, you can return to work." She crossed her arms.

Well, wasn't she a bundle of joy?

"How long will his physical therapy be?" Piper asked.

Dr. Kennedy turned her gaze to his girlfriend. He smiled. Just thinking of Piper as his girlfriend cheered him up and kept the dark thoughts about surgery and recovery at bay.

"Therapy can be anywhere between three and six months."

Tuck groaned. That did not sound good.

"Will he need any follow-up appointments after surgery? Maybe to remove stitches or . . ."

"He will. We'll want to check on the healing, and that appointment is typically six weeks later. I won't be doing follow-up care, but I'll leave you with the name of a doctor who can take over after surgery."

"I'm sorry if this question is intrusive, but why can't you do it?" Tuck asked.

"I'm actually in Kentucky on vacation visiting my sister." She gave that grimace-smile once more. "I leave for home in a few days."

"Oh. You're licensed here, though?"

"Yes." She nodded. "And a few other states. The ER doctor knew I was in town and called me to perform the surgery. I'm one of the best in the field."

"One of or *the* best?" Piper asked with a grin.

For the first time since she walked into the room, Dr. Erykah Kennedy softened and looked almost joyful. "*The* best."

Piper let out a breath. "Fantastic. And the doctor you'll recommend will be able to do Tuck's follow-up care adequately?"

"Yes. I wouldn't recommend someone I didn't trust."

Good enough for Tuck. "Thanks, Dr. Kennedy."

"Sure thing. You'll meet with the anesthesiology team next, then I'll see you in the OR."

Tuck gave her a salute, and she smirked, shaking her head. But he thought he saw a genuine smile on her face as she walked out of the room.

"Good morning," Piper whispered before placing a kiss on his forehead.

"Morning." Tuck reached out with his good arm and attempted a half hug. "How's everything? Reporters still at the gates?"

Piper scrunched her nose. "Unfortunately. A few articles speculating about the incident yesterday have appeared. They suspect you or someone else who works for Maisha Farms to be hospitalized. I wouldn't be surprised if someone tried to sneak into the hospital to gain information."

Tuck wouldn't be surprised either. That had happened to Nevaeh when she was in a car accident last year. Then again, this wasn't Hollywood.

"Don't worry about it," he said, urging her not to. "As long as we maintain our no-comment stance, they'll eventually get fed up and leave us alone."

"I hope you're right. I don't know how Lamont and Nevaeh handle the scrutiny. I want to hide from the articles, but I also have this compulsive desire to click on every notification with the McKinney name in it."

"Don't do that." He frowned. "Erase those alerts."

"I didn't set them up. I think it's just the algorithm—or maybe our phones listening to our conversations," she quipped.

"Then be strong and don't click."

Piper laughed. "Easier said than done."

A knock sounded, and a doctor and nurse walked in. They introduced themselves as the anesthesiology team who'd be overseeing his beauty sleep. After that, the scrub tech came in to wheel him away.

"I'll see you when you wake up," Piper said.

"Don't fall in love with the other guy while I'm sleeping."

She laughed. "Aren't you glad you don't have a brother?"

"Very." He loved how she'd got his reference to *While You Were Sleeping*. He'd maintain his belief that Sandra Bullock made for a better rom-com actress than Julia Roberts. Her movies had been more enjoyable for him to watch when Piper forced him to view an endless number of chick flicks.

"I'll be waiting," she murmured.

Tuck closed his eyes to avoid seeing the ceiling tiles pass in his field of vision. This was the first time he'd be under the knife, and the thought had kept him awake most of the night. It didn't help that the hospital also made him sign paperwork saying he could die due to complications. He'd wanted to ask Dr. Kennedy to further explain what the risks were, but then again, he hadn't. No need to up his unease. Instead, he practiced drawing in deep breaths and exhaling slowly as he prayed.

Lord God, please fill me with Your peace. Please be the hands of the surgeon. May there be no complications, and may I wake up on the road to recovery. He swallowed, searching his brain for other things to pray for. *Oh yes. Please bring peace to Piper and my folks. I'm sure they're all nervous too.*

When his parents visited yesterday, Tuck had been in and out of consciousness. When awake, it was to see tears in his mom's eyes and a furrowed brow on his dad's face. He so badly wanted to ask his mom to leave so he could talk to his dad about the RMTC, but getting answers would have to wait. He didn't want to bring more worries than a broken shoulder had already caused.

Still, with all the possible scenarios his mind had gone through, his gut felt like a bone being gnawed by a dog. How could his dad possibly know what was going on at Bolt Brook? Had *he* doped the horses before he retired? Or maybe Aaron Wellington was just trying to drum up more drama.

None of the scenarios had a very uplifting outcome, so Tuck forced himself to meditate on something good—aka Piper. From the moment he'd wakened in the ER, Piper had been a rock. She offered countless hugs and even comforted his folks. He already knew she was awesome. It was the reason they'd been friends for so long. But seeing her in a nurturing capacity after an injury had Tuck thinking of the next step.

He loved Piper McKinney with every breath in his body. Maybe when he woke up, he'd take the risk and let her know exactly how he felt. No hesitation, just the simple use of three words.

The hospital staff pushed the button to open the OR room doors.

"Welcome to the OR, Mr. Hale," one of them said. "We're gonna need to move you on over to the operating table."

He nodded and followed their instructions. They had him spread his left arm out on a cross pad, and as they strapped it to the cushion, he thought about how Jesus must have felt. Guess he should be thankful his other arm wouldn't be stretched out and strapped down as well.

"Relax," the anesthesiologist said. "You'll be asleep in no time."

"You're gonna wake me back up, right?" Tuck cracked.

"In a blink of an eye. It'll be the best sleep you've ever had."

"If it's not, do I get a refund?"

The doctor laughed. "Sorry. My services are nonrefundable."

"Good thing I just earned some horse race purse money. Who knew I'd be spending it on a hospital bill."

"God's timing is often mysterious."

Tuck breathed out. "You're a Christian?"

The doc nodded.

"Then I think I'll rest well."

"Told you I'd take care of you." The anesthesiologist held up an oxygen mask. "Take a few whiffs of this and you won't even have to count backward before you start feeling the effects. 'Kay?"

Tuck nodded as the doctor placed the mask over his nose. The air smelled a little weird and made his nose want to twitch, but he followed instructions and inhaled deeply. A drowsy sensation came over him, and then his eyes fluttered as he thought of Piper and her comment about his not having a brother.

All he knew was this better not be . . .

Twenty-One

Now that Tuck was home and recuperating from his surgery, I could focus on what I'd been avoiding: facing my parents. Driving up the driveway to Bolt Brook filled me with trepidation. I had no idea if my folks would be honest with me about what was going on. I didn't know how they would respond to my queries, but I had to ask. I had to know if they intentionally used illegal substances, or if someone on staff had without their permission.

It was time for their silence to end.

I got out of my truck and walked up the sidewalk steps leading to the double front doors. A twist of the knob told me my folks had finally locked them—something they never did in the past because someone was always coming or going. I pressed the doorbell and listened to the echo chime throughout the house.

A minute later, the sound of the lock releasing greeted my ears, and with the opening of the door, my father stood before me.

"Hey, Dad." An empty pit widened in my stomach.

"Piper." He swallowed. "I'm surprised you haven't been by sooner."

"I would have, but Tuck got injured and had surgery yesterday." His mom had wanted to be the one to take him home today and pamper him, so I made myself scarce to face the dragon in my own backyard.

"Is he okay?" Dad closed the door behind me.

"He will be."

"Hmm. Your mother is in our bedroom." He pointed down the hall. "Hasn't come out in days."

I searched his blue-gray eyes. "Why? Is she . . . okay?" Was she upset by the news articles, or did she know the truth?

"She's mad at me. Won't even speak to me."

My chest started to tingle. "Did you . . ." I drew in a shaky inhale. "Did you do it, Dad?"

Silence greeted my ears, then just when I thought I couldn't stand the tense quiet anymore, he spoke. "Yes."

The room spun, and I placed a hand on my heart, trying to steady myself and comprehend the three-letter word he'd just lobbed my way. I swayed backward, and Dad reached out to steady me.

"Don't." I shook my head, stepping back. "How could you?" I raised my hands, but then dropped them. "*Why* would you?" My voice cracked.

"Sweetheart, it was just one time. But then . . . it wasn't." He ran a hand over his head. "The horses started performing better. We won more races. Then buyers were willing to pay a higher stud fee." He gulped. "Things got out of hand, and before I knew it, I couldn't keep myself from making it a common practice."

"Did you administer the drugs yourself or use a staff member?" I thought of Tuck. He'd never firmly said whether he believed my dad did it or not, had he?

"Our vet did. Since he often came to check the horses, it made sense to ask him."

Was it awful of me to thank the Lord I didn't use the same veterinarian? When I chose Mordecai, it was to make myself feel independent of my folks. Now I was thankful it made me less culpable.

Focus, Piper. "How much did you pay him to keep your secret and do your dirty work?" Disgust dripped from every word. I couldn't hide it. I didn't even recognize the man standing before me.

Dad's lip twisted. "Don't ask questions you don't want the answers to."

"Did Mama know?"

He shook his head, dropping his chin to his chest.

Now her anger made sense. My heart hurt for her.

"Suppose you'll take her side, huh?" He lifted his head, but his gaze remained downcast.

"Dad, there's no side between you and her. But there is right and wrong, and I know what side of that I stand on."

"That's easy for you to say." Bitterness flashed in his eyes. "You're just starting out, and your colt is doing well. Wait until the pressure rises. Wait until people expect you to produce winners on a regular basis. Will you stick to your morals then?"

"Yes!" I shouted. "Because *you* taught me we were nothing without integrity. You taught me to always be honest. You always said not much in life could be trusted, but as long as you could tell God you were trustworthy, that's all that mattered." Tears streamed down my face. "Who *are* you?"

"I'm still your father, Piper."

I shook my head again. "You're not the same man who raised me. He would've never hurt Mama with his actions. Would've never hurt me," I whispered. "I don't know who you are."

"You do." His face looked haggard as he took a step toward me. "Your mama feels the same way, but if y'all would just stand by me, you'll see I'm the same man."

I stared at the only father I'd ever known. This man taught me what it felt like to be loved by an earthly father without question. He taught me how to ride a horse and took me to the track to explain the facts of racing. We'd sit up at night and talk about old horse races, like the beauty of Secretariat's

Derby win or how American Pharaoh came back from an awful start in his road to the Derby to end up winning the famed title. Dad and horse-racing memories were wrapped up into one.

"Do you know what reporters have said about me? You?" I pointed at him.

"I know it hasn't been easy."

I scoffed. "Please, you make it seem like the world hasn't done a hatchet job on you in the media—and me by extension."

"Piper—"

"Dad." I took a deep breath. "At the end of the day, can you tell God you're trustworthy?" No tears made my vocal cords wobble, and anger did not show its face.

Still, the change in my father came instantaneously. His mouth trembled, and his shoulders shook as he curled into himself. While I wanted to hang on to my outrage a little longer, I couldn't ignore someone who appeared contrite. I walked forward, tentatively placing a hand on his back. The next thing I knew, he was sobbing into my shoulder as I rubbed soothing circles across his back—as though he were a child in need of comfort.

Lord, please let Your presence be known to my dad. Please give him a repentant heart and show him how to walk in forgiveness. I bit my lips. *Please help me and Mama learn how to forgive him and what that looks like.*

It looks like this.

The thought was so clear in my mind that it was almost audible.

We stayed in the hall until Dad's tears subsided and my shoulder began to protest the weight of his head. As he stepped away from me, he turned his back, wiping at his face.

"Will you be okay?"

Dad shrugged. "I just want you and your mom to forgive me."

"Maybe you should desire God's forgiveness more than ours. His is what will sustain you."

He turned and gave me a soft smile. "How did you get so wise?"

"I listened to my parents despite what they believed during my teenage years." I never was huge on rebellion, but I may have argued back more than once.

"Go see your mother. She needs you."

I nodded.

My tennis shoes squeaked against the marble floors as I maneuvered around the big house. Soon I found myself in front of the primary bedroom. I knocked and placed my ear to the door, listening for any signs of life.

"Go away, Ian."

"Mama, it's me."

I heard shuffling, and then the door opened wide enough to show Mama's bourbon-colored eyes.

"Your father's not with you, is he?"

"No, Mama."

She sighed and opened the door. "Then come on in before he uses this as an opportunity to sneak in here."

I would have laughed had the situation not been so serious. Mama looked like a warden guarding her domain, daring anyone to cross the threshold.

"I just spoke to Dad."

"Did you, now?" She placed a hand on her hip. "Did he tell you he did it? That he actually gave blood-doping agents to our horses?"

I nodded.

She threw her hands into the air just like I had. It was kind of eerie.

"I cannot believe that man. Doesn't he know I'm listed as part owner of Bolt Brook? It's not only his name he's dragging through the mud."

I grimaced inwardly. "I know, Mama."

"Do you? Because I had to turn off my cell phone just to get the calls from the media to stop. I can't even check my email for legitimate messages because they're spamming that. Not to mention our social media manager wants to quit because your father keeps trying to say no comment and people are spewing hate in every single post on Bolt Brook profiles."

She sank to the bench in front of her bed, a handkerchief magically appearing in her hands. "How could he do this to me?" she wailed.

"If it's any consolation, I believe he's truly sorry."

She snorted. "Did he turn on the waterworks for you, then say how important it is for you to forgive him?"

I tensed. "Yes," I replied cautiously.

"He was probably faking. He's diabolical," she groused.

My mouth dropped open. I'd never heard my mother talk badly about Dad. *Ever.* They were a little less affectionate than Tuck's folks were, but I'd never doubted their love for each other. Yet this . . . this I was not prepared for.

I sat next to her. "So you don't think he's sincere?"

"Now that I know his true nature, I think he'd do anything to keep the wealth he's amassed, Bolt Brook, and whatever else on his list of items he cares about. But mark my words, it's certainly not the people in this house."

I didn't want to believe her. Dad had seemed contrite, and those tears had been real. But if the man I thought I knew, the man who taught me about integrity yet turned out to be a liar . . . who's to say he couldn't put on an A-list performance for his family? Too bad I didn't have a clip of his actions to send to Lamont so he could assess whether my dad had been acting.

"What are you going to do? Are you going to prepare a statement?" Surely Mama wanted to get Bolt Brook back in good standings.

"What can I do?" Her eyes drooped as she blew out a noisy sigh. "If I throw him under the bus, there will still be those who won't believe I had no clue." She let out a bitter laugh. "I don't blame them, either. I feel like a *fool*. If I want Bolt Brook to survive the onslaught, it might be better to stand with him. To have him prepare a contrite statement."

I asked the question that had been on my mind ever since Dad admitted his guilt. "Will he go to prison?"

Mama's face paled. "It's a very real possibility," she murmured.

"What are you going to do?" I asked again, closing my eyes against the assault of awful scenarios and consequences my brain had already conjured.

"Honestly?"

I nodded.

"I want to leave him. I almost packed a bag and hightailed it to your farm yesterday."

Uh . . .

Was I supposed to encourage my mom to stay with Dad? To seek counseling? Or invite her to use my guest room? *Lord God, what do I do?*

"I'm here for you, Mama."

She wrapped me in a hug. "Oh, my sweet girl, thank you." Then she sniffed and pulled back. "I'm sorry I haven't been there for you more these past few months. Seeing you leave was hard to get used to, and then the investigation . . ." She huffed. "It's been a lot."

"I get it." Life was a bit much at times.

Mama sighed. "I can't imagine what our friends think. A few called when the news first hit, but no one has since our farm was found guilty." She sniffed again. "All those years of trying to do what was right, and look what happened."

I rubbed her back, and it hit me. My mom had subjugated herself to keeping up appearances as much as she'd required me to do the same. Only, I didn't know what to do with that revelation, so I reverted to drawing soothing circles on her back.

"They'll come around. Your true friends will still be there."

She nodded. "At least you have Tuck. He's always been dependable."

"He has." I wanted to smile just thinking of him. "He means a lot to me."

"Are you two . . . ?" Mama's watery gaze studied me.

I grinned, remembering that first kiss and all the ones since.

She smoothed my hair. "Tell me. I want to know everything."

Twenty-Two

Tuck
Help me.

Lamont
What's up?

Chris
Is this a serious call for help, or just you whining?

Tuck
Serious. If my mom spoon-feeds me one more time . . . 😣

Lamont
Must be rough having your mommy wait on you hand and foot.

Chris
😂

Tuck
It's like I've reverted back to childhood.

Chris
Tell her thank you and to go home. Then tag team your dad in for help.

Tuck
Speaking of dads . . .

Lamont
What's up?

Tuck pressed the video call button. This was something he didn't want to text nor let his mom overhear.

"What's wrong?" Chris asked. He appeared to be outdoors, though Tuck couldn't say he recognized the landscape. Then again, if Chris wasn't outdoors he was working at the wildlife nonprofit he ran.

Tuck looked from his place on his living room couch into the kitchen. There was a small, open doorway, but judging from the singing his mom was doing, there was no chance of her hearing.

He faced the camera once more. "The day of my accident, I got a tip that it was my dad who turned in Piper's folks."

"Are you for real?" Lamont's eyes bugged out.

"That's what I was told."

"Did you ask your dad if it was true?" Chris ran a hand atop his head and rested it there.

"I was going to, but then I broke my shoulder. Since then, we haven't had time alone."

Sympathy filled Chris's gaze. "Then take my earlier advice. Tell your mom to switch places with him. You need to know if this is true or not."

"What am I going to tell Piper?" It was one reason Tuck tried to keep their visits short. It wasn't difficult to get her to agree since he was still in a considerable amount of pain.

"The truth, man." Lamont sighed. "I can't imagine what you're going through, but that's not a secret you want to keep. Trust me, honesty really is the best policy."

But what if Piper couldn't handle the truth?

Ugh. Now he had the Jack Nicholson GIF from *A Few Good Men* running through his mind.

"You afraid Piper will kiss your ugly mug good-bye?" Chris smirked.

"Something like that." He wouldn't tell them how deep that fear ran.

Suffice to say bad dreams with that exact scenario had woken him every night since Aaron Wellington III suggested such a tale.

Lamont shook his head. "I don't think you have anything to worry about. She looks at no one but you."

Tuck prayed that was true. He only saw Piper, but he couldn't guarantee the reverse.

"Get off the phone with us, and call your dad over," Chris reiterated. "And know we'll be praying."

"Amen," Lamont echoed.

"Thanks, guys."

Tuck ended the call, then leaned back against his recliner. Talking it out helped, but he still felt like he was in limbo. Probably would stay there until he did like they suggested and talked it out with his dad.

"Are you hurting, hon?"

He opened his eyes to see his mom walking into the room. "No. Just have something on my mind."

"Are you sure? Because it's time for another bout of pain reliever. We don't want you hurting too much. Remember the doctor said the pain could get ahead of you."

"I remember." Tuck studied his mom. Lines framed her brown eyes, hinting at her age. But her perfect brown bob didn't show a strand of gray, courtesy of her standing salon appointments.

Did Mom know what Dad did? Could Tuck ask her and avoid the awkward conversation with his father? *No.* If his dad had indeed made the anonymous tip, he needed to hear it from him. "Mom, you've been working so hard since I came home. Why don't you go home and send Dad over?"

She bit her lip. "I don't know . . ."

"It'll be good. You'll get some rest, and Dad will have something to do."

A mischievous glint lit her eyes. "You do have a point."

"He's probably streaming reruns of *The Dukes of Hazzard*

or *The Incredible Hulk*." Tuck knew his mom couldn't stand how often Dad sat in his recliner just to watch old TV shows. She'd always needed something to do. His dad, not so much.

"You're right. I'll call him right now." She pulled out her phone and walked toward the back of the house. Tuck wasn't sure why she wanted a private conversation—unless she was giving his dad a list of dos and don'ts.

He grinned. *Yeah, that's exactly what she's doing.*

A half hour later, his mom kissed his forehead and said good-bye. Meanwhile, Dad sank into the sofa cushions, peering around the room. Tuck reached to the left, where the remote sat on the end table, then extended it toward his dad.

"I'm sad to leave my recliner, but that was smart thinking giving your mom a break," his dad said, still making the admission a little grudgingly.

"She was driving me a little batty. Insisted on spoon-feeding me."

A bark of laughter fell from Dad's lips. "Sounds like her. She told me she'd check on us tomorrow. Gave me a list of things to do." Dad held up his cell. "Texted them to me."

"Then she'll definitely check on us."

"She'll give us peace tonight, though."

That gave Tuck enough time to ask what he wanted. *Do it now. Get it over with.*

"What do you wanna watch?" Dad asked.

Tuck shrugged, then winced. "I don't care. I can't really focus lately."

Dad's brow furrowed. "You in pain? Your mom said you haven't taken your latest dose."

"Wanted a clear head." Tuck swallowed. "I have something to ask you."

"Of course. Anything." Dad motioned for him to go ahead.

Now that Tuck had the floor, he wanted to backtrack. Did he really want to rip off the bandage now?

TONI SHILOH

"Tucker?"

"I got a strange phone call the day of the accident." He rubbed his chin.

"What about?"

Tuck met his dad's concerned gaze. "The person said you tipped off the RMTC about Bolt Brook's doping practices."

Dad sat back, and the silence between them stretched. And stretched. And stretched some more.

"Dad?" Tuck prodded. *Say it ain't so. Please.*

His father blinked, then cleared his throat. "I did."

"How did you even suspect?" There was no way his dad was involved, right?

"You remember John, right?"

Of course Tuck remembered Bolt Brook's veterinarian.

"Well, apparently he arrived at The Bourbon in the early evening and drank whiskey until the bartender cut him off. Anyway, I'm listed as a DD for the bar. I'd rather be inconvenienced than have someone drive home drunk." His dad sighed. "So the bartender called me to pick up John. As I helped him into my truck, he started talking about how he wanted to stop, but the money was too good to turn down."

"Did he say how much he was getting?" Tuck's gut clenched.

Dad shook his head. "Nope, but I admit the comment made me curious. I asked him what he was trying to stop, and it all came spilling out. I was shocked. Had no idea anyone at Bolt Brook would authorize such a thing. I prayed all that night. The next morning, I called the tip line. The rest is history."

Tuck sat there, trying to process what his dad shared.

"You upset with me, son?"

"No." Tuck cleared his throat. "Can't say I would've done anything differently."

"But it puts you in a tight spot with Piper." It was a statement, not a question.

Knowing Aaron had been right about Tuck's dad being the

one to put the whole media storm in motion was a weight Tuck couldn't bear. "How am I supposed to tell her, Dad?"

"Son, I was only trying to do what was right. You know how I feel about horses. It's not right for them to suffer for sport."

Tuck rubbed his face. "I agree. I just don't know how this'll affect our relationship."

"Y'all've been friends since you were knee high to a grasshopper. Ain't nothing stopping that now."

Tuck looked at his dad. "Well, I have news. Piper has agreed to be my girlfriend, and eventually, I want her to be my wife. I'm not sure how she'll take this. I don't want her to feel like I betrayed her or took advantage of the situation."

"I'm happy for you, Tucker. Piper's a wonderful girl, and it's about time. She won't feel like that. She knows you as well as she knows herself."

Tuck could only pray that was true. He didn't want to break Piper's heart with this news. Because as Lamont stated, Tuck *had* to tell the truth. He couldn't let their relationship go forward knowing what he knew.

But, Lord, I don't want her to break up with me, either.

He'd seen enough rom-coms to know that reaction often happened. Maybe not every movie portrayed a breakup, but they all experienced some type of bleak moment. Tuck didn't want that. He wanted the happily ever after Piper loved so much without the heartbreak.

But is it real life if there's no heartbreak?

He couldn't escape trials. Jesus Himself said mankind would experience tribulation. Tuck would just rather it come any other way than an issue that could threaten their relationship.

"It'll be okay, son."

Tuck's breathing had turned a little shaky. "I think I'm ready for some pain meds." His shoulder was burning with a fierceness. Now that his dad had shared his story, Tuck didn't need to stay awake. He could take a pain reliever and get a nap. Maybe when he woke up, he'd have a plan of action to implement.

Until then, he'd ask God to give him wisdom and keep his and Piper's relationship intact. *Please, God. I can't bear the thought of this being the end before we even really have a beginning. More than that, I don't want Piper to hurt, and I don't want her relationship with my folks to be strained.*

After all, he wanted an in-law relationship sooner than later.

"I'll grab them and some water. Do you want me to help you to your bed?"

"It's my shoulder that's broken, not my legs."

Dad smirked. "Bet you didn't talk that way to your mother."

"She's scary. Plus she would have rolled her eyes and helped me there regardless."

"Then head on back before I take a page from her book."

Tuck laughed. "Yes, sir."

Twenty-Three

The sound of the doorbell pealing had me rushing from my office to the front door. No alert that someone was at the gate had come, which meant someone who had the code was at my door. Tuck would normally knock.

I peered through the peep hole and blinked a few times. Yet with each close of my eyelids, the image before me never changed. There stood Mama on my front porch with a couple of suitcases flanking her.

Lord God, see me through this.

When I'd offered the guest bedroom in my place, I hadn't actually believed she'd take me up on the suggestion. I figured she and Dad would work through their differences as they'd always done. That was probably the inner child in me wishing for reconciliation versus the grown-up who still couldn't believe her father was a liar and a cheat—in sports, that is.

Now that Mama stood on the other side of the door, I wasn't quite sure what to do.

Let her in first, then figure out the next steps.

I twisted the knob and stepped back. "Hey, Mama."

Her thin lips pursed as she struggled to pull her luggage behind her. "I just couldn't take another minute in that house with *that* man," she snapped. She looked around my living room as if seeing the inside of my home for the first time.

She'd received a tour of my place when I first moved in, then promptly told me all the ways I could decorate the space to make it look the best. I didn't listen, which was probably why she stood there staring at my rustic chic décor in shock.

More like horror that you didn't go upscale country.

"It's so . . . so . . ."

"Cozy?" I supplied, folding my arms across my chest.

"Mm." A forced smile appeared across her lips. "Will you take my luggage to the guest bedroom?"

"Of course, Mama." Was it too early for me to ask how long she planned to stay?

I wanted to text an SOS to Tuck and tell him to come over. Only knowing he spent the majority of his days napping and healing kept my cell in my back jeans pocket. Maybe once Mama was settled, I'd text Nevaeh and ask her to pray for the situation.

She'd been sending me encouraging Bible verses every morning since Bolt Brook first made the headlines. Knowing she was praying had bolstered me and gave me direction for my own prayers. Her texts usually came closer to midday—thank you, time zone difference—and gave me the pick-me-up I needed.

With all the commotion arisen from the RMTC's positive test results, I wanted to spend most of my days with my head buried in the proverbial sand. I was keeping off my socials unless I needed to post something specifically for Maisha Farms.

I'd also ignored all calls that weren't from someone in my contacts. I didn't need another reporter trying to ask me about my feelings about Bolt Brook's guilt. *I* didn't know my own feelings. Once I figured them out, it wouldn't be the local news who got the scoop.

Now that Mama was here, maybe I'd be too busy to think and could let my mind relax some. Comforting her through this season might be the distraction I truly needed.

I pushed the suitcases to the corner of the guest bedroom. Mama would be unpacking as soon as her nerves allowed her to. Good thing I'd had the foresight to change the sheets yesterday. The room rarely got used, but after issuing the invitation to Mama, I'd felt the need to dust and clean up a bit just in case.

I headed back to the living room.

"Piper, sweetie, could you pour me some tea?"

"Yes, Mama." She followed me to the kitchen, where I pulled the pitcher out of the fridge. "Are you hungry?" It was that awkward time between lunch and dinner, or afternoon tea, as hobbits would call it. I just happened to have the iced and sweetened variety.

"No, dear, just a little weary."

I handed her a glass.

"A Mason jar glass, sweetie? So cliché." She shook her head but sipped the drink anyway.

I wanted to ask what was so wrong with the cute glassware. But knowing Mama, she thought it too basic. She was all about flaunting her wealth as an accomplishment. Not that what she and Daddy had managed to achieve wasn't such.

No wonder she was mad at him. She probably thought it all moot now that Bolt Brook would suffer some type of ban.

"What do you think will happen next?" I asked.

"Who knows?" Her lips flattened. "Your father has his head so far stuck in the clouds I think he's lost oxygen to his brain. Keeps thinking I'll pull some Tammy Wynette nonsense and stand by my man," she scoffed.

I bit my lip to stifle a laugh. Not because the situation was at all comical, but the country music reference tickled me. Mama always quoted older country stars when she was particularly flustered. Usually it was Patsy Cline.

"What am I supposed to do now?" Mama's head flopped onto the back of the couch.

I reached out to rub her shoulder. "I'm so sorry, Mama." But I had no actual words of wisdom. I felt just as stuck.

"So am I, sweetie. To think of all those so-called wins we celebrated. Knowing what I know now, it sickens me. He altered those beautiful beings. Based our name and brand on deceit." A tear rolled down her cheek.

I felt the same way, but this was Daddy we were talking about. How could we just sever our relationship? We had a duty to forgive him as Christians, but just thinking about it hurt my heart.

"Will you forgive him, Mama?"

She let out a small sigh. "Eventually. But I may never forget."

"Will you divorce him?" I asked cautiously.

"I don't know what to do at all, Piper." Mama's bottom lip quivered. "I can't make my mind believe the headlines or even his own confession. Not to mention I'm waiting for him to be handed over to the authorities soon."

My stomach heaved. "Do you really think he'll be arrested?"

I'd seen such a thing in the past, but it had all seemed so fanciful. Not a consequence I'd ever worried over, considering I'd never crossed a line. Now I had to wait to see what charges would be brought against Daddy—and if the word *leniency* would be part of our new vocabulary.

"Any day now."

"Goodness," I muttered under my breath.

"But don't you worry. I'm sure your operation will be untouched. I read a small caption in the newspaper saying your horse was found clean. Tuck's horses too."

"Oh, so someone cared to mention that fact?" Everyone in the media as well as on social media acted like that was a lie. One person's comment literally stated, "Stop the cap."

"They did, but I'm not sure if society believes it." Mama's mouth turned downward. "A person is reasonable, people are not."

I hated that the saying made sense. Unfortunately, experience had taught me how true it was.

I had to believe not everything Daddy had taught me was a lie. "All I can do is keep showing up and showing up with integrity."

Mama nodded. "I'm sure you will. You've always been honest." She winked. "Must have got that from me."

I smiled, but my heart ached. Was anyone in my biological family honest to a fault? My bio mom? Bio dad? Or some extended family I'd never know? Sometimes I thought of the unfairness of it all. I was so thankful to Mama and Daddy, but I also craved knowledge of my biological family. Yet with one awful accident, the orphanage and all my records had burned to a crisp. Unless both my bio family and I used some DNA kit service, I'd never know who they were.

All connection lost with one flame.

"Well, sweetie, I'm going to lie down." Mama rose.

"Sure. I'll probably be in my office if you need me."

Mama nodded.

"Anything in particular you want for dinner?" Dining out was *not* an option. We didn't need to hit the news like Nevaeh was prone to do when she and Lamont went out.

"I don't have much of an appetite these days. Make whatever you want. If I'm hungry, I'll nibble a bite or two."

I nodded, and she left the room.

I dropped my head into my hands. This situation was so overwhelming. I'd been crying out to God ever since I first saw the headlines and doubly so once the RMTC revealed evidence of guilt at Bolt Brook. Now I didn't know how to pray. Pray for reconciliation between my parents? Intellectually, I could say yes. Emotionally, that felt like choosing sides.

Lord God, what do I ask for? What is Your will?

Because I didn't want to go outside of His will, not even in my prayers. But I didn't know what He wanted in this situation.

Surely God would choose justice, which probably meant Daddy would need to be arrested. But in my earthly limitations, was that the only option I could see? Was there a better outcome that would glorify God and meet the demands for justice?

I sighed.

I feel so lost, God. Please help my family. Please work on Mama and me. We need to forgive, but hurt runs deep. I swallowed. *Please save my parents' marriage in the way that's best. Please give justice in Your will. Please just help.*

I shook my head, trying to jostle all the confusing thoughts away, then whispered an "Amen" and walked to my office. I couldn't let anything else distract me. Decisions needed to be made for Maisha Farms, and I needed to ensure I handled it all in a way that honored God.

Twenty-Four

Tuck winced as Piper drove over a pothole. His shoulder hit the seat, and hot, searing pain vibrated through his whole right side. He should probably be at home on the couch with his mom standing over him and offering homemade chicken noodle soup. Instead, they were making the two-hour drive to the racetrack for their first April race.

"Did you take some pain meds before we left?" Piper asked.

Of course he didn't. Those narcotics made him feel fuzzy. But he'd taken some over-the-counter pain reliever. He was done with the prescription meds. "Yep."

Piper glanced at him. "Prescribed or over-the-counter?"

"Um . . ." He struggled not to shift in his seat. "Over-the-counter," he mumbled.

"Tucker Hale." Exasperation coated every syllable and sounded a lot like how his mom used to say his name when he did something she thought unbelievably foolish. She'd just had the grace not to come right out and say so.

Piper's so cute. He wanted to tell her that, but remembering the secret about his dad had him clammed up and more than a little awkward.

"I'm okay," he said.

"Sure. That's why you're wincing every time the truck jostles you. Glad those OTC meds are helping you out."

He smirked. "You're so adorable when you're irritated." There, he let it out. He'd just have to make sure he stuck to talking to her. If he leaned over and pressed his mouth to her beautiful lips, his dad's secret would tumble out.

Or the guilt would compound further.

"I can't even with you." She shook her head, but a smile flitted across those sexy lips.

"I think we should go on a date tonight," Tuck said. He grimaced inwardly. *Not what you were supposed to say. Dating a woman whose dad has been arrested because your dad's a whistleblower is beyond complicated.*

Piper glanced at him, surprise coating those ebony eyes, then faced forward. "You do, do you?"

Could he backtrack, or should he use the opportunity to come clean? "Yes. What do you think?"

"I think when a girl gets asked out, she likes to hear it all proper-like." She slowed to a stop as the light went from yellow to red.

"Darlin'"—Tuck reached for her right hand—"would you do me the immense pleasure of going out with me tonight?"

"Of course I will, Tuck." She placed a quick kiss on his lips, then tugged her hand back. "I need that to drive."

She'd kissed him. He loved it. But yep, there was that guilt growing by the second.

She stepped on the gas, and Tuck sighed.

"You miss driving?" Piper asked.

"Being an invalid is a pain."

"You make a cute one, though."

Tuck scoffed. "No man wants to be called cute."

"And no woman either. Remember that."

He laughed.

"How's your mom handling your recovery?"

A Run at Love

Tuck winced for a different reason this time. "Still hovering. I thought after she returned to her own house and had a break, she'd be okay." Dad had convinced her to return home for good. Only now she'd taken to helicoptering via text.

"And she's not?"

"Calls me every morning to remind me to take my meds. Then every four hours on the dot to remind me to take the next dose." He sighed. "Plus she's still bringing me suppers. I mean, they're good and all, but I don't need her spoon-feeding me. I thought Dad would've nipped that in the bud for me."

Laughter burst out of Piper. She covered her mouth trying to muffle her delight, but it was too late.

"Glad my girlfriend is on my side."

Her smile dropped as quickly as the temperature on a winter night.

"What did I say?"

"Just reminded me of my folks and their situation."

Tuck hated that for her. When the news of her dad's arrest hit the headlines, she'd been distraught. On the other hand, her mom seemed to have grown increasingly bitter. "How's your mom doing with it all now?"

"Still not very well. She spends most of the day streaming romance movies and crying through them all."

"Ouch. Have the reporters multiplied in front of your place?"

"They have, but honestly, I doubt we'll escape them anytime soon. Not with the world wanting everyone and anyone at Bolt Brook held responsible."

She wasn't wrong. The clamoring need for justice was why Tuck had turned off his ringer and told people he needed to do business through text or email. He was tempted to change his number, but that would be a bigger hassle.

"Did I make the wrong choice offering my guest room to her, Tuck?"

"What else could you have done?"

"My thoughts exactly." Her lips pursed. "Still . . ."

Tuck's phone vibrated in the cup holder. He reached for it with his left hand—his *non*-dominate hand. Using his weaker hand for everything was annoying, but the sling holding his right arm was worse. He wished he could rip it off and be instantly healed. Where had his patience gone?

A few texts popped up in quick succession.

Lamont
Hey, where should we stay for the Derby?

Chris
So you're going?

Lamont
Yes, and you should too. If you don't, how will you be the official fifth wheel?

Chris

Lamont

Lamont
I think I saw a Hilton and Crowne Plaza.

Chris
If I'm coming, I need something in my price range. We're not all rolling around in movie-star dough.

Tuck
We booked a few rooms ahead of time when we attended last year. The hotels fill up pretty far in advance.

Chris
He lives! How's the arm?

Tuck
Hurts.

Lamont

Praying for you. How much do we owe for the rooms?

Tuck

No charge. My treat.

"Hey, darlin', how many rooms did we reserve at the Galt for the Derby?"

Piper frowned. "Quite a few. You were standing right next to me when I did it. Don't you remember?"

"I don't have a head for details like you." He winked.

Seeing her blush was heady to his senses. *And damaging to your soul! How long are you gonna wait to tell her what your dad did?*

He drew in a breath. He'd tell her on their date. Surely that was the best time to do it.

"Charmer," she muttered.

"You say that like it's a bad thing."

Piper gripped the wheel. "It's not. I actually need the distraction. Knowing Dream will race next week has me nervous. I know he has enough points to advance, but I still want him to win regardless."

"He'll do great." Tuck smiled.

"Why did you ask about the Derby rooms?"

What could he say that wouldn't give away the surprise? "We need to finalize the guest list, right? I couldn't remember if we were booking for my folks and yours plus us and Gabe or . . ."

"That was our thought initially." She frowned. "Though now who knows if my folks will go."

"I'll handle the rooms. You have enough to worry about."

That would allow him to secure a spot for the guys. He'd already talked to his folks about the Derby. They apparently had booked a room the moment Tuck started training for Piper, though, which meant the guys could definitely stay in one Piper had already booked. And there should be enough rooms in the block for Nevaeh to have her own, but if she had to, she could stay with Piper after they surprised her.

Maybe one day he'd show up to the Derby with Piper as his wife and no need for them to have different rooms.

"What are you thinking about? You're wearing a grin a mile wide."

Tuck startled. "Uh . . . just thinking of the future."

"Yeah? Future of horse racing? Or something else?"

"Us. Me and you." He didn't mention the twisting of his insides or the intense feeling of trepidation going through him.

Lord, please don't let her hate me when she finds out what Dad did.

"*Us* is a beautiful word," she breathed.

Marry me.

Fortunately, he kept that thought to himself. He'd almost said it aloud. *Almost.* But first he needed to take Piper on a proper date, drop a bombshell, and pray the collateral damage was survivable. If God willed it, Tuck would take her on another date, and another, until an appropriate length of time had passed for him to share how his feelings were more of a lifetime-attachment deal.

There you go planning everything again. Haven't you learned anything?

Apparently not. Yet the idea of dating her filled him with a calm that had been absent since talking with his dad.

"You zoned out on me again," Piper said softly.

"Sorry. Just thinking."

"Well, now's the time to switch gears. We're here." She pointed ahead.

Soon a groom was unloading Dream and then leading the horse around the paddock. He'd let the Thoroughbred stretch his legs before putting him in the racetrack stables. Tuck would text Gabe and make sure he arrived on time. They needed one good work to acclimate Dream and hopefully jog muscle memory as well. Then again, this wasn't their first time at Mountain Laurel Grounds.

As soon as Tuck checked into his hotel room, he reached for his toiletry bag and grabbed some pain relievers. The generic store brands would hopefully dull the pain enough for him to tolerate it. The throbbing heat in his shoulder was the worst. For the past couple of weeks, he'd attended physical therapy and performed the prescribed exercises, but that didn't make the pain go away.

A quick look around the room showed nothing to drink—not even a bottle of water. He huffed.

A knock sounded on his door, so Tuck shuffled across the carpet. Piper stood on the other side with a tote in hand.

"What's all that?"

"I brought you gifts."

"How? You were supposed to be checking in."

She smirked. "Yeah, because it takes so long to drop a suitcase in a room."

"It does when you're you. What happened to unwinding with a book, taking a shower, or just deciding on what you're wearing for our date?"

"Don't worry. I'll knock your socks off tonight." Her grin said *checkmate*.

Tuck's mouth parted. Using one hand was making time crawl by while it apparently sped up for two-handed people. "I've got nothing."

Piper laughed, then motioned to the chair at the desk in front of his bed. "Come sit."

He ambled over as she began pulling stuff out of the bag. First she held up some weird wrap concoction.

"What's that?"

"One of those instant ice packs. It'll feel good on that shoulder." She placed it softly against his body. "How's that?"

He groaned. "Perfect."

"I also brought you a shoulder pillow."

"From the hotel gift shop?"

"No, silly." She grinned. "I ordered it from Amazon, and it arrived yesterday." She slid the pillow under his slinged arm. "There. Now you can rest in comfort, let the ice pack do its thing, and . . ."

She searched his room, then saw the pain meds. With a quick pop of the bottle's top, she handed him two pills. "I got you a sports drink to wash it down."

"Thanks darlin'. I really appreciate you." Which made the news he had to tell her all the more difficult.

"Of course." She kissed his cheek. "Do you feel a little better, at least? I know it won't take the pain completely away—"

He grabbed her arm. "With you this close, I feel nothing but the beauty of your presence."

"Tuck . . ." She grabbed the sides of his face and kissed him.

Thank goodness he didn't need two arms for this. He could still pull her close with his left arm and let his lips do the rest.

And later, *much* later, he'd tell her what his dad had done.

Twenty-Five

A date with Tuck? What was a girl to wear?

Contrary to my earlier confidence, I actually had no idea which of the boring outfits in my luggage would knock Tuck's socks off. I'd filled my suitcase with clothing good for horse racing. Jeans for time in the stables, a dress for race-day photo ops, and a couple of casual options for being out and about. None of it was date wear.

Fortunately, I could always go shopping. Now that Tuck was icing his shoulder and Dream was being cared for, all that was left for me was finding a cute outfit. Unlike the last time I tried to impress Tuck without trying to be obvious, I wanted to be as noticeable as possible.

I left the hotel in my truck and headed for the boutique an internet search had assured me offered my perfect outfit. Since Tuck always saw me in jeans, I wanted to go for a dress. Though he did see me in those a lot for race days.

Ugh. What could I find different from anything else he'd seen me in? Guess that was the problem—and the blessing—of dating your best friend. They'd seen everything and still wanted to be with you.

I took in a calming breath. Tuck literally knew every single look. There was no surprising him. Still, he gazed at me like I hung the stars and he was happy being in my light. My heart fluttered. It didn't matter what I picked as long as I felt pretty in it. Since spring was here, maybe I could find something in pastels to remind me of the season.

GPS got me to the right place, and I pulled into the parking lot and took the key out of the ignition.

An employee greeted me as I entered, and I smiled back before heading toward the closest dress rack. It had a bunch of A-line dresses right up my alley. Some were bold colors and others more muted. As I flipped through dress after dress, a niggling sensation tickled the back of my neck. After rubbing the area and confirming nothing was crawling there, I discreetly peeked around the store.

I locked eyes with a woman who was obviously recording me with her phone. I arched an eyebrow, and her face flushed. Was she a fan of the sport or one of the keyboard trolls leaving nasty comments about my parents and my obvious moral corruption? If the latter, the fruit didn't fall far from the tree.

Seriously, you'd think that expression would have died off decades ago or at least be totally unknown to my generation. But apparently not.

"Can I help you?" I asked.

The woman pursed her lips, then stepped closer. "Do you really think it's right for *you* to be here?"

My teeth locked. "And what's that supposed to mean?"

"Your dad was arrested. You were investigated. And you *still* have the nerve to show up for the stakes race?" She shook her head. "You're tainting the sport."

I would *not* cry. I lifted my chin and considered a counter-argument. "I'm not my father. I was never under official investigation because my horses have never been given any illegal substances. So yes, I showed up to a stakes race I rightfully earned a spot to be in."

"Money can buy innocence these days."

"Do you work here?"

Before she could answer my question, a woman wearing a name tag stepped between us and looked at me. "Is everything okay?"

"This woman is taking a video of me without my permission and maligning my character." I nodded toward the offender. "I was just asking if she's a customer or an employee. Regardless, I think I'll go elsewhere."

Her face blanched. "No, please. She's not an employee." She cleared her throat. "Um, I didn't want to get involved, but we can ask her to leave."

"I was here first!" the woman protested.

Yep. Time for me to go. I headed for the door.

"Please, Ms. McKinney."

The pleading tone didn't sway me one bit. It was bad enough being harassed by reporters and keyboarding trolls. I didn't want to put myself in the line of fire from everyday citizens. There were some dangerous people in the world, and I wanted to make it back to my hotel safely.

Now what are you going to wear?

I didn't want to go to another store, but I didn't want to return empty-handed either. Did I have enough clout to ask someone at the hotel to shop for me? Give them my size and ask them to pick something out? Or maybe one of the boutiques had curbside pickup.

I climbed into my truck, but before I could make a search, my phone rang. Anxiety filled me as *Daddy* flashed on the caller ID. I couldn't believe he was out on bail already.

"Hi," I said cautiously.

"Piper girl, how are you?"

"All right."

"You make it to Mountain Laurel?"

It was great that my dad was taking an interest in my life,

but ever since the RMTC shared their investigation results, I didn't know what to say to him. I hadn't even seen him since he was released on bail.

"I did. Just trying to do a little shopping now."

I stared at the store and gaped. Police were talking to the woman who'd been filming me. Guess she objected to being asked to leave the store. Of course, that was pure speculation on my part.

"Oh, good, good."

But it didn't sound like he was doing so well. I bit my lip. "Is everything okay?"

Dad scoffed. "Kind of an ironic question, don't you think?"

"Well, yeah. I just meant, are you all right in this moment?"

"No." There was a long pause. "I'm doing an interview tomorrow."

My eyes widened. "With who? Why?"

"With a reporter. Your mother keeps accusing me of not taking personal responsibility."

That was definitely a line in her latest rants about Daddy. "And an interview will allow you to do that?"

"I don't know, Piper. But I want your mama back. I want you to call me every week like you did before instead of debating whether or not you'll answer my call."

I wanted that, too, but I didn't know how to reconcile my dad's guilt with the vision of the man who had raised me. That man had been full of love, encouragement, and integrity. This man I didn't know.

"I'm sorry," I whispered. What else could I say?

"You have nothing to be sorry for, Piper girl. I know it's on me. If being accountable will win the respect of your mother, then I have to try."

"But will admitting guilt help the charges against you?"

"I plan on pleading guilty regardless of what my attorney thinks."

My stomach dropped. Wouldn't that mean he'd incur the maximum penalty?

Shouldn't he?

I was tempted to lay my head on the steering wheel. "Dad, maybe you should ask your attorney's advice on talking to a reporter. It just doesn't seem wise. This is no one's business but the court's and our family's. Everyone else can stay out of it."

"You say that, but shouldn't I speak publicly now that the whole world knows?"

"I don't know. If you have anything additional to say to me or mom, just talk to us. That should be said in a personal conversation at a private location. You know, at Bolt Brook or some neutral place where Mama would meet you. Not on the evening news."

"I just want things to go back to how it was before."

I thought of the days before he'd made the news. The days when our family unit was the best thing ever, and I wanted to visit my parents often. But we couldn't go back, and I wasn't sure if a redo would solve our present anyway.

"Daddy, have you talked to the pastor?"

Breathing filled my ears. "I haven't been to church since the news broke."

"Don't you think that'll help you? The church offers counseling."

"I don't need therapy, Piper."

I winced at the brusqueness in his voice. Somehow, I doubted he'd appreciate the *You need Jesus* thought running through my mind. *Lord, please guide my words.*

"Maybe you don't, and I can't make that call. But you need to seek God's guidance in this situation. Let Him examine your heart, then submit to His spiritual makeover." Okay, so using a makeover metaphor might not be the best way to reach a man, but it was what came out of my mouth.

"I appreciate you, Piper, but . . ."

"Give it some thought. 'Kay? And talk to your lawyer too."

"Fine. I will."

I could only pray he meant it. "I'll talk to you later?"

"You can call me anytime."

After hanging up, I did lean my forehead against the steering wheel. The incident inside the store and now the phone call with Daddy had zapped me of strength. How was I supposed to shop for my date with Tuck now? All I wanted to do was curl up on my hotel bed and stuff my mouth with bourbon balls or something equally chocolatey.

Pull yourself together, girl. This is a date with Tucker Hale! You've been wanting to date him forever.

I blew out a breath. I could do this. I could mentally dust myself off and refuse to let anyone steal my joy. When Tuck knocked on my door, I wanted to be excited, not weighed down by today's woes.

I found a place that offered curbside pickup and purchased four dresses—technically two dresses but in two different sizes. I didn't want to worry about their not fitting. I'd either return the ones that didn't or drop them off at a donation center.

After picking them up, I headed back to the hotel. I'd have time to shower, try on the dresses, then do my makeup before Tuck came knocking. Because tonight would be perfect regardless of the lemons life was throwing my way.

Twenty-Six

Tuck growled at the button that refused to go through the button hole. Didn't it know getting dressed at the pace of an octogenarian wasn't going to make him any more patient? All he knew was a gorgeous woman expected him to knock on her hotel room door and take her to a fancy dinner. Thanks to Lamont's generosity—he'd paid for Tuck's hospitable bill, and no amount of texting, video chatting, or cajoling would make him accept a reimbursement—Tuck could afford the fanciest restaurant in Lexington without feeling like a penny pincher.

He'd already made sure Piper's favorite flowers would be waiting at the table, that her most-requested candies would accompany said daffodils, and that the restaurant had some of her favorite foods for her to choose from. While Tuck would most likely be ordering a steak, they had plenty of seafood options for Piper. Though the dessert menu was the real catch of the day.

Finally, the button slipped through the hole, and Tuck smoothed out the front of his button-down shirt. No way he was going to attempt to stuff the hem into his waistband. That seemed like too much effort. Putting on a blazer would have to be the work-around for going without a belt and a tucked-in look.

He grabbed his going-out Stetson as the final accessory and opened his door to get to Piper's room across the hall. Only, his feet came to a halt as he stared at the door. Could he really sit her down on their first date and tell her his father got hers arrested?

Tuck squeezed his eyes shut. *Lord God, why is this so difficult? I've never kept a secret from Piper, minus the whole feelings thing, which made sense to keep quiet about. But this . . . this is huge.*

He didn't want to do any mental gymnastics for what constituted a lie and what was okay under omission. He also didn't want to ruin their first date by springing this on her. They weren't in Eastbrook. It's not like anyone would tell her before he could. It'd make more sense to come clean when they were on their home turf, right? Give her a chance to talk to his dad?

And the mental gymnastics have begun anyway.

"Tucker Hale, are you going to stand there all day or knock on my door," a muffled voice said, reaching his ears.

Just like that, the burden lifted, and he was looking forward to seeing his best friend. His lips quirked in a half smile, and he rapped his knuckles on the door.

The chain lock rattled, and then the door swung open and his breath whooshed out.

He was half-cognizant of blinking way too many times as his brain temporarily shut down. Then the rebooting slowly took effect as Tuck's gaze roamed Piper's figure. She wore some floral-type dress that stopped at the knees and showed shapely legs that went into a heel that had his mouth watering. Piper had terrific calf muscles, though that seemed like a weird body part to get hung up on.

"Don't drool."

His brain righted. "You look amazing."

"You think?" She twirled in a circle, a sassy expression covering her cute face.

"I *know*."

"Then mission accomplished." She swung her purse over a shoulder and shut the door. "Where are we going?"

"To that one place."

"Oh, I see. We're being all secretive."

He leaned over to whisper in her ear. "The better to woo you with, darlin'."

She shivered, and goosebumps appeared on her arms. Tuck ran a finger down one of them, then placed his palm against hers. He brought the back of her hand up to his lips and left a soft kiss there.

"Tucker Hale, you're not playing fair."

"I hear all's fair in love and war."

"I have no comeback."

He chuckled. "That's okay. I already know I'm winning."

"What are you winning?" Piper's ebony gaze studied him.

"You, of course." He kissed the tip of her nose. "Now stop distracting me. We've got a reservation to make."

"What will we talk about on our date?" Piper asked after he opened the truck door for her.

"What do you mean?"

She bit her lip. "We already know everything about each other. Will we just stare at each other awkwardly trying to find something to say that hasn't been said?"

"Or will we be flirting and sharing our dreams together?" Tuck kissed her forehead. "I thought I was the overthinker."

"You are. I'm just helping out." She smirked.

"You can't steal my play."

"Again. We know everything about each other. There can't possibly be anything that'll surprise us or make dating . . . exciting. Right?" Her voice came out whisper soft.

Tuck took a step forward and another until Piper had backed up against his truck. Thank goodness he'd run it through a car wash before dressing for their date. Using his good arm, he rested his palm against the truck, crowding her further. Her mouth parted, her gaze focusing on his lips.

"Do you know I love the way you look in cowboy boots?" He placed a kiss on her cheek. "Do you know how hard my heart thumps when you nibble your bottom lip while you're thinking?" He brushed her mouth with his. "Or can you even fathom how often I dreamed of kissing you before I knew you liked me almost as much as I liked you?"

"Tuck . . ."

He pulled back and stared into her eyes. "You don't know everything, Ms. McKinney."

Her breath shuddered, and she gave a slight nod. "Consider me properly schooled."

"Then in the truck you go." He held out a hand to assist her. She never did well climbing into his vehicle when she wore heels.

"Wait," Piper called out.

He halted.

"You can't drive, remember?"

Tuck looked at his slinged arm and began mumbling under his breath as Piper climbed down from the truck. This time, he helped her into the driver's seat. Then he put the restaurant address into the GPS himself so it would hold some semblance of surprise.

Piper was strangely quiet as she drove to the restaurant, which had Tuck's mind overacting. Her insinuation that she knew everything about him had the guilt rising again—and the resolve to wait as well. He needed to prove that dating wouldn't make them go backward. It would only enhance their relationship. Telling her about his dad would muddy the waters, as his grandpa used to say.

The moment the hostess seated them at the table for two tucked into the corner of the room, Piper spoke, pulling Tuck into the present.

"Daffodils," she said with a sigh.

"I know yellow can sometimes mean friendship, but they *are* your favorite."

She grinned, a sheen in her eyes. "They're perfect."

"Good." He swallowed. Then suddenly he wanted to reach for her hand like it was a lifeline. Maybe she was right. Maybe there would be nothing more to say, and they'd find themselves wishing they hadn't crossed the line.

But watching Piper cradle the flowers, the look of pure joy rosying her cheeks, Tuck realized that as long as he was with her, everything was right. He didn't want to miss a single moment with her. He wanted to be there for them all, from the mundane everyday living moments to the victorious moments of accomplishment. Being with Piper settled something deep in his soul, and he wasn't going to let doubt disrupt him.

"Did you know daffodils mean new beginnings?" he said.

Her eyes widened. "Seriously?"

"Yep. I needed to make sure I wouldn't friend zone myself if I bought them."

She chuckled. "You did good."

"Open that and tell me I exceeded your expectations." Tuck nodded to the brown box to her right.

"Okay." Confusion marred her forehead. She pulled off the label, then lifted the box lid. Inside lay sixteen Kentucky bourbon balls made with a sugary bourbon-pecan mixture covered in dark chocolate and topped with a pecan half.

They were too sweet for Tuck, but Piper enjoyed the chocolates.

"Thank you so much."

"Of course." He leaned forward. "Now let's stare at each other with panicked expressions until we figure out what to talk about."

She laughed. "How about you tell me how long it took you to dress yourself?"

He threw a fake glare her way. "We don't talk about my invalid status."

"We don't? Then how about training?"

"No horse talk."

She pouted. "But I love horses."

"Love me"—Tuck cleared his throat—"love them tomorrow." He almost said *love me more.* Thank goodness he'd changed his words, but judging from the light in Piper's eyes, she was already speculating on his true intention.

"Fine. Then if I can't talk about those things, what *should* I talk about?"

"Your favorite subject—me." He winked. "Now that we're not hiding our feelings, you can tell me all the ways you admire me and have come to realize I'm the best."

"I so hate that I really can't argue with you. Only, how did I not know you're so egotistical?"

"It's confidence, darlin'."

Her lips twitched. "You've been talking to Lamont too much."

"I'm not saying I'm the sexiest man in Kentucky, but we all know men naturally gravitate to other males of the same caliber."

Piper spit out her water. Her gaze darted around the room, trying to ensure no one was paying attention to her faux pas. Tuck did his very best to keep from letting his laughter loose.

"You are so easy to tease," he quipped.

"You'd think I'd learn by now."

"Until you do, I'll keep coming up with jokes."

"I need to have a talk with your mama. Make sure she keeps you in line."

"Kiss me every day, and I'll behave."

"Likely story."

Miraculously, conversation continued to flow, and Tuck was no longer worried that he'd run out of clever things to say.

Instead, he had to battle guilt while smiling and turning on the charm. He didn't want to hurt Piper more, and he feared his silence would do exactly that. But he also didn't want to distract her from the Mountain Laurel Stakes. Everything else could wait. He just hated that plan.

Regardless, by the time he walked her back to her room, Tuck felt assured that their date had gone off without a hitch, and that they were closer than ever before. He could only pray that would work in his favor when he revealed all.

Twenty-Seven

No matter how many races I'd watched with a horse I wanted to win, I still got nervous at every single one of them. The anticipation of watching the colts line up at the start. Then waiting to see how your horse would move out of his stall and onto the track. Not to mention if an injury happened during the race—that was enough to tear up your stomach.

What made today worse was seeing Tuck disgruntled. He wouldn't tell me if it was due to Dream's work earlier that week or his shoulder. Then again, having screws in your shoulder and only over-the-counter pain relievers probably tipped the scales in that direction.

I got it. He hurt. But he didn't have to take his negative emotions out on me. I wanted to shake him—*That's gonna hurt him more*—but I settled for glancing at him occasionally and furrowing my brow.

"Darlin', you do that one more time, and we're gonna duke it out old-fashioned style."

"You can't race me to the water hole. Doctor's orders." I barely restrained myself from sticking out my tongue. *Barely.*

His eyes flashed fire. "Doc's not here."

"*I'm* here."

He muttered something that suspiciously sounded like "Women."

"Tucker Hale, you better tell me what got stuck in your craw, or I'll . . ." What? Tell his mama? Wag my finger at him? Take an idea from a rom-com and tell him to leave?

Seriously, why were the female leads always making the guy go when they *knew* they wanted him to stay?

"You'll what?"

"Kiss you silly."

"Is that a *kiss you* comma *silly*, or no comma?"

I sighed. "You're impossible."

"Is that better than incorrigible?"

I grinned, thinking of the captain's children in *The Sound of Music* introducing themselves to Fräulein Maria. "No fair. You made me smile."

"Then I'm definitely incorrigible." He winked.

I placed the palms of my hands on his cheeks, then placed my forehead against his. "What's going on inside that head of yours?"

He closed his eyes, his breath fanning against my lips. "I'm a little antsy. My shoulder itches and hurts. How it's possible for it to do both, I don't know, but it's making me slowly lose touch with reality."

He paused.

"What else?" I asked. I don't know how I knew, but he was holding something back.

Tuck pulled away and shrugged his left shoulder, a trace of pain tugging at his mouth. "Nothing that needs to be talked about before the race."

"Do you want me to pray for you? Maybe the whole shoulder thing has you a little off-kilter this morning?"

"You're probably right." He kissed my cheek. "Don't worry. I've already prayed over the situation, but sorry I didn't pray not to be a grump."

"Everyone's allowed a bad day."

I studied his profile. What was going on that he wasn't sharing? We shared everything.

You both kept mute about liking each other as more than friends.

True. I bit my lip.

But . . .

"The horses have reached the starting gate."

Tuck and I both sat up in our seats, and my brain immediately switched from its focus on him and proceeded to be nervous with anticipation for the race. I scanned the number two stall and smiled at how still Dream was. He was probably already envisioning the commands Gabe would give him. My Thoroughbred reminded me of Secretariat in that regard. Only he was nowhere near the dream horse Big Red had been.

The bell went off, and the horses sprang out of the gate. The two in the last stalls bumped into each other, and one stumbled so hard he tossed his rider.

Lord God, I hope he's okay. Please don't let him have any serious injuries.

Fortunately, the other horse and jockey regained momentum but trailed the rest of the colts. My gaze jumped back to the front, searching for Dream. Only, AlwaysaWinner was leading, not my colt.

"Come on, boy. You got this," I whispered.

But something was wrong. Dream looked lethargic, and the distance between him and AlwaysaWinner increased. No amount of cajoling or anyone yelling "Come on!" made him go any faster. Though the race wasn't a long one, time slowed until he finally crossed the finish line.

He placed sixth. *Sixth.* The race was merely to keep him in top form, but it seemed to have had the opposite effect.

"I'm so sorry, Piper." Tuck wrapped his left arm around me.

I shrugged. "We can't win them all."

"No, but I know how much we wanted a good race to keep the momentum going."

"What place for the Derby did he fall to?" Thank goodness there was an app to show the twenty horses going there. We'd been in tenth place, but I wasn't sure how far this would drop us.

Tuck checked his phone. "Hold on. The app is updating."

I held my breath as I waited for the verdict.

"Eighteenth place." He blew out a breath. "Maybe he's not feeling well?"

My eyes drifted close. It wasn't what I wanted going into the Derby, but the more important thing was that Dream *would* go. "Okay. I'll call Mordecai and ask him to look him over when we get home."

"Somehow it'll all work out," Tuck rasped.

I nodded, squeezing his hand. Right now, he looked like he needed encouragement more than I did.

Tuck came to his feet, wincing as he reached for his shoulder.

"Need that ice pack again?" I asked as we walked away from the track.

"Yes. Hopefully that tiny freezer kept it cold."

The freezer in the hotel mini-fridge was pretty compact. "I'm sure it did."

Before I could formulate another thought, a flash went off, blinding me, and questions flung about. It was almost reminiscent of the last race we attended.

"Ms. McKinney, how do you feel about Dream's performance today?" a reporter asked.

I drew in a calming breath. "I'm a little disappointed but thankful he'll be in the Derby."

"Ms. McKinney, what do you think of his competition? Do you think there's a better horse than Dream?"

What kind of question was that? Seriously, how did he expect me to answer? I conjured up a serene smile. "I'm sure racing at the Derby will answer those questions."

"Ms. McKinney, Robert from KLA News. Did Dream do poorly today because you stopped giving him illegal substances?"

"Excuse me?" It took everything in me not to lose my temper. "I have *never* given my horses anything illegal."

"How can we be so sure of that? After all, you *are* a McKinney."

My cheeks were on fire. I licked my lips. "The RMTC has already been to Maisha Farms and cleared us of any wrongdoing. Maybe you should do your due diligence before flinging accusations that could get you sued for libel."

His face blanched, and he stepped back.

I took the opportunity to push through the reporters, and I vaguely felt a palm on my back. Part of me relaxed at Tuck's sure touch. His presence gave me the strength to keep walking with my head held high instead of curling up in a ball and crying.

By some miracle, the reporters all seemed to fade into the background, allowing Tuck and me to walk side by side.

"I'm so sorry you're going through this, Piper."

"Sometimes life stinks." I glanced at him. "Make sure you text Lamont and tell him to do something to gain media attention and take the heat off us."

Tuck laughed. "Yeah, I'm sure he'd be willing to jump back into the fray after the reporters have finally stopped hounding him."

"What do you mean *stopped*? They were just talking about Nevaeh having a supposed baby bump at some gala, suggesting they're no longer celibate now that they're engaged." *Reporters.*

"What business is it of theirs what they do? They need to talk about actual news," he grumbled.

"We don't have a royal family to harass in this country, so we might as well put celebrities under the spotlight."

Tuck sighed. "I get it, but it annoys me."

"I'm pretty sure media annoys everyone they target until they need it to work for their good."

"I hate that you're right."

I threw a fist in the air. "About time I get to use prevailing logic to get under your skin."

"You're adorable." Tuck stopped walking and pulled me to him with his left arm.

I had to admit, there was something sexy about being close to a man with a sling. Did that make me weird or just horribly in love? I wrapped my arms around his neck, careful not to jostle his right shoulder. "At least you didn't say cute."

"I almost did," he whispered.

"Then I wouldn't kiss you. I can't kiss a man who would dare call me cute."

He kissed my nose. "What about beautiful?"

"That works." Why was my voice so airy?

"Stunning?" He kissed my eyelids.

"Mm-hmm."

"Lovely?" he rasped.

"That one is perfect."

Kissing Tuck was becoming my favorite activity, but I didn't want to do it anywhere paparazzi might spot us. Not because I was ashamed but because it was none of their business. I stepped back, letting my arms drop to my sides.

"I'm pretty sure it's against the rules to kiss before a date." Tuck had been wonderful about taking me out each night since we got here. Though with his recent moodiness, I wondered if the strain of being my boyfriend might be too much, like he'd rather go back to being friends.

You're overthinking it.

"Darlin', we're dating. Pretty sure that means I can kiss you whenever. Plus, you did say it would make me behave." His lips crooked in a half-smile.

"You said that, Tucker Hale. I just agreed for the benefit of feeling your lips against mine." I pointed my finger at him, a mock scowl on my face.

He simply kissed the tip of my pointer. I stared at the digit, surprised at the tingles erupting from such a small finger and from such an innocent gesture.

"See you later for our date?"

I nodded, coming out of my stupor. "Where are you taking me today?"

"You'll see." He winked.

My stars! That man was doing that on purpose. I couldn't remember Tuck being much of a winker before we started dating. "'Kay."

If he wanted to wine and dine me under the guise of romance, I wouldn't stop him. I loved seeing this side of him. After our first date, he told me he intended to take me on as many dates as I could handle.

Nevaeh convinced me to go shopping in celebration—online ordering and curbside pickup for the win, because she said I had a figure that could wear anything. When I mentioned my underwhelming bust size, she merely said a sheath dress would enhance what I did have. Thank goodness for girlfriends who understood body insecurities. And one who answered an endless number of texts with photos of me trying on outfits for her opinion.

It was really too bad she didn't live in Kentucky. Maybe I needed to make another friend in Eastbrook. People weren't unfriendly there, but I let my insecurities keep me a little distant from my peers. Maybe it was time to stop that.

Something to think about later.

Maybe I should focus on whatever made Tuck upset earlier and what I could do to help. I didn't want dating to create distance and room for secrets. I wanted to tear down walls and build a fortress around us. The whole us against the world thing. Idealistic maybe, but the dream of my heart regardless.

Twenty-Eight

An incoming call popped up across the news article Tuck was reading about yesterday's stakes race. At breakfast, he and Piper had decided they weren't in any hurry to leave, so he was relaxing on his hotel bed. They still had another couple of hours before checkout.

His lips flattened at the interruption, but then he pressed the green accept button. "Hello?"

"Hey, sir, it's Joel."

Why was their groom calling? He sat up and placed his feet on the floor. "Everything all right?"

"No. Something's wrong with Dream, Mr. Hale."

Tuck's heart picked up speed. "What?"

"I'm not sure. Every time I try to get close to check, he backs away. I hate to bother you, but can you come down here?"

"I'll be right there."

His gut clenched. *Crap.* Was it the strangles? Did Dream have a virus? His mind raced as he put his boots back on and grabbed his wallet and cell. He didn't want to give Piper more bad news on top of Dream's not placing. Not to mention he still hadn't told her about his dad. Was that why he hadn't seen the signs that something was wrong with her horse? *Lord, what's going on?* This would explain why the colt hadn't run faster yesterday. Having him place in sixth was a huge letdown.

Tuck raced out of the hotel, thankful the stables were within walking distance.

Lord God, please give me wisdom. Please help me see what's wrong with Dream. I pray it's nothing serious and that it can be easily managed. Please keep my thoughts centered on You and not on a path that won't help me or Dream. Please don't let him be so sick he loses his opportunity to race in the Derby.

Piper would be devastated if that happened.

When Tuck entered the stables, his eyes slowly adjusted from the bright light outside to the dimmer light inside. Joel met him in front of the colt's stall.

"Anybody else have a sick horse?" Tuck scanned the stalls, but the other horses appeared calm.

"Actually, yeah." Joel pointed over his shoulder. "They removed one from the stables an hour ago. Said he might be sick and they'd let us know if it was something contagious."

Tuck had some not-so-great words to say to that, but instead, he clenched his jaw. "How far away was that stall from Dream's?"

"At the very end."

Could be a blessing in disguise.

"You want me to call a local vet or Mordecai?" Joel asked.

Tuck shook his head. "Let me examine him first." Tuck slipped into the stall, whispering soothing noises as he extended his hand.

Dream's nostrils flared, but he didn't back away. Tuck continued his slow pursuit until he was rubbing the colt's muzzle. Drool hung from his bottom lip, but Tuck couldn't see anything amiss otherwise.

"What's wrong with you, boy?" Tuck ran his hand all along the Thoroughbred, examining him from head to hoof. Nothing appeared out of order. No swelling in the joints, no palpable heat or painful area that made Dream jerk away. Puzzled, Tuck faced the colt once more.

"Are you just antsy? Or is there something more?"

Tuck's gaze narrowed on the clear saliva dangling from the horse's bottom lip. He grabbed a glove, and while whispering soothing noises, slid his finger along Dream's upper lip and lifted the flesh away from the teeth.

Dream whined.

"Aw, poor guy."

A burr had nestled itself right in the upper fold of the horse's mouth, and an abscess had already begun to form.

"Found the culprit." Tuck jerked his head, signaling for Joel to take a look.

The groom blanched. "I swear I didn't see anything on race day. I would've said something."

"I believe you. I know Gabe would've said something as well." Though people had been known to ignore an issue in order to let a horse still compete, they weren't the ones Tuck chose to work with.

"Can you make a warm saltwater solution for me, Joel?"

"Sure thing."

"Good. I'm gonna remove this and see if he starts feeling better."

Lord God, please don't let Dream get a fever. Please don't let this get infected. We just want him healthy and whole and ready to race in the Derby.

Tuck needed to update Piper. He pulled out his cell and called her.

"Hey, you. What's up?" she said.

"I'm in the stables." He cleared his throat. "Dream's got a mouth abscess."

Piper inhaled sharply. "How bad is it?"

"It looks pretty nasty, but he doesn't seem feverish. Just a little skittish right now."

"No," Piper moaned. "I'll be right down."

"You don't have to come. I've got this. I'll watch over him."

"Of course you will, Tuck. But Dream needs to know everything will be okay. I'll comfort him and get to hang out with you. Two birds."

"Then come on down," he drawled.

She laughed. "Oh, hey, are you gonna be able to remove it yourself?"

"Never had any trouble before."

"But you're right-handed."

He stared at his slinged arm. How could he have forgotten about this blasted contraption for even a minute? "Joel can do it if I can't."

"Or you can stop being stubborn and let *me* help."

He wasn't stubborn. "Dream's under my care, and I'm pretty sure I can take care of him myself. I don't need your help."

"And I think that's called being stubborn." Piper chuckled.

Tuck sighed. "Fine. I'll wait for you."

"Good. Be there in a jiffy."

This was the perfect time to ask for prayer. Tuck opened his text messages and wrote one to Chris and Lamont.

> **Tuck**
> Dream has a mouth abscess. Please pray he heals with no issues so he won't lose the chance to race in the Derby.

> **Lamont**
> On it. Nevaeh is right next to me and said she's praying too.

> **Tuck**
> Thanks y'all.

> **Chris**
> 🙏 Please keep us posted.

> **Tuck**
> Of course.

219

Is this why he placed so low?

Could be.

"Tuck."

He turned at the sound of Piper's voice, and his brain went into hyper focus. Tuck noted her gleaming eyes, the wisp of a smile across her full lips, and the way her jeans hugged her body. And because he could, Tuck took his time appreciating her beauty without having to hide the fact that he found his best friend attractive.

She came to a stop before him and placed a kiss on his cheek. "You okay?"

"Me? You're the one I'm concerned about."

"Tucker Hale, when will you realize I'm good as long as you're by my side?"

Joy bloomed inside him. Whenever he contemplated the Scripture that talked about abundant joy, he couldn't help but think Piper was part of that. The Lord had blessed him with this woman, and Tuck prayed he'd give thanks all his days.

He hugged her to him. "I feel the exact same way."

"Good. Now that I know we can face whatever, what are we looking at?" She studied Dream.

"Obviously, we need to remove the burr. After that, we'll rinse his mouth with a saltwater solution. I want to make sure he doesn't get a fever."

Piper's brow furrowed. "He's gotten so far on the road to the Derby. Will this prevent him from racing?"

"It shouldn't. The recovery should be straightforward as long as he doesn't get an infection and need antibiotics." Tuck ran a hand through his hair.

If it came to that, Piper's Derby dreams would end right here. Well, for this season. There was always the next.

"I just keep thinking about the horses who never got to race because of tragic medical issues. Remember Wild on Ice?" She sighed. "He qualified for the Derby only to break his leg after a work. He never even got to leave the starting gate before he was euthanized."

"I know anything can happen"—Tuck cupped the back of Piper's head—"but remember, God wants us thinking on what's true, noble . . ." Tuck paused, trying to recall the rest of Philippians 4:8.

"Lovely, good report," Piper added.

"Right. All those things. Let's focus on removing the burr and getting Dream comfortable."

She nodded. "Okay. You're right."

Piper entered the colt's stall, and then soft murmurings cascaded from her lips as she slipped a halter around him.

"I can pull his lips back if you want to grab the tweezers to pull out the burr," Tuck said, suggesting a plan.

"That'll work."

Joel walked up. "Got the saltwater ready."

"Thanks, Joel."

"Need anything else?"

"We're good. Thanks," Piper said.

Joel walked away, and Tuck turned to the task at hand.

"It'll be just fine, boy." Tuck slid his fingers under Dream's upper lip and folded it back from his teeth. "Can you see, darlin'?"

"Yep. I'll get that removed right about . . . now." Piper held up the burr triumphantly.

"Make sure there are no remnants."

"It's all good. Want me to check his lower lip?"

"Yep."

Once she gave the all clear, Tuck let go of Dream and reached for the saltwater solution. He filled the syringe, then handed it to Piper so she could squeeze the solution into the colt's mouth. They worked in silence until Piper pronounced the site clean and free of debris. That and the solution was almost gone.

"We need to get him home so he can rest. Give him some soaked mash to eat until he's all healed." Piper placed her hands on her hips.

"I've got some softer grass hays we can try too."

Piper nodded. "Sounds like a plan."

"Good. Do you still want to make the trek back today, then? Rather than let him rest here another day?"

"Yeah."

"All right. Let's get packed and check out."

Tuck wrapped an arm around Piper's shoulders. Telling her what Dad did now didn't seem like a great idea. With what was happening with Dream, Tuck didn't want to compound the drama. Maybe tomorrow he'd sit her down and share all he knew. Starting with the phone call with Aaron Wellington and moving to Tuck's conversation with his dad.

Until then, he'd have to take his own advice and meditate on what was good and true. Yes, it was true that Dad outed Piper's dad. But it wasn't necessarily true that she would dump him because of it. He couldn't entertain the unknown, because it would make him spiral quicker than a spinning ride at the carnival.

His relationship with Piper mattered above all else. His feelings had ranged from a crush to feeling like he was in a pathetic, unrequited one-sided relationship. Knowing she felt the same way, had been trying to repress her feelings as well, unleashed his in an almost overwhelming fashion. He loved her.

Loved her the way God called a man to love a woman. If she decided to end their relationship because of his father's action . . . well, Tuck wasn't sure what he'd do. That fear was enough for him to keep quiet and pray for the right time, even though his gut kept prodding him to speak.

Could he do it? Could he turn to her right now and just lay it all bare?

He opened his mouth and—

"I sure hope God doesn't have any more surprises," Piper murmured.

"What do you mean?"

"It's been storm after storm. I feel like I've been in a very real battle." She laid her head on his good shoulder. "It's exhausting."

He squeezed his eyes closed. No, today wasn't the right time. He didn't want to cause Piper any more turmoil. He placed a kiss on the top of her head and said nothing. For once, he had no words of encouragement, only a hope that they truly would get through the storm.

Twenty-Nine

EHV-1 at Mountain Laurel Stakes
How Many Thoroughbreds Will It Take?

I winced at the news headline. AlwaysaWinner had been put down, his infection too severe and suffering too great. I wept for his owners, trainers, and all those his short lifespan had touched. Their Derby dreams were now just that—dreams. Oh sure, they'd have more chances, but not with AlwaysaWinner. His death brought the end to their racing season.

Thank goodness we'd left Mountain Laurel as soon as we had. Though we'd been notified to quarantine—which Dream was doing at my farm—there were no signs of the virus, just recovery from the abscess. Unfortunately, two other horses in the stakes race had come down with the highly contagious virus. They'd both been euthanized as well. Neither had been Derby contenders, but that didn't make the loss any less heartbreaking.

Mountain Laurel's stables were being cleaned from head to toe according to a statement put out by their PR firm. Their social media page showed them cleaning the stalls and making sure anything that might be contaminated was removed.

Reporters had reached out to me for a comment, wanting to

know how Dream fared. In a turn of events that was absolutely a miracle—and pointed to God, in my opinion—people had been leaving well wishes on Maisha Farms' social media post updating everyone on the colt's health. It wasn't an official statement like news journalists were hoping for. Just a simple photo of me hugging his neck and a lengthy update on how he was healing from an abscess—the cause of his poor race-day performance. People had been posting encouraging comments ever since.

I was sure any moment someone would turn out to be a troll, go against the trend, and post something hateful. But I wouldn't seek out the comment or dwell on it. Instead, I would do what Tuck had encouraged the other day—focus on what was true.

I wanted to go over to Tuck's house and check on him. The day after we got home, he'd been shifty and even a little sickly looking. But he claimed he wasn't ill. I'd check on him now, but he was at physical therapy. So that left me trying to figure out which two-year-old I wanted to buy from an upcoming auction.

I'd received a catalog book and wanted to purchase a few horses that would complement what Dream had already done by putting us on the map. My goal was for him to win the Derby, then turn him into a stud. But one did not become the owner of a great Thoroughbred farm with a single horse.

The other idea I had was so new that I hadn't even shared it with Tuck yet. Mostly because this one hinged on the idea of our being married. I sure hoped it was normal to date the man you'd loved your whole life and immediately start thinking matrimonially. Like, if I became Piper Hale, how easy would it be to merge my operation with his? Tuck could continue to train, and I could continue to purchase and raise horses that would make us a household name in the horse-racing world.

No illegal substances allowed.

I blew out a breath. That felt suspiciously like throwing

shade at my father. Since we'd last talked, I'd been waiting to see an exclusive interview with him appear, but nothing had been released. Had he truly listened to my advice and consulted his lawyer? Regardless, I was glad he was keeping under the radar. His trial date had been set, and Mama was a nervous wreck.

My quiet moments with God had been spent trying to figure out if I wanted Daddy to avoid a prison sentence or for him to come to justice. Bolt Brook's main veterinarian had been arrested and released on bail as well. From the attention in the local news, people expected him to go straight to prison without collecting two hundred dollars. The public believed someone dedicated to healing animals shouldn't be blessed with grace. I'm not so sure the verdict regarding my dad was as clear. After all, he hadn't been the one administering the illegal injections. The vet had.

Lord, this is such a headache. I don't know what to think or hope for.

Kind of. I didn't want my dad in prison even though he admitted his guilt and should face punishment. My mind refused to comprehend such an outcome. I believed praying for God's will was the best thing to do, but my selfish desires kept me mute. Instead, I kept pouring out my angst and hoping God knew what to do with my incoherent groanings.

Mama certainly was no help in the matter. When she wasn't watching TV or sad movies, she spent much of her time muttering under her breath about how she'd been bewitched by a smooth talker and lied to for decades.

"*Piper, that man is a liar and a tiger,*" she'd recently said. "*Tigers can't get rid of their stripes no matter how hard they try. No amount of scrubbing will remove something ingrained in their DNA.*"

"*But Jesus can make an entire new creation, Mama. Daddy could become a dolphin or something.*"

That had been the only dependable mammal I could think of at the time. Mama hadn't liked my rebuttal. She'd tilted her chin, shaken her auburn hair, and flounced away. Funny enough, I'd often done the same thing when I argued with Tuck—minus shaking hair since my short afro didn't move like the stereotypical shampoo commercials. Then again, he always had me laughing before I could complete my extraordinary exit.

Noticing things like that made me thankful for my parents and the mannerisms they'd bestowed on me. It was nice to see I had *something* of them, even if I'd never share their DNA.

I got up, stretching my arms above my head. I'd been sitting in my office chair far too long. Maybe I should go out and check the goats to make sure they were behaving. The fresh air would do me good and keep me from thinking about the Derby next month.

My phone blared, the security gate alarm sounding. I quickly opened the app, and my mouth parted. Someone was attempting to hop over the fence. I squinted at the video trying to identify the perp, but a hood was drawn, and a face mask covered any feature identifiable.

The phone rang.

"This is Amber with TS Security. Am I speaking to Ms. Piper McKinney?"

"Yes." Oh boy. This was real.

"Are you safe?"

"I am."

"Please verify your security code."

I relayed my four-digit pin.

"Thank you, Ms. McKinney. We've already notified the Woodford County Sheriff's Department of the perimeter breach. Were you able to identify the suspect on footage?"

"No, ma'am, I don't know who the person is."

"They'll be arriving in two minutes. It appears the intruder is heading for your stables."

Now my mouth dropped completely open. "No! Are they close?" What if they planned to harm Dream or kidnap him?

"Not yet. Do you hear the sirens?"

"No." I placed the phone between my ear and shoulder and slid on my boots. "I'm going out there."

"Ms. McKinney, I don't advise that. Please wait for the sheriff's department to arrive and apprehend the intruder."

"If they mess with my horse—"

When I opened my door, I hadn't expected to see the intruder, obviously a man, fleeing. Hot on his heels were Ice Ice and Baby, bleating like they were guard dogs, not goats who liked to escape their enclosure at will. Seriously, how had they escaped this time? Nothing left near the pen could be used as a step stool or tool to open the gate latch.

Ice Ice lunged forward and nipped the man's leg. He screamed like a prepubescent tween at a young Justin Bieber concert. I laughed, covering my mouth.

"Ms. McKinney? Is everything okay?" Amber asked cautiously.

"Everything is just fine," I said. "And the sheriff is here."

The intruder jumped into the law officer's arms, screaming incoherently and pointing to my two Pygmy goats, who stood in the field looking as innocent as lambs.

Hanging up with the security team, I met one of the deputies—a man I knew.

"You all right, Ms. McKinney?" Deputy Waller asked.

"I am. Thank you for arriving so fast."

"Happy to serve. Besides"—his lips twisted into a sly grin—"looks like your goats did the work of a K-9 unit."

I laughed once more. "Best thing I've ever seen. Even better, I've got the footage."

"We'll need a copy of that."

"Of course."

"We'll take him in and find out what the deal was. He didn't have a chance to do anything nefarious, did he?"

"No, sir. Ice Ice and Baby stopped him before he got to the horse stables."

"You named your goats Ice Ice and Baby?"

I bit the inside of my cheek, trying to squelch my laughter. "Who doesn't like Vanilla Ice?"

"He might be more of a guilty pleasure." Deputy Waller's lips twitched this time.

"No guilt here." Even though I could rap along to the intro, I didn't know the lyrics of the entire song. I just liked the names for my goats.

A voice from the deputy's radio on his shoulder was garbled for me, but he pressed a button, answering into the receiver. "Roger that." Then he looked at me. "Seems he's some reporter who was trying to get a photo of your horse. Do you wanna press trespassing charges?"

Yes but no.

"Just escort him off and ensure he doesn't come back."

"Sure thing." He tipped his hat. "Have a good day, Ms. Mc-Kinney."

"Will do."

My phone buzzed in my pocket, and at the sight of Tuck's name on the screen, my heart immediately lightened. "Hey there," I said. "You okay?"

"I should be asking you that. My phone alerted me to a breach at your place. Everything all right?"

"I'm fine, but you won't believe the story I have to tell you." I headed back inside the house. "How about I order some takeout and come over?"

"Sounds great. My folks are playing Bingo tonight at the church, and my mom's finally convinced I'm okay and can fend for myself."

"Hooray! I thought you might turn into chicken noodle soup before she gave up feeding you."

"I think I sneezed out a carrot the other day."

I chuckled. "Okay. What's your poison?"

"Burgers. Bonus points if they have BBQ sauce and grill marks."

"Got it."

I hung up and immediately opened the best takeout app to place an order. The barbecued burgers and seasoned fries would taste a lot better if I grabbed them versus having them delivered. Plus, I didn't know how many more photojournalists lingered outside my and Tuck's gates. It didn't sit right to put that kind of pressure on some Eastbrook High teenager trying to deliver food to earn tips for prom or whatever else kids spent their money on these days.

By the time I arrived at Tuck's, my mouth watered in anticipation. The smell of the burgers had tantalized me all the way from the restaurant to Tuck's front door. I held up the takeout bag. "I come bearing gifts."

"Mm. Smells great." He moved aside, letting me pass through. "Let's head to the living room, and you can tell me why there was a breach at your place."

"'Bout had a heart attack when my phone blared and I saw someone hopping over the fence." I started unpacking the bag. "I got the bright idea to go out and make sure Dream would be safe."

Tuck's face flushed red, and his eyes flashed. "Darlin', tell me you didn't."

"Tuck . . . you know how much I love Dream."

"Who's insured."

"And going to the Derby," I countered stubbornly.

Tuck squeezed the bridge of his nose. "Continue."

"I opened the front door to see Ice Ice and Baby chasing the intruder right into a deputy's arms."

We sat down on the couch, and I showed him the video footage on my phone. This time he laughed until he cried. It was great seeing him look so lighthearted. I knew he felt responsible for not catching signs of the abscess sooner and Dream's disappointing ranking at Mountain Laurel. But Tuck wasn't God, all knowing or seeing. He was simply Tucker Hale, fantastic horse trainer and the man who delighted me with every blue-eyed smolder.

"Tuck?"

"Hmm?" He wiped his face with a napkin.

"What's been going on with you? You've been really moody and almost . . . secretive." I bit my lip.

He blew out a breath. "Guess that's because I have a secret."

Thirty

Tuck wished he could text Lamont and Chris to pray for his conversation with Piper right this moment. He could use some courage.

But you already told them about this. You already know they've been praying.

It was time to come clean.

He met Piper's gaze. "I'm sorry. Can I just start by saying how sorry I am for keeping a secret?"

"What secret have you kept?" she whispered.

Tears were already welling in her eyes. Tuck slid across the couch and wrapped his hand around hers. "I haven't told you I found out something about your dad's situation. Aaron Wellington called and told me he knew who tipped off the RMTC."

"Aaron?" She scoffed. "You can't believe everything he says, Tuck."

"I completely agree." He ran a hand over his bearded chin. "But I, uh, know the person he accused of being the snitch." He squeezed his eyes shut. Great, he was calling his dad a snitch for doing the right thing.

Tuck shook his head. "I'm sorry. I need a moment to gather my words."

Piper placed a hand on his cheek. "Whatever it is, I can handle it. Just don't keep secrets."

Easier said than done, but she was right. She deserved the truth. Deserved the chance to operate with all the knowledge. "My dad tipped off the RMTC, Piper. It was *my* dad who got *your* dad in trouble." His throat was raw. He wanted to back away yet simultaneously wrap her in his arms and never let go.

Piper blinked. Then her mouth parted, yet no words came out.

Great, he'd shorted her brain. "Please say something," he rasped.

"No."

The stark reply seemed to echo around his living room.

Tuck reached for her, only for Piper to immediately slide backward, widening the space between them.

"No, Tuck. He didn't. Right?" Her voice cracked, and a tear spilled over.

"I didn't want to believe it, but I asked him."

Her luminous gaze locked onto his. "When did you find out?"

"I . . ."

"How long have you known?"

"Aaron called me the day I broke my shoulder."

She reared back, and the joy that had seemed to be a permanent fixture in her evaporated in the blink of an eye. "That long ago?"

"I didn't know if he was right. I was on my way to talk to my dad when I fell. Then, of course, I was in the hospital. When I was finally able to ask Dad, he confirmed it."

"Then why wasn't I the next person you talked to?" She held up a hand. "Please tell me just you, Aaron, and your dad know this. *Please*, Tuck."

He licked his lips. "Piper . . ."

"Oh. My. Word." She stood and started pacing from the couch to the foyer and back. "Chris and Lamont know?"

"Yes."

"Nevaeh?"

"I don't think Lamont told her."

"So you told Chris and Lamont before you told me?" She pointed at her chest, coming to a stop before him.

"Darlin', there was so much going on in your life. I didn't want to drop one more bomb when you were still recovering from the shrapnel of the last one." He rubbed the back of his neck. "You're telling me when I was in the hospital waiting for surgery, I should have said, 'Oh, hey, my dad might have outed your dad'?"

She rubbed her cheeks, eyes closed.

"Or maybe when your mama showed up on your front step with suitcases because your dad had been arrested. Or how about on our first date? Maybe when we were at Mountain Laurel waiting to race and all the paparazzi drama that followed you there." Tuck snapped his fingers. "Better yet, when we discovered the abscess."

Tuck knew he should shut up. The hole he'd dug was growing larger with each word out of his mouth. But he wanted—no, *needed*—Piper to see there had simply never been a good time to tell her.

"Are you trying to manage me?"

If her question hadn't felt like an ice bath, the broken look on her face would've done the trick. "No. *No.* How could you even ask me that?"

"Because you made a decision that concerned me without my input. Instead of asking me what we should do with that information, you just made choice after choice, all without asking *me* what to do. The very person it affects!" Her voice ended in a shout.

Tuck sat there, too stunned to refute her claim. Piper had never yelled at him. Sure, they'd had arguments, but they always ended with them laughing and moving on good-naturedly.

"I didn't want to cause you more pain. You've been through so much these last few months."

"Tuck, you're not God. You can't just make a plan with your limited view and think it'll succeed."

Ow. That arrow sure met its mark. "I'm sorry. I wasn't trying to manage you. And I'm sorry I didn't tell you sooner." He dropped his chin to his chest. "I'm plain ol' sorry."

"Yeah, well, so am I." She shuffled to the door.

He shot up, wincing at the twinge in his shoulder. "Where are you going?"

"Somewhere you aren't."

"Can we talk about this?"

She shook her head. "I'm done talking about it. I'm done talking to you."

Just like that, she turned and walked right out of his house. He winced as the door slammed, the picture frames on the wall rattling from the force.

Lord God, what did I do? Why did I wait so long? Why did I ignore those warnings and opportunities to just come clean?

He groaned. "Tucker Hale, you've got to be the most senseless man alive."

Twenty plus years of friendship with Piper, and he'd never screwed up this badly.

"I'm done talking about it. I'm done talking to you."

Did that mean they were *done* done, or did Piper just need to process everything he'd said?

His phone rang, and he groaned again when he saw *Lamont* flashing on the caller ID.

"What?"

"Whoa. What's wrong with you?" Then just as quickly Lamont said, "Oh man, she knows?"

"Yep." Tuck smacked his lips together.

"And you've just *now* told her?"

"Throw a little more salt on it. I don't think that burned enough."

Lamont chuckled. "Glad you can crack jokes at least."

"I'm not. That burned, but I was already suffering from the gaping wound Piper left me. Should we get Chris in the conversation to see if he can throw a flaming dart at me?"

"Bro, I'm sorry the conversation didn't go well, but maybe it would've if you'd talked to her when you first found out."

"I'm pretty sure I didn't throw *I told you so* at you when you were going through your fake dating fiasco. You know, the one with the whole lying."

"Wow, so when you're wounded, you get mean. Good to know."

The wind left Tuck's sails. He closed his eyes, asking for God's forgiveness before speaking. "I'm sorry. That was uncalled for. Please forgive me."

"Nothing to ask forgiveness for. I was gonna let love cover up that sin."

Tuck's lips twitched. "You're in rare form today."

"Nevaeh and I set a date."

"For real?"

"Yep. I was calling to ask you to be my best man."

"Ouch. Did I just remove myself from the running?"

Lamont snorted. "Please. We all have our bad moments. You're lucky I love you like a brother and remember I was once a jerk."

Tuck laughed.

"So will you?"

"I'd be honored."

"Good. Make sure you make up with your lady before the wedding so we don't have any awkward moments or longing looks across the aisle."

"You get overbearing when you're happy, huh?"

"You know it."

"Shoot me the details about the wedding. I'll make sure it's on my calendar."

"And I'll be praying for you. I'm sure Piper will come around."

Tuck hoped so. He didn't know what would happen if this was a breakup. "Thanks."

"Keep your head up."

Thirty-One

Moving on autopilot, I found myself sitting in my parked truck before I'd even registered where I'd been driving. It only made sense that I would come to Tuck's parents' house. That the need to know exactly what happened had propelled me to the one place I could find answers.

I thought that would've been with Tuck, but knowing he'd kept quiet all these weeks had shattered something within me. I wasn't sure what, though, because although my heart ached, it still felt intact.

Figure that out later. Now's the time for answers.

I knocked on the front door and waited for some kind of movement or sound to reach me. After a minute, my knuckles rapped once more on the frame. *Lord God, please let them still be home.* Tuck hadn't said when his folks would be leaving for the church.

Finally, the lock turned, and Mrs. Hale stood in the doorway, pushing the screen door out to let me in. "Piper honey, what brings you by?"

"Hi, Mrs. Hale. I actually came to talk to Mr. Hale." My voice shook, and I couldn't stop twisting the edge of my T-shirt.

Mrs. Hale was astute. "Is this about Tuck?"

"He's just fine."

238

Her shoulders sagged. "Well, Leslie's sitting in the yard out back. Should I bring something to drink? Do you want a snack before we head to Bingo night?"

"No, thank you." I couldn't let anything past my lips right now. My stomach hadn't stopped heaving upward and back down like I was trapped on a sailboat out at sea.

I walked through the house and out the back door. Sure enough, Mr. Hale sat in a lounge chair, gazing at the rolling landscape as the sun made its descent. He turned at the sound of my footsteps.

A sad smile covered his face. "Hey, Piper. I figured you'd be visiting sooner or later."

"It would've been sooner had Tuck told me when he first heard."

Mr. Hale winced. "Aw, don't be mad at him. You know that boy thinks of every possible outcome and then plans his way. He's not the impulsive one. We are."

I wanted to argue, but he wasn't wrong. Then again, I didn't really want to hear logic right now.

"Can I sit?"

"Of course you can. I'm sure you have questions," he said, giving me his full attention.

"Yes. I mean . . . I don't know what to ask. My brain won't stop spinning."

"You're probably wondering what even made me suspect?"

I nodded.

Mr. Hale sat back, his hands intertwined and resting on his middle. When he spoke, his words were assured but calm. Measured yet steady. Not once did he falter. It was almost like a bedtime story, his voice was so soothing, but hearing his perspective had me oddly stoic. I thought I'd be crying. I thought I'd be yelling.

All I did was listen.

"So that's that?" I asked when he finished.

"That's that." Lines etched his brow as he studied me. "I'm sorry it was me. I'm sorry your dad was actually giving illegal substances to his horses. I never wanted to hurt you. I love you like a daughter. I hope you know that."

I tried to swallow around the ball in my throat. "I know," I whispered.

"I'll apologize to your mama as well, if you think I need to."

I shook my head. Who knew how she'd take the news? Not once did I even think about the person who shed light on the banned act. I'd been so sure it was just a rumor to disrupt the racing agenda and throw us all off track. Then after Daddy admitted his wrongs, I was too shocked to consider who'd first discovered them.

I wanted to feel betrayed. I wanted to rail at Mr. Hale and tell him how he destroyed my family. But logic was working in my favor and kept me quiet. Daddy was the one who set this all in motion the moment he gave the okay for the vet to dope one of the horses. All this time, I'd been trying to figure out how to deflect some of the blame away from my dad. I didn't want him to be guilty.

Only, he was. Had admitted it to me, to Mama. Mr. Hale wasn't to blame, and if I was honest, neither was Tuck. Yeah, he should've told me the moment he knew about his father's involvement. But I knew how kind and good Tuck was. He wouldn't knowingly hurt me. He was so meticulous when it came to planning his next move that it wasn't a shock he kept quiet. But I guess I thought our newly expressed feelings meant we'd continue riding that cloud off into the sunset and never come down.

Shame on me. As many rom-coms as I've watched, I should've known better.

I looked at Mr. Hale. "Thank you for sharing with me."

"I'm sorry I had to be the bearer of bad news."

"Life's little ironies, huh?"

He cracked a smile. "Guess so." He rose to his feet. "Can we hug it out? I want to make sure we're good. I know how much Tuck cares for you."

I melted into his hug. Mr. Hale was like a second father to me. And if I had my way, one day I *would* be a Hale. Of course I didn't want our relationship to be strained.

"You gonna go talk to our boy?"

I shrugged. "It might serve him right to stew in his mistakes a bit."

Mr. Hale laughed. "Oowee. I'm glad you came to Eastbrook, Piper. You could only ever be the one for our Tuck."

Tears smarted, and my heart warmed. "You think so?"

"Without a doubt."

I grinned for the first time since I'd heard the news. I'd often wondered why I had to be adopted in the first place. Why I couldn't have stayed with my bio family and lived a good life. But if it all happened so I could meet Tuck, well, that was a gift I'd thank God for. And eventually, I'd let Tuck know that so he wouldn't be sweating bullets wondering how long I'd stay mad.

Thirty-Two

Chris
How's the shoulder?

Tuck
Hurts like the dickens.

Lamont
Exactly how painful is that? Is the Dickens scale literary or . . .

Chris
I don't know whether to laugh or groan.

Tuck
Groan. That was painful. But not as painful as my shoulder.

Lamont
Can't your girlfriend give you a massage?

Chris
Nice. Threw that in there all inconspicuous like. Now we can ask how they're doing.

Lamont
You're ruining the subterfuge, old man.

Tuck
Don't worry, Chris. We'll be all right. You're now officially the fifth and oldest wheel.

Chris
I don't like you guys.

Tuck laughed and slid his phone onto the coffee table, then sat back against the sofa cushion and focused on his breathing. Texting had distracted him from the pain a little bit, but using his left hand to text was aggravating. He didn't need to develop carpal tunnel from overuse. What he needed to do was sit back and relax. It wasn't like he had a day booked with business or anything.

Since the people of Eastbrook and neighboring towns had decided the McKinney name was tarnished, he'd been unable to get any more horse-riding lessons scheduled. And if Dream developed a fever from that abscess—though so far he was looking fine—Tuck wouldn't be making any more money off his winnings either. That would leave him with just the filly, since the other two horse owners had dropped him.

Tabloids were lamenting the EHV-1 development and asking if horse racing was a business that needed to be stopped in order to ensure horses lived a long healthy life. Tack on last year's debacle at Churchill Downs with a dozen horses dying, and the journalists were having a field day. Reporters seemed to have forgotten that investigations had been conducted by every race organization to ensure horse racing remained humane and there wouldn't be a repeat of deaths at Churchill or other tracks. EHV-1 wasn't in the same bracket as that disaster.

Something could be said for the practice of stabling the horses at communal race track stalls, giving them time to acclimate to the different track surfaces. But other countries let the horses remain on independent farms until day of race.

Tuck ran a hand over his beard. All this thinking wasn't relaxing. Maybe he should go for a walk around the farm. Being stuck in the house was driving him bananas. He wanted to rip off the sling, but every time he removed it to shower, his shoulder protested the weight of gravity. Wearing it during the day made sense. Tuck just couldn't handle the restrictions. The six weeks were dragging on forever.

He rose to his feet, then paused at the sound of the doorbell buzzing. He grimaced as his head rang with the echo. Most of his visitors knocked rather than pushing the offensive button. He should get it rewired and install a new bell sound.

Tuck ambled toward the front door and twisted the knob. *Oh boy . . .*

"Mr. McKinney." Tuck blinked. *Yep, he's real.*

"Tuck." Mr. McKinney eyed the sling. "Heard you were in an accident."

"Had surgery. It'll heal."

Mr. McKinney visibly swallowed. "May I come in?"

"Sure." Tuck moved to the side. His insides had tensed, and every muscle went taut with awareness. Why was Mr. McKinney here? Had Piper told him what his dad did?

Help me, Lord.

Tuck stood there for a moment, trying to gather his thoughts and make a plan of action. "Uh, do you want something to drink?"

"No. I don't want you to go to any trouble." Mr. McKinney gestured toward the one living room chair. "May I sit?"

"Of course, sir." Tuck sat catty-corner on the sofa. "What brings you by?" *Please don't be furious with my dad.*

Ian McKinney's blue-gray eyes stared right into Tuck's soul. "How long have you and Piper been dating?"

"About a month, sir."

"A month?" Shock dropped Mr. McKinney's jaw.

Tuck leaned forward. "Is that a problem?" he asked cautiously.

"Not at all. I honestly thought y'all had been dating a lot longer."

"Really? Why?" He thought he'd played the role of a mere friend pretty well.

"You're always together. When Piper lived at home, you came over to hang out often, and I know she did the same at your parents' house."

"I didn't gather up the courage to tell her how I felt until a month ago. At the Jeff Ruby Steaks."

Mr. McKinney nodded slowly.

"Is that why you came by?" If Tuck could just figure out what Piper's dad wanted, then he could respond accordingly.

"Actually, I came because I believe your relationship with Piper could help me."

Come again? "What do you mean, sir?"

"I want my family back, Tuck." A weary sigh tore from his lips. "I understand why they're upset with me. I know Piper's working toward forgiveness, but . . ."

Piper was one of the most gracious people Tuck had ever met. However, she had a temper. It had just never been directed at him until yesterday.

Tuck ran his fingers through his hair. Okay, so he wouldn't describe her personality as having a temper, but when wounded, the hurt ran deep and so did Piper's need for distance to process. It was the reason he hadn't reached out to her yet, even though Tuck was desperate to know they'd be okay and get on the other side of his mistake.

"Sir . . ." Tuck thought a moment before continuing. "Piper probably just needs a cool-down period. The shock of your admitted guilt and arrest was a lot for her to take in." Even Tuck couldn't shake the feeling of betrayal from his former employer. And if Tuck had those emotions, he could only imagine the depth of hurt Piper carried. "Maybe you reaching out to her now would be better received."

If she *hadn't* told her dad about his dad, it might be some weird bridge to reconciliation. Then again, if Piper somehow sided with Tuck's dad, the choice could widen the gulf between father and daughter. Guess hoping for a happy future in-law situation was a no-go at this point.

Mr. McKinney looked skeptical. "I don't know about that. That's why I'm here."

"I'm still not sure exactly what you want me to do. How do you think I can help?"

"Talk to her. Ask her to see me." Mr. McKinney's expression became downtrodden. "I want a chance to resolve our issues before I go to prison."

Tuck jolted backward. "But what about your trial? You haven't even been sentenced." His shoulder hadn't kept him that far out of the loop.

"I'm going to make a guilty plea. I've talked it over with my lawyer, and I think it's the right decision. Taking accountability"—Mr. McKinney gulped—"well, I think it's the best way to move forward with my girls."

"Have you told them?" *Because this might break Piper.*

"I told Piper. However, my wife is ignoring all forms of communication. If you could somehow get Piper on board to paving the way, then maybe Jackie would speak to me. I'll be seeking an earlier sentence hearing, and I want them both to know."

Oh man. This was a big deal. Once again, Tuck knew something Piper didn't. He squeezed his eyes shut. "I wish you'd go straight to Piper, sir. She's already upset with me because I didn't tell her something I knew. She hates not being involved in . . . plans."

Mr. McKinney's mouth drew down. "What did you do?"

"I didn't do anything." And truly, that's why he was in trouble. He hadn't told Piper about his dad's whistle-blowing when he was in the position to do so.

"Piper doesn't get mad over nothing."

Tuck sighed. "I found out who reported on Bolt Brook. I didn't tell her until yesterday even though I've known for a couple of weeks."

"You mean you didn't know your dad reported me?"

Tuck's mouth dropped open. "You knew?"

"Yes." A faint smile covered Mr. McKinney's face. "You must

be proud of a man who has such integrity." His eyes dimmed. "Unfortunately, Piper can't say the same for me."

"But you can change, sir. There's a God of miracles."

He heaved a sigh. "I know you're right, but in here"—Mr. McKinney tapped his chest—"that knowledge isn't real."

Tuck knew a broken man when he saw one. The world might not believe Ian McKinney was sincere in his regret, but Tuck recognized the light had gone out of the man's eyes. He no longer looked assured of anything. Tuck could only imagine what being estranged from his wife was doing to him.

"I'll pray for you, sir."

Mr. McKinney bobbed his head. "I appreciate that."

They each came to a stand. Tuck simply waited to see if Piper's dad would say anything more. Then after a couple of awkward beats passed, Tuck broke the silence. "Will you be at the Derby?" Bolt Brook had been banned from racing for the next two years by the racing commission, so Mr. McKinney was no longer competition.

"Will Dream be well by then?"

"I believe so."

Mr. McKinney rubbed the top of his head. "I don't think it's a good idea. I'm kind of like a bad stain."

"Understood. Maybe show up for Piper in some other way, without prompting. Women like that kind of thing."

Take your own advice. Show Piper how sorry you are.

Mr. McKinney chuckled. "You might have more wisdom at your age than I did."

"I doubt that. But if you hear any wisdom from me, know it's actually from God."

"He's not talking to me right now."

"Or maybe He's waiting for you to talk to Him." Tuck cocked his head. "This doesn't have to end your relationship with God."

Mr. McKinney slowly nodded. "I'll think about what you said."

Once Tuck closed the door behind Piper's dad, he leaned against it. If he could encourage Mr. McKinney to patch up his relationship with Piper and her mama, then Tuck could trot on over to Piper's house and apologize. He'd wanted to be there for her yet not make her life more difficult, but in making the decision to keep quiet, he'd taken away her choice.

He should've known that was a bad idea. After all, the one thing Piper wanted her parents to accept was that she was a grown woman capable of making her own decisions. And good ones at that.

Lord God, forgive me for once again letting my desire to plan my steps come to the forefront. I should've leaned on You and sought You for courage to tell Piper the truth. I pray You forgive me, and I pray she will too.

Tuck headed outside and, unable to drive or ride Nutcracker, walked across the fields. He needed to seek a woman for mercy.

Thirty-Three

'm so glad you're getting better, Dream. I don't know what I would've done if you were feeling worse." I placed a kiss on the colt's nose.

Mordecai said the abscess was healing nicely. The mash Tuck made had also helped a bunch. Now Dream was on soft grass, and Mordecai said he could go back to regular feed next week.

He was much happier now, and the skittishness had all but left him. Thankfully, no signs of EHV-1 or positive nasal swabs had appeared. I rubbed a hand down his muzzle, reveling in the softness that was as familiar to me as the feel of my own skin. Touching the Thoroughbred soothed me in a way only a horse's presence could.

Dream was supposed to be the one constant. The one thing that was mine, no matter what. He was my companion through the mess with my parents, through the turmoil between Tuck and me. Dream was supposed to have remained untouched by life's tragedies.

He's going to be okay. Everything will work out according to God's plan.

Telling myself God was still good over and over despite all the surrounding chaos was centering me. I didn't feel as panicked as I had. I felt reassured that God truly would get me and my family to the other side of this. One day I'd wake up and wouldn't see the McKinney name in the headlines. One day.

But it was not this day.

My cell vibrated in my back pocket, jolting me into the present. I removed it and checked the notifications, grinning when I saw Nevaeh's name.

Nevaeh
Guess what.

Piper
You got a request from Aline Brosh McKenna to do the next *it* Netflix rom-com?

Nevaeh
Nope 😄 I got asked to be the key stylist for the next Marvel movie.

Piper
Oh my word! Are you serious?

Nevaeh
As a heart attack. In fact, I took my blood pressure to make sure I wasn't having one.

Piper
Can you tell me for what film, or should I just use my imagination and assume the best?

Nevaeh
Imagine away!

Piper hit the call button. She had so much to say and didn't want to use her fingers to talk.

"Hey, Piper!" Nevaeh said in greeting.

"Are you excited? What about your salon? What does Lamont think?" Piper took a deep breath to give her friend time to respond.

"I'm super excited. The request seemed out of the blue but is very much welcomed. My salon . . . well, if I take the position, I'll probably have to promote one of the ladies to manager while I'm away for the film."

That made sense. Last year, Nevaeh wanted to work on a film or TV set more than anything. But after much prayer, she decided to open her own shop that catered to women going through health issues. They could come get pampered and leave with tips on how to maintain their hair during illness. Nevaeh even offered in-home services for some clients.

"What does Lamont think?" Piper asked.

"He's happy for me and will cheer me on no matter what I choose."

"Aww."

Nevaeh sighed. "He's the best."

"Y'all are too cute."

"I think so too."

They both laughed.

Then Piper asked, "How will you decide?"

"Pray first. My gut says yes, but I don't know if that's because it's an old dream I thought was no more or because God wants me to say yes."

"I get that. Praying for clarity for you."

"Thanks, girl. I also have a question for you."

"Ask away." I left the stall and headed for the stool near the tack room. I wasn't ready to leave Dream completely, but he didn't like cell phones.

"Lamont and I set a date for the wedding, and I was hoping you'd be my maid of honor."

My mouth dropped open. "Are you for real?"

"Very."

I gave a light squeal. "I'd be happy to. Thank you so much for thinking of me."

"Oh thank goodness. I really feel like we've become fast friends, but I was still worried you'd say no."

"I'm not going anywhere. I'm an official member of the Nevaeh Richards fan club."

She laughed. "At least someone's heading it up. It's a vast difference from the haters attacking me."

"They're not still doing that, are they?"

"Some people will die on that hill. I've chosen to take the high ground . . . which might be a mountaintop?"

"There you go." Nevaeh's stance was #lifegoals.

"How are *you* doing?"

I sighed. "Life's been so up and down lately. I'm ready to get off this roller coaster and get into one of those boats that just coast."

"I bet. I can't believe how often you've been in the news. You and Tuck trying to outdo me and Lamont?"

I laughed. "No way. The news circus is for the birds. I'd be happy if people forgot our names altogether."

"I don't think there's any sign of that happening. Since I've been following the races, I keep getting alerts on my phone related to anything equine. Girl, if I see your dad's name in the news one more time—" Nevaeh sucked in a breath. "That was so insensitive of me."

"No, you're right. His name is in there more than mine."

"Have you talked to your dad?" Nevaeh asked hesitantly.

"Not recently." My mind went to our argument. "But I need to."

"Remember, nothing gets resolved if you're ignoring it."

Ugh. I hated that she was right. "Thanks, Nevaeh."

"Anytime. I'll talk to you later."

"'Kay. Let me know what you decide."

"Will do."

I sat there in the quiet of the stables. Other than the puffs of air from Dream and the sounds of birds and other wildlife outside, it was pleasantly quiet. Perhaps that's why I noticed the sound of footsteps way before I saw a body enter the stables.

Tuck moved slowly, arm in sling, hat on head, looking extremely too good for my heart. I watched him check each nook

252

and cranny before his eyes landed on me. My lips curved of their own accord as I stared into a face I knew as well as my own. "Hi."

He approached me slowly, a wary look on his face. My welcoming grin probably threw him off. Last he knew, I wanted to punch his good-looking face.

"Hey there," he said cautiously. "I didn't really expect to find you in here."

"Expected to see me chasing the goats?"

"Without a doubt."

I laughed. "They're the only ones not giving me grief today." I gave him a pointed look.

His face flushed, and he stared at his boots before meeting my gaze once more. "I'm sorry."

"I know."

He took a step closer. "I won't do that again."

I studied him, noting everything that was the same and seeing the contrition in his gaze. "I hope not."

"Will you forgive me?" He took another step.

"Already done."

He closed the gap and wrapped his free arm around me, kissing me just below the ear.

I sighed, nuzzling my cheek against his beard. I looped an arm around his neck and kissed him soundly. "And what have we learned from this?"

"To not keep secrets." He grinned at me. "And that you're the most forgiving woman I've ever met?"

"Don't forget that, Tucker Hale."

He chuckled.

"How's the shoulder?" I asked.

"Hurting like you wouldn't believe." He sighed and laid his head on my shoulder. "Make it stop."

I ran my fingers through his hair. "Do you need some pain meds?"

"No."

"Ice pack?"

"Not if that means you'll move and disturb my pillow," he mumbled.

"Maybe we should shift to the floor so you can be more comfortable."

Tuck raised his head. "Actually, I have something else to tell you."

"Tucker Hale!"

"No, wait!" He held up a hand. "Before you get mad, please note that I literally just learned this new bit of information, and I came to talk to you straightaway."

I blew out a breath. "Noted."

"Your dad came to see me. Wanted my help talking to you and your mama."

"Really?"

He nodded, then told me the rest of the conversation. It almost sounded word for word. I held back a smirk. Tuck obviously wanted to stay in my good graces.

"He even knew about my dad."

I blinked. "He *knew*?"

"Yep. Wasn't upset or anything."

I tilted my head. "Your dad and I talked yesterday."

Now it was time for Tuck to show surprise. "About what?"

"You know."

Unease filled his eyes. "Are y'all good?"

I nodded, and Tuck's shoulders sagged. "Thank goodness."

"I know how important your family is to you."

He cupped my cheek. "And same for you."

"I think Mama misses Daddy."

"What about you? Do you miss him?" He withdrew his hand.

I swallowed. Did I? I missed the daddy of my childhood. The one who took me to horse races. The one who taught me to love Jesus and others. The one who was there at the drop of a hat when I needed something. I missed being a daddy's girl and feeling safe with him.

Only, now all I could remember was his confession back at Bolt Brook. The regret I heard in his voice talking to him when I was at Mountain Laurel. How he'd knowingly endangered the lives of horses for monetary gain. Did I want to know this new version of Ian McKinney?

"I don't know how to answer that."

"I know he did a terrible thing. He knows it as well." Tuck grabbed my hand. "But doesn't he deserve a second chance?"

"I know you want me to say yes."

"Only if you believe you should. This isn't me trying to pressure you. I'm simply offering another perspective."

I gave a short laugh. "Tuck, you've always been the one to offer me another perspective. And I don't mean that in a negative way. You're the whole iron sharpens iron. When I need to come to my senses, you're often the one encouraging me to do so. You do it patiently and without judgment. So you coming here, talking to me about my dad . . ." I lifted a shoulder in a helpless shrug once more. "It means it's the right thing. I'll come to that realization sooner rather than later because you make me want to be better."

Tuck kissed my cheek. "You're the best, Piper McKinney."

"This time I think you're the best. I'm pretty sure my dad isn't your favorite person."

"Wanting your forgiveness as well made it easier for me to come on his behalf. I know how badly I wanted to resolve the rift between us. I can only imagine how much more your father wants to with you and your mom."

I thought about my parents, how long they'd been married. "I'll talk to Mama."

"I'll be praying."

I sighed and placed my forehead against Tuck's chest. "Why is being an adult so difficult?"

"I don't know, but Peter Pan had the right idea."

"No kidding. No bills. No life-and-death decisions to make."

"Unless fighting Captain Hook."

A huff of air left me at my slight chuckle. "Why do we always forget that when we say we don't want to grow up?"

"Right?"

I straightened, meeting Tuck's gaze. "You know, no kisses either."

"Yeah." Tuck frowned, but then his face brightened. "I guess falling in love is the best thing about being an adult."

I froze.

Had he meant . . .

Did he just say . . .

My brain stuttered, then started up again. "What's that?" I asked as casually as possible.

Tuck turned bright red. "Um." He rubbed the back of his neck. "I'm just saying that . . . you know."

I couldn't stop the grin on my face. "I know what?" I tilted my head. "What are you trying to say?"

"Get over here." He hooked his thumb in my belt loop and tugged me off the stool. "I love you, Piper McKinney."

I wrapped my arms around him. "I love you, too, Tucker Hale."

"Yeah?"

I nodded, pure pleasure filling every part of me.

"Thank the Lord," he whispered before kissing me.

Thank the Lord is right.

Thirty-Four

Piper's declaration yesterday had Tuck wanting to visit his parents. Since he still wasn't cleared to drive, he'd asked his girlfriend—the label still made him grin—to drop him off at their place on her way into town. Now he sat at the dining table while his mom sliced homemade bread and slathered freshly churned butter over the pieces.

"Here you go, son."

"Thanks, Mom."

"Of course." She sat down with a plate in front of her. "What brings you by? I thought you were done with my hovering."

He laughed. "I am. That's not why I came." Tuck looked at his mom, then his dad. "I'd actually like some advice from the both of you."

"I hope it's what I think it is." A gleam entered his dad's eye. "What's that?"

His mom turned to his dad. "Yeah, what are you thinking?"

"I think he and Piper finally stopped fighting that lovin' feelin'."

Tuck laughed as Dad broke out singing the Righteous Brothers' song.

"Honey, I'm pretty sure that song is called 'You've *Lost* That Lovin' Feelin'.' I don't think losing is something you want to project onto their relationship."

Dad's voice came to a halt, and the lines in his forehead grew more pronounced. "Huh. You're right." He shrugged. "They won't lose it, though. Haven't yet."

"Dad . . ."

"What? You've been moon-eyed over Piper since the day she walked onto Bolt Brook. Never thought children could fall in love like that."

"We didn't fall in love. She was five when she moved here." Which made him six. That wasn't a falling-in-love age.

"I don't know, Tuck," Mom started. "You two were thick as thieves. It was hard to separate y'all at the end of the day. You never wanted to leave her and vice versa."

Tuck ran a hand down his face. "Regardless, I love her now."

His parents' eyes widened, and then his mom broke out into a grin and his dad whooped.

"'Bout time, my boy." Dad patted him on the back like he was giving him some version of the Heimlich. "Glad you let God's timing work perfectly."

"I kinda had to. You were telling me to let Him take charge, and then Lamont challenged me. . . ." Tuck grinned begrudgingly. "I couldn't ignore both of y'all."

Mom chuckled. "I'm surprised you didn't wave your planner in the air and entreat the Lord to bend to Your will."

He scowled. "I wasn't that bad about planning."

His parents did that wordless exchange where they met each other's gaze and spoke with their eyes. Okay, he might have worn an identical smirk on his face. *Now I know where I get that expression.*

"So what advice do you need?" Dad asked.

"How soon is too soon?"

"Too soon for what?"

His mom gasped and leaned forward. "Do you want to propose?"

"Yes." He hated the way her shiny eyes made his own want to water.

"Oh, my baby is gonna get married," Mom wailed.

"Good grief, Caroline. It's not the end of the world."

"I'm happy. I promise," she said through tears and hiccups.

"You sure you want to hitch yourself and have to deal with that for the next lifetime?" Dad hooked a thumb toward Mom.

She'd somehow made tissues materialize as she dabbed at her face. "Oh, hush, you ol' man. You act like you've never cried."

"Of course I cry. I've got tear ducts, don't I? I just have the sense to do it in private—in the shower, or when it rains outside. Not in mixed company."

"Is the company mixed because I'm here?" Tuck asked in amusement.

"Hush," his parents chorused.

Yep. He was the mixed company.

"Back to your question." Dad met his gaze. "Y'all've been tiptoeing around each other for years. No reason why you need to keep dancing just because ya finally admitted your feelings. Propose. Plan the wedding. Then say *I do*."

"Well, it may not be that simple, Leslie," Mom interjected.

"It is." He thumped the table for emphasis. "I didn't waste a bunch of time proposing. I saw you, then dated you long enough for it to be respectable."

"Three months is respectable?" Mom had a rosy glow on her cheeks.

Tuck wanted to make his escape before his parents started reminiscing, but he still needed advice.

"It is when you know. The extra two months were for your folks."

"Oh, Leslie . . ."

Tuck made gagging noises. "There's a child present. Please stop with the gross display of affection."

Mom giggled, and Dad rolled his eyes.

"I can't wait until you have kids and discover how fun it is to embarrass them," Dad said. "Actually, embarrassment is more the icing on the cake. Making your mama fall for me all over again, that's the goal."

"Mission accomplished, dear."

Maybe deep down Tuck liked that his parents were still so in love with each other. "Can we focus?"

Mom looked at him. "Just ask her, sweetie. That's all there is to it."

"Then you don't think it's too soon?" Because he really hoped not.

"No," they said in unison.

"Good grief. Sorry I asked."

"No, you're not," Dad said. "We'll fund the wedding. Gotta do something with the money sitting in our account."

"Y'all gave me a down payment on my farm. You've done more than enough already."

"It was a pleasure to do so too," Mom said. "So don't go grumbling or thinking you owe us. We're your parents, Tuck. It's a blessing to us, so don't go throwing our pearls back."

When they threw Scripture at him like that, all he could be was thankful. "Thanks, guys."

"Anytime. Now, do you know what kind of ring you're going to get?" His mom rubbed her hands together.

"Nope." Tuck sighed. "We've never discussed marriage or anything like that before."

"How could you, with you both pretending you weren't in love?" Mom shook her head. "Children really are foolish."

"Ouch. I can hear you."

She waved a hand. "You're not shocked."

He laughed. He really wasn't.

Tuck stood. "Guess I'll go figure out where to get a ring."

"You'll do just fine, son. Think about what she likes and go from there." Dad winked.

"Thanks." Tuck hugged his father, then rounded the table to hug his mom.

"Try to get a video of it so I can see her reaction."

Tuck laughed again. "Yes, because capturing it on video is what I'll be thinking about. Not sweating and worrying she'll say no."

Mom rested her hands on his cheeks, looking up into his eyes. "No way she'll say no, Tucker Hale. That girl loves you as much as you love her."

"Thanks, Mom," he whispered.

She placed a noisy kiss on his cheek, then let go. "Don't forget the video."

"Yeah, yeah." He waved good-bye and headed for the door.

"Tuck, wait." His mom raced behind him. "Did you drive?"

He groaned. "No. Piper dropped me off." How could he have forgotten?

"I'll give you a ride."

Once he arrived home, he sat on the couch and carefully removed the sling, then took the pillow Piper bought for him and placed it under his arm. Now that he had his parents' approval, he felt better about assuming it wasn't too soon to propose. Only thing was, he knew nothing about rings.

Tuck
Hey, can I get Nevaeh's number?

Lamont
No pleasantries? Just straight up ask a man for his fiancée's phone number?

Tuck laughed.

Tuck
I want to get her help picking out an engagement ring.

Lamont
😲

Lamont
No joke?

Tuck
I'm serious.

Lamont
Okay then.

Tuck clicked on the link for Nevaeh's number.

"Hello?" she answered cautiously.

"Hey, Nevaeh. It's Tuck."

"I was about to ask who's calling me from Kentucky other than Piper."

"Lamont passed on your number. Hope that's okay."

"Sure. What's up?"

His mouth dried. Why did he feel like his nerves attacked every time he wanted to say the *p* word? "I want to propose to Piper."

Nevaeh shrieked.

Tuck held the phone away from his ear until her squeals turned to some words, though they were garbled. "I'm sorry, what's that?"

"I said it's about time. I knew this would happen the moment I met you guys."

"How?"

"Anytime two people who are so-called friends can complete each other's sentences more's going on than they're saying."

She wasn't wrong.

"How can I help, Tuck?"

"I need ideas for a ring and how to propose."

"Aw, and you're asking me?"

"I know you two have become friends. I'm hoping Piper said something when she found out you and Lamont were engaged. Maybe about what kind of ring she likes."

He still couldn't believe his friends were engaged. They hadn't even been dating a full year. Granted, neither had he and Piper.

When Nevaeh didn't answer, he said, "You know what? Maybe it *is* too soon."

"No!" she shouted. "I hear that doubt in your voice. Ignore it. This is the right thing, I promise. I can feel it in my heart. I was only quiet for so long because I had to think over our past conversations."

"Then do you have any ideas?"

"Well, Piper has never said anything about dreaming of a wedding. Maybe she was afraid to hope. Unfortunately, she also never said anything about rings. You could always ask her. But if you surprise her, you get to watch her eyes light up."

"You really think she'll say yes?"

"Without a doubt."

He blew out a breath. "Okay. Thanks."

Looked like he'd be spending time with the Lord to determine if he was being ridiculous no matter what Nevaeh thought. After all, who was to say his wanting to marry Piper wasn't him still working an imaginary timetable? Only, it didn't *feel* that way.

Lord, this is me checking in. Hoping You'll provide wisdom. Is this the right thing to do? Am I moving too fast? And if I'm not, what kind of ring am I supposed to give her?

He sat in silence until the perfect idea dropped into his mind. "That'll work, Lord. Thank You."

Thirty-Five

If Mama cleaned the countertops one more time, I was going to lose what little patience I still had. I walked into the kitchen, drawing a breath and saying a prayer.

"Hey, Mama, do you want to go out for lunch?"

She looked up from her scrubbing, then back to the granite top. "I'm not done cleaning."

"Um, didn't you do that earlier?" *And the day before that and the day before that one.* I stifled a sigh.

"Before we ate. Don't you clean up after you eat each time?"

Of course I did. I just didn't have a compulsory scrubbing issue. Yet this was always what Mama did when her nerves were taut and she was anxious about something.

"You know I do, Mama."

She stopped rubbing the surface raw and finally stared at me. Her auburn hair had been pulled into a messy bun on top of her head, and the unkempt look contradicted her pristine, all-white sweats. Not a speck of dirt or lint could be found on the fabric. How did she still manage to look effortlessly beautiful?

"I'm doing it again, aren't I?" A small V appeared in her forehead.

"If you mean worry-cleaning, then yeah. Big time." I widened my arms for emphasis.

A wry grin shifted her lips. "Sorry." She threw the sponge down. "I just can't be still."

"Can't or won't?"

"Both?" she asked sheepishly. She tilted her head. "Yes, we should go somewhere for lunch. Where do you want to go?"

"It doesn't matter. I just can't watch you clean again. That, and I *am* getting a little hungry."

Working on a farm, even when I spent time in my office, meant I needed a little higher food input. At least that's what I told myself when I ate a slice of pie after supper or drank a large sweet tea. After all, corralling goats back into their pens was tough work. I deserved to be rewarded.

Mama flung an arm around me and gave a slight chuckle. "Okay. Let's get you fed."

We headed for the front door and were soon in her car, rolling down my driveway, Mama driving. Fortunately, the reporters had finally vacated my premises. I had no doubt they'd show up to Dad's hearing, but thanks to some prima donnas in Hollywood, no one was bothering me. Granted, daily articles still appeared in our local paper, but the national news no longer cared.

I drew in a breath and let the air of my exhale fizzle like helium from a balloon.

"It's good not being hounded anymore, huh?" Mama asked.

"So good." I stared at her. Was now the time to point out the very large, very gray elephant in the room? "Have you talked to Daddy?"

Her face blanched. "No. I don't plan on it, either."

My heart ached for her. A father betraying you was different from a spouse doing it. Though I didn't know by experience, I could sympathize. "Never?"

"I don't know," she murmured. "We were supposed to celebrate our fortieth wedding anniversary the same time we celebrated the 150th year of the Derby. Now I feel . . . stuck."

Didn't we all get stuck at one point or another? "Maybe talking to him will help you gain momentum." *And right our family.* Had I been maintaining my distance from Daddy out of respect for Mama?

The thought made my insides clench, but I couldn't tell if it was conviction or something else.

"What do you expect me to say, Piper? Hmm? Do I tell him how disappointed I am? How ashamed I feel to be his wife?"

I grimaced. *Definitely not that.* Disappointment was something a person could get over hearing. But learning your wife was ashamed to be your spouse? I wouldn't want to be in Daddy's shoes.

Then lend support.

"I don't know the right words, Mama. But I imagine it starts with you listening to what he has to say. Hopefully he apologizes profusely, and you try forgiveness on for size."

"Do you plan on forgiving him?"

My body froze. This was definitely one of life's tests. I didn't want Mama to feel alienated, but I couldn't abandon Daddy, either. I knew what that felt like.

I swallowed. "Yes. It's a slow process, but I've asked him to have dinner with me to start." Talking with Tuck made me realize I couldn't ignore Dad. Seeing him face-to-face would be the real test.

"Really, Piper?" Mama shook her head.

"He's my dad."

As much as I disagreed with what he'd done, I couldn't pretend like he didn't exist. It wasn't what God would want. It wasn't what *I* wanted. Even though Mama would be upset with me, I'd rather face her frustrations than God's. No way I wanted Him to say He was disappointed in me.

"I know, honey." She sniffed. "I don't know why life has to be so complicated."

"Because people always mess things up."

She gave a watery laugh. "True."

"We'll get through this somehow." Now I sounded like Tuck.

"I don't know how to do life without your father. We've been tackling problems together longer than you've been alive, Piper."

"Then don't stop now. Dad needs your grace more than ever." She pulled into a space in front of an Italian restaurant. "How's pasta for lunch?"

"Great. Their bread and oil here is the best."

She turned off the ignition. "Let's eat."

Subject changed.

I got out of the car just as a flash went off. I blinked, trying to regain vision after the bright light. I thought the journalists were done with us. When the circles stopped dancing in my eyes, I saw a local reporter accompanied by a photographer.

"Mrs. McKinney, Ms. McKinney, what do you think of Ian McKinney's statement?"

What were they talking about? How had they known we'd be here? Had we been *followed*?

"Will you forgive him, Mrs. McKinney?"

I turned to Mama just as she turned and looked at me. Saying nothing, she hooked our arms together, and we went around the reporter and into the restaurant. Fortunately, he didn't follow.

"What's going on?" Mama whispered.

"I have no idea." But then an image of Daddy telling me about an exclusive interview wormed its way into my heart. Had he done that? He said he'd talk to his lawyer first. Surely he didn't think it wise to publicly admit his guilt.

Something tickled my senses, and I scanned the premises. An overwhelming silence greeted us as every single patron stared. Some leaned in close to whisper, and others faked disinterest. Yeah, because all this wasn't obvious.

I pulled my cell out of my purse, then typed in Daddy's name and waited for the search engine results.

Ian McKinney Issues Formal Apology in
#McKinneyGate Scandal

My mouth dropped open. I showed Mama the headline.

A similar headline caught my attention as well, but here wasn't the place to click on either article.

"Maybe eating out isn't such a good idea," she said into my ear.

"Agreed."

We turned around and left. The photographer was still there snapping photos, but I tucked my chin to my chest and ignored him.

As Mama drove us back to my house, I placed an order for pickup at a nearby sub shop. Surely there wouldn't be a crowd there, allowing me to run in and out without being accosted and asked my opinion. A glance in the rearview mirror didn't reveal any cars following us, though I wasn't an expert at this. Watching spy movies just made me feel like a spy.

I itched to be alone and read Daddy's apology. Had he only penned the op-ed to get Mama's attention? Would she believe he was sincere?

By some unspoken agreement, neither one of us spoke again. Mama took her sub to the guest room, and I headed for my office. As soon as I sat down, I had the article open on my laptop, devouring the words faster than I nibbled on my sandwich.

It recently came to national attention that I authorized administration of illegal substances at Bolt Brook Thoroughbred Farm. Despite media speculation, I enlisted only the help of the veterinarian who worked for me. His name has already been released. No one else was aware of my scheme. I am ashamed of my actions and apologize for the hurt and various consequences my family has suffered because of my crime.

That was it. Nothing more.

Do you expect him to bare his soul to the local news?

I scrunched up my nose and put the article aside. Did I really need an apology letter? Daddy had already asked for forgiveness in person, and I agreed to give it. I needed to remind myself of that fact daily and make efforts to remove the distance and distrust between us.

Mama stuck her head into the office, and I jumped.

She frowned. "Are you busy?"

"No."

"You don't have anything going on with Tuck?"

I shook my head.

She came in and sat in the accent chair in front of my bookshelves. "Right now y'all are like peas and carrots." She tucked an auburn strand behind her ear. "I hope he doesn't ruin your relationship like your father ruined ours."

"Mama," I breathed. "I'm so sorry for what you're going through, but please don't talk like that. Tuck's a good man."

"I thought your father was too." Her lips flattened, and she stared out the window. "You know, people said I wasn't good enough for Ian McKinney."

"Really?" Why had I never heard that before?

"I came from a poor family, and though your grandparents weren't as wealthy as we are, they were still somebody." She sighed. "I worked so hard to get good grades, work my way through college, wear the right things, talk the right way . . ."

Little bits of my life came together like a puzzle taking shape. "Is that why you always picked out my outfits?" And shoes and everything else she could control.

"Yes. But not just because of how I grew up." Concern showed on her brow. "Piper, life in America for an African American . . ." Her hands twisted in her lap. "I love you. I love you with my whole heart, and I have ever since we decided to adopt you. But I didn't really *know* what life I was subjecting you to when I signed those papers. You became part of my heart before my head ever considered the ramifications."

"It hasn't been all bad, Mama. Having two parents means the world to me." Severe understatement.

Sure, I wondered what it would have been like to be raised in a majority Black community or even in my homeland. But that's not how my life turned out. I couldn't stay in those thoughts, because they wouldn't help my present.

"But what did being picked on by white kids do to you? Somehow, I thought if I could change your clothes, make sure you had the best education, it would somehow lessen the stigma of you having white parents."

I'd always known Mama loved me, but having her explain the reason she was so controlling made all the difference in the world.

"Thank you for all you did."

"But was it enough, Piper?" Her brown eyes studied me.

"Well, adoption, just like being in a biological family, is what you make of it. You married Daddy, and he became yours. Y'all adopted me, and now I'm yours. I love Tuck, and now he's mine." I gave a grin. "It's the beauty of relationships. We reap what we sow, and you sowed love. Please don't forget that." And I wouldn't forget Daddy was part of that as well.

Mama's eyes went glassy. "I love you, sweetie. And I can't believe you finally admitted you love Tucker." A huge grin lit her face. "It's always been obvious he loves you too. You two are so good together."

I came around the desk, we hugged, and I nestled my face in her chest and breathed in her scent. This was my mom, no matter what.

I pulled back. "Please don't leave Daddy," I whispered.

"What?" She sputtered. "I . . ." She shook her head. "I'm not going to leave your father."

"Yes, because this resembles Bolt Brook." *Oops.* That was too snarky and maybe slightly disrespectful.

"I just need some time to gather my wits. I don't want him thinking he can get away with this."

"Mama, he might go to prison. I'm pretty sure he knows he can't get away with this. What he needs to know is whether he still has a wife."

I bit my tongue and held back the *for better or worse* hanging there. Because honestly, I'm not sure what I'd do in her shoes. It was easy for me to forgive the man I so desperately wanted in my life. I didn't want another parent to abandon me. Not that he had. He just made a huge mistake and got stuck in a pit of his own making.

I wanted to be there to see him climb free from the muck and mire and grow in grace.

"I'll try," she whispered shakily.

"That's all I'm asking."

Mama nodded, then left the room and me with my thoughts. Only I wasn't going to spiral. I was going to pray and pray and pray some more. We needed God's intervention if our family would regain any similarity to what it was before darkness fell.

Lord, please see us through this.

Thirty-Six

Tuck
Right now I kind of think Bucky was lucky.

Chris
Who?

Lamont
You don't know who James Buchanan Barnes is?

Chris
🙂

Tuck
White Wolf?

Lamont
Winter Soldier?

Chris
☹

Tuck
Captain America's best friend

Chris
A Marvel reference?

Lamont
Yes!

Tuck
Yes!

Chris
Is he that dude with the metal arm?

Tuck
Something like that.

Chris
Man up. Your arm will heal in no time.

Lamont
Don't be afraid to cry. We're here for you.

Chris
Make sure you get it on video for future blackmailing evidence.

Tuck
Blackmailing me for what?

Chris
Whatever is necessary

Tuck shook his head and slid his phone into his pocket. Now that he was in front of Piper's door, the distraction of walking up to her front stoop was no longer needed. He smoothed a hand down his shirt. The solid navy color looked good with his complexion and eyes—or so Piper had told him once upon a time. He could only hope she'd been attracted by the image and that's why she'd urged him to purchase the shirt.

He rapped his knuckles on the door.

A shuffling noise sounded before the door opened. Piper's eyes gleamed, then a slow smile lit her face.

Man, she's beautiful.

"Don't you look handsome." She rose up on her toes and kissed his cheek. "Mm. And you smell good too."

He snaked his good arm around her waist and angled his lips to meet hers. After his greeting, he pulled back. "You look magnificent." Then he held out his arm, giving her a twirl.

Her giddy laughter made his chest puff out.

She came to a stop and put her hands against her cheeks.

"Goodness. It's a good thing I'm so brown you can't tell when you make me blush."

"Oh, I can."

"How?" She held out her arm as if assessing its shade and wondering how he could possibly see a rose tint.

Tuck laughed. "Because you always glance down, and your cheeks bunch just a little higher than usual. I figured you were blushing just now."

"Huh. So if I'd never done that, you wouldn't have been able to tell?"

"Probably not. I've always explained away the blush when it came to me, after all."

She chuckled. "True. So where are we going on our date?"

"Come out and I'll show you."

She slipped on her brown boots that somehow made her yellow dress shine all the brighter.

Tuck threaded his fingers with hers and headed toward the back of her property.

"We're walking to your house?"

"Sort of. You'll see. Just be patient." He winked at her, then grinned when she made that telltale move.

"You know you don't have to take me on a date just to prove your love, right?" She looked up at him. "I figure as long as we've known each other and as many times as we've hung out, we've been dating and didn't realize it."

If she felt that way, maybe proposing wouldn't come as a shock. "You think so?"

"Yeah." She nodded.

"Good." He stopped and placed a kiss on her forehead. "Because it feels like we slid right into a relationship like putting on a favorite tee."

"Or that perfect pair of jeans that bends when you need to bend."

He chuckled. "Bending's a problem for you?"

"Hey, every girl has bloat days."

"Don't I know it." Tuck shook his head. "There was that whole year in middle school when all you did was eat chocolate and lament the wiles of Eve. Pretty sure you wore sweats that whole year."

"You try going through puberty."

"Right," he drawled. "Because I didn't have to live through the embarrassment of my voice cracking every time I tried to talk to my best friend, who was also my crush. The one who just happened to die laughing each time it happened."

"Aw, Tuck. You were so cute."

He groaned. "Not what a man wants to hear, darlin'."

"What do you want to hear?"

"That I'm yours." He winked at her.

"Smooth talker. Did you learn that from your dad?"

"I hope I have better skills than his."

"Ha!"

Who was he kidding? His dad was great. "Nah. If I have a future like him—right woman, wonderful job—then I'll know I've done something right."

She sighed. "I love your folks. That's marriage goals right there."

"What? Canoodling in front of your children to gross them out?"

Piper bent at the waist, laughter floating in the air. "*Canoodling?* Who says that, Tuck?"

He only said it because he knew certain words caught her attention. *Canoodling* seemed like a good one to insert and see how she reacted. The uninhibited laughter did something to his insides. He loved Piper so much.

"Quit your laughing, and let's go."

"So bossy." But the grin she threw his way made up for any censure.

"Not bossy. Eager."

"Is your date-night plan that epic?"

"Well . . . it's not really a plan, per se. Just an idea of how it'll go." He looked at her. "I'm trying really hard not to plan everything so much."

"I like that about you. Always have. Don't let it go, but don't let it rule you either."

"Yes, ma'am." He placed another kiss on her cheek. "How often can I kiss you and get away with it?"

Amusement danced in her ebony eyes. "I wasn't aware you were getting away with something. Are you stealing kisses, or am I simply handing them out freely?"

"Hopefully that last one, because I feel another itch to kiss you."

Piper placed her lips against his. "There. Now I'm doing the stealing."

"Nope." He shook his head. "I'm giving them out freely as well."

"Then it sounds like there's not a—" Her gaze widened at the scene before her.

Tuck swallowed, nerves suddenly present where they'd been miraculously absent before.

"Tucker Hale, what is this?"

"Um, our date."

He stared at the red-and-white checkered picnic blanket he'd borrowed from his mom. Fortunately for Tuck, she'd also had a literal picnic basket, and he'd stuffed it with items for their very own charcuterie board. He'd bought Piper's favorite red seedless grapes and all the cheeses, crackers, and meats the lady at the grocery store recommended. His neck heated up remembering the exchange.

"Um, excuse me, but is this the kind of cheese you'd use in one of those board thingies?"

The woman blinked at him. *"A charcuterie board?"*

"*Yes.*" He snapped his fingers. "*I'm taking my girlfriend on a picnic.*"

"*How romantic.*"

After that, the stranger got serious and loaded Tuck's cart with all the items she claimed would make the best pairings. Had even shown him where he could find a cheese knife and board to lay everything on.

"You packed us a picnic by the watering hole?"

When Tuck bought this place, the watering hole at the back of his property had piqued his interest. It reminded him of the time he and Piper spent at the one at Bolt Brook. Though this pond happened to be on a smaller scale, it was no less special, considering it bordered her property as well as his. A gate opened on her side leading to his with no problem.

He lifted the latch and gestured for her to go ahead. "Hope everything's to your liking."

"I don't see how it won't be." She beamed. "I love this."

They sat down, and Tuck started unloading the basket with one arm. "We've got some sparkling lemonade."

"My favorite," she breathed.

He stared into her eyes. "I know."

Piper fanned her face. "I'm not sure if you meant that to be a Star Wars reference, but I'm over here with my heart dropping to my toes."

He grinned, then pulled out the wooden board in the shape of a circle. Piper's forehead scrunched when he pulled out the cheese knife next. Once he placed the package of crackers on the blanket, understanding lit her eyes.

"Is this for a charcuterie board?"

"It is."

"How do you even know what those are?"

"Adult Lunchables? Not too difficult to figure out they're your favorite. All that's missing is the Capri-Sun."

She laughed. "The sparkling lemonade is an upgrade."

"I'll say."

"Can I help you unpack? You look like your shoulder is bothering you."

It was, but nothing some pain reliever wouldn't fix. He'd taken some before leaving the house so the throbbing wouldn't worsen. "I'm fine. Since this date is my idea, I'll put it all together."

"What if I starve before then, Tuck?" she whined.

He grabbed a grape and popped it into her mouth. "There."

"Mm. These are the best."

While he continued unloading the basket, he also continued feeding her grapes. Some part of him thought to feed her grapes one by one meant he was completely gone over her, but watching the delight in her eyes kept him at it.

"Piper, if you eat all the fruit, I'll have nothing for the board."

"With all that meat and cheese, I doubt that." Piper looked at him. "What gave you the idea of a picnic?"

"In high school, I almost got up the courage to take you on one. It was after Bobby Deter asked you to homecoming. When you told me you turned him down, I was so relieved I almost asked you out."

"Almost? What stopped you?" She tilted her head, studying him.

"Your mom said she was planning a family dinner the same night as homecoming. I kept quiet after that."

"I remember that. She was trying to keep me from being sad about not going."

"Did it work?"

"It did." She grinned. "We had a fancy dinner, and I still got to wear a pretty dress."

Tuck leaned on his left arm. "Why did you say no?"

"I overheard Bobby tell his friend he'd never kissed a Black girl and wanted to see if it was any different."

Tuck growled. "If he wasn't married and a dad now, I'd go to his house and . . ." He blew out a breath.

"And what?"

"Tell him thank you?"

She laughed. "Sure. We'll go with that."

They laughed and talked until it grew too dark. A few times Tuck felt the little ring box in his pocket. But it just didn't feel like the right time, so he never brought it out to ask the question that now burned brighter than the strength of Piper's smile.

He'd asked God for wisdom and knowledge to know when it was okay to propose. Judging by the feeling in his gut, it wasn't today. But that was fine. Being around Piper was enough for Tuck, because he had no doubt that one day God would say "Now."

Thirty-Seven

Before I could leave for the Derby, I needed to do one last thing to prepare. I checked the knob, relieved when it twisted. *Unlocked*. Surely that meant Daddy was hoping Mama would return and find him waiting with welcoming arms. Hopefully, he wouldn't be disappointed it was just me.

"Daddy?"

My voice didn't echo thanks to all the furnishings Mama had brought in to decorate the foyer over the years. I turned down the hall that led to his office, where he spent most of his time. If not there, then the stables. But I was pretty sure the latter were off-limits to him until the RMTC believed all illegal substances gone and the horses tested free of such substances.

After rapping my knuckles on the office door, a peek inside told me he wasn't there. I walked to the living room near the kitchen only to discover it empty as well. I paused. No way was I walking every square foot of this place to find him. I pulled out my cell and dialed his number.

"Piper?"

"Hey, Daddy. Where are you?"

"I'm at home." He scoffed. "Nowhere else to go, really."

"*Where* in the house are you?"

"Are you here?" His voice lightened. "I'm sitting by the pool. The time got away from me."

I hadn't thought to go outside. "Okay. I'll be right there."

When I was young, we spent most of our time outdoors. Either we were riding horses or Daddy was playing Marco Polo with me in the pool. Mama would sit on a lounge chair with a coverup and a hat as wide as the state of Texas. She was always conscious of the risk of being burned by the sun and developing skin cancer later in life. I saw her get sunburned only once, and that was the day she joined us *in* the pool. She'd been super red for the next week and moaned in misery every day.

Was that the memory pulling Daddy outside, or did he just like the scenery out there?

I made my way through the house and out the back door. The pool beckoned to me, the water still as could be. It was a warm April day, which was quite a change, because last week I'd needed a jacket. Now I was using the AC in the truck as I drove around town.

Sitting on the side of the pool, Daddy had his feet in the water, but his face held a downcast expression. My heart turned over as I took in the picture. He looked broken. That was the only word that came to mind.

His head popped up as I drew near. "Piper." He stood and opened his arms, then hesitated.

Taking a deep breath, I stepped into his embrace and hugged him back. "Hey."

His frame seemed thinner, his clothes a little looser.

"Are you eating well?"

He pulled back, gaze darting away. "I gave the cook a paid vacation for a few weeks."

"Daddy . . . at least tell me you're eating something, even if it's junk."

A shadow of a smile curved the corners of his mouth. "I have consumed my share of junk food."

My breath steadied. "Good." If I'd thought about it, I would've brought some groceries with me to cook him a meal. "Do you have food in the fridge?"

"Mm-hmm." He gestured toward the pool. "Want to dip your feet in first?"

"Sure." I sat on the deck and rolled my jeans up to my knees, then slid off my boots and socks. "How long have you been sitting out here?"

"I don't know." He stared at the sky. "Since I woke up, I guess."

"Are you sleeping through the night?"

"I can't." He sighed. "I'm used to your mama lying right beside me. It feels awful with her gone. I just toss and turn until I give up and get up."

Lord God, please reunite my parents. Please help Mama to forgive and Daddy to do whatever You require so they can be one again.

They were both so miserable without the other.

"I'm praying she comes around."

His head bobbed. "Me, too, Piper girl. Me too." He faced me. "Is she doing okay?"

"Won't stop cleaning." I flicked the water with my feet. "It's a little much to watch."

He wrapped an arm around me and placed his chin on my head. "Daughters shouldn't have to worry about their parents."

"Maybe when we're young. But as you both age, I'll eventually be in the position to care for you as you cared for me. So I think daughters *should* worry over their folks. Especially when people are being stubborn."

Daddy jerked away from me. "How am I being stubborn?"

"Have you tried talking to Mama?"

"I've called her, but she won't answer." He hung his head. "She still doesn't want to talk to me."

"How do you know for sure? Why give up with the phone?

Why not actually get in the car and attempt a face-to-face?" Must I tell my folks everything?

"She told me she didn't want to hear from me."

"Yeah, the day she moved out. That was how long ago?" *Sixteen days.* Not like I was counting or anything.

"She's never been this mad before."

"You've never done anything this bad before," I said bluntly. He winced. "True."

"You need to stop throwing a pity party and win back your wife. You have to show her you're contrite and that you'll *never* do something like that again. Before it's too late." Before he was behind bars . . . or worse.

"You're right." He rubbed his stubbly chin. "Got any tips for me?"

"No, but do something soon. I can't watch her clean one more day. I can eat off my floors now."

He chuckled. "I'll figure out a plan."

"When's your court date?" I asked quietly.

"My lawyer is trying to see if he can just enter a plea for me so we can bypass the trial."

I blinked. "What kind of sentence will that entail?"

"That's the question. I'm not sure the judge will go on the lenient side considering how long I was breaking the law." His face flushed. "But my lawyer thinks sharing all the information about how and when the vet administered the injections, even showing them accounting statements, will help."

"How is a plea different from going to trial?" And was he really throwing the vet under the bus to save himself?

"It might prevent me from going to prison. The outcome we're trying for is a hefty fine—though the RMTC and other organizations have banned me from buying and selling horses as well as racing them."

My mouth dried, and I swiped my sweaty palms against my jeans. "But just for two years, right?"

He looked away, staring out over the pool once more.

"Daddy?" I whispered.

"They might extend the sentence based on a trial outcome, but don't worry about it, Piper. I don't know yet what it means for Brook Bolt's future, but trust me." He looked me in the eyes. "It's not for you to worry about."

"I'll be praying for you. That you'll have wisdom in this time."

I hoped this season in Dad's life would draw him to his knees and increase his faith despite the deviation from the right path.

"Thank you. I've been talking to God more." He gave a self-deprecating chuckle. "Well, mostly whining."

"Hey, take a page out of Psalms."

He gave me a quizzical look. "What do you mean?"

"The writers lament but never stay in their pity. After recalling what God has brought them through, they're moved to praise Him."

He nodded slowly. "All right, then. No more pity party. I think you've hinted and stated it quite obviously."

"Good." I stood. "Dinner at my house will be postponed, because I'm going grocery shopping with my boyfriend, and we're going to take our time. I may even stay at his house *the rest of the evening*." I needed to give my parents the opportunity to start communicating once more.

"I get it. You're about as subtle as a bucking bronc."

"Sorry, not sorry."

We hugged again, then I left. I prayed Daddy would take the initiative and visit Mama. Hopefully, she wouldn't be stubborn and bar him entry.

Lord, please soften her heart. Please pave the way to reconciliation.

I probably could've kept my mouth shut and not inserted my opinion in their affairs, but I wanted my folks happy again. I wanted our quirky family with the best memories to continue making more. They were my family, and I wanted nothing but goodness for us all.

When I got to Tuck's place, I honked the horn. I'd texted him before leaving Daddy's. Since we were leaving to get groceries, he'd told me not to come inside.

Was it sad that I was excited about our outing? It wasn't a date to a fancy restaurant. It wasn't even a date to listen to some bluegrass and eat foods with bourbon in them. It was simply a stroll down the aisles while we bought items we were both low on.

My face glowed as I imagined what married life would look like with my best friend. Was it too early to think about marriage? Sure, we hadn't been an official couple very long, but we'd known each other forever. Didn't that mean our dating life had included all the times we got together as friends keeping our feelings secret? Would that mean I could give in to dreams about how Tuck would propose or what I'd wear on my wedding day?

Hmm. A floral wreath in my hair maybe. Maybe a simple white gown with no adornments.

The passenger door opened, and I jerked from my imaginations.

"You just honked. How did I startle you?" Tuck asked as he attempted to buckle himself in with one arm.

I took the seat belt away from him and clicked it in. "I was thinking."

"Must have been some thought. You looked completely zoned out."

I put the gear in reverse. "It was a good thought."

"Want to tell me about it?"

"Maybe later. First, don't you want to know how my talk with Daddy went?" I glanced at him.

Tuck nodded. "Of course."

"Really well."

"Yeah? I'm proud of you."

I scoffed. "I didn't do anything to be proud of."

"Of course you did. You showed up when most people would have severed all ties. That couldn't've been easy."

"It was once I saw how sad he was." My dad had always been the man who entered a room with his head held high, daring anyone to think anything but good about him. To see his shoulders slumped, head hanging low, tore something inside me.

"Did he say anything about your mom?"

"Yeah. I encouraged him to talk to her. Told him we were going to take our time shopping, then I'd stay at your house for the evening."

"Oh man." Tuck laughed. "I don't know if I should feel sorry for him or your mom."

"Neither. Pray they make up. She needs to stop running, and he needs to make more of an effort."

"Give him some credit. He did ask me for help."

"Because he's scared of us. And that's a shame."

Tuck squeezed my elbow. "Darlin', y'all can be fierce."

"I don't think so, sir." I tilted my head. "Should I pick out a nickname for you?"

"Like what?"

"Honeybunch?"

He laughed. "Please no."

"Good-looking?"

"Not bad."

"McDreamy?" I asked, thinking back to *Grey's Anatomy* and the battle between #McDreamy and #McSteamy.

Tuck laughed again. "Pass."

"Dreamy for short?"

"I expected more from the rom-com queen."

I came to a stop at the grocery store, shut off the engine, and looked Tuck straight in the eyes. "My heart?"

He groaned. "Way to show me up."

"Face it. I'm superior."

Tuck laughed and motioned for me to come closer. I gave him a quick kiss, then unbuckled his seat belt. "These groceries won't buy themselves. Let's go."

"Yes, darlin'." He winked.

Thirty-Eight

Lamont
We just landed.

Tuck
Great. Our ETA: 2 hrs.

Chris
I just got to baggage claim, so I should be checked in and settled by the time you two arrive.

Lamont
Do you need a ride? I rented a car.

Chris
A gas guzzler?

Lamont
No, Mr. Conservative. An EV.

Tuck
Guess you don't want to hear we're driving diesel trucks.

Chris
That's too much to unpack in a text.

"Who are you texting?" Piper asked.

Tuck looked up, hoping he seemed normal. He didn't want

to spoil the surprise. "The guys." It was the week of the Derby, and festivities were already going on in Louisville.

"How are they? I haven't talked to Nevaeh in a couple of days."

"They're all good." He shifted in his seat. "How are your folks? Your mom's coming, right?" Maybe a shift in topic would distract her from asking more pointed questions.

"I don't know. She was oddly silent when I got home the other day. All she said was she talked to Daddy. Nothing else." Piper frowned. "Of course, Daddy can't come."

"I'm sorry he'll miss it. Did your mom say how long he was there?"

"No. Do you think the conversation didn't go well since she hasn't moved out?"

"I don't know. She could still be processing."

Piper nodded. "Yeah, I honestly don't know what to think."

"Did your dad say if he could go to the racetracks as a spectator?" Or was the man truly banned from all racing events?

"Actually, we didn't really talk about that. I just assumed he was banned completely." She frowned.

"I'm sure your mama's coming. She knows how much this means to you." Tuck had half a mind to call Mrs. McKinney and make sure she'd be there. Surely she'd put up with the press in order to support Piper.

He squeezed her hand. "Are you excited about the festivities?"

"Somewhat. I'm too antsy to really look forward to them. They're just distractions from the main event."

"Fun distractions." Tuck slowly rotated his shoulder. It felt weird to be out of a sling. He'd been allowed to remove it the day before they left with advice to still be cautious. His physical therapy wasn't over. "You're sure there isn't an event you're excited about?"

"Hmm." She tilted her head. "The gala. I can't wait to show off my dress."

Tuck knew the Barnstable Brown Derby Eve Gala was *the* event in Louisville society. This would be his first time attending. "I can't wait to see it." Piper would make any dress look good.

"After we get the horses settled, what will we do next?" she asked. They'd also brought the filly Tuck had been training for the Kentucky Oaks, held the day before the Derby.

"Go to our rooms, change into dinner clothes, then . . . food." Where their friends would show up to surprise her.

"All right. I'll set aside some worry for some fun." She blessed him with a smile.

"Good."

There was a welcome wagon when they arrived at Churchill Downs. Also journalists milling about with photographers hoping to get a comment from the trainers and owners—or anyone who would stop and give them the time of day. In silent agreement, Tuck let Piper go ahead to the stables as he walked up to the reporters.

"Jim Bleu with the *Louisville Sun Times*." He pronounced the city Loo-a-vul, like most Kentuckians did. The others said Loo-ee-vil like the French pronunciation of King Louis XVI's name. "Mr. Hale, can you tell us what your plan is for Dream going forward?"

"We're gonna introduce him to the track and see what he can do. I'm sure after the first run, everything will look good." Tuck tried to remain ambiguous, remembering all the times he'd seen famous trainers offer similarly vague lines. As a viewer, it had been frustrating, but as a trainer, he understood their desire not to give anything away.

"When can we get a photo of Dream?" Bleu asked.

"Come out tomorrow. He'll be running early." Tuck would probably have the colt on the field about six or seven in the morning, depending on how many trainers had the same thought. Then again, hadn't Churchill sent a schedule of track times? He'd have to recheck his email inbox.

"Thanks for talking with me." The reporter held out a hand.

Tuck shook it, trying to hold in a wince when a jolt went through his arm. The OTC meds didn't make his pain go away, just lowered it to tolerable levels. His right arm wasn't used to such vigorous movements.

When he first visited Nutcracker after the incident, Tuck had to convince the gelding he was okay. His horse hated seeing Tuck with a sling. He'd been out to the stables the other day to show him he was fine now, and Nutcracker acted like his usual self. Tuck still wasn't allowed to ride, but he would be soon.

Tuck texted Piper to let her know the interview was over and he'd be in his room. He wanted to hurry and change, then find his friends.

> **Tuck**
> Chris, you make it to your room?

> **Chris**
> Yep. You guys finally here?

> **Tuck**
> Yeah. Just finished talking to a reporter. I don't know yet if Piper is at the stables or headed to her room.

> **Lamont**
> This is Nevaeh. I saw her in the hall. She almost saw me, but I hid behind a wall!

> **Tuck**
> What room are y'all in?

Both replied in quick succession.

Tuck
How 'bout we meet in the guys' room?

Chris
Sounds good.

Lamont
I'm already here so works for me. I can't wait to see my girl!

Tuck
She'll be happy to see you too.

Tuck grabbed his key card and entered the room. Fortunately, a porter had already dropped off his luggage. He took out his garment bag and hung the nice dress pants, tux, and dinner jackets in the closet. Tonight they'd be eating at a place Lamont booked for them. All Tuck had to do was get Piper over there after their friends arrived first.

Truly, he probably didn't need to go to the guys' room before he saw Piper, but he hadn't seen his friends since last July when he and Piper traveled to California. As great as texting and the occasional FaceTime chat was, he'd rather see them in person. The likelihood of any of them moving to Kentucky was slim to none, so he'd have to settle for the occasional visit.

He grabbed a blue blazer and paired it with his dress jeans, cream button-down shirt, and dress boots. He'd leave the Stetson behind for once.

Tuck opened the door and froze. Piper stood there in some kind of jumpsuit that was classy and breathtaking all at once.

"Wow."

"Yeah?"

He nodded. The emerald color did something to her skin that made it seem like it was glowing. "Definite yeah."

"Were you racing out of your room to mine?" Her grin emerged. "I figured you'd still be getting ready."

"Uh . . . yeah." *Think, Tuck.* "I thought *you*'d still be getting ready." Banked on it, but obviously he'd been wrong.

"Nope." She shrugged. "Our groom had everything under control with Dream, so I came back to the room and got dressed."

"Cool." He made a show of patting his pants pockets. "Forgot my phone. My wallet too. Give me a sec."

She nodded and stood in the doorway. He stepped to his suitcase, pretending to look for both. How could he text the crew without Piper knowing?

His cell rang, and he pulled it out of his jacket. "Oh, snap, it was here the whole time."

Piper laughed. "Thank whoever's calling. Otherwise you'd still be looking."

"No kidding." He answered Lamont's call. "Hey, Gabe, you make it in?"

"Oh, Piper's there?" Lamont said in a low voice.

"Yeah. Will you be ready tomorrow?"

"We'll leave right now."

"Fantastic. See you then." Thank goodness actors recognized cues. "Okay. I'm ready now."

As he drew closer to Piper, she laced her fingers with his. "You know I have a wallet in this purse filled with credit cards, right?"

"I can't ask my girlfriend on a date, then expect her to pay."

She rolled her eyes. "You can if you lost your wallet."

He pulled it from another pocket. "Lucky I didn't, then." He smirked at her.

"Men," she scoffed. "Don't even remember what you've put in your pockets."

"Yeah, but you love me."

She beamed. "I really do."

This woman! He fingered the ring box in his jacket pocket. He'd been praying ever since he bought it. Every time he was with Piper, he'd ask God, *This time?* and wait for a response. Except right now. He didn't want to go down on one knee in the hallway of their hotel and have to tell their children and grandchildren that's how he proposed. So he said nothing as they walked into the elevator.

Hopefully, Lamont, Nevaeh, and Chris were already in their rented car and headed to the restaurant. He couldn't wait to see Piper's face when she realized their friends had flown across the country to support her. He hoped she'd shed tears of joy and then spend the rest of the evening laughing over their antics.

They drove in his truck to the restaurant in silence, and the closer they got, the quieter Tuck became.

"Are you okay?" Piper asked from the driver's seat. "Did something happen with the reporters?"

"No, it was okay. They didn't ask anything about the drug situation or your dad. I gave the standard line."

"You pulled the ol' 'We'll have to see how it goes after I introduce him to the track' nonsense?"

Tuck chuckled. "Something like that."

"Infuriating."

"But no less expected."

She pulled into the circular driveway of the restaurant. "They only have valet here?"

"It's cool. I can afford it."

She frowned. "Who said I wanted someone driving my truck?"

"You let me drive it."

"It's you, Tuck."

He smiled. "It'll be fine. Let's go eat."

Once they'd handed over the truck, Piper threaded her arm through Tuck's and leaned in close. He should have texted Nevaeh to tell her to record Piper's reaction. Or maybe even Chris. He was a bona fide YouTuber, after all.

But it didn't matter. When the hostess led them to their table, Tuck knew the instant Piper saw them. Her body tensed, and her breath hitched.

"Surprise!" Nevaeh practically shouted.

Thirty-Nine

I couldn't believe the sight before my eyes. Staring back at me were Nevaeh with her happy self, Lamont with his star-studded looks, and Chris with his charismatic yet laid-back persona.

"I'm speechless."

"I was kind of hoping for happy tears," Tuck commented.

I shook my head. "It would take something amazing for those."

"Ouch," Lamont, Nevaeh, and Chris chorused.

"Sorry." I covered my face.

"Girl, don't worry about us. We just wanted to come and support you."

"What she said." Chris pointed toward Nevaeh.

"Thank you." After a round of hugs, I sat and put my hands in my lap. "It really means a lot that y'all came out here. It couldn't have been a quick flight."

Nevaeh waved a hand. "I listened to a podcast while Lamont slept."

"Hey, it's not my fault my new schedule is exhausting."

"You're the one who wanted to play a pilot," Nevaeh shot back.

I looked at Lamont in confusion. "What does playing a pilot have to do with an exhausting schedule?"

"They wanted some realism, so instead of just using a green screen, they've got me in the air with a real pilot. It's twelve-hour days."

"Not counting the commute," Nevaeh added.

"Say"—I looked at my friend expectantly—"you never told me your decision. Did you take the Marvel job?"

A sly grin curved across her face and made her dimples pop. "I sure did. It's been a whirlwind, so I haven't had time to call and talk."

"Who did you promote to manage the shop?"

"Charmaine. She has amazing leadership skills, which made it a no-brainer."

"Congrats," Chris added.

"What about you, Chris?" Tuck asked. "Catch us up on anything new with you."

"Let's see." Chris took a sip of ice water. "The board of the nonprofit I work for really wants to target Gen Zers in hopes that getting them to care about the planet will spiral upward and affect the older generations."

"How are you supposed to do that?" I asked. "Make more YouTube videos?"

"Naturally, but they actually want something more sensationalized. They're thinking of doing a documentary series for YouTube that would have me out in the wild showing the current state of the environment."

"Are you going to say yes?" Lamont asked.

"I'm praying about it. As much as I love being outdoors, I don't love the idea of cameras on me twenty-four-seven like I'm on some reality show."

"But could you survive?" Nevaeh asked.

"You know it." Chris grinned.

I laughed. "Then I say go for it. A lot of documentaries are making a difference. Zac Efron's docuseries seems to be a hit on Netflix. Surely your documentary could show us what we could do to help the planet and maintain the circle of life." Did that make sense, or was I merely babbling at this point?

"Wait, sorry." I still couldn't believe they were really here. My brain was running slowly. "Are y'all here this whole week?"

They all nodded. "But what about y'all's work?" If Nevaeh was so busy she couldn't find time to tell me she'd taken the Marvel job, how could she take a vacation?

"This is a trial run for Charmaine. If she can handle the shop while I'm on vacay in Kentucky, then she can handle it when I start my position as key stylist."

"I was fortunate to have a break in between locations," Lamont said. "I'll fly to Nevada after I leave here to start another part of filming."

"And you?" I looked at Chris.

"When I come back, I have to give the board my decision."

"We'll be praying for you," Tuck and I said simultaneously.

I faced him. "Was this why you were so quiet in the car? Were you worried you'd blurt out the surprise?"

He chuckled. "No. I don't know why I was so quiet. Nervous maybe? Afraid you wouldn't like that I kept it a secret."

Considering the whole fiasco about his dad, I could understand that. Only this was different. "You should know I love surprises." I leaned over and kissed his cheek. "Thank you," I whispered.

"Aww," Nevaeh said with a hand over her heart. "You two are absolute perfection. I'm so glad you stopped pretending to be just friends." She rolled her eyes. "Biggest pile of poo I've ever heard."

"We *were* just friends then," Tuck insisted.

"Right," Chris drawled. "I have to agree with Nevaeh. There was no friend-zone vibe anywhere. Nothing but sparks."

I could feel my face heating and fought the urge to look

down and bunch my cheeks. According to Tuck, I just had to look normal and no one could tell I was blushing.

"You're doing it again," Tuck murmured.

"Hush." I met his gaze. "How can you tell?"

"I just can."

Now my cheeks were on fire, but my heart said, *Who cares? Who wouldn't blush at his dreamy gaze?* I was so head over heels for this man. I wanted to shout that he was mine to the world and let my heart rejoice in that fact. "I can't believe I once thought he'd reject me. How had I missed the signs?"

"I don't know, girl. They're brighter than the Big Dipper any day."

I looked at Nevaeh. "I said that out loud?" *You* have *to stop doing that.*

She nodded, and Lamont laughed. I simply shook my head.

Our food arrived with pomp and a server who was robotically polite yet always appeared when someone's drink was low as well as when Tuck signaled for the dessert menu.

"Since when do you want dessert?" I could count on one hand the times I saw him eat it.

"I don't, but you will."

I grinned. "Want to split with me?"

"No, thanks." He grimaced.

"Chris, Lamont, do y'all eat dessert?" I asked.

"All the time," Chris said.

"Only when I'm not working on a film."

Which might as well be all the time." Nevaeh smirked. "I'll share with you if you don't want a whole one, or we can get two different desserts and share."

"Oh, let's do that. They've got bourbon chocolate cake and peanut butter pie." Complete opposites but no less good.

"What about the bourbon bread pudding," Nevaeh said, suggesting a third option. "That sounds divine too."

"Hmm. It does. How about all three?"

Her eyes lit. "Let's do this."

Tuck laughed, and when the server came, he ordered them all, then stood. "I'll be back."

As soon as he was out of earshot, Nevaeh leaned forward. "Okay, you have however long it takes that man to use the restroom to give us the scoop. Are you thinking forever? Is dating him all you imagined?"

Lamont shook his head. "No, we really want to know how he slid out of the friend zone."

"Right?" Chris laughed. "And whether you plan on putting him back now that you've tried dating him."

"Y'all are speaking nonsense." I smiled. "I love everything about being with Tuck. I didn't think going from friends to this would be a huge difference, but . . ." I thought about the picnic, the way he cared for me, and even the grocery shopping. "It's so much better."

Nevaeh sighed. "I love you guys as a couple. Seriously the best thing ever."

"You're not bad," Lamont said.

Chris shrugged. "I'm not sure how I feel since it makes me the official fifth wheel."

"We'll just have to find you a girlfriend," I said.

He faked horror, eyes wide and hands waving back and forth in front of him. "Been there. Have the scars and memory branded in my mind. I'm good."

"The right woman makes all the difference," Lamont said. He smiled down at Nevaeh, who beamed up at him.

"I'm so glad your fake romance worked out," I said.

"Me too. The fans have been much calmer since Lamont told the truth," Nevaeh said.

I still couldn't believe he went on social media—live for goodness' sake—and told the world he'd lied to prevent being canceled. Somehow, his sincerity had shown through, and people cheered them on.

"The engagement ring also helps." She wiggled her left hand.

"It's gorgeous." I'd seen a photo, but seeing it in person made such a difference. They were obviously happy, and I couldn't be more pleased for them. "Praying many blessings over y'all's future."

"Thanks, Piper," they said simultaneously.

"Have y'all been shipped yet?"

"Yep," Lamont said.

"What in the world does that mean?" Chris asked.

"You can*not* be that old." Nevaeh placed a hand on her hip. "You know, when two people get in a relationship—celebrities, mind you—the world gives them a relation*ship* name. They get shipped."

"Like Bennifer," I supplied.

At Chris's blank look, Nevaeh chimed in. "Ben Affleck and Jennifer Lopez."

"Brad Pitt and Angelina Jolie were Brangelina," I added.

Chris groaned, then looked toward Lamont and Nevaeh. "I'm afraid to ask what your shipped name is."

Before they could answer, the waiter walked up. My mouth watered as I looked at the trio of desserts. "This looks amazing. Thank you."

"Of course."

Suddenly the lights in our booth dimmed, and the LED candles sitting on the border lit up. I frowned. Why the sudden ambiance for a group of five? Clearly, whoever just lowered our lighting did so by mistake. But then a song came over the speakers that had my heart speeding up. One that had good memories associated with it. Maren Morris's "Good Friends." It was Tuck's and my song.

I gasped at the realization. We had a song!

I turned to my right, and there he was. My best friend. My boyfriend. My heart on bended knee, holding a ring. My breath caught in my throat.

"Piper Imani McKinney, you've been my best friend for as long as I've had memories." His Adam's apple bobbed. "You've been it for me for as long as I could grasp the concept of love. Nothing would make me happier than you becoming my wife. Would you please marry me?"

"Yes!" Tears streamed down my face as he stood and wrapped me in his arms. The kiss he placed on my lips set me on fire as I wound my own arms around his neck, careful to avoid his healing shoulder.

We kissed for an amount of time appropriate in a restaurant, but which left me whimpering when we broke apart.

"I love you," he whispered.

"I love you so much, Tuck."

He held up the ring. "You forgot this. Your yes prize."

I chuckled through tears and held up my left hand. After he slid the ring on my finger, I wiped at the tears to get a good look at it.

"Oh my word. This is fantastic." A horseshoe of diamonds cradled a heart-shaped diamond. "Where in the world did you find something like this?"

Tuck simply grinned.

"Let me see!" Nevaeh said.

I laughed and sat back down in the booth, then held my hand across the table.

"Look at you, Tucker Hale. I knew you'd find the right one."

"You knew about this?" I studied my friend.

She nodded. "He asked for advice, and I gave him unhelpful advice. But it looks like he didn't need my help anyway."

"It's perfect." I stared at the ring, my heart rate slowing from the gallop it had been. Then I stared at my friends, at Tuck—my fiancé—and sighed. This was the best night of my life.

Thank You so much, Lord, for abundant blessings.

Forty

He was engaged.

Tuck smiled up at the ceiling. The shades were drawn, and his hotel room was still pitch black, but that didn't matter. Piper had said yes. More importantly, God had said "Now." He'd been so grateful that the server understood how important it was for Tuck to get the song and ambiance for the booth.

The guys had given him congratulatory pats on the back once they'd returned to the hotel, then he and Piper had spent some time in her suite, sitting on the couch and dreaming of the future. She'd shared her dream of a rustic farm wedding at Bolt Brook, and he shared his dream of running a Thoroughbred farm with her.

It had been amazing to finally tell her all the thoughts he'd had about the two of them and not worry about ruining their friendship. It didn't matter that she had more money than he did. It didn't matter that he hadn't attended an Ivy League school like her folks and Piper had. Piper loved him for him.

Honestly, that was mind-boggling in and of itself. He was so grateful. *Thank You for Piper. Please help me be the man she needs. Help me help her.*

Tuck grinned, then hopped out of bed and grabbed a pair of

jeans and a T-shirt. Soon, he'd have to be on the track watching as Gabe took Dream for a run. Tuck prayed over the colt and all the other horses racing in the Derby. He could only hope there would be no deaths this year.

Too much had happened last year at Churchill. Horses had broken their legs, and some mysteriously died. The 149th Derby had been under a cloud of death with people demanding answers. Fortunately, new rules had been applied, and so far, so good. Still, Tuck couldn't help but be a little wary. If he had to tell his fiancée—oh yeah, he'd be using that term at will—that her horse had to be euthanized, he didn't know what he'd do.

Tuck went down to the breakfast area, grabbed some food to go, and headed for the track. He shifted the Stetson on his head to block the slight breeze as he turned toward the stables. The horses were all in stalls labeled with the number of the gate they'd shoot out of on Saturday, Derby day.

The smell of hay and horses calmed the nerves drumming through him.

He found Dream being saddled by Gabe. "Hey."

"Hola, Tuck. You ready to see what this boy can do?"

Tuck grinned. "Absolutely. Did you even get any sleep, or have you been partying since you got here?" There were so many Derby parties to attend during the week's festivities.

"Nah. I got here and crashed. I knew we'd have to be here about now."

They'd be on the track by six. Tuck had managed to grab an early start time for both Dream and the filly, which meant he'd have a bunch of free time later on. Maybe he and Piper could plan how they could turn some of their dreams into reality. He'd love to be married to her by the end of the year. He was done waiting and sticking to a rigid timetable.

Gabe got Dream in the starting gate as the other jockey did with the filly, and Tuck turned his focus to both horses.

They were the only ones in the gate. They lifted their hooves as if feeling the track and taking in the sensation. Tuck pulled out his cell to take notes. So far, he was pleased with Dream. The Thoroughbred wasn't doing anything unexpected or that needed correction. And he was all healed, so this should be a good training session.

At this point in the season, the colt knew the drill. Warm up on the track and get a sense of how he moved across it. Listen to the prompting of the rider and try to outrun the other horses. It was simple, yet it wasn't. Racing was always a gamble on how a horse would perform. He could be pure perfection in training and then fail a race because of something as trivial as an upset stomach from a delayed bowel movement.

Tuck had seen horses eliminate waste in the middle of a race and jockeys fall off and land in it. Horse racing wasn't a clean sport, but it gave the riders the same feeling as winning a medal or trophy. It just so happened they also got roses.

And Tuck was betting on roses draped across Gabe Moreno's lap. Then Piper could stand in the owner's box with pride and realize her dream had come true.

Or maybe Tuck had done that by proposing last night.

Focus, man. Think about the colt, not about your fiancée.

The gates opened, and the horses galloped out. Tuck noted their form and the speed with which they ate up the track. As they rounded the curve, Tuck whispered "Go" at the exact spot he wanted Gabe to spur Dream on—only, the Thoroughbred lagged behind the filly.

Tuck frowned. "What are you doing?" he whispered.

This wasn't how he'd envisioned training would go. Dream should've passed the other horse, not come in second. He needed to see if the colt was sick or favoring a leg.

Lord God, please let him be fine.

Tuck checked Dream's run time. *So bad.* It wasn't a winning number, though Tuck felt good about the filly. Hopefully, she'd do spectacularly in the Kentucky Oaks. Tuck hopped off the track railing and made his way toward the stables.

"Hey, you're Tucker Hale, right?"

He turned to see a man proffering his hand. "I am."

"Kerry Shaw."

Kerry Shaw? The trainer who had three Derby wins under his belt? "Nice to meet you."

"I've been watching your journey. This is your first time being lead trainer, if I understand that right."

"Yes, sir."

"Hmm. Bolt Brook seems to be making a lot of reckless decisions lately."

Tuck flushed. On the one hand, he appreciated the backhanded compliment. On the other hand, the McKinneys were his future in-laws. "People make mistakes, but they can recover from them."

"Ah, so the rumor about you and Ms. McKinney is true?"

"I don't listen to rumors, so I'm not sure what you're referring to."

"They say you're dating."

"We are. She's my fiancée." Bonus points for dropping that casually into the conversation.

"Congratulations."

Tuck nodded.

"Anyway, I've been thinking of forming a small organization of trainers. We'd have a lawyer on staff to oversee any contracts and basically be a company owners could approach to find their next trainer. I'm wondering if you'd be interested in joining."

Huh. Tuck had never thought of something like that. He liked being his own entity. But if he and Piper decided to merge their operations, it might be wise to have a network of trainers to pull from. Maybe he should hear more and get Piper's take before automatically saying no. "I might be. I'd need to hear more first."

Kerry nodded. "Understood. I've invited some of the other trainers here this week to a lunch today at noon." Kerry named a local restaurant. "Can you come? You can meet them and get a feel for how things would work."

"I'll be there."

"Great. See you then." Kerry jogged away.

Tuck met up with Gabe, who was hosing Dream down.

"Hey, Boss. Sorry that run wasn't faster." Gabe sighed.

"What happened?" He tilted his chin toward Dream. "He okay?"

Gabe grinned. "Just a delayed bowel movement. He's good now."

Tuck let out a breath. "If we can get that to happen sooner on race day . . ."

"Understood. I'll talk to the groom. Make sure he notifies me or you."

Sounded weird getting a bowel movement update, but Tuck didn't want anything to spoil Derby day. "Thanks for hosing him down."

"No problem. Tell Ms. McKinney *hola*."

"Will do." Tuck wished he could avoid telling Piper the training session wasn't great, but hopefully, she'd understand.

Back in his room, he made use of a quick shower. By the time he was dressed and ready, the clock said nine. He could wake up his lady love and see if she wanted to grab second breakfast—well, her first.

His cell rang, *Dad* flashing on the caller ID.

"Hey, Dad. Y'all make it in?"

"We're actually just pulling out of our driveway. We'll be there in about two hours. You know we'll have to stop and stretch after an hour."

"Don't rush. I have a lunch at noon, but we can definitely do something later."

"Oh, don't worry about us, son. Your mom wants to go

shopping. We know your friends are in town, so hang out with them."

"You sure?"

"Positive, except that's not actually why I called."

"Why did you?"

"Your mom keeps hounding me about your proposal. Wants to know when you'll ask Piper to marry you."

Tuck grinned. "Doesn't she think I'd let her know?"

"You know you'll drag it out, son," she yelled in the background.

He laughed. "Well, your timing couldn't be better."

"Does that mean what I think it means?" Dad asked.

"You proposed, Tuck?" his mom shouted.

He winced. She'd never learned talking so loudly wasn't necessary with Bluetooth, no matter how many times he'd told her.

"I did."

"She said yes, of course. Oh, I hate to have missed it. Did anyone record it by chance?" Mom rushed out.

"Actually, yes. Our server did. I didn't even realize it until he asked for my email address to send the video to me."

"What are you waiting for, Tucker Hale?" Mom whined. "Send it to me stat. I have to see if I should be proud or ashamed."

"Hush, Caroline. He's a Hale. Be proud. I know he made sure the proposal was perfect."

"He's right, Mom. I think you'll even like the ring."

"Send it now, Tuck."

He laughed. "Yes, ma'am. Y'all drive safely, 'kay?"

"We will. See you later."

Forty-One

I studied the ring on my left hand as the diamonds sparkled in the hotel lighting. I couldn't help but think they would give a little something extra to my evening gown for the charity event.

Tonight was the annual Barnstable Brown Derby Eve Gala. The black-tie event was where the who's who of the Derby world congregated before the big race. Not to mention the event would be filled with celebrities who wanted to have fun. Tuck and I would be going, but we'd also secured tickets for Lamont, Nevaeh, and Chris. Actually, getting Lamont's ticket had easily secured Nevaeh's and Chris's. The ticket secretary had practically drooled at the mention of Lamont Booker.

Some days I looked around and wondered how an orphan from Ọlọrọ Ilé landed in a place where she was surrounded by wealth. Surely my bio parents had no clue my life would be like this when they dropped me off at the orphanage. At times I wished I could find them, if only to tell them they were successful. I'd received a better opportunity in life.

Of course, I didn't know if that was their hope when they left me there. They could have simply thought one more mouth to feed was one too many. Regardless, they gave me abundance in their sacrifice. Even if I never completely overcame the feeling of rejection because of that, I would remind myself I wouldn't be here if they hadn't made that choice.

Beauty from ashes like God promised.

My phone chimed, and I checked the text.

Nevaeh
Do you need me to do your hair, makeup, accessories?

Piper
A short afro means I never have to do my hair. But I wouldn't mind the makeup done by a professional. 😊

Nevaeh
Girl, I always travel with wigs. I can bring one in if you want to change up the look.

I studied my face in the mirror over the hotel desk. I'd worn braids before courtesy of extensions, but I wasn't too sure about wearing a wig.

Piper
I think I'll pass on the wig.

Nevaeh
Ok, I'll be over with my makeup bag and jewelry case. I have some great statement pieces. Rings, necklaces, earrings.

Piper
Sounds fun. Come on over.

I washed my face with my favorite cleanser, then applied toner serum. By the time I finished, Nevaeh was in my room, laying out her goods across the hotel vanity.

"Goodness. When you said makeup bag, I was thinking something the size of a clutch." I pointed to the roll out hanging over the width of the furniture. "That's not a clutch."

Nevaeh chuckled. "I don't do anything in small measure."

"Something I love about you. What will you do to my face?" I sat down in the chair in front of the mirror.

"How about we go bold? You're always wearing safe choices. I think you'd rock the bold look just as well."

I looked at the color palettes laid out. "I don't know. They seem a little daring."

"But that's you! Who else could make such a presence in the Derby world? You've made more African Americans interested in the sport. That's daring."

I bit my lip. Maybe so, but the only place I ever attempted a little boldness was in colorful dresses. Even then, I was still a little sedate. I thought back to my conversation with Mama, how she felt the need to fit in. Maybe Nevaeh was right. Maybe I needed to be more daring.

"Trust me," Nevaeh said. "I won't make you look like a trollop."

I burst out laughing. "That's an old-fashioned word if I ever heard one."

"One of my good friends is an older woman." Nevaeh grinned. "She's always supplying me with terms from the past."

"That's awesome. Maybe we can add some Kentucky phrases to your vocab."

"Oh, I studied up before I came. Ask me anything about horses, though, and I still might get the answer wrong."

We laughed.

"I've been living horses since I was five. That's the only reason I get it."

"But you love it. I can tell." Nevaeh brushed foundation over my face.

I closed my eyes at her prompting. "I do. It's in my adopted DNA," I quipped.

"Have you ever wanted to know about your bio parents?" she asked softly.

"So many times. Only the trail is pretty much dead. The

orphanage burned to the ground in 2000. All paperwork lost. So even if I wanted to know who they are, they wouldn't have the information I'd need to find them."

"I'm so sorry, Piper."

I was, too, but I kept mute in case tears decided to make an appearance.

"Do you mind me asking what it was like growing up in Eastbrook?"

"I don't mind at all." Nevaeh was a safe person to talk to. "It was kind of difficult. I was the only Black kid in my school."

I told her about the comments kids made and explained how hard it was to feel like an oddball every single day yet wanting to enjoy life regardless of whether I fit in.

"It's why I don't have many friends." I sighed. "I'm not sure why my race didn't bother Tuck, but I'm thankful he saw me and not just the color of my skin. I'd probably have grown up bitter if it weren't for his friendship."

"I can understand that. I've felt uncomfortable going to all-white churches, so I can only imagine what it was like to grow up in a town that had no diversity."

"Guess that's just how God's plan worked."

"He is doing something amazing in you. I can just feel it."

I opened my eyes. "You really think so?"

"Of course." She placed a hand on one hip. "If you win tomorrow, think about the hope you'll bring to a little girl or boy who looks just like you. They'll know the sky's the limit and to not let adversity or good ol' fashioned racism stand in their way."

My insides warmed. "Thank you for that. Sometimes I get so me-focused I forget the whole world is watching."

"Don't let the weight of that keep you from doing." She picked up some eye shadow. "Believe me. I got paralyzed last year with all the judgments from the keyboard mafia." She shook her head. "If I'd been stronger in my faith and remembered my purpose is to worship God, I wouldn't have let their words have any power over me."

"How do I find that boldness?" I closed an eye as Nevaeh swiped the wand over my lid. "I've been trying to blend in most of my life. The equine atmosphere is the only place I feel really confident. I know horses. Everything else feels like a gamble."

"Then remember who's betting on you—God. He calls you His and already knows the great plans He has for you, so you don't need to dim your light for fear of making anyone else uncomfortable. *Or* because you're uncomfortable with all eyes on you. All that matters is you walk in the joy and boldness that believing in Jesus and accepting Him as your Savior brings."

She finished, and I opened my eyes, gaze lasered right on her. "Okay. Then I need you to help me choose my dress."

Nevaeh stepped back to give me space to stand. "What do you mean?"

"I brought two." I bit my lip. "One seemed like the best choice, the choice I'd always pick."

"And the other?"

"It's daring." My heartbeat picked up speed as I thought of the two gowns.

"Show me."

I went to the closet and slid back the mirrored door, then pulled out the safe choice.

"That's gorgeous. Is that chiffon?"

I nodded.

"I bet that ice blue is stunning with your complexion."

One of the reasons I chose it. It's something even Mama would like. "I agree and I don't."

"Okay. Is this the safe choice or the bold one?"

"Safe."

Nevaeh's mouth dropped open. "Show me the bold one!"

I laughed and hung up the chiffon gown. Then I grabbed the

red dress that had caught my attention. The sleek silhouette followed the shape of my curves almost giving me the semblance of a figure. The wide straps crisscrossed, leaving a tiny triangular keyhole in the center of my neckline. My arms would be bare as with the chiffon gown, but somehow this one seemed more audacious. I held it up in front of me and met Nevaeh's gaze.

"You have to wear that one," she whispered in awe. "You'll look amazing in it. I also have the perfect shade of red lipstick to match. You'll knock Tuck's socks off."

"I definitely want that result."

"Then go for it. Choose this one."

"Okay." I grinned. "Let's do this."

Nevaeh gave me a high five. "Great. Let's finish your makeup, then you can put it on. I should have brought my dress down here so we could get ready together."

"Go get it." I glanced at the hotel clock. "We've got plenty of time. The guys know where to find us."

"Okay. I'll be right back."

I laughed as she headed out the door. The gala was going to be great. My favorite singer and band—Holiday Brown and Every Breath—would be performing as well as a few other famous entertainers. I couldn't wait for the fun to start. A night of dancing with Tuck and being with friends to commemorate a wonderful time in my life.

I thought about what Nevaeh said. Of the importance of shining for God.

Lord, sometimes that seems so egotistical. Please show me how to shine my light and let You remain my focus.

Forty-Two

"Nevaeh said to pick them up at Piper's room. The ladies got ready together," Lamont said.

Tuck slid his hands into his tux pockets. "Good to know. You ready?"

"Yeah. Just waiting on Chris."

"Great." Tuck moved to the full-length mirror near the door. He stared at the haircut he'd gotten at the hotel salon. The man had trimmed the length up at the top and shaved off his beard.

"Stop worrying," Lamont said. "You look clean. Piper's going to love it because she loves you."

He sighed. "Right. I don't know why I'm so nervous."

Someone knocked on the door, and Tuck moved to look through the peephole. "Chris is here."

Chris's mouth dropped open when Tuck opened the door. "You got rid of the beard."

"Does it look bad?" Tuck rubbed his bare chin.

"Nope. You clean up nicely. Piper will love it." He clapped a hand on Tuck's good shoulder. "Where are the girls?"

"Waiting on us in Piper's room," Lamont responded.

"Then let's go get them."

They headed for the elevator. Piper's suite was on the floor above, which made it a short ride up. As they exited, Tuck moved ahead of the other guys and soon found himself knocking on her door. He leaned against the doorjamb, feigning nonchalance. He had no idea if she would hate the lack of beard or not. He hadn't been clean shaven since high school.

The door swooshed open, and Tuck's breath swooshed out.

He was vaguely aware of his mouth being wide open and Chris and Lamont's voices in the background. But all he could focus on was the woman of his dreams looking absolutely stunning in a red dress that cinched in where her waist dipped and curved out along the lines of her hips.

Piper blinked, then a slow smile curved her ruby red lips, showing off her high cheekbones.

"Say something, Tuck."

His heart stuttered back to life. "Amazing."

"You like?" She made a three-sixty turn with an impish grin on her face.

"Darlin', I have no words."

Piper trailed a finger across his chin. Tuck wasn't ashamed to admit tingles erupted down his spine.

"This bit of skin has left me speechless." She placed a small kiss where her finger had been. "Ready to party, Mr. Hale?"

"Put me on your dance card," he countered.

She laughed and linked her hand with his. "Let's move out of the way so we can watch Lamont's jaw drop," she said quietly. "Nevaeh looks magnificent."

Tuck moved out of the way and couldn't control the smirk that appeared on his face as Lamont stared, slack-jawed. "You're right. It's a lot of fun watching that."

"I need more friends," Chris groaned. His blue eyes rolled, almost appearing to make the rotation twice. "Both you couples disgust me."

"Now, Chris," Nevaeh commented, leaning on Lamont's arm, "jealousy doesn't look good on you."

"Maybe we can set him up with a friend," Tuck offered.

"Who do we know around here who's single?" Nevaeh asked.

Piper tilted her head, then rose on her toes and whispered in his ear. "What about that ortho doc? She was single."

"How do you know?" Tuck frowned. "Is that something women just tell each other?"

"No." Piper shook her head. "She didn't have a wedding ring, but she seemed like an awesome person. So I tried to figure out some basic info about her just in case."

"Just in case what?" Tuck turned to study Piper. "In case you needed to set up a friend? You do know your friendship pool is small, right?"

"What's going on?" Lamont asked.

"Tuck is pointing out my obvious lack of friends." Piper squinted her eyes at him. "And probably thinking I was trying to set *him* up, which I wasn't." She rushed on before the others could interrupt. "But I like knowing interesting tidbits about people I meet since you never know when the knowledge comes in handy."

Nevaeh moved closer to Piper. "So do you know someone who could be a fit for Chris?"

Chris held up his hands. "Wait a minute."

"I think so. She was the ortho surgeon who did Tuck's surgery back home."

"That's an impressive job," Lamont said.

"She was pretty too."

"Pretty, smart . . . Sounds like a good combo for Chris," Nevaeh said.

"I can hear all of you," he deadpanned.

"Good," Piper shot back. "And if this worked out, you wouldn't be lonely anymore."

"I'm not dating a twenty-something, barely-on-the-brink-of-thirty woman. Remember, oldest member of the group?"

"Doctors are rarely in the twenty-something stage considering how long they're in school." Lamont folded his arms. "Surely she was in her thirties at least."

"Actually," Tuck interjected, "I think she mentioned being in her forties." Or was that some anesthesia-induced dream?

"Call her up, then," Nevaeh said.

"I can't. I never got her number, and she doesn't live local," Piper said.

The group groaned.

Oops. Tuck had completely forgotten she wasn't from Kentucky. "I don't even think she said where she was from. She was visiting Kentucky to see her sister."

"That's right." Piper's bottom lip pocked out. "You should have found out where she lives. It could've been close to Chris."

"Aww." Chris feigned a sad expression. "Too bad, so sad. Guess we have to go to the gala without an extra woman. I'll have to put one foot in front of the other and make it on my own for at least another decade."

"Mark my words, Chris Gamble." Nevaeh wagged a finger. "We'll find you the right woman."

He shuddered. "I'll pass."

"Never say never, brother." Lamont patted him on the back and headed for the elevator.

Tuck pushed down a chuckle and walked up to Chris. "You should have invited someone to come with you just to keep Nevaeh and Piper from plotting," he murmured.

"Now you tell me."

Fortunately for Chris, the women forgot their plans as soon as their limo pulled up to the red carpet in front of the Barnstable mansion.

"Oh, wow," Nevaeh said. "I think I just saw the GOAT walk into that tent over there."

"Michael Jordan's here?" Chris looked out the right side of the limo.

"No, not MJ."

"Lebron?" Lamont asked.

Tuck laughed. Chris and Lamont were always arguing over who was the greatest of all time to play in the NBA. They never agreed.

"No. Ugh. I meant the GOAT for football," Nevaeh said.

Tuck tried peering out the window now. "Jerry Rice is here?"

"Tom Brady!" Nevaeh cried.

Piper covered her mouth, shoulders shaking with suppressed mirth.

Nevaeh turned her glare onto her fiancé.

Lamont raised his hands. "What? It means something different to everyone."

"How? When you have a player who's arguably the best—"

"Arguably," Chris interjected. "I can say Michael Jordan is the GOAT because of the records he set, championships he won, not to mention what he did with Air Jordans."

"*Or,*" Lamont stated, "you could say Lebron actually has better stats—"

"But fewer championships. Not to mention he played more games, and MJ still did more."

"Guys"—Tuck cleared his throat—"I don't think Nevaeh cares."

"I really don't. I was just surprised to see an NFL player at the gala."

"Expect to see actors, singers, and other celebrities," Piper told her. "It was easy to get three extra tickets once I mentioned one of them was for Lamont."

"It looks good to have celebrities attending the gala," Lamont told his fiancée. "After all, it's a charity event."

"What charity?" Chris asked.

"They're raising money for diabetes research," Tuck supplied.

A knock sounded on the limo window.

"That's the cue. Everyone ready?" Lamont looked around the car, and they all nodded.

One by one, they exited the car, made their way to the tented red carpet, and posed for photos. Lamont even answered a couple of reporters' questions, as did Tuck and Piper.

As soon as they entered the mansion, they heard music filling the air. Tuck raised Piper's arm and twirled her in a circle, and they immediately moved into each other's arms. He sighed and pulled her closer. Somehow, someway, God had seen fit to bless his life with this amazing woman.

"No matter what happens at the Derby . . ."

"We'll thank God for getting us this far." She squeezed him.

He leaned close to her ear. "I love you, Piper McKinney."

"Oh my goodness. Is that Aaron?" She pointed over his shoulder.

"I'm having a heart moment, and you're noticing other people?"

Piper clasped his face and turned his head.

"Oh. *That* Aaron."

Tuck could do without seeing Aaron Wellington III again. Unfortunately, the journalist took that moment to scan the premises and spotted Tuck and Piper. Surprise colored his eyes, then with a resolute expression, he walked toward them.

"Piper. Tuck."

"Aaron," Piper responded.

"Fancy seeing you here."

Tuck raised both eyebrows. Really? Fake pleasantries?

"Uh . . ." Aaron cleared his throat. "I just want to apologize again for how this all started. I shouldn't have tried to direct the narrative of your story."

Piper tensed, but then her shoulders sagged. Tuck wound his fingers through hers.

"Apology accepted," she said.

"Thank you for always being so gracious." Aaron briefly met Tuck's gaze, dipping his head in acknowledgment. "You two have a good evening."

Tuck watched the man until Piper squeezed his hand, getting his attention.

"You okay?" His gaze roamed her face.

"Yeah. I'm glad I got to hear him apologize in person. It somehow meant more than him being annoying through voicemail or text."

Tuck chuckled. "Are you sorry you didn't finish the story with him?"

She shook her head. "I've had enough of the media. I'd like to go back to the occasional social post and then spend the rest of my time with you." She ran a finger down his cheek. "I can't get over this new look."

"I thought I'd try to upgrade for tonight."

"Tucker Hale, you look fine no matter what your facial hair is doing."

He kissed her. "They really do say love is blind."

She pinched him.

"Hey, now that you're my fiancée, don't you think the teasing could stop?"

"You'd miss it too much."

"So true." He pulled her into his arms, then swayed around the dance floor. "Let's boogey."

She groaned. "Don't say that again."

He grinned cagily, then proceeded to say all the cringe words he could to get a laugh out of her. As she giggled, his heart soared. No matter what happened tomorrow, he'd bank this memory as a keeper.

Forty-Three

A bottle of antacids wouldn't be enough to get through this day. How had I landed at Churchill Downs in my finest outfit and matching fascinator? My emerald-green wrap dress was pretty simple except for the large bow tied against my left side. The blue statement earrings that hung in beaded adornment and matching necklace added some oomph. Not to mention my green hat covered in green and blue feathers.

But my fascinator wasn't the only covering that caught attention today. All the ladies were wearing them. Too bad staring at all the Derby hats was doing nothing for the suspense coursing through me.

"Breathe, girl. You made it this far, so hold your head up high." Nevaeh threw an arm around my shoulders.

"Is it that obvious I'm about to freak out?"

She laughed. "You look like you're gonna have a *Jerry Maguire* flip out moment."

I gave a genuine smile for the first time that day. "Where have you been my whole life, Nevaeh Richards? Tuck doesn't get my desire to quote movies all the time."

"Fortunately for me, I've got myself a movie man. He'd

get his SAG card taken away if he couldn't quote from rom-coms."

"Oh, Tuck can quote them, but not with obvious delight and abandon like I do."

Nevaeh shook her head. "If movie quotes didn't make you fall in love with him, what was it? The Stetson?"

I looked at Tuck across the way, being interviewed by a reporter. "It was the way he saw me." I turned back to her. "No one on earth can ever know us completely. That job has only and always been intended for God. But if I had to pick a person who knows me the best, it would be Tuck. He's never made me feel ashamed for anything I've liked. May have teased on occasion, but he's more inclined to take notice, knowing how important it is for me."

"I just love you two." Nevaeh placed her hands on her cheeks. "I'm so glad we got to come out and support you. I only wish you could move your operation westward."

"It would be great to have you closer as well, but Kentucky is me and I'm Kentucky." I linked my arm with Nevaeh's. "There's always FaceTime."

"Don't forget texts."

"Can't forget that." I tilted my head, studying Lamont and Chris talking. "Do you think the guys text more than we do?"

"Most definitely." Nevaeh grinned. "Lamont is always reaching for his phone, and since I'm right next to him, I know it's not me he's texting."

I laughed. "I think Tuck secretly lives for those moments."

"If only Chris had a woman in his life."

"We'll just have to agree in prayer that God brings it to fruition."

Nevaeh sighed. "Would it be awful to say that's my least favorite part of believing in Jesus?"

"Praying? Or waiting?"

"Waiting. I so want to just *do*, you know? But I also know

how doing just makes me look like a hamster on a wheel. I think I'm going somewhere, but only the person watching me—ahem, God—can tell I'm not."

The mental image was so perfect I lost my composure. I may have even snort laughed.

Chris and Lamont turned to stare at us, and Nevaeh waved. She looked fantastic in her red sheath dress. The ruffled capped sleeves matched the ruffled concoction on top of her straw hat, which even had a white feather poking out of the center.

"You know waving to them is just going to make them wonder what we're talking about," I said.

"Of course. I'm hoping they'll come over here so I can tease Chris some more about being the fifth wheel."

Trust Nevaeh to bring life to the party. A few seconds later, the guys did come over, and Tuck slid his arm around my waist. I would never tire of touching him just as I'd always wanted to when we were repeating the just-friends mantra.

"Were you talking about us?" Lamont asked, then placing a kiss on Nevaeh's lips.

"Absolutely." She beamed up at him.

Chris shook his head. "Yeah, right. Probably talking about the oldest one in the group is more like it."

"You, too, guess correctly, sir."

Chris stared at every one of us, then groaned. "Fine." He slid his hands into his pockets. "When I go back home, I'll attempt dating."

We all cheered. He tried not to smile, but soon his dazzling pearly whites showed, and his eyes sparkled. "I'll admit seeing you guys is an inspiration."

"Do you think you'll use an app?" Nevaeh asked.

"Nah, not my thing. I'd like to meet someone the old-fashioned way."

"What? Roller skating?" I quipped.

"Hey. I'm not *that* old."

"Keep us updated," Lamont said. "I'll be praying God brings you the right person."

"Someone who likes animals, hopefully," Tuck added.

"Yes, please." Chris smiled.

An announcer came over the intercom mentioning the start of the race commencing soon.

"I need that pink stuff," I whined to Tuck.

He pulled out a small container and shook two chalky substances into my hand. "Couldn't find the pink stuff, but here's the ever-helpful calcium tablet."

I popped the antacids. "What if Dream loses? What if he has to go to the bathroom again?" I still can't believe he did poorly in training because of that. I mean, I *know* it's possible, but I didn't want it happening to my colt.

"Then we'll come back next year with another colt."

My mouth dried. "What if he wins?"

"Then we'll deal with the media." Tuck grinned. "God's got us either way."

He was right. Win or lose, God had us. I repeated that as we walked forward to view the Thoroughbreds lining up at the starting gate.

"We're praying, Piper," Lamont said.

I nodded, too overwhelmed to do anything else.

Chris squeezed my shoulder, and Tuck held on to my hand.

I had to remember that as much as I wanted to win the Derby, I wasn't the only one who had something at stake. If we won, Tuck would have his first win as lead trainer. That would do wonders for his career. And Gabe would have a second Derby win under his jockey credits.

Not to mention, maybe, just maybe, the limelight would move away from Daddy. With his plea deal now national news, the reporters had once again started writing scathing articles about him. At least Mama was still talking with him on a daily basis, something she said they were attempting to rebuild the broken trust.

Speaking of . . .

I scanned the stands, looking for her. She'd arrived last night but chosen to hang by herself and not disturb our time with our friends.

Tuck pointed. "Over there."

My bottom lip trembled as I found her in the crowd. Mama blew a kiss, and I clutched my heart in return. She'd chosen not to sit in the same box as us in hopes it would keep the reporters from asking us insinuating questions that had nothing to do with the Derby.

I love you, I mouthed to her.

Mama shaped her fingers into a heart.

My body jumped at the sound of the start of the race. We were too far away to hear the gates open, but that didn't matter thanks to the siren they used for the Derby. All twenty gates parted, and the Thoroughbreds galloped out of their pens. I leaned forward as number five, Mystery, took the lead.

"Why did they do that?" Tuck asked. "The jockey shouldn't have told Mystery to take off like that."

"Maybe he has the stamina."

Tuck scoffed. "That horse will lose the lead by the time they hit the clubhouse turn. Just watch."

He was right. Number ten moved into the lead with Dream in second. "Oh, Tuck, I can't watch. How is the race lasting this long?" This was supposed to be the fastest two minutes in sports.

"Time slows when adrenaline kicks in."

I bit my lip, afraid to look and afraid to look away. What happened if I blinked and another horse passed number ten and Dream? I'd be bereft. Instead, I widened my eyes to watch as they neared the finish line.

"Come on, boy. Come on!" I muttered to myself.

Dream jolted forward, and I blew out a breath. Gabe had been practicing that move all season, and it looked like Dream did it without a hitch.

Around me, I could distinguish the different horse names shouted by the spectators. Every owner was cheering for their horse, and those who had bet on the races were screaming for their champion. As my body got another jolt of adrenaline, my senses focused on Dream. All noise faded as my heartbeat seemed to sync with every hoof landing on the Churchill Downs track.

This was it. They were near the finish line.

Then I saw it.

Dream's head passed the finish line before any other horse's.

"Did that just happen?" I shouted. I whirled toward Tuck. "Did he win? Did. Dream. Just. Win?"

Tuck stared back, dazed. "I think he did."

"He won!" Nevaeh shouted, doing a little shimmy.

Lamont clapped Tuck on the back, and Chris gave me a side hug.

Tuck and I met each other's eyes, then fell into each other's arms. He kissed me, sweeping me off my feet and twirling me in a circle. When he lowered me to the ground, I held on, the box spinning around me.

"He won," I whispered.

"He won," Tuck said, amazement lighting every portion of his face.

We'd done it.

EPILOGUE

JULY

Lamont
Tell your fiancée the article was amazing.

Chris
Yeah, looks like that Aaron dude turned things around.

Tuck
She's happy with it.

Lamont
She'll have to sign my copy the next time we meet.

Chris
Same

Tuck smiled at the texts. He'd been skeptical when Aaron sent Piper a finished article with a plea to read it before making a decision. And he did give her the choice whether or not the article would be published.

Seeing the photo of her, Tuck, Gabe, and Dream in the winner's circle to the left of the printed article was pretty bizarre.

"Unreal, huh?" Piper asked as she snuggled her back into his chest.

"Very."

"I'm glad I agreed to it. Aaron was sincere in his regret, and the article reads well."

"Mm-hmm." He kissed the top of her head. "It's certainly garnered us a lot more attention."

"Nah." She tilted her head up, grinning at him. "Think that was the Derby win."

"Oh, that ol' thing?" He pointed toward the trophy on his mantel.

Piper laughed. "Want to go for a walk and daydream?"

"Let's do it." They put on their boots, and soon they were walking his portion of their land.

They'd filed paperwork with the county to merge the properties, and already they were having the fencing between his land and hers removed. They were also still praying over what to name their new operation.

"So whose house should we move into after the wedding?" Piper sat up to look at him this time.

"Depends on our needs, I guess. You have two guest bedrooms."

"So do you."

Oh yeah. "But you have a basement."

"You have a track."

He smirked at her. "We could always remodel one and keep the other as a guest house. Maybe then Lamont and Chris would visit more often."

Piper nodded slowly. "I like the idea of a guest house, but it probably doesn't need to be the size of either of our houses. So maybe we live in your house while we tear mine down and build our dream home."

"I like."

Piper paused and met his gaze. "Are you sure you made the right decision not joining the other trainers?"

"I am. Kelly Shaw was offering an awesome opportunity, but I'm betting on us. That's our future."

She kissed his cheek. "I like the sound of that."

"And I like your idea of turning our operation into a full-fledged training venue. Are you sure you won't regret not raising your own racehorses?"

Piper wrapped her arms around his waist. "Not at all. You know I didn't buy those horses at the auction because my thoughts were already beginning to shift. I've got a Derby win to remind me of this season, but it's not one I want to stay in. Training with you is a lot better than deciding which horses to buy and the whole siring process. I don't want our business to turn into another Bolt Brook."

It had been hard to see her dad stripped of all rights to run his farm, part of the plea deal agreement. Fortunately, though, Piper's mama had returned home, and she and Mr. McKinney were in the process of selling their property and downsizing. They were also going to weekly marriage counseling.

"Then we won't raise them."

"I also want a dog."

He tugged her closer. "What kind?"

"Australian shepherd?"

"To chase the goats?"

"But of course."

"Then let's get one." He'd give her everything in his power. "Promise me something." He pulled back to stare into her eyes.

"What's that?"

"Promise we'll continue to dream with each other. To share our ideas and ensure we're on the same track."

"I promise, Tucker Hale."

He cupped her face and grazed his lips against hers. When she wound her arms around his neck, he pressed his mouth firmly to hers, cementing the promise, reminding her how much he loved her and their life together.

Together.

It was what he wanted with Piper for the rest of their days. He prayed they'd always communicate, stay on the same page, and support each other in every endeavor. Because what they had was bigger than friendship. It was a partnership that melded them together in every way, and Tuck hoped he'd always remember to foster their love above all else.

AUTHOR'S NOTE

Dear Reader,

Thank you so much for reading *A Run at Love*. This book went through many revisions as I struggled to adapt to the racing world and incorporate that knowledge. I wanted to take you along the racing season without overwhelming you with information.

Mountain Laurel Stakes isn't a real place or race. Since the horses in my story got sick with EHV-1 (a real virus), I didn't want to use a real place and insinuate that would happen at their facility. All the other locations and stakes races are real.

Also, the 149th Derby was taking place as I wrote this book. A lot of horses lost their lives, and investigations were conducted to determine why. I tried to keep abreast of the information as it was available and be as accurate as possible, but eventually I had to stop editing and let the book go to production.

Lastly, Piper was adopted from the fictional country of Ọlọrọ Ilé. I could've used a real African country, but it was fun to reference the country of Queen Brielle Adebayo from *In Search of a Prince*. Though I did a lot of research on transracial adoptions, it wasn't a central plot point. I could've gone deeper, but it wasn't necessary for Piper's story. Still, I hope I did justice to this thread.

Thank you for taking the time to walk with Piper and Tuck. I pray this book blesses you.

Blessings,
Toni

ACKNOWLEDGMENTS

Thank you so much to Janine Rosche, Nicole Deese, and Katie Ganshert for talking to me about your experiences with transracial adoptions. I'm humbled by your honesty, vulnerability, and willingness to share. I pray I did this story justice and shed light on transracial adoptions and families. Readers, any mishaps are my own.

Thank you so much to my Book Troop for helping me name characters and places in the book. Special shout out to Michelle Leverette for naming Mordecai, Martha Artyomenko for naming Piper's daddy, Candy van Holbrook for the Mountain Laurel Stakes, and Melissa Pettersen for naming Piper's mama. Y'all are the best!

Thanks to Mr. Fischer for answering my questions about shoulder fractures. I appreciate your time.

Thank you to Elizabeth Knoll for your expert knowledge on horse racing. You saved me! I so appreciate the time you took to correct my blunders. Readers, any remaining mistakes are mine.

Thank you to Carrie Schmidt for being my alpha reader and encouraging me when I thought this story wouldn't amount to what I'd hoped. I value your friendship.

I also can't forget to thank my critique partners, Andrea

Boyd and Sarah Monzon. You two are the very best, and I'm so thankful we're friends. I love you both!

Lastly, thank you to my husband for helping me stay the course when I'm on a deadline crunch. Thank you for telling random people at bookstores I'm the author. I love you. And to my sons, thanks for listening to me talk about my characters as if they were real people. I love y'all so much.

Read on
for a *sneak peek* at
the final book in the

LOVE IN THE SPOTLIGHT

series

Available Spring 2025

Drilling a hole in the middle of a person's femur was my least favorite thing to do. Not because I wasn't capable. Technology had made a way for me to drill a precise hole exactly where I needed to insert the metal rod and screws to repair the midshaft femoral break. However, I couldn't do anything to stop the intense pain this sweet woman would feel when she woke up. A broken femur was one of the hardest injuries to overcome. Couple that with the woman's occupation—an Olympic ski jumper—and she'd have an uphill battle.

I would do everything in my power to ensure she'd get back on the slopes.

"Ready for the rod," I murmured now that the sound of the drill had stopped overtaking the classical music floating through the operating room speakers.

I'd been listening to classical composers in the OR since the first time I'd scrubbed in. One of my med school professors had insisted that listening to the music while learning would guarantee a good grade. I played while studying, when learning new procedures, and now in the operating room. Classical music represented my career. On the other hand, my at-home playlist consisted of '70s music that would help me unwind from the long day of surgeries.

"Rod," the second-year student replied.

I slid the rod right down the middle of the femur and into the broken piece. Next, I inserted the screws to ensure a close bond and allow the healing process to begin. I gestured for the fourth-year resident to suture the incision. "Close up, Dr. Bryner."

"Yes, Dr. Kennedy."

I walked out of the operating room, breathing a sigh of relief that nothing had gone wrong. I was also on call at the nation's Olympic sports injury clinic up in Vail, so I'd done this procedure multiple times before. But I still couldn't perform one of these surgeries without my gut clenching and twisting like a gymnast during a floor routine.

I removed my surgical gown, placing it into the dirty bin, then washed up before heading into the hall. A glance at my smartwatch told me I'd have about thirty minutes to look at my email and answer any phone calls that were urgent before I clocked out.

Today had been a good day.

"Have a good evening, Dr. Kennedy," Nurse Jones said as she passed me.

I nodded. "You too." My throat constricted.

Whenever I interacted with my colleagues, my mouth dried out. My throat seemed to get tighter as my mind grappled for words. What should I say to them? Did they expect more than simple small talk? I'd heard whispers behind my back. Most of my colleagues found me stuck up and abrasive. Just because I didn't share what I did on the weekend or gossip about the other hospital workers didn't mean that I was silently judging them.

I simply had no idea how to respond.

You'd think a world-class doctor would be able to navigate the basics of small talk, but I didn't earn my accolades by making friends. No, I obtained my status by working my tail off until the only person I knew, *really* knew, was my baby sister. And even that relationship had become strained. Not that we were at odds, but she'd built a life separate from me. One that I had to get weekly phone call updates on because she lived in Kentucky and I was happy in Colorado.

Or at least satisfied.

After making the last follow-up call of the day, I turned off my office computer, grabbed my purse, and headed to the employee parking lot. I'd already changed from scrubs into jeans and a sweater. My peacoat would give added protection against the cooler temps October had brought. It was firmly in the fall season, and I was here for it.

I got into my white Range Rover, inhaling the scent of the leather seats. Pressing the seat warmer, I took a moment to settle in, letting the weight of today's surgeries fall from me. Now wasn't the time to analyze what had gone right or wrong, but to simply empty my mind.

My stomach rumbled, and I glanced at the dashboard. *6:07 p.m.* Time for some dinner. I was ravenous and knew just the place to grab a bite.

Colorado Springs was pretty walkable, depending on where you lived. It just so happened that my work (Peak University Hospital), my home (right on West Pike's Peak in Old Colorado City), and food (a stop at Skirted Heifer was a must) were all within a couple of miles of each other. I could be at the hospital in a jiffy by car, but on my off days that wasn't necessary unless I wanted to stay warm.

I slid into an empty parking spot, then climbed out of my Rover. A cool breeze fluttered the leaves, and I peered up into the clear sky. The sky was making its way to sunset, but I didn't care that I'd missed the sunshine by being in the OR all day. It was enough to feel the breeze on my face and know I had a show to binge when I got home.

I made my way to the front door just as a man reached for the handle. I paused, and he stared at me, a hesitant look on his handsome face.

"Um, would you like to go in first?" he asked in a smooth tenor.

For some reason, the question made tiny goosebumps pebble my arms. Was it the thoughtful request or the tone of his voice?

"If you don't mind."

"Please." He gestured me forward.

I walked ahead of him, conscious of his stare behind me. *Don't be ridiculous. He's not staring.* But I wanted to.

I wanted to turn around and stare at his warm blue eyes once more. I'd never seen a Black man with eyes that particular shade, unless you counted the movie star Michael Ealy. Now that I thought on it, the guy behind me had similar features, but he was more handsome in my opinion.

Erykah, what's gotten into you?

I didn't stare at men. I didn't note their voices or their eye color, and I certainly didn't try to talk to them. I was the woman who couldn't carry a conversation in a bucket.

Ignoring his presence, I placed my order for a naked heifer, adding my favorite toppings—this girl couldn't live without bacon, guac, and pepper jack on her burger—and requested a side of fries with their handcrafted soda.

I moved on, finding a spot to wait in the dining area. Maybe a spot that earned me a portrait view of the man's face. His beard was on the scraggly side, as if he'd just come down from the camping in the mountains and enjoying all that Colorado had to offer. Or maybe that was his style.

He wore a black beanie and black-framed glasses. He looked studious but masculine at the same time. I watched as he placed his order and then scanned the area as if searching for someone. Shock coursed through me when his gaze landed on me. A small smile lifted his full lips, and he walked to my table.

"Hi," he said.

"Hello." I straightened in my seat.

"May I sit for a moment?"

I nodded, not sure what else to do.

"So I don't normally do this."

"Order food?"

He chuckled. "Sit at a stranger's table."

"Then why mine?" I winced inwardly. Had that sounded rude?

"Because you ordered your burger just like I order mine."

Okay, a little surprising, but considering the odds—not that I knew them—not totally stunning. "And that made you want to sit here?"

"It made me want to introduce myself."

"Fair enough." I held out my hand. "Erykah Kennedy."

"Christian Gamble, but my friends call me Chris."

"Nice to meet you, Christian."

His eyes twinkled. I wasn't sure if I'd said something funny, or if he was just one of those happy guys.

"What do you do, Erykah?"

I swallowed. *Here it goes.* Whenever I encountered a similar line of questioning with men in the past, they always got defensive when I said I was a surgeon. Or they treated me as if it was so cute that I tried to be more than just a homemaker.

My shoulders tensed. "I'm an orthopedic surgeon." My breath caught in my chest as I waited for his reaction.

He let out a low whistle. "So you're unbelievably smart and talented."

"Uh . . ." Why were my cheeks heating? "I am." It was the one thing in life I was sure about. The rest was freestyling. Remembering niceties, I replied, "What do you do?"

"Official title: wildlife conservationist."

"Unofficial?" I asked, curiosity piqued.

"Animal wrangler."

My lips curved upward. "What kinds of animals?"

"Whichever are in the house."

"Erykah," an employee called out.

"Oh, um, my order's ready."

"I hope you enjoy that burger," Christian said.

"You too." I stood, fidgeting with my purse strap. Was I supposed to say anything more? Invite him to dine with me even though I had placed a to-go order?

I opened my mouth, then promptly shut it and headed for

the counter. Sitting at my table didn't mean anything. I'd go home, eat my dinner, and watch another episode of *Nadiya Bakes*. Her accent soothed me, and in another life, I imagined myself baking everything she did.

As I grabbed my food, I glanced over at Christian Gamble one last time, marking every single feature of his face in my mind. A sigh tore from my lips as I pushed the door open and headed to my car.

Erykah Kennedy, you are a coward.

Toni Shiloh is a wife, a mom, and an award-winning Christian contemporary romance author. She writes to bring God glory and to learn more about His goodness. Her novel *In Search of a Prince* won the first ever Christy Amplify Award. Her books have won the Selah Award and have been finalists for the Carol Award and the HOLT Medallion. A member of American Christian Fiction Writers (ACFW), Toni loves connecting with readers and authors alike via social media. You can learn more about her writing at ToniShiloh.com.

Sign Up for Toni's Newsletter

Keep up to date with Toni's latest news on
book releases and events by signing up
for her email list at the link below.

ToniShiloh.com

FOLLOW TONI ON SOCIAL MEDIA

Toni Shiloh, Author   @ToniShiloh   @ToniShilohWrite

More from Toni Shiloh

Hollywood hair stylist Nevaeh loves making those in the spotlight shine. But when a photo of her and Hollywood heartthrob Lamont goes viral for all the wrong reasons, they suddenly find themselves in a fake relationship to save their careers. In a world where nothing seems real, can Nevaeh be true to herself . . . and her heart?

The Love Script
LOVE IN THE SPOTLIGHT

Fashion aficionado Iris Blakely dreams of using her talent to start a business to help citizens in impoverished areas. But when she discovers that Ekon Diallo will be her business consultant, the battle between her desires and reality begins. Can she keep her heart—and business—intact despite the challenges she faces?

To Win a Prince

Brielle Adebayo's simple life unravels when she discovers she is a princess in the African kingdom of Ọlọrọ Ilé and must immediately assume her royal position. Brielle comes to love the island's culture and studies the language with her handsome tutor. But when her political rivals force her to make a difficult choice, a wrong decision could change her life.

In Search of a Prince

BETHANYHOUSE

 Bethany House Fiction

 @BethanyHouseFiction

 @Bethany_House

 @BethanyHouseFiction

 Free exclusive resources for your book group at BethanyHouseOpenBook.com

 Sign up for our fiction newsletter today at BethanyHouse.com